Somebody I U

Eve Ainsworth is a public speaker, creative workshop coordinator and award-winning author who draws from her extensive work with teenagers managing emotional and behavioural issues to write authentic, honest and real novels for young people and adults. Eve's adult debut, *Duckling*, was published by Penguin Random House in 2022. She has had short stories published in magazines such as Writers' Forum and Prima and articles posted online for the *Guardian*, *Metro* and BookTrust. Eve is also a champion for working class voices, has set up the Working Class Writers Network and is an experienced mentor.

EVE AINSWORTH

SOMEBODY I USED TO LOVE

CANELO

First published in the United Kingdom in 2024 by

Canelo
Unit 9, 5th Floor
Cargo Works, 1-2 Hatfields
London SE1 9PG
United Kingdom

A CIP catalogue record for this book is available from the British Library.

Print ISBN 978 1 80436 774 2
Ebook ISBN 978 1 80436 775 9

Cover design by Head Design

Cover images © Shutterstock

Look for more great books at www.canelo.co

Printed and bound in Great Britain by Clays Ltd, Elcograf S.p.A.

1

MIX
Paper | Supporting
responsible forestry
FSC
www.fsc.org
FSC® C018072

To Cherry – my brave and beautiful sister

Love you always xx

Before

'You can open them now.'

His hand lifted from my face, and I flicked open my eyes in excitement, a nervous tingle still trembling down my spine. It took a moment to register where we were standing. The significance of it. The familiar street wrapped itself around me: the green on the corner, the collection of parked cars to my left, and in front of me the looming tower of Beckett Court. For a second it was like I was thirteen again – young and skinny, chapped lips and dry hair, clutching my broken bag and staring up at the looming building as if it were a castle, rather than a faded 1960s development.

Hope swelled inside me.

Will's arm whipped around my body, hugging me close. He stank of cigarettes, but this wasn't the time to tell him off. Anyway, the acrid scent was quite soothing, in a weird way. I pressed my body deeper into his, almost wishing I could completely absorb myself into him.

'Did you guess?' he asked.

I shook my head. No. No, I hadn't – I really hadn't, but perhaps I should have. This was so like Will. It was just what he would do. So bloody, completely perfect.

'Is it—'

I

The words tumbled from my mouth before I could stop myself – I barely dared to ask, but Will wasn't in the mood to answer anyway. His eyes twinkled as he tugged me forward.

'Come on,' he said keenly. 'Follow me.'

I knew where we were going as we trudged over the mashed-up grass on the verge, towards the dark wooden doors of the main entrance. My heart thumped nonetheless, as we swept across the threshold and thundered up the concrete steps, worn down through use over the years. Faded graffiti still stained the walls. The same words that I used to read as a kid – 'Grifter was here', 'Peace before Profit', 'call Mandi H for a good time'.

I counted the floors as we passed them – 1… 2… 3…

I could feel the blood pumping in my veins, my head was giddy with nerves. I chewed on the inside of my cheek, a habit I'd had since I was little. There was so much I wanted to say to Will, but I couldn't quite bring myself to do it. I still couldn't believe that he had brought me here.

How long had he been planning this?

I remember running up these stairs fresh from school, full of chatter and gossip to share, my school bag thumping against my back, my knackered trainers catching on every step, daring to trip me at any moment.

4… 5.

My heart was beating faster now. My hand gripped tight on the rail. Will turned to me, his face red with exertion, dark hair plastered against his forehead. His smile was wide and bright, like a light welcoming me home. I continued to cling to the rail, terrified that my fuzzy head might make me tip back if I let go too quickly.

'Will…'

'This is it! The fifth floor.' I knew this already, but his words only cemented the trembling inside of me. My God, we were here. We were back.

He took my hand again, easing me down the narrow, dark hallway. It still stank of damp and, faintly, of wee. Through a heavy glass door and then we were into the main corridor, closed doors facing us on each side. Some were brightly painted or adorned with plaques, or tubs of flowers by their steps. Others were still painted their original council grey.

Others, like number sixty-five.

Will stopped outside the door, his hands planted neatly on his hips. He nodded towards the faded paint, at the numbers in their tarnished bronze. I remembered how much she used to polish those numbers, until they shone bright like a new penny.

'Why are we here?' I asked at last.

Will chuckled softly. He dug into his coat pocket and pulled out a key. Such a simple thing, but for a moment I was mesmerised. I licked my dry lips.

'Will? Are you messing me around?'

'Course I'm not.' He looked hurt. Carefully, he handed it to me, like it was a precious jewel. I held it tenderly in my hand, wondering if it was the same one she used to have. She used to have a keyring attached to it. A cat, wearing a top hat. I wondered what happened to that; it was such a sweet little thing.

'It's ours, Gem. It's ours now.' He paused. 'I put the deposit down for the rent this week. For you.'

'For me?'

He coughed. 'For us.'

'But... how?' I shook my head. This didn't make sense. How did Will get his hands on that money? 'I don't understand how you could put down a deposit for the rent…'

He shifted on the spot. 'The money Mum left me. I thought it was the best use for it.'

The shock hit me fast. 'Will! That was for your future! For your travelling. For America.'

'This is my future.' He pecked my cheek gently. 'You are.'

I dangled the key between my fingers. Only Will really knew how much this flat meant to me. How I'd spent my childhood behind these walls, safe and sheltered in Nan's company until she died, two years ago, when I was eighteen. I remembered how I'd wept on his shoulder once again when I heard the council was selling it off. I'd been living in crappy bedsits and horrible rentals ever since.

My nan's flat. My precious place.

'You did this for me…' I whispered.

Will had had plans for his inheritance. He was going to travel to the USA with his brother, try to make a go of it out there with their band. I never for one minute expected him to spend it on this.

On my past.

'I did it for us,' he said, carefully taking the key back from my hand. 'It's our start together. Our new beginning.'

As I watched him open the door to our new life, a realisation suddenly hit me. This was a man who knew me better than I knew myself, and he truly loved me. He had to, to do something like this.

I knew in that moment that I would be with this man forever.

God, I was so wrong.

Chapter One

Gem – 2022

I hated Mondays at the best of times, but today I'd woken up with the kind of sludgy headache that I knew I would have difficulty shifting. The thought of standing in front of my class of thirty-two, switching on my brightest smile and attempting to teach them about the Tudors was already making my heart sink, despite loving the little buggers desperately. Why were the weekends so short?

I stared into the mirror. A smear of lip-gloss and flick of mascara weren't enough to lift my flat and colourless reflection. My frizzy ginger curls refused to be tamed by my hurried ponytail, and my skin was so ghostly pale that I swear I was glowing.

Giving up on my appearance, I instead checked my phone for updates, while slugging my too-strong tea. Usually there was a flurry of bright and positive social media posts from 'friends' desperate to show that their lives were exciting and fulfilling. But it was the negative posts which, more often than not, caught my eye. Call me cold-hearted, but I was a sucker for a more realistic entry. What did the Germans call it? *Schadenfreude* – enjoying someone else's misfortune.

One particular post this morning had lots of exclamation marks and sad little emoji faces, guaranteed to grab my attention.

Marshbrook Lane closed!!!!! Avoid!!!

It was typed in a hurry by Matty101, a regular poster on the neighbourhood group. I'd never met him, but I imagined he was the type of fella who stood glued to his window, waiting for bad things to happen.

> Be careful out there everyone!
> There has been a car crash on Marshbrook Lane.
> Just one car is involved. Looks pretty nasty. Suspect
> a drunk driver. Possibly a boy racer hitting a tree.
> Either way, I hope they're OK.

Marshbrook was the country road that looped around the town of Crowbridge, and my main route into work. Now I was going to have to take a horrible detour, through the congested town centre, to avoid it. Crowbridge was a new town that had been expanded over the years. I had lived here all my life but at times I was quite bored of the place; the only good thing about it was that it offered a convenient commute to both London and Brighton.

'This always happens on a Monday. I bet some idiot was speeding again,' I said, resisting the temptation to type out an exasperated reply. After all, someone was hurt.

Richard, downing a protein shake by the sink, had his gaze fixed on his own phone, a tiny frown etched on his face.

'You don't know that, Gem. It's an awful road, so many blind spots.' He thumped his glass down and swiped at his face. 'Two of our students have been hurt there recently, caught out by the bends – or for all you know, a car might have been forced to avoid an animal or something.'

'Yeah, well, that's not the point...'

7

'I'm sure they didn't crash to inconvenience you,' he replied mildly.

'Whatever – now I'll have to leave earlier to make sure I'm on time. There are always tailbacks through the High Street, and I bet the level crossing is down.'

'It'll be fine, Gemma.'

I busied myself trying to get my stuff together and ignoring the thumping headache that was threatening to explode behind my eyes at any moment. Richard was always so level-headed about everything. I guess that was what made him a good teacher. Better than me, anyway.

Richard walked over and wrapped his arms around me. He was so tall that I had to stand on tiptoes to kiss his bristly chin. I could smell the mint chewing gum on his breath. He was such a stupidly stereotypical secondary teacher; I almost expected him to rock up one day in a corduroy jacket with the patches on the sleeves. Vee always joked that he was the perfect boyfriend to take home to your dad.

If you had a dad, of course.

'You could always get the train, like me?'

'I hate trains.' I wrinkled my nose. 'Besides, the school is nowhere near the station.'

'You keep saying you want to be more environmentally friendly. Walking would be good for you.' He patted my bum as if to make a point. I tried not to flinch. We both knew I'd put on a bit of weight the last couple of years. Wasn't that meant to be a good sign? Didn't it show I was content or something?

'Or bored?' Vee had joked when I'd tucked into another biscuit round at hers. It was easy for Vee to joke, though. She had the perfect life, the perfect relationship with lovely Brandon. She didn't seem to understand that

8

what I had was good too — it was just a different sort of good.

'I say a lot of things, Richard. It doesn't mean I truly mean them.'

He grinned at me. A toothy grin that I'd found so endearing the first time I'd met him. It was probably the cutest thing about him. Nan had always told me that people with gaps in their teeth were lucky. Richard said he agreed with that, because he was lucky to have me. Although I usually cringed over smoochy stuff, I had to admit that was kind of cute, so I'd let him off.

Richard was so different to anyone I'd met before. OK, he wasn't my usual type. But like Vee said, I had to stop comparing other men to Will. Besides, surely it's best to avoid anyone that looks like your ex? That relationship didn't work for a host of reasons, so I needed something new. Someone unlike Will. A totally fresh start.

Richard was lanky and in a constant battle with his body. His hair was blond and wispy, and his eyes so pale blue that they resembled clear-cut glass. A clumsy incident had led me to Richard: a spilt drink down the local pub and a heartfelt apology that made me melt a little bit inside. The cheeky, gappy grin that followed had been the icing on the cake. Soon we were talking about our shared love of the Beatles and the fact that we were both struggling teachers, something that only fellow professionals would understand. The stain on my new skirt was quickly forgotten as we moaned about the government and latest Ofsted inspections.

Richard just had that way about him; he made me feel comforted, safe. He was what I needed. Everyone said so. A breath of fresh air after an awful, awful storm.

He bent down and kissed my hair. 'Today will be a good day, Gemma. Just you wait.'

I closed my eyes, taking a moment or two to simply breathe him in. It was so quiet in the flat, so perfect. For that split second it felt like it was just us in the world, totally protected and cushioned from the madness around us. The news on my phone was soon forgotten; even my headache melted away a little. With a gentle sigh, I nestled into his chest. Why did I worry about these stupid things? I really had to stop getting myself into such a knot.

'I hope you're right, Richard. I could really do with today going right.'

But despite my resolve to be more positive, deep inside a voice was pressing me, demanding to be heard.

Because he'd forgotten.

He'd forgotten what today meant to me and why I was in the state I was in.

And that hurt.

–

By some miracle I wasn't late, and my class were fairly well-behaved. Archie Edwards (the main ringleader) was off school sick and three of my girls (Macy, Marnie and Melody) were getting along for a change. By lunchtime, I felt like I was going to get through the day unscathed.

In the staff room, the gossip was all about the crash that morning. Fiona was sitting centre stage, telling everyone what she had heard. I wasn't sure how Fiona always managed to find stuff out – it was like she had contacts everywhere. I tried to pretend I wasn't interested as I microwaved my grey-looking soup, but it was hard not to be drawn in.

'It was only one car, so I heard. It was speeding and careered into that old tree near the crossroads. Really messy.'

'That's awful,' said Dana, the dramatic Year 6 teacher who always looked like she was about to cry. 'Were they hurt, do you know?'

Fiona pulled a face that said, 'Oh I don't know if I should say.' Spare me. She shook her head slightly, making her neat black bob shake. 'Well, I've only heard talk, but it's not good.'

'How did you hear this talk?' I asked, not able to stop myself. 'There's nothing online.' I knew this because I'd looked, nosy bugger that I was.

'My best friend is a paramedic. Of course, it's top secret what she tells me.'

'Of course.'

Trust Fiona to know the bloody paramedic. She probably knew the Prime Minister too. My soup pinged in the microwave and I pulled it out, nearly burning my fingers on the lava-like dish. I banged it down on the side, cursing.

'So, what did you hear?' Ben, Year 3 and all-round loved teacher, asked gently, tipping his boyish, good-looking face towards Fiona.

'Well, I heard that the driver was badly injured. Like, *really* bad. They say he was lucky to make it out alive.' She tutted. 'It's so horrible. Too awful to think about. Someone must have been watching over him.'

I stirred my soup bleakly. It really was too awful. I just hoped it was no one I knew.

Chapter Two

Gem — 2022

I met Vee at The Swan at six p.m. By then I was a sweaty, tired mess and guzzling my soda water like it was nectar. My head was still pounding, and I was already dreading going home and thinking about dinner. I wondered if I could convince Richard that a takeaway was the way to go. It was annoying that he generally hated them.

Vee rushed in twenty minutes late as usual, looking apologetic but unflustered. I wasn't sure why we kept agreeing to this time, when she could never keep to it.

Vee was my oldest friend. We had latched on to each other at secondary — two lost and slightly weird girls that ended up in the same form group. I had been marked out by my unruly ginger curls and clearly second-hand uniform. Vee had been marked out by her height (super tall) and acne (which had now cleared up). She was now a stunningly beautiful, tall leggy blonde with a great job in a modelling agency, and I was still a short, dumpy weirdo with messy hair and barely a pot to piss in.

But she was my best friend and the best person to ever have entered my life.

Well — one of the best.

'I'm sorry.' Vee kissed me lightly on the cheek and then slid in the chair opposite. 'It's been a nightmare day.'

'Tell me about it.' I tugged at my hair. 'I'm still picking the glue out. I don't know how they managed to coat me in the stuff.'

Vee wagged a finger at me. 'You're too slow, that's your trouble.'

'You sound like my head. She was on at me for not being focused this morning.'

'Are you still having trouble sleeping?'

'A bit.'

The truth was, it wasn't so much the falling asleep bit, but rather the waking up in the middle of the night which was draining me, finding Richard's arm like a heavy weight across my middle, his snore a repetitive hammer drill in my ear. I would end up lying there, my thoughts tumbling over me like waves, unable to slip back into any form of relaxation. Why did overthinking go into overdrive in the middle of the night? It could be something as simple as worrying if I'd locked the front door, or something altogether bleaker, like reliving mine and Will's break-up again and again – a relentless and painful broken record.

'You need to listen to that podcast I told you about,' Vee said. 'It worked miracles with me. I'm onto a new one now.'

'Oh yeah – what's this one? More meditation?'

Vee knew I didn't have the patience for those sorts of things. My God, Will had spent enough time trying to convince me of the benefits years ago, and look where that had got us. Even he'd given up on it all in the end. I couldn't imagine the Will of today taking time out of his busy life to practise mindfulness. Those days were long gone.

Vee's voice broke me out of my thoughts.

'Well, mine is on conceiving, actually.'

Her voice was quiet now. I felt my stomach dip and roll. Oh God – I went too far. I knew how important this was for Vee and Brandon, and I hadn't even bothered to ask her how it was going. My best friend was going through hell and all I kept doing was focusing the conversation on me.

'I'm sorry, Vee. I should have thought.'

'It's OK, you weren't to know.' She sipped her drink again. She was being nice, of course – I *was* to know. Vee and Brandon's struggle to conceive had been so painful for them. I knew what amazing parents they would be.

'We have another consultation next week. More tests. Maybe they can give us some answers then, eh?' she said carefully.

'You're still so young, Vee.'

We're so young, I wanted to say, even though I was as aware as Vee of how quickly time was flying. I was thirty-two and I wasn't sure if my life was going exactly how I'd planned. The years seemed to be racing by and I had so little control.

'I know. I've just always wanted a big family.' Vee smiled softly. 'Every passing year reduces my chance of achieving that.'

I squeezed her hand.

Another thing we had in common was that we both loved children. However, while I struggled to detect a single maternal bone in my body, Vee seemed to long for the family she never had growing up.

'Let's not focus on me anyway. I wanted to see you today, because… well, you know—'

'I know.' I squeezed her hand tighter. 'I can always rely on you to remember.'

'How can I forget? It's so bloody horrible.'

I felt the tears pressing behind my eyes. 'I just wanted to keep busy today, that was all. You know how hard it is.'

She nodded softly, stroked my hand. She didn't have to do anything else, just be there.

Sometimes it felt like I never had a dad. But I did once, a long time ago.

I had a mum and dad who were together and in love. I was part of a happy little family.

Thinking of the facts hurts too much.

I don't remember the fire. I was only five. I think what memories I did have are now shut away at the back of my mind, festering and burning a scar deep into my brain. I may not remember, but the pain never seemed to go. Cruel, really. Why can't the pain disappear too?

All I know is that we got pulled out in time, Mum and I.

But Dad didn't.

Twenty-seven years ago today, on 18 July, everything changed for me.

It's a date that has haunted me ever since.

'Has he contacted you?' Vee glanced at my phone knowingly.

I shook my head, took another swallow of my drink. I didn't want to think too much about it.

Vee frowned. 'That's not like Will – he always checks in at this time, doesn't he?'

'Usually...' I shrugged. 'I guess I couldn't expect him to keep it up, Vee. He has his own life now. He's probably too busy with that—'

I screwed up my face. I still couldn't bring myself to say her name, even after all this time.

'Nicola,' Vee provided helpfully. 'The very-nice-but-very-posh Nicola.'

'Nicola…' I took a sip of my drink. I swear, the very fact I had uttered her name out loud had made it taste sourer.

Really, there was nothing wrong with the woman. I had met her a handful of times, at mutual friends' parties, where Will and I were still forced to mix. These were few and far between now, as Will had distanced himself from us all. And with reason, of course. I don't think he could ever face up to what he did to me. To us.

Nicola was one of those girlfriends that you wished your ex would never end up with – skinny, beautiful, clever and just a little condescending.

'He still checked in with you, though, didn't he?' Vee said. 'He knows how important today is. I hope that bloody girlfriend of his hasn't stopped him.'

I snorted. 'It doesn't matter anyway. I don't need his messages, I'm fine.' I studied my hands for a moment, considering my next words. 'Besides, I have to let go of him eventually, Vee. Even now, he's still there in the background of my life and I can't bear it.'

Although all of this was true, I was a little hurt not to have heard from him. Every year on this date, I'd usually wake up to Will's text, saying something like:

> You know I'm with you today, right? You'll get through it. Keep smiling.

I expected he'd set a reminder or something and the messages these past two years had been a little more 'off' and less friendly, but it had been something. Despite everything he had done, this had been something familiar and reassuring. It was the only good part of Will left. Perhaps that part of him had gone too.

'Did Richard say anything?' Vee asked gently.

I shook my head. 'No, I don't think he's remembered.'

'You've been together nearly two years now, Gemma. I would have thought—'

I batted her concern away. 'Richard is different, you know that! He might not be as thoughtful and romantic, but he's kind and reliable. He makes me happy.'

'Like a warm dressing gown. Snug and cosy...'

'Yes, I suppose so.'

'...But not particularly sexy.'

'Vee!'

Vee was laughing and I knew she didn't mean it. She was fond of Richard.

'Richard is good for me,' I said softly. 'Remember how he helped me? How he picked me up when I was broken?'

Vee reached forward and squeezed my hand. 'Babe, I'll never forget that. I'll always be thankful.'

'Like I said, it's probably good that Will hasn't texted me. I need that break, Vee. I need to finally move on.' I took one last slug of my drink. 'I need to accept that Will can never be part of my life again.'

-

The drive home seemed to pass in a blur. I was dog-tired, almost wishing I had cancelled on Vee and gone straight home to a hot bath and some crappy, brainless TV show. But Vee was good to come out and meet me. She knew I'd be feeling sad today. In fact, sad wasn't the right word, it was more lost – a reminder that most of my childhood and the life that followed had been destroyed by one reckless accident. It could have been so very different.

I clicked the indicator and drove down Marshbrook Lane. The road was open again, but as I passed the main intersection by the small parade of shops, I saw glass glittering on the road and a broken wing mirror in the grass verge. I shivered, passing carefully. People always drove down this section too fast.

'That's why you should always be slow and steady,' Richard would say, tutting as some lunatic overtook him. 'There's no point trying to race to your death.'

I knew he was right, but even I found myself longing to hit the gas pedal every time I was a passenger in his car. There was driving steady and then there was driving too slow, like a granny.

Blowing out a deep breath, I pushed my lips into a smile and tried to reframe that thought, knowing I wasn't being fair to him: Richard was so lovely, so careful. I was glad I had defended him to Vee. I pictured him now, back in our scruffy flat, probably marking some homework with half an eye on the evening news. If I was lucky, he might have put the dinner on.

I pulled into the communal car park and found myself in the usual space next to the overflowing bin store. Every day some helpful neighbour added something else to the bulging contents. This time it was a stained mattress, lolling out of the door like a diseased tongue.

Switching off the ignition, I took a breath. I often spent a moment or two just sitting and looking up at the block that had been my home for so long. When I was a kid, I had pretended it was a castle, even though it was the least-likely-looking castle in the world. The monumental, grey looming towers had always impressed me, with their large balconies and brightly lit windows.

My council–estate castle…

My mobile broke the spell, buzzing in my pocket urgently. I frowned, guessing it was Richard, wondering what time I'd be home. Ready to reassure him that I was on my way, I froze when I realised it wasn't him at all.

It was the last person I expected to call.

'Jack?' I answered, even as my stomach surged. Jack never called me. Why would he? It had been so long now. Jesus, he wasn't even in the country.

'Gem?' His voice was sharp, jumpy almost. 'Gem? Thank God I got hold of you.'

'What is it?'

My body was now ice, my gaze still fixed on the tower block, on the fifth–floor window that contained my lovely boyfriend, my lovely safe life. Intuition prickled me. Was this all about to be destroyed?

'Gem, I'm so sorry…' His voice cracked. 'It's Will…'

'Will?'

Jack's little brother. My ex-boyfriend. Why was he calling about him?

Suddenly, everything made sense. The overwhelming bad feeling this morning, stronger than before. The crash in the road. The driver speeding. The horrible shitty date.

It was Will.

I gripped the phone and fought the urge not to scream – 18 July was confirmed forever as the worst date in the world.

'What is it, Jack? Is he dead? Just tell me!'

Even though I didn't want to be told – not now, not ever.

I just wanted it all to go away.

Chapter Three

Will – 2022

Bleeping. Too much bleeping.

God, my head hurts.

Mouth tastes of shit.

Can't move – everything is too heavy.

That bleeping. Stop it, will you? Cut it out!

My head! Fuck.

Still too loud. Hurts to open eyes.

Body is heavy. Like lead.

Am I dead?

Fuck that bleeping. Shut it up…

'Bleeping… Fuck! Fucking bleeping…'

Words tumbling out, finally. Mouth is still so dry, though.
Urgh, tastes awful. Someone squeezes my hand. Too hard. I
want to pull away but can't.

'Will. Will, it's OK, baby…'

She smells sweet, too sweet. Who the fuck is she?

I want—

Fuck.

I opened my eyes.

It was bright and I hurt badly. I could still hear the machine beside me, constant little bleeps like something from a TV show. The ceiling light above me was round and bright. It made me think of an eye staring down at me.

I tried to turn my head a little. Two deep breaths and I found I could focus better. There was a chair in the corner. Green – plasticky-looking. The place reminded me of an old people's home. In fact, the smell was similar. There was a window on my right, with blue blinds drawn, and next to me, alongside the bed, was a high table, pushed to one side. There was a plastic cup of water on it, but nothing else. I licked my lips, realising just how dry they were.

'Will?'

I turned my head the other way. God, it was so stiff. I felt like I was trapped in a brace. I suddenly remembered the time I got into a fight with Jack, when we were kids, how he'd held me in a headlock and refused to let go. The same feeling of panic was building inside me now.

'Where... What's going on?'

A nurse was on my other side, fiddling with tubes and drips that threaded out of my arm like spaghetti. She smiled at me. She was in her forties I guessed, with blonde hair cut into a neat bob. She looked a bit like an old actress my mum used to like – I couldn't think of her name.

Marilyn? No.

Greta? No.

Grace? Was that it? Grace Kelly?

'I'm your nurse, Will. You can call me Geri.'

'Like the Spice Girls?'

She giggled. 'If you like – although I look nothing like her and I can't sing!'

I wasn't sure the real one could either, but I didn't say that. Although words were forming in my brain, they felt sludgy on my tongue, like I couldn't move them into place properly. I wiggled my mouth around, not realising it was possible to feel this stiff.

'You've been unconscious for a little while,' Geri said softly. 'The doctors put you in an induced coma to reduce some swelling to your brain.'

'My brain?'

Fuck, my brain! That wasn't good.

'Am I... Am I OK?'

Stupid question, Will! I was in a hospital. Of course, I wasn't OK. Why couldn't I come up with better questions? Why was nothing making sense? The need to go back to sleep was also clawing at me: a lovely, swirly dark pit where I could rest my mind and not worry about this for a moment or two.

'You've bruised a rib, got yourself some nasty cuts to your face.' She touched my cheek to indicate, but I couldn't feel anything, as it was all numb. 'You haven't lost your good looks, though, don't worry.'

'Good looks?' I snorted. 'Maybe *you* have the brain damage.'

Her grin widened. 'I see your sense of humour is still working.'

'But my brain?' I tried to reach up to touch it, but my arms felt too heavy.

It had never been that great, if I was honest, but I knew I needed it to get through everyday life. A brain was a big deal, right? It wasn't something you could just mess around with. It wasn't a spleen or, I don't know, a little toe.

'The consultant will need to see you – but the fact that you are awake and talking, joking even, is good. Reassuring.' Nurse Geri nodded. 'You just need to rest now, give your body time to recover. It's been through a lot.'

I screwed up my face, trying to think back. Everything was a thick blur. I could remember leaving the flat, but where was I going? And where was—

'Do you know what happened?' Geri asked carefully, perhaps reading my expression.

'No – no, I don't. Did I fall or get into a fight?' A sharp fear suddenly exploded inside of me. 'Oh God, is my girlfriend OK? She—'

Geri put her hand on my arm to calm me. 'She's fine, Will. She's been here the whole time, holding your hand, talking to you. She only went home to have a shower and get a little rest. I will call her now and tell her you are awake. She'll be so relieved.'

I felt everything inside me relax.

Thank God.

'You were in a car accident, Will. Quite a nasty one. That's how you ended up here.'

'Car?' I frowned. 'But I don't own a car.'

'Don't worry about that now. Everything will make sense soon, I'm sure. You just need to take some time, OK?'

I sighed, reality hitting me. I was in a hospital, one of the places I hated the most, and I had no idea how I got here – and, somehow, I had managed to batter my brain.

I'd had better days.

'When did this happen?' I asked.

'Well, like I said, you were in an induced coma overnight. The accident was yesterday morning.'

'What was the date yesterday?'

'It was the 18th of July.'

Something whirled and dipped inside of me. That bloody date. It had always been such a horrible one, trust me to make it worse.

'You're joking! I need my phone. I need to—'

'And you will have that soon. Just be patient – you're not going anywhere.'

Geri fluttered around me, making me sip water that slipped down my dry, parched throat beautifully. She checked my blood pressure and my heart rate while talking in her soothing nurse-trained voice.

By the time she left, I couldn't fight it any longer. Sleep was insisting on taking over. I just hoped the next time I opened my eyes, things would make more sense.

–

I don't know how long I slept. Hours maybe. A voice woke me up, deep and official. Blinking my eyes open, I saw a man standing over me, his white coat and serious expression telling me he wasn't here for the entertainment.

'Ah, Will! Good to see you back with us!'

Where had I been before?

I tried to shift on the bed. It was tilted slightly. My bum cheeks were aching, and I could now feel a dull pain in my left side.

'I still don't understand—'

'You were in a nasty crash. Your head took most of the impact. Fortunately, you were wearing your seat belt, and your car is one of the best for safety.' The man stepped forward. He had deep wrinkles, more like crevices, and his thick grey hair was clipped short. His dark grey eyes looked me up and down like he was re-examining me. 'I'm your consultant, Mr James. I've been taking care of you.'

'Well, of course I'd wear a belt.'

I wasn't stupid, was I? I blinked, no longer sure – why was this man still frowning at me?

'I don't even have a car,' I muttered. 'Who was driving? Was it Jack?' He was normally a sensible enough driver, but who knew. Another thought struck me with horror. 'Shit – is Jack OK?'

Mr James frowned. 'Will, you were alone in the car. No one else was driving. At some point the police will need to speak to you, to work out what happened.'

'Driving?' I shook my head. This didn't make sense. 'Doctor, I haven't got a car.'

'I see...' His eyes seemed to bore into mine, judging me. I had to turn my head away, suddenly feeling quite shamed.

Why couldn't I remember? Why on earth would I be behind the wheel of a car? No wonder I crashed. I was lucky I didn't—

Oh God.

'Did I hurt anyone else?'

'No, thankfully. You crashed into a tree. Luckily, no other vehicles were involved.' He stepped forward. 'Will, we found bruising to your brain and a small bleed. We managed to stabilise that, but you will need some time to recover. Aside from your other injuries – your ribs, for example – we will need to do some neurological rehabilitation with you, to ensure your brain is functioning as it should.'

I felt like my brain was already struggling with all this new information. It was too much. I was a criminal. I had driven and crashed a car that I didn't own, and now I had a brain injury to worry about. How long would it be before the police arrived to arrest me?

'Will I recover?'

'Well, you're in the right place to do so and you certainly seem to be on the right track.' Mr James flashed a bright light at my eyes and peered carefully into them.

'I'm just going to ask you a few questions, if that's OK. Tell me your full name, please?'

'William Henry Manning.'

'The date?'

I remembered what the nurse had told me before. 'I know I crashed on a bloody bad day – the 18th of July – so today is the 19th of July, right?'

Mr James nodded, clearly not interested in those details.

'Who is the prime minister?'

I told him the answer and watched his face darken. He stepped back, the light still gripped between his fingertips.

'Will, what year is it?'

'It's 2019.' I paused. 'Why are you frowning like that, is something wrong?'

'Will, I...'

I pulled myself more upright – a struggle because of the pain in my side, but I managed it. I felt so disgusting and sweaty. All I wanted to do was get out of here. I wanted to be home. I wanted—

'Where's my girlfriend?' I demanded. 'I need to see her.'

At that moment, there was a movement in the doorway and a figure strode confidently in, dressed in a cut-off top and skinny dark jeans. She had a mass of shiny blonde hair and a pretty made-up face. She beamed in my direction like I was the best thing since Christmas.

'Will! I'm here. I'm here now.'

'What?'

'I'm here! I'm sorry I wasn't here when you woke up, but the nurses called me straight away. I rushed to come back.'

She leant in towards me, as if to give me a kiss, and I immediately pulled back.

I couldn't help it. The words leapt from me in both disgust and confusion.

'Who the hell are you? And where is my Gem?'

Before

Gem – 1995

'No. No, I'm sorry, darling, I can't.'

Mum was curled up on the sofa, still wearing the dressing gown that she had had on for weeks. The TV was on, and she stared at it bleakly, even though I knew she wasn't watching it – not really.

According to my diary, we had been in this new house for three months now, but it didn't feel like it. There were still boxes everywhere. The few clothes I had were still bagged up in bin liners. There were no toys. I had lost those. All I had left was my bedraggled teddy that still stank of smoke if I breathed him in too hard and the doll that Nan had given me years ago.

'I just want to go to the park,' I said.

I was grumpy. I didn't like it here. I knew the park was just across the estate, probably only a few minutes' walk. I was sick of sitting in this poky house that smelt funny and I was sick of staying in the tiny garden. It was just a small patch of grass with some unruly shrubs growing around the edges. The only thing to do was to watch the birds swooping in the trees. I liked watching them: they were so busy, so free.

Unlike us.

'I miss Nan,' I said, louder now.

28

We should've been allowed to stay with her, in the flat. It was what Nan wanted but Mum said it wasn't fair. She said Nan was too old now, too tired, and that she needed her own space.

At five, I was old enough to know when adults lied, and I could always tell when my mum was, because she could never look me in the eye.

It was happening more and more lately.

'I can't take you out, Gemma, I'm too tired,' she whispered. 'Maybe tomorrow. Maybe tomorrow I'll feel better.'

Another lie tripping off her tongue, and another day of more of the same.

–

Later, she fell asleep. I saw the mug sitting on the table. It still had the drink inside that smelt funny. I knew she would wake up with a headache and a grumpy voice.

I was sick of being in the house. Outside, the sun was shining. I slipped on my tatty trainers and pulled open the front door. The Osbourne estate seemed huge now, limitless. I took a few steps out onto the main footpath, fascinated by the cacophony of sounds around me. There were kids playing everywhere.

I moved slowly, suddenly a bit scared. The park seemed too far away, and lots of the children were staring at me. I wondered if they didn't like my boyish haircut, for which I was teased a lot at school – or maybe it was my mismatched clothes and the way my too-short trousers skimmed above my ankles as I walked.

'Hey!'

I looked up: two boys were standing on the patch of green opposite me. The taller one was holding a ball. They both had dark, floppy hair but the shorter boy had dark blue eyes that seemed to be staring at me intently.

'What's your name?' he asked. 'You're new here?'

I pulled a face. I didn't much like boys. The ones at my school were mean and pushed me in the playground. 'I'm Gemma. Gem.'

'You moved in the Hendersons' old house,' said the older boy. 'He died, you know?'

I felt sick. 'What, in the house?'

The boys both laughed. 'No – in hospital. He was really, really old.' The older boy kicked the ball towards me. 'You play?'

I didn't. But that day I decided I would.

I soon learnt that Will, a year older than me, and Jack, four whole years older me, only lived down the bottom of the road. They had lived here all their life, with their mum Gayle. Their dad had 'run off years ago'. Both boys pulled a face when they spoke about him, so I knew it wasn't a good thing.

When they asked about my family, I got a bit worked up. I didn't want to cry, but the combination of someone being nice to me and my worries about my mum made it hard for me to keep my emotions in check. To my surprise, Will and Jack weren't nasty about the tears – they didn't tease me or make fun of the snot drizzling out of my nose.

Instead, they told me to sit down on the low wall and Will gave me a scrappy old tissue that was buried deep in his pocket.

'It's clean,' he promised me. 'I think it's even been through the wash.'

I dabbed at my nose and told them about the house fire. About how my lovely, brave dad had died, and me and my mum had to live with my nan for a bit while the council tried to re-house us.

'We lost everything,' I said.

Will sat down beside me. 'That sounds horrible,' he said.

'And now my mum isn't the same. She cries all of the time and she won't leave the house.'

'She needs to meet our mum,' Jack said. 'She is an expert at fixing people. She'll know what to do.'

Will took my hand. His was a bit sticky, but it was warm and soft.

'Come on,' he said. 'We'll introduce you. She's really nice.'

'Really?' I said, unsure.

'Really,' Will replied. 'You've got us now. I'm going to look after you.'

Chapter Four

Gem – 2022

My first instinct was to call Mum.

You could never describe my relationship with Mum as being good. She'd been badly affected by the house fire, for good reason, and I couldn't remember a time when we didn't struggle. In the years that followed we were finally moved into a poky little maisonette across town that stank of mould and decay. Mum didn't really see the point in anything. She spent most of her days in bed, or down the pub, drowning her sorrows in gin or prescription medication.

I guess I didn't have what you would call a 'happy childhood'.

There was a barrier up between me and my mum, and I wasn't sure it could ever be knocked down, but the one thing we shared was our love of Will. Sometimes I was convinced Mum loved my ex-boyfriend more than she could ever love me.

Telling her the news over the phone wasn't an easy thing to do.

'Oh God.' I could hear Mum was breathing a bit too fast. I pictured her pacing the room, her hands clenching and unclenching. She was never good with bad stuff, and there was always a risk it would send her spiralling again.

'Oh God, Gem,' she said, her voice cracking. 'It's awful. Poor Will.'

'I know,' I said. 'I can't even get my head around it.'

'I should go,' Mum muttered. 'I should, but I can't – you know I can't, Gem. You know how I feel about hospitals. I just can't stand that... I can't – not since your dad—'

I could hear the break in her voice, so familiar. I tried to force back the little bit of frustration that was building inside me. *Why can't you see him, Mum? He loved you too. You were like another mother to him...*

'I don't know what to do,' I said instead. 'Jack wants me to be there and see what's going on. He won't get a straight answer from Nicola.'

Mum sucked in a breath. 'That bloody bitch wouldn't tell us anything.'

I shook my head. This wasn't helping.

'I guess I could go,' I said finally. 'Just pop in? I'm not sure it's a good idea, but—'

'You have to go,' Mum interrupted firmly. 'You have to, Gem. I know you might not want to, but right now Will needs you. You have to do the right thing.'

The right thing! Yeah, of course. Didn't I always.

I hung up the phone, feeling both defeated and frustrated. So now I was going to have to visit the man that nearly broke me. I wasn't sure how I felt about that.

And I wasn't sure how Richard would feel about it either.

—

Richard was, as I expected, on the sofa, marking textbooks. In the background the TV was quiet, the voice of the newsreader like an annoying drone that I wanted to swat away. I hovered in the doorway, my handbag still clasped in my hands. The sofa was so tatty now, grey and faded at the arms – my attempt to conceal it with a shaggy throw and scatter cushions was no longer working. To be fair, the bloody thing had been in a state when we had collected it from the charity shop ten-odd years ago and Will lugged it into the van with Jack. God, had I really had it that long? I still remember giggling behind the two brothers as they tried to manoeuvre the thing up the stairs, because of course the lift was on the blink again.

'We should've bought new,' Will grunted. 'I told you. Debt would have been better than a ruptured spinal disc.'

'This was a bargain!' I sang back, still happy that I'd managed to swing £50 off the asking price because of some loose stitching on the seams. I could sort that – no problem. Our entire flat was crammed full of random bargains that I had secured either second hand or via friends and family. It was an eclectic mix of colour, vibrance and a little hint of tat.

We christened that sofa on its first night home, so Will called it a welcome-home present. In fact, it happened in about the same spot where Richard was sitting now.

Richard didn't like having sex on the sofa. Sex was for bedtime, safe beneath the covers and with the lights turned low.

'Gemma? Are you OK?'

He was looking at me now, peering over his glasses in that stereotypical way that made me want to scream with laughter. But instead, I felt my body sink and I clung to the door frame, wishing I could be somewhere else.

'I've had bad news – I've been talking to my mum.'

'Oh no, is she all right?' He pushed aside his papers and gestured for me to sit beside him. 'Come over here! You look like you need a hug. My God, you're so pale...'

I staggered over and perched on the edge of the cushion. Richard's arm felt too heavy, too overbearing, as it twisted around my waist, but it seemed too rude to shrug him off.

'Could you maybe get me a water?' I licked my lips. I could still taste that soda water, and it seemed to be making my mouth even drier.

'Of course!' He leapt up, as if keen for something to do.

I watched as he rattled about in our small kitchen, finding a glass, carefully rinsing it out, and letting the water run some more before he filled it for me. Richard preferred bottled water, claiming it tasted 'so much better'. I had finally worn him down with my argument that tap water was just as good, as well as better for the environment and cheaper. It was one of the smaller battles I had won.

'What's happened?' he asked, as he walked back over to me, passing me the glass carefully. 'Is your mum – well, uh, is she in trouble?'

'No, no, she's fine...' I sipped the water.

Was that even true? I wasn't sure my mum would ever, really, be fine, but she was safe for now.

'I called her because I'd had some news.' I placed the glass between my feet. My hands were shaking, and I had to grip them together to make them stop. Inside, my stomach was still doing somersaults. 'I spoke to Will's brother, Jack.'

'Will, your ex?'

There was a sharpness there. I chose to ignore it.

'Yes… Will, my ex…' Even saying his name made that pain come back, right in the middle of my chest. I pressed my hand there as if to force it away.

I thought of Jack, Will's lovable, slightly goofy older brother. Both of them had taken my mum under their wing a bit. At the time it had annoyed me, as I'd assumed they wanted a replacement mum, someone to nurture and cherish, but looking back at it now, I think it was much simpler than that. They just saw something in my mum that I didn't. They brought out the best in her.

'Will has been hurt. Badly hurt,' I said finally. 'He's been in a car crash. I couldn't get much out of Jack; he was in a bit of a state, but he said something about an induced coma – about a head injury…' I shook my head, feeling the sickness rise inside of me. 'He's stuck in America. He can't come back yet but he's sorting stuff out.'

My voice broke, and I swiped at my face, trying to stop the tears.

'I always nagged Will about getting himself a car. He never wanted to, all the time we were together. It wasn't important to him at all, but then he got that shitty job and met those arseholes and everything – everything changed… and now look…'

Richard sat down beside me again.

'And why can't Jack rush back?'

I shrugged. 'Jack wants me to see Will, check how he is, and he'll make a decision then. He's got a few tour dates booked out there, and it's not easy for him to give everything up. Also, I don't think he can face him yet. He's still hurting.'

We both were, even after all this time.

'What do you want to do?' Richard asked quietly.

'What do I want to do?' My voice was louder than it should have been. But none of this was Richard's fault. I shook my head, tried to calm myself. 'I want to rewind the day. I want to start all over. I want not to have taken that call...'

I found myself crumbling into Richard's arms, my wet face pressed up against his white shirt, breathing in his lovely, reassuring, clean smell. He enveloped me in a hug, making me feel safe once more, his lips gently pressing against my neck.

'I want to see him, Richard...' I said finally. 'I need to see Will.'

–

The last time I'd seen Will was at the flat, when he'd come back for the last of his stuff. It wasn't much, really, just a bag of clothes, some records I'd found discarded under the bed, an old pair of trainers that he'd probably sling out straight away. Will took it all gratefully, like it was precious. He couldn't look at me properly – he never could in those days. I think we both knew that if we held eye contact, we would burst into tears.

'Here.' He passed me a wad of paperwork.

I knew what it was. He had signed over his half of the flat. No arguments, no questions. This place was mine now.

'Will you manage?' he asked, his voice soft, almost a whisper.

'I'll cope.' I knew my tone was still brittle, but I didn't care. This used to be ours. We had such plans, such dreams. I couldn't bear to have him in this space a minute longer, in case he tainted it even more.

'Gem...'

I didn't look up. My eyes were still fixed on his stupid shoes. Shiny leather. He must have spent hours polishing them. So unlike him. The Will I knew, *the Will I used to know*, lived in scruffy trainers and holey socks. Yet, now here he was, in a neat, well-fitting suit and a pink tie that I would quite happily have strangled him with.

'Gem,' he tried again, stepping forward so that he was in my light. 'Gem, I never wanted this. You know that, right?'

I shook my head. 'You made your choice, Will. You fucked up.'

'I know... I know, I just wish...' His hands combed through his hair, which was slicker now, not long and floppy like it used to be. 'If I could turn back time, you know—'

'I know. I know, you would.' My words were like little bullets flying at him. 'But you can't, Will, can you? You did this to us. You created this mess. It is what it is.'

His head hung low. 'I just wish—'

'There's no point wishing.' The papers were clutched tightly in my hand and I held them in front of him. 'This is the proof. It's over now.'

'I still love you, Gemma.' He turned slowly towards the front door, defeated. 'You know that. Everything we've been through... You know we're meant to be.'

'No.' I was flat, deflated. 'I thought I knew, but I was wrong.'

'It'll never change for me,' he said. 'Just remember that.'

I slammed the door on his face and then fell to the floor, the stupid papers now crumpled in my fists.

Will had destroyed everything. He had shattered every part of me and I knew in that moment that I could never let him get close to me again.

And yet, here I was, three years later, standing outside a hospital ward, plucking up the courage to actually walk in.

Three years was a long time in theory, but in reality it felt like no time at all. Everything had been a blur of work, family commitments, hiding myself away... and then the horror of Covid and the months that followed that. I'd been so thankful to meet Richard just before the lockdowns. He had understood the position I was in and hadn't wanted to rush anything, happy to go at my pace. Perhaps if lockdown hadn't happened, he might not have moved in, but we were two lonely people, so what was the harm? When everything went back to normal, Richard just stayed. I was used to him by then.

And I needed him. Richard stopped me thinking about Will: the scars had started to heal, and I was moving on.

So how was I here, standing outside Will's ward?

Richard had questioned what good it would do before I left the flat in the morning. 'You're not his girlfriend now. He's not your responsibility. Won't Nicola be with him?'

I flinched, hating myself for the instinctive unkind thoughts towards Nicola. Like Vee said, I needed to give her a chance. 'Yes, probably,' I replied. 'I just think... I don't know, Richard. We've known each other for so long – since we were children. We always used to look out for each other, the three of us.'

'I know. I get that, but he's still your ex.' Richard eyed my carefully straightened hair with suspicion. 'It just feels odd.'

'I'm going to check on him, that's all. Jack asked me to, and Mum wants me to as well.'

And when had I ever done anything that Mum had asked me to do before? I couldn't blame Richard for looking slightly confused.

I could have turned back, of course. I was pretty sure I would be the last person that Will wanted to see anyway, but something held me back. I found myself lingering outside the doorway of Steyning ward, one hand clutching my phone as if I was hoping a sudden call might save me from making a decision.

'Can I help you?' A nurse was beside me, clutching a load of files. She smiled warmly and gestured with her head towards the ward. 'Have you come to see someone here?'

'Well… I don't know. Sort of.'

'It can be scary, can't it?' she said softly. 'Is it a relative?'

What could I say? He had been the love of my life once, the most important man, but now I wasn't so sure.

'I've known him forever…' I said instead. 'His brother can't come so he asked me. He wanted me to check…'

'What is his name?'

'Will. Will Manning.'

'Oh!' The nurse shifted her files onto her other arm. 'I've been keeping an eye on Will. He's not long been awake.'

'He's awake?'

'Yes. I think the doctor has just finished with him, so you are in good time. His girlfriend has been here, of course, but no one else—'

'There is no one else,' I said quietly. 'His mum died years ago. His brother, Jack, is abroad.'

For so long it had just been the two of us. Just like the song.

You and me, always – and forever.

The line that he loved to sing to me.

'I really just wanted to make sure he's all right. I won't stay long.'

She smiled again. 'Come on, follow me. I promise you there is nothing to be scared of.'

God, she couldn't have been more wrong. As I followed her like an obedient little puppy, I could feel my insides jumbling about like a washing machine. We drifted down a corridor with rooms curtained off; it was quiet down there and a feeling of doom washed over me. This was a bad place. This was where people came when they were in a very poorly state.

'Will is just in here,' the nurse said, stopping outside the second-to-last doorway.

I stood outside, frozen again. What the hell was I thinking? This was madness, pure madness.

'You could just tell him I came…' I said, my confidence wavering. 'Just tell him I was here. I'm Gem and I wanted to—'

'Gem?' she interrupted, raising one eyebrow. 'He's been saying that name a lot. He's been asking for you.'

'Really?'

She nodded. 'Yes. Look, it's up to you what you do, but I think he would really appreciate a visit. You don't have to stay long, do you?'

'No,' I whispered. 'I don't suppose I do.'

I stepped in.

I don't know what I was expecting to see. Perhaps Will, sat up in bed, that cheeky grin plastered across his

41

face, a naughty wink greeting me and telling me off for worrying.

It was scary to see him hooked up to so many machines, staring vacantly at the ceiling, his head wrapped in bandages, his face thin and bruised. There was another bandage stuck on his left cheek, with the stain of blood beneath.

He looked broken and lost. Not like my Will at all.

My. Why had I said *my*? He hadn't been mine for a long time.

'Will?' I gasped. 'What the hell happened?'

His head turned quickly. His blue eyes blinked in recognition.

'Gem? Gemma? Is that really you?'

And he burst into tears.

Chapter Five

Will – 2022

The woman that wasn't Gem was not happy. She snatched her hand away from me and started pacing the room.

'What's wrong? How can you not remember me? This is crazy!'

Yes, it was crazy. This entire situation was. I felt like I was in a bad film, one of those trashy ones that Gem always made me watch. My head was swimming and sickness was washing over me again. I hated feeling so grumpy, so out of control, and I just wanted this woman gone.

Mr James, my smooth-talking doctor, immediately took control. He walked over to the woman and tried to reassure her. I heard words drifting over me:

Head injury.

Substantial memory loss.

Temporary.

Trauma.

I wanted to interrupt. I wanted to shout that there was nothing wrong with me and they had this all back to front. My brain was perfectly fine: I knew this woman had nothing to do with me, nothing at all. There had to have been some kind of mistake. Perhaps she was some kind of nutter?

'I want Gem. My Gemma,' I demanded loudly. 'Can someone just call her? Please? Tell her I need her. She's probably at work, or—'

'Gem's not coming,' the woman snapped, breaking away from Mr James. 'I'm here! Nicola! Your girlfriend.' She thrust her hand in front of me and I noticed a large ring sparkling on her finger. 'Your *fiancée.*'

'I – this is crap!'

I was going to say more, but my eyes were fixed on the ring. I knew this ring. I recognised it instantly. I had kept it for years in a blue velvet box in my wardrobe, sure I was going to give it to Gem one day. One day soon. It was the most precious thing I owned.

My mum's engagement ring – one of the few things I had left of hers.

'How did you get this?' I hissed, gripping her hand.

She tugged it away. I saw her face was streaked with tears, ruining that pretty make-up. She looked like a doll that a toddler had smeared with crayons – beautiful but ruined. Had I really done this to her?

'You gave it to me, Will.' She sniffed. 'Last month. In Paris. You don't remember?'

'I've not been to Paris. I've *never* been to Paris,' I said, rubbing my eyes. 'This can't be happening.'

I'd never even left the country. Gemma used to tease me that the furthest I'd ever been was Scotland, and even then I still ended up getting travel sick.

See! I could remember that. My brain couldn't be that bad. What was this stupid doctor on about? I glared at him, but he was looking at this woman with an expression of concern.

'You have, Will – you've been to Paris with me, to Cyprus too.'

44

Her voice was rising now, drilling painfully into my head.

'Miss Young, this isn't helping.' Mr James rested a hand on her shoulder. 'What Will needs is rest, and plenty of it. His brain has suffered an awful shock.'

'I don't understand...' I whispered.

'I don't either.' Nicola sniffed, stepping back. 'You must remember me – us! It's just so wrong...'

'I'm sorry.' It's all I could find to say. I wanted her gone.

'Maybe you could get yourself a drink? Have a little walk in the fresh air? You've been here for some time, haven't you?' Mr James said gently to her. 'We can have a talk when you get back. It might help you to process things.'

'I don't want to leave Will,' she said.

It made me sad that I felt absolutely nothing when she said this. I hated seeing those blue, tear-filled eyes staring down at me. Her nose was pink, and her cheeks still streaked with moisture. She was very small and petite, like a fragile bird. When she lifted her arm to rake her thick hair away from her face, I noticed how thin it was.

I wish I knew who she was.

After all, she had Mum's ring – that meant she was important to me. That meant I must love her but if that was the case, what the hell had happened to Gem?

A sudden blast of ice opened up inside me.

'Where is Gem? Where is she? She should be here!'

I saw the look of pain in Nicola's eyes, another bullet that I had needlessly delivered. She turned and fled the room.

Mr James stood at the end of my bed. His face had that kind of sympathetic smile that doctors adopt when they are about to deliver bad news. Another memory pierced me, this one much further back: my mum, sitting in a similar hospital bed, a drip attached to her arm, skin thin and yellow in the poor light. Jack and I were there by her side. I hadn't been old. Fourteen, that was all. I had only just had my birthday. I remember I was wearing the bright white trainers that mum had got me especially. They were a bit too big, but I didn't care. I preferred looking at them rather than the heavily bearded doctor who had just walked in.

'*Miss Manning. Maybe I should speak to you alone.*'

'*No. My boys are always with me. They need to be here.*'

He had the same expression, that doctor, that same sad expression that didn't quite reach the eyes.

'*Miss Manning, I'm sorry to tell you, but the treatment—*'

'Will?' Mr James snapped me back into the moment. I blinked, embarrassed that I had been caught daydreaming like a stupid kid.

'Had you remembered something?'

'Yes – but from long ago.' I frowned. 'It just hit me quite hard.'

And vivid, too. I could smell that room, remember the squeaking noise the soles of my shoes had made on the beige-coloured floor. I never did wear those trainers again, not after that day.

'You might find that,' Mr James said quietly. 'If you picture your mind like a storage cupboard, it's like its contents have been tipped upside down and spilt all over the place. Things that may have been stored tightly away might come to light – and other things might, well...'

'Be lost?'

'Perhaps.' He rubbed his chin thoughtfully. 'The brain is a complex thing, Will. It has a wonderful ability to restore itself, but we can never predict how and when.

Your scans were positive and didn't indicate any long-term damage, but there's always a possibility that some things may not be as they were. You had a small bleed and swelling, and we are not sure at this stage what damage that might have caused.'

I frowned. 'How much have I actually forgotten? I mean, I didn't know that woman who was in the room with me. She was talking about trips abroad I've never been on. I have no idea who she is.'

'She is your girlfriend, Will. She was on your phone. Your brother Jack confirmed it too.'

'Jack? Where even is he?'

'Abroad. In America. He's in a band, I believe? That's what your girlfriend—'

'No! We're in a band! I'm the lead bloody guitarist.' I could hear my voice rising. 'We have been for years. Why is he out there without me?'

I saw that expression again. That sad, pitying look. The reality was kicking in, but I didn't want to accept it. I just couldn't.

Gingerly, I found the words, even though I practically had to choke them out.

'How much have I forgotten?'

'Will, you still think it's 2019. It's actually 2022.'

What. The. Fuck.

I slumped back. This was too much. It had to be a sick joke, right? How had I lost three years? How could this be happening?

In that time, apparently, I'd been driving and travelling abroad. I was shacked up with some blonde woman and my brother was touring the world without me. And Gem – Gem, was fucking nowhere.

'But will I get my memory back?' I asked.

'There is no way of knowing that, Will. We will keep you with us for a while, work on some rehabilitation, but with things like this it's usually time and patience that are needed, a lot of wait and see.'

Wait and see? I had to wait and see if I could get my life back on track?

'Will?'

'I think I'd rather be alone now, Doctor. If that's OK.'

It was a lie, of course. I didn't want to be alone, any more than I wanted this stupid broken brain of mine, but I couldn't stand to look at his sad expression.

It was making me want to punch him.

–

I tried not to think, I really did. I just wanted to clear my head of everything. I figured that if I was completely relaxed and my mind was empty, maybe my memories would drift back, like birds returning to roost, but nothing seemed to change.

Instead, my thoughts were muddled and blurred.

I remembered Gem at the door of the flat.

I remembered kissing her, before I left.

And I remembered a bike – yes, that's right, a bike. Wobbly and knackered and far too old, and I clambered on.

But then nothing.

What happened next?

I tried desperately to piece together the next images, but nothing came to me.

Nothing at all.

'Will?'

A shudder ran through the entire length of my body. For a moment, I could barely stand to look. Was my brain playing tricks on me? I'd only drifted off for a second or two, so it was possible I was dreaming.

Either way, I'd know that voice anywhere. Some things become embedded so deep inside a person that they're like DNA, they can't be removed.

'Gem?' I knew I was crying, big sobby tears as she stepped into the room.

It was Gem, except it wasn't.

I blinked a few times and tried to force back the sickly feeling that was taking over. My world seemed to be tipping and racing out of my control. I gripped the sheets of the bed as if I could stop it.

This was wrong, so wrong.

This Gem looked different. Too different. Her hair was no longer a vibrant red, hanging in thick waves around her face. I used to joke that she was my 'strawberry bomb' – everything about her had been healthy, rich and stunning.

She was still stunning, of course, but not as I remembered. Her hair was shorter, cut bluntly just below her chin. Her curls were now replaced with straight, glossy locks. She was skinnier, too, and somehow frailer-looking.

The worst thing, though, was her expression. There was something there I didn't recognise: a hardness, a coldness that immediately pushed a barrier up between us. Her eyes were sad, but distant.

She might as well have been a stranger.

'Gem?' I said, feeling my entire resolve break in two. 'What the hell has happened to us?'

She stared back at me, her eyes wide with shock.

My next question came out in a desperate cry.

'What did I do?'

Before

Gem – 2003

No more! I couldn't stand this any longer. In my room, I managed to throw a few things into my rucksack while Mum screamed abuse from the bottom of the stairs.

'*You think you're the only one that matters!*'

I slammed my bedside drawer, desperately hunting for my diary, for a few pairs of clean underwear.

'*You never listen – that's your trouble! You're too selfish!*'

I tugged at my duvet, pulling it down and exposing the sheet that hadn't been changed for weeks. There was no point me doing it. I didn't even think we had clean bed linen anymore.

'*You just don't care. You don't know what I've been through…*'

I grabbed Teddy. At thirteen, I was too old to still have him, I knew that, but it was the only part of Dad I had left. His rough fur brushed against my fingers as I rammed him into the bag. I couldn't leave him behind. I didn't before and I wasn't going to again.

I left my room, throwing my bag over my shoulder and bracing myself for a further onslaught. Mum stood on the bottom step, looking up at me bleakly. I couldn't even remember how this argument had started. Was it about me wanting friends over? Having no food in the fridge?

The fact that Mum could never grant us permission to be happy?

I'm not sure it even mattered. All I knew was that I needed to get out.

'Are you going to Nan's?' she asked.

I nodded. Usually, I only popped over there for a break, a few hours' respite from the chaos here, but now I knew I had to stay away for longer.

I came down the stairs slowly, my bag feeling suddenly heavy. I wondered if she might reach out to me at that moment. If she might say she was sorry, or even pull me into a hug.

I hesitated when I passed her, thinking that the moment might come.

Mum sighed. 'Well, don't drive her mad too,' she said finally, before shuffling back into the living room.

Nan's flat was a different world, like walking in from the dark to the light. The minute I entered, I could smell beef stew cooking and my stomach rumbled. Nan rushed to meet me. She was taller than my mum and very thin, too thin maybe. Her hair was blonde and curly and so fine that it reminded me of candyfloss. While my mum crumbled and hid, my nan stood strong and proud.

She complained about my creased uniform, moaned about the lack of clothes in my bag and told me she was going to get my unruly hair trimmed.

'Your mum can't help it, you know,' she said, pulling me into a hug. 'She blames herself for what happened. It's too much for her. Your mum suffers so much because she loved your dad to death. What they had was a magical thing, a special thing,' she said wistfully. 'They completed each other, made each other feel alive.'

'That sounds wonderful.' I sniffled, wishing I could remember my dad more.

'One day you might have the same thing and it might help you to understand your mum better,' she said. 'Losing the one that you love is a hard thing.'

'But I'm still here,' I whispered.

'I know. I know you are.' Nan touched my hair, so much like hers, except in colour – I'd inherited my ginger from a man I barely knew.

'She loves you,' Nan said softly. 'She loves you so much, but her love makes her scared now.'

I couldn't understand how love could be scary. It sounded crazy to me. I screwed my eyes shut and just hoped that one day I would meet someone who would make me feel as good as Dad had made Mum feel.

I wanted love.

The closest thing I had was Will – my best friend and protector. When I started secondary school, he was there to make sure I was OK and that the bullies left me alone. When I moved in with Nan a year later, he was also there, helping me go back to Mum's and pick up some bits. He stood in the kitchen, chatting to her while I filled up a case. For the first time in ages, I heard her laughing.

'She really loves you,' I said, trying not to let the bitterness show.

Will looked unfazed. 'She doesn't love me,' he said. 'She just thinks I'm a bit daft. I take her mind off things.'

Rather than me, who reminded her of everything.

A few months after I moved permanently into Nan's, Will came to see me. I could tell he was upset. His face was pale, and his eyes were red-rimmed. We went for a walk together, and as we started to walk out of Beckett Court, towards the Osbourne estate, he finally spoke.

'My mum is really sick. Her cancer is back.'

I looked at him shocked. 'I didn't even know she'd had cancer. Will she be OK?' I asked.

Will shrugged. His dark hair flopped in his eyes, and he pushed it away. 'She keeps telling us not to worry, that she will fight it, but Jack has done some research. It's in her pancreas and really aggressive...'

'Oh, Will – I'm so sorry.'

He shivered, looked away from me. 'It's OK, there's nothing you can say, really.'

'Will you be OK?'

'I have Jack. We'll always look after each other.'

'And you have me.' I tugged on his arm. 'Always.'

He held my gaze and smiled weakly. 'Thanks, Gem. That means a lot.'

We stood for ages like that, me just gripping his arm and Will staring off somewhere far away, but it felt natural. It felt good.

'I like being with you,' he said finally. 'You're good to talk to and make things feel better.'

'Do I?'

He nodded. 'Yeah – you really do.'

Chapter Six

Gem – 2022

I was standing in a cold hospital room, staring at a man who had become a stranger to me. And now he was asking a question I didn't want to answer.

'What did I do, Gem?' he repeated.

I shook my head.

This wasn't what I was expecting. I don't know what I was expecting, really, but it wasn't this – a pitiful Will, laid up and looking at me with big fearful eyes.

I wanted to run out of there and get myself far away from this sterile room, back to the safety of my flat. But instead, I stood rooted to the spot, feeling uncomfortable and out of place.

Looking at Will was like looking at a small child. He seemed so desperate, so needy, but what was I expecting? Him sitting there in bed in his suit and shiny shoes – untouched and unflappable, laughing the whole thing off? Or the other version of Will: the distant, hurtful one that I could barely bring myself to think about. What version of Will did I think I'd see?

'Will, I'm not sure I understand.' I glanced around the poky space. There was just Will's bed, a machine monitoring something, a drip and a chair, which was shoved up close to his bed. But I couldn't bring myself to sit there. It seemed wrong – too familiar. Instead, I stood at the foot of the bed, awkwardly fiddling with the strap on my bag.

'I was told you were in a car accident. I'm guessing you were speeding again. Jack said you loved showing off in that bloody thing...'

Will was rubbing his hands frantically. 'No, no, Gem. You don't understand. I mean, what did I do to us?'

'Us?' I felt a horribly familiar swooping sensation in my stomach. That sinking feeling I had managed to ignore for so long. Three years; it sounds like a long time, but it's really not when your insides have been reduced to ash. Sometimes I wondered if I would ever be myself again. Why was he bringing this all up again?

'Will. We don't need to go over this now,' I said quietly. 'I'm not staying long. I just wanted to pop in, to send my...'

What? Love?

No. Not that.

'To check on you,' I continued numbly. 'I promised Jack I would. He will be here to see you himself soon. He's getting on the next flight, I think.'

And then this won't be my problem anymore. I can move on – again. I can try to forget all about you.

Again.

Will swiped at his eyes; he was still crying, and it made my chest ache. Will wasn't a crier, not really.

'I can't remember stuff, Gem...' he said. 'They think I've lost three years or something. I thought we were still together. None of this makes any sense: me driving, me not being in the band.' He sniffed loudly; his watery blue eyes were now fixed on mine. 'Me not being with you.'

'You've lost three years?' I whispered, not quite under-standing. 'What, of your memory?'

'Yes… I can't – I don't even know if I'll get it back. All I know is that I'm in some kind of hell where nothing makes sense.'

It was all I could do not to rush to his side and grab his hand, but I held back, gripping the bedrail instead, making myself stay firm and steady. This was the man who had broken me, who had destroyed everything we had.

'It's probably just temporary, Will. You need to stay calm.'

'But it might not be…'

And so what? What do you want from me?

I took a deep breath and moved slowly away from the bed.

'I know the date,' he said, his voice cracking. 'I crashed on your bad day. I should've been with you.'

I blinked back at him, stunned that in the chaos of everything, he'd remembered that.

'Is Nicola here?' I asked.

He shook his head. 'No – I mean, she was, but she got upset. I didn't want her here.' His glassy eyes stared up at me. 'Who the hell is she? Why would I be with her and not you?'

I drew a breath. 'So much has happened. I'm not sure now is the time.'

'But I still think I'm with you. This feels so wrong, Gem. So wrong.'

I looked around, desperate to grab a nurse or a medic. Surely, they would have an answer to all of this. The only stuff I knew about amnesia was what I had picked up from TV dramas, and I was guessing they wouldn't be very accurate.

'Has a doctor talked to you? Do you know how long you could be like this?'

'They don't know.' I could hear the frustration now in his voice. The shake that was there when he was just about to lose his temper. 'They don't seem to know anything. It's all just "watch and wait", like I'm a bloody cake in the oven.'

'Well…' I attempted to soothe him. 'You have to let yourself heal. You've been through a huge trauma. Time is probably the best thing for you right now.'

He didn't reply. His entire body seemed to slump in the bed. For a moment or two neither of us spoke. I went to grip the end of the bed again, terrified that I might lose my balance if I didn't. Across the ward I could hear a peal of laughter, the clatter of what sounded like a tea trolley. My mind raced, thinking of Richard back at the flat and wondering what he would be doing. It was a Tuesday, we'd usually meet up in town, grab some dinner. Instead, he was probably indoors, watching an old film, and I was here – visiting an ex-boyfriend. My only ex-boyfriend.

An ex-boyfriend who thought we were still together.

I swallowed and made myself speak again.

'Will, so much has changed. I'm with someone else now, and so are you. We are both happy.' I paused, the tremor in my words almost giving me away. 'We weren't good together, Will, but thankfully we found that out in time. It was hard for both of us, but we had to move on. That's all. It's just a sad thing that happened.'

'And you're OK?' His voice was so gentle, laced with compassion. 'You're happy?'

'Yes – yes, I am. Busy and stuff, but I'm happy.'

He looked away, towards the window. 'I can't even picture you with someone else. It feels like a bloody nightmare.'

'I've been with Richard for two years, Will.'

'Two years...' He shook his head, like it was a joke. 'And he's nice to you, yeah?'

I smiled despite myself. 'He's really nice. He's a teacher like me. He's...' I tried to find the right word. 'He's what I need.'

'And you're busy?' he asked. 'You're still writing?'

I flinched, like he had touched a sore point on my body. 'No – I haven't for a while, Will. I've just not been in the right headspace.'

I thought of the laptop – stashed under my bed – and the unfinished story that remained on its drive. At one time I had thought it might be something good, something original, but now I knew different.

'That's sad,' Will said. 'You know how much I love your stuff.'

I didn't answer. I couldn't bring myself to. This was all getting too much.

'What did I do?' he asked again, his voice a little louder now. More insistent. 'How did I mess this all up? I can't remember anything, but I have this nagging feeling deep inside that I did something bad, and it won't go away. Gem, I need to know.'

Guilt? I almost laughed. It seemed that emotion was a stubborn bastard that wasn't going to leave him alone easily, brain injury or not. But I wasn't ready to rake over it all. I couldn't stand to talk about it again and bring back all that pain. He might be injured, but I didn't owe him anything.

'You fucked up,' I said finally. 'You fucked up in a big way, Will, and you nearly destroyed me.'

I saw him shrink further back in the bed, his eyes wide with shock. He was so much like the Will I used to know; it almost made me feel sorry for him.

Almost.

'I'm sorry,' I said. 'I promised I'd come and check on you, and I have, but now I never want to see you again.'

I walked straight out of there.

And I didn't look back.

–

I ended up in the loos, scrunched up on the seat, sobbing into a handful of tissues. On my lap, my phone flashed a flurry of messages. One was from Vee, asking how I was and demanding I call her. The others were from Richard. The first asking if I was OK, and the second asking if I wanted him to pick me up. The only thing I knew with any certainty was that I couldn't face Richard just yet. If he saw my tear-streaked face, he would be bound to think the worst. He wouldn't understand that I wasn't crying over Will because I still felt something for him.

I was crying over Will because the situation was so completely messed up and cruel.

Years ago, I would've prayed for this – for Will to bang his head and come to his senses. To go back to being the man I fell in love with. I never for one minute expected our relationship to become the screw-up it did – and, scarily, so quickly. Almost overnight Will became a person I didn't recognise.

Selfish.

Cold.

Distant.

Able to hurt me.

And yet, here he was, propped up in a bed, all wide-eyed and shaken – convinced that we were still together. That we were still in love.

I stuffed my manky tissues down the loo and flushed it violently, taking out my frustration on the stupid metal handle. Why was life so bloody messed up?

I stepped outside the cubicle, and quickly filled the sink and splashed my blotchy face with ice-cold water. I didn't care about my make-up. Most of it had run off anyway. I rubbed at the dark smears under my eyes and tried to smooth down my fuzzy mess of hair. My nose was a bright red bauble. I looked like a clown having a particularly bad day.

The door flew open and in waltzed Nicola.

As usual, she looked just gorgeous. Her hair was shiny and straight, lying against her shoulders in a perfect sheen. Her lips (though definitely artificially aided) were pouty and soft; her eyes, framed by expensive eyelash extensions and perfectly made-up, were now regarding me in complete horror.

'Gemma? What the hell are you doing here?'

'Nice to see you too, Nic.'

I saw her flinch at the shortened use of her name. I guess I still grabbed my cheap kicks where I could. Only Will was ever allowed to call her that.

She snorted and moved past me towards the sink. I watched as she placed her small handbag on the side and carefully pulled out an expensive-looking compact, a tiny hairbrush and a lip-gloss. She fussed over herself in the mirror.

'I can't believe how much this mascara runs,' she muttered, rubbing at her face. 'It's meant to be hard-wearing, but look – most of it is on my face.'

'I think most mascara would struggle in these situations,' I said softly.

She turned to face me. Without her carefully applied make-up, she did look so much younger and less threatening. The first time I had met her, I thought she was some kind of model – with the same kind of aloofness and hostility that seemed to come ready-made with a lot of these types. But here, stood before me, she was vulnerable and bare.

'Why did you come?' she asked, her tone flat.

'I didn't want to, but Jack called.'

Her lips tightened. She had never met Will's beloved brother, my best friend. It was another connection to Will's past I had that she didn't.

'Why would he want you to?' She shook her head. 'You're his ex. You are not part of his life now.'

'Jack was in a rush, he was worried. I don't think he knows what to do. He's so helpless out there,' I said. 'Maybe he should have called my mum instead. He probably considered it... She practically adopted those two.' Loved them more than her own daughter, I thought bitterly. It certainly felt like that at times. 'Jack just wanted me here to see Will. To represent him, I suppose...' I was floundering. 'I was in and out quickly. It doesn't mean anything.'

'Is Jack coming?' she asked.

I shrugged. 'I think so. It's difficult for him.'

I saw the flicker in Nicola's eyes. She knew Will and Jack were no longer talking – and probably knew the reasons why. I wondered how she felt about that.

'I only came to check, that's all,' I repeated. 'It's not a big deal.'

'But he recognised you.'

A small flutter danced in my throat when I thought of Will's expression. The way he had lit up when I walked into the room. How I felt something move inside of me that I thought I had destroyed long ago. How he had remembered my date.

'Yes – yes, he did.'

Nicola's shoulders slumped a little. She returned her gaze to the mirror and continued to apply make-up with small, violent moments – her mouth was set in a thin grimace.

'He called your name – when he woke. Called and called for you. I had been sitting there all night, stroking his hand, praying he would make it – and what happened? He asked for you! It made me—'

She hesitated and then shook her head, clearly not able to say more.

'Nicola, I—'

She snapped the compact shut. 'Don't. Don't say anything. You shouldn't be here. I don't care what Jack said. It wasn't your place to come.'

The door opened and another woman walked in. She looked at us both a bit uneasily, before moving into the furthest cubicle.

'I'm sorry,' I hissed at Nicola. 'I didn't mean to upset you. Today doesn't mean anything.'

'Of course, it doesn't,' Nicola hissed back. 'Will has a brain injury. We've been told it's temporary and that he needs rest. The worst possible thing that could happen now is for him to have you around. It'll confuse him and stop him healing. He needs to come back to his current life, not be reminded of his past.'

'Of course...' I nodded, feeling small now, even a bit silly. Had me coming here today really made things worse for Will? As much as I was still angry at him for all the crap he had put me through, I didn't want to cause him unnecessary pain.

Nicola zipped up her bag and straightened her body. 'Good. I'm glad we've got that all cleared up. Now, in the nicest possible way, I hope I don't see you again.'

'No. You won't.'

'In that case, I'll go back to my boyfriend.' She slung her bag over her shoulder and flashed me a more familiar grin. It made me want to kill her again. I saw the sparkle then, on her left hand. The ring, still as beautiful as I remembered, was snug on her third finger.

He held it in front of me, still nestled inside the velvet box. My breath caught in my throat. I'd never seen something so precious.

'One day this will be yours, Gem…'

'Oh God, Will, I couldn't have that – you'd never trust me, surely?'

'I couldn't think of anyone more suitable.' He planted a kiss on my head. 'I know how much Mum loved you. She wouldn't want anyone else to have this.'

'But not yet…'

'When you're ready, Gem. Only when you're ready.'

He snapped the box shut.

'It's in there waiting, just for you, and when the time is right, you'll put it on your finger.'

'Oh, I will, will I?'

He kissed me again – this time full on the lips. 'Oh, that is a promise.'

Now Nicola was peering at it, with a satisfied look on her face, like she had only just noticed it.

'Oh yes, I should say *fiancé*, shouldn't I?' she said sweetly, before leaving the room and slamming the door behind her.

The toilet flushed and the stranger plodded out. She took one look at me and tutted under her breath.

'You look like you've lost a tenner and found a penny.'

'No...' I muttered. 'I've lost my old boyfriend and found him again.'

The problem was, I wasn't sure that I wanted him to be found.

As I walked out of the hospital, my phone buzzed again in my pocket, but I ignored it. I would call Richard in a bit and tell him not to come. Vee could also wait until later. There was someone else I needed to see first. Someone who probably loved Will more than I did.

Someone who, for once, might be able to help me.

Chapter Seven

The rest of the day passed in a blur. I hated every part of it: the tests, the long, protracted conversations with consultants, who seemed more interested in treating me as a guinea pig than anything else, and the police, who had more questions that I couldn't answer. The prodding. The poking. The long, sleepless nights that followed.

No one could tell me anything useful and my head throbbed with the unfairness of it all. I was still living in 2019: a new memory came to me of being in The Swan with my old boss Mel – I could even smell the beer, hear the music playing on the jukebox. Anything after that was a dark, unending hole.

Even worse, Nicola insisted on being beside me throughout my stay. She held my hand. She talked to me in her sweet, but almost cloying voice. She told me everything would be OK – and what else could I do but nod along like a numb dog? The doctors kept telling me my memory could come back at any time and I had to remain hopeful. I had to keep believing that one day, all of this would make sense and this woman – who seemed very loving and kind – would ignite some kind of emotion in me.

And maybe then I would stop thinking so much about Gem.

'We have so much to plan for,' Nicola said cheerfully, squeezing my hand. 'We have big plans. The house to finish, the wedding…'

I stared down at the ring, I couldn't help it: every time, my eyes were drawn to it like a magnet. It was the biggest nagging doubt I had. The one thing that didn't seem to make any sense.

'How did I do it?'

'What? Propose?' She lifted her hand and touched the ring gently. 'I told you before: we were in Paris.'

'But how did I do it?'

'Oh… it was lovely. So sweet.' Her cheeks flushed pink. 'We were on the Eiffel Tower, right at the top, and I was busy admiring the view, chatting away while thinking you were behind me, watching too. Then I spun round to find you on your knee, clutching that box. You looked so worried. So earnest! But I said yes straight away!'

'I proposed on top of the Eiffel Tower?'

'Yes, what's wrong with that?' She looked hurt.

I shook my head. 'I don't know, I just can't imagine doing anything like that. It feels a bit… cheesy.'

Nicola puffed out her chest. 'Well, it wasn't, Will. I can't believe you're saying that. It was beautiful and really romantic. I thought it was perfect.'

'OK…' I tugged at the blankets, pulling them closer to me. I guess that made sense. If Nicola was into that kind of romantic, showy kind of stuff, I probably did it for her. I just knew that Gem would've hated it. She would've cringed and probably shouted at me for being too public.

I'd had such different plans for her. For that ring.

Some things were difficult to forget, even though I didn't seem to have much trouble with that at the moment.

Nicola leant forward so that her hair was brushing against my arm. I could smell her perfume, which was rich and sweet.

'One more night, Will, and then you'll be home. Aren't you excited?'

I blinked. I didn't even know where home was.

'It'll help,' she said, rubbing my arm gently. 'Seeing all your things around you again.'

'Where do we live? What's it like?'

'Oh, it's lovely. You live with me in one of those newly developed places on the other side of town. It's very minimal and modern. You love it. You told me it's "very you".'

'Very me?' I frowned again. Who was this 'me' that Nicola kept spouting about, so different from the 'me' that I felt like? The 'me' I knew didn't even like cars much, let alone own one. I wanted to travel the country in a camper van. I liked clutter and comfort, and interesting design. The words 'minimal' and 'modern' sent a cold shudder through my body.

'It'll feel so much better when you see it,' Nicola insisted. 'Just you wait. All these things will help your memory.'

'Maybe,' I said, uneasiness heavy in my words.

'And the lads from work are going to come and see you.' She giggled softly. 'I mean, they are a bloody nightmare, but I'm guessing it might help your recovery if you saw them.'

'Work?' I hadn't even thought of that. I knew I wasn't in the band anymore – that was clear, as Jack had continued without me. I wasn't even sure I wanted to know what happened there. But there were no 'lads' that I knew. I worked in a bar, with Mel, my manager. A fifty-year-old grump with a mean sense of humour. She was my mate, wasn't she?

'Isn't Mel coming?' I asked hopefully.

'Mel?' Nicola looked confused. 'No – it'll be Pete, Matty and possibly Freddie, if he can be arsed. They were going to come and see you here, but I put them off. I thought it might be too much for you.'

'Who are they?' I asked desperately.

Nicola stopped stroking my arm. 'You work with them, Will, at the recruitment agency. I thought maybe you might remember that, but I guess you did start there about three years ago...'

Three years ago? Did my break-up with Gem cause me to go in a completely different direction? To change everything about myself? Did I have some kind of break-down? That certainly seemed logical.

'Don't worry, babe,' Nicola said, planting a kiss on my lips. It missed. 'When you are back with me, things will get better again. You'll soon be back to normal.'

I smiled at her because I wanted to reassure her, but the truth was I had no idea what normal was anymore.

And I wasn't even certain I wanted it.

After Nicola left, I reached for my phone. It had survived the crash with only a small scratch on the screen, doing better than me.

And, unlike me, it had memory.

The nurse had handed the device to me yesterday, like it was a precious gift, though of course it really meant little to me. I didn't recognise the cold silver case, the flashy phone inside. When I powered it up, I saw my battery was low and felt a sudden anxiety about not killing it too soon. I wanted to find out all I could, and this small little friend might just be able to help me. Luckily, it accepted my old password. Probably the only thing that hadn't changed!

I flicked to my messages first. Names flashed up that meant nothing to me – the same ones that Nicola had mentioned, and I had barely reacted to: Pete, Freddie, Matty. I skimmed through the texts, noticing how the majority were in group chats, and impersonal and dull.

> Drinks after work. Your shout.

> That one was particularly hot, mate.

> Last night was mad!

The last messages, on a chat named the 'the lads' (God, even that gave me a sick feeling), were sent a few nights before my accident.

> Pete: I'm going to be hanging tomorrow.
> Might need a pep.

> Matty: You know me. Happy to deliver.

> Me: Can't believe you lot bailed so early.
> Disappointing! I will be having words.

Fred: Fuck me, Will, are you back yet? Nic is going to kill you.

Me: Nah. Night is still young, right?

Pete: Yeah and so is that girl you were wrapped around.

Me: LOL

Matty: It'll all catch up with you one day, William.

I stared blankly at the screen. What kind of arsehole was I? Nicola had been sitting with me, talking about our romantic trips and long-term plans, and here I was, messing around with another girl behind her back. I didn't care what anyone said – this wasn't me! I had never cheated in my life. Both Jack and I had seen the pain and devast-ation that had caused our mum, and we both swore we would never be that type of prick.

So how had I become this person? Had I fallen into some kind of parallel universe? Was I still in a coma and this was all some kind of sick dream? I smacked my head with my palm, in an attempt to bring myself round.

This had to be a dream. It had to be.

'You keep doing that, you'll just give yourself a head-ache.'

My nurse, Geri, had walked back into the room. I couldn't help smiling. She was my favourite nurse here. She didn't look at me like I was stupid, or someone to feel sorry for. She just treated me normally.

'I need to do your blood pressure again,' she said and then nodded in the direction of my phone.

'Has that helped you at all?'

I held out my arm and watched as she looped the monitor around it. 'If by helping you mean telling me that I'm a complete and utter knobhead.'

'Oh.' She started the machine. 'Well, if it's any help, I really don't think you are.'

The machine tightened and constricted around my bicep, a similar feeling to the one I got in my throat every time I tried to make sense of things. I felt like my world was crushing me.

'All good.' She nodded, unwrapping my arm. 'It looks as though you will be allowed to leave tomorrow.'

'I'm hardly better, though,' I muttered.

I was scanning through the contacts on the phone now, desperately looking for names I recognised. So many men I didn't know – and women. No Gem. No Mel. The only name that I immediately recognised was Jack's.

'It's like these last three years I've become a completely different person.'

'A lot can change in that time,' Geri soothed. 'If you had broken up with your girlfriend, you probably lost a lot of mutual friends too. Sadly, that's what happens. That, alongside a new job...'

'I'm a recruitment agent now, apparently,' I said. 'I'm not even sure what one of those does.'

'Try not to worry about that now.'

'And I have messages, look...' I held up the screen. 'So many messages from girls I don't know. Thanking me for "last night", asking me to call them... I was obviously messing them all around, messing Nicola around, but that doesn't make sense. That's not me!'

Geri gently eased the phone back out of my grasp. 'Maybe this is a bit much to take in right now, Will. It's bound to be a shock, but I'm guessing there was a reason why you acted in that way.'

'Yeah, it's because I was an arsehole.' I stared glumly at my hands. 'That must have been why I lost Gem, and why my brother no longer speaks to me. I checked! There's no calls at all from him, no messages either. And we were close, Geri. We were in the same band. We spoke every day.'

'He'll call soon, I'm sure. Maybe he's just waiting for the right time.'

'I've done something awful to both of them. I've really messed up, I know it.' I took a breath, trying to fight back the tears that were threatening to come. 'But the worst thing of all... I'm scared that he *will* call. I'm not sure I can face that. I don't know if I want to know.'

'Then why don't you call him? Take control,' Geri replied gently. 'You might not like what he has to say, but at least you'll have heard him out? The waiting is probably what is driving you mad.'

I stared back down at my phone again. She was right, I couldn't leave this any longer.

I had to call Jack.

Geri found me a battered old charger to keep my phone going, and I eased myself off the bed and onto the chair. My ribs screamed in pain as I moved and my body was as stiff as a board, but it was good to get off the bed.

From this position, I could see out into the ward. An old man was passing by with a walking frame and he tipped me a nod as he went past the open curtain. Across the way I could see inside another room, where a man was propped up in bed with what looked like an oxygen mask fixed on his face. A woman sat beside him, fussing with the covers. I hadn't noticed before how busy and noisy it was in here. It was so easy to shut myself away in my little bubble and pretend I was the only one who was suffering. But I wasn't.

For a while I simply held the phone, staring at his number. It was seven o'clock here, but I had no clue where Jack was in America. Was he five hours behind, or more?

When did he go? And why? Finally, I pressed the button.

I tried to recall the last time I had seen Jack. I was pretty sure it was down at The Swan, where I used to work. He had popped in late after his cleaning shift and we had sat in the corner of the pub. Jack had flyers that he'd printed out and was showing them to me. They had our band name on the top, RiffRaff, followed by a list of dates.

'Aby printed these up for us. She shouldn't have done, really, her boss will kill her – but don't they look ace?'

He'd shoved the flyers towards me. I had picked one up, rubbing the glossy paper between my fingers. We were posing on the front, looking mean and cool in black and white, and I could barely recognise myself. I looked like Johnny bloody Marr.

'Aby did this? Amazing!'

I loved Aby. She and Jack had been together for two years, perhaps a little bit more – that would be five now, if they were still together. She was outgoing. Optimistic and

73

a little bit dizzy, she kept him positive when his self-doubt kicked in. She was as good for him as Gem was for me.

'Aby is a star! She's buzzing about this, even thinks she can arrange some PR for us. She has the connections.'

We had been excited that day, talking quickly and over one another about the gigs. We had a new drummer. Shit, how could I forget about him! Vic was one of the best in the area and we'd nabbed him. Jack had clapped me on the back.

'This is it, bro. I think this could be our chance.'

Me on lead, Jack on bass and vocals – our perfect harmonies syncing together the way only we could. What could go wrong? I thought back to that day and I could feel the same feelings: the bubbling excitement in my belly, the tingling in my skin. The fucking hope.

So, what the hell happened? And why was Jack in America without me?

I tried hard to think back, to make my mind work properly, but my last memory of Jack was him hugging me at the bar and clapping me on the back.

'This is it, mate, I really think we are going to make it. I really do.'

Except we didn't, did we?

Or at least, I didn't.

'Jack?'

The phone had taken a while to connect, and I had to fight to control the stutter in my voice. I heard a sharp breath and then what sounded like a door being shut. The seconds that passed seemed to take hours.

'Will?' A pause. 'Are you... Are you OK?'

'I'm a bit bashed up.'

'Yeah, I know. Slammed your car into a tree or some-thing? Fucking hell, Will, you were lucky you didn't kill yourself. Or someone else.'

'I know… I know.' I rubbed at my side, which was really throbbing now. 'I miss you, Jack.'

There was another quick intake of breath, but then silence. It hung between us like a heavy wet sheet.

'You're in America? Gem told me…'

'Yes, you know I'm in America, Will.' He sighed. 'But Gem came, did she? She said she would. I didn't like to ask, but I wanted one of us to be there.'

'She said you're going to try and come back.'

'Well, yeah. I'm sorting some bits this end. The tour is going well, Will. We've sold out. It wouldn't be fair on Vic and Deano for me to leave right now.'

'Deano!' My heart caught in my throat. 'Dean Franks. That little scrotum. Why is he there with you?'

'Yeah, of course he is, you know that. Will, what the fuck is going on? Are you all right?'

'Deano fucking Franks,' I muttered. 'So, you piss off on tour without me and replace me with the one arsehole I can't stand.'

'Will, we went through this already. Dean has a decent voice and he's not—'

'Not, what?'

Another sigh. 'Well, he's not you.'

I stared blankly out at the ward. The little old man was trundling back now. I guessed he had gone for a piss, or maybe just for a walk to get away from the confines of his space. A nurse walked beside him, talking softly in his direction. They both looked at me and smiled. My face was frozen, I couldn't even bring myself to frown.

'Will… Look, I'm sorry that you're hurt and stuff. The hospital called when it happened. Obviously, I was worried, but they told me you had woken up. You have to understand that, even with all of this, I still struggle with the thought of facing you. Maybe it's better that I don't?'

'Better?' I repeated the word. Such a positive word, usually, yet now it sounded so cruel and cold.

'I'll call Gem later; she'll update me on everything—'

'I can't fucking remember, Jack,' I hissed. 'I can't remember anything that happened in the last three years. I don't understand why I'm like this, why I'm not with Gem, why I'm not with the band… why you can't stand me.'

'You can't remember?' He sounded stunned.

'No. The last thing I knew, we were planning our tour. We were happy.'

'Jesus.'

'Jack, what happened to us?'

There was a long silence. I heard movement and I could picture Jack pacing the room, like he always did when he was stressed or wanted to escape something.

'Jack, please tell me. What did I do?'

'I'm sorry, Will. I really am, but I can't do this right now.'

And the phone went dead.

Before

Gem – 2007

It was Jack's idea to arrange the Christmas party. Gayle had been dead for two years by then and the boys had spent most of that time just trying to make the best of things. Jack had an apprenticeship at the garage and worked evenings cleaning offices. He was determined that he and Will should stay together and remain in their council house. Will and I were still friends, sort of, but school had come between us. We were both in sixth form, but Will was one of the cool kids. I was a year younger than him and a plump, unpopular kid with frizzy hair, hanging around with Vee, who was equally geeky and unpopular. Now I was living at Nan's all the time, I didn't run into the brothers, and our friendship had drifted. Girls like us didn't get invited to the party of the year, even if I knew the host. Kids like us just learnt to fade into the background.

Everyone was talking about it at school. It was going to be at the local pub, The Swan. Will was giving out invites to people in his year like they were candy. He wanted to fill the place up, play Christmas songs loudly, make it the festive hive of the street.

About a week before, Will passed us in the corridor and smiled, the way he smiled at everyone – friendly, almost cheeky. His eyes settled on mine, and it was like he had seen me for the first time.

'Gem! Oh my God! How are you?'

I wished I could've fought back the blush that was spreading across my cheeks. I dipped my head slightly, hoping my hair would conceal my red face. 'I'm good, thanks.'

'I never see you on Osbourne anymore. Do you remember how we used to hang out all the time?'

I felt Vee nudge my side. Remember? How could I forget? It was all me and Vee used to giggle about – that, and the fact that I'd once seen Will's willy in the paddling pool when we were little. I was guessing he didn't need reminding of that.

'I still live with my nan,' I explained. 'At Beckett Court.'

'Ah, shame. How's your mum?'

'Good… Good…' I nodded. It was a lie, of course. At that point, my mum hadn't left the house in a month, was refusing to take her medication and was still accusing my nan of stealing me – but apart from that, everything was fine.

'Hey!' His face brightened. 'You should come to our party on the 18th. It'll be like old times having you back.' He gestured to Vee. 'And bring your mate too. The more, the merrier.'

'I'd… We'd love to.'

'Great! See you then.'

We watched as Will walked away, and then collapsed into hysterical giggles. It was only later that the nerves kicked in. How could I go, really? I was ugly and unpopular, and I didn't even have anything decent to wear. It was bound to be a disaster. Nan was poorly. She needed me home. I had a thousand reasons why I didn't want to go and only one for accepting the invitation – and I wasn't sure that one reason was enough.

Vee nagged and nagged me. We had never been invited to a party before, not even Claire Bishop's, and she was an even bigger geek than both of us put together.

'It'll be OK,' Vee said. 'We only have to go for a little bit.'

'But Nan…'

'She'll be fine for a few hours, and besides, she'd want you to go.'

This was true. Nan was tired a lot of the time now and often went to bed soon after dinner so I knew she wouldn't miss me, really.

'You could always ask your mum to come over.'

I laughed. 'You're joking, aren't you! Mum is likely to be in the bloody pub too.'

Mum had found ways to help her leave the house, but they usually involved alcohol or prescription medication. I wasn't sure if the loud, fake mum was an improvement on the withdrawn, hidden one.

'What will I wear?' I asked hopelessly.

Vee grinned. 'You leave that to me.'

–

The pub was heaving. I was already wobbly and that had nothing to do with the stupid heels I was wearing. Clinging on to Vee's arm, we staggered across the uneven car park. I was decked out in one of her mum's dresses, and the black Lycra kept creeping up my legs, revealing the tops of my thighs. My heels were a last-minute charity-shop purchase, higher than I wanted but I could hardly rock up in my usual trainers.

Vee reached over and fluffed my hair; my curls were out and proud tonight, and moussed to perfection.

'You look beautiful,' she said.

I didn't believe her. Not really. But there was something in the way she said it that made my stomach swirl.

Something about tonight seemed different – special, like anything could happen.

Inside the pub, I tried to ignore my nerves and followed Vee to the bar. She wasn't a local and her height meant she got away with ordering us both a vodka. We then stood in the corner, sipping our drinks. I hated the taste but liked the warm feeling it gave me at the back of my throat. Dance music pumped out of the speakers a bit too loud, making it difficult to talk.

I kept looking around. Luckily, there was no sign of my mum, but sadly there was no sign of Will either. Was he even here?

After a while, a tall, muscular boy came over and started chatting to Vee. He told her his name was Brandon and that he liked her dress; he was a bit awkward and had a nice laugh. Vee lit up in a way I'd never seen before and after a while I started to feel like a third wheel. I made my excuses and slowly crept away.

There were people from school there, mean girls that looked me up and down and pulled faces; popular boys who made gestures and leered at my exposed cleavage.

I wanted to go home so I walked to the bar to put my sticky glass back and head out. Someone jostled me, pushing me off balance and into another person's back. My cheeks on fire, I muttered a hasty apology.

'It's OK, Gem. It's no problem.'

Will. He was grinning at me and looked so good. He was wearing a crisp white shirt and dark jeans. His eyes seemed to actually sparkle in the dimly lit room.

'You came,' he said.

'Yeah...' I shoved my glass down and rubbed my hands on my dress. 'Yeah, but I'm thinking of going, actually.'

'Why?' He looked shocked.

I glanced back at Vee. She was deep in conversation with Brandon, her body turned towards him, his hand touching her arm.

'I think... Well, this isn't really my scene.'

Will laughed. 'It's not mine either... Jack chose the music because he thought everyone else would like it. It's doing my head in. Shall we escape for a bit? Look, come here...'

He took my hand and dragged me outside. It was already dark and the sharp, crisp air made me catch my breath.

'You look really good,' he said. His eyes darted away from me. 'I'm sorry, that sounds so crap.'

'Don't be sorry.'

He nodded towards the sky. 'Look, look up there – the stars are so bright tonight. It's like they're having a party too.'

I followed his gaze. The stars were twinkling so fiercely that they did seem more intense than usual.

'Beautiful,' I whispered. Then I shivered despite myself, and Will gently eased his arm over my shoulders, pulling me close.

'Is that OK?' he asked gently. 'I don't want you to be cold.'

'It's fine,' I said, trying to keep my voice casual, but internally my thoughts were muddled. The shivers had now moved deeper inside my body and I felt a little dizzy.

'I miss how close we used to be before you moved off the estate,' he said. 'How we played together.'

'We're a bit too old for hide-and-seek now,' I said.

He laughed. 'Yeah, probably, but I did say I was always going to look after you, didn't I?'

'I remember.'

'I always thought you were cute, even when we were little.'

I was no longer shivering; instead, burning heat was building inside my body. Was this happening? Was Will actually saying these things?

Gently, he moved me round to face him.

'I don't want you to go,' he whispered. 'Not yet anyway.'

'Really?'

'Really. I was hoping…' He stuttered a little, something I'd never heard him do before. 'I was hoping to talk to you tonight, spend some time with you…'

His hand touched my face, his fingers lightly tracing my cheek, my chin. My legs were wobbly again, and my heart felt like it might actually be beating too hard in my chest.

'I want to kiss you,' he whispered. 'Can I? Is that all right?'

I couldn't answer. My words were lost by then so I simply nodded. His lips found mine, warm and soft. I could taste beer. He moved against me carefully, his hands in my hair, then stroking my back, seeming to be every-where all at once.

He pulled away. 'I'm sorry. I've wanted to do that for so long. I didn't want to risk you going and never...' His expression suddenly turned stark. 'I'm sorry, Gem. Have I moved too fast? Have I ruined everything?'

I couldn't answer him. I didn't think I could say the right words. Instead, I reached up to his face and guided it back towards my lips. This time the kiss was far more intense; his tongue slipped into my mouth, and I groaned softly. I didn't want it to stop and when it did, we were both breathless and wide-eyed.

'I don't think we can be friends anymore,' he said, his gaze burning into mine.

'That's a shame,' I replied, before pulling him back for more.

Chapter Eight

Gem – 2022

Being back on the Osbourne estate always made me feel strange. The place had hardly changed in all these years; it had just got a little more tired, a bit more frayed around the edges. I couldn't fit my car in the jammed car park, so instead parked up the street, a few roads away from Mum's house.

As I stepped out and pressed the key to lock the door, I realised I was only a few doors away from Will and Jack's old house. Without stopping to think too much about it, I carried on walking until I was right outside number forty-eight. This place was distinctive because the facia had been painted white. Apparently, Will's dad had done this long ago, just before he decided to leg it with his new, younger girlfriend.

Poor Gayle. I stared up at the peeling walls, at the once-bright door that was now losing its shine. She had always kept this place so nice: growing flowers in the borders, washing down the front step. She must have struggled so much, after her husband left her with two young boys while she was battling cancer, but she always wanted to present a clean and tidy home. Even after her death, Jack and Will had done their best to keep the place looking good.

Today, number forty-eight looked dirty and forlorn. There were rubbish bags strewn in the garden, and the windows were dark and smeared. I felt sad just standing there, in this place where I had experienced so many happy memories.

But like a lot of things, this was ruined now.

I walked quickly to my mum's, keen to get away. For a weekday afternoon, it was quiet here. There were a few kids playing with a football in the street and one man was washing his car on the grass verge. I guess the sun had driven most people into their small back gardens, or to the parks nearby. It wasn't like when Mum and Gayle used to plonk their deckchairs on the paths at the front and drink wine together as we played, other women soon joining them, on rugs or chairs of their own. It used to be quite a thing. I think Mum enjoyed the company, and it took her mind off her dark thoughts. I know Gayle was good for her, for a short time at least.

Number thirteen. Mum's house. Our house.

I had never loved it and neither had she. She used to joke that it could never be as unlucky as our last place, despite the number, but it was easily just as depressing: a dingy, shabby-looking house that had never really been cared for. The front door was grey, with grubby glass above the letter box. The front garden was cemented over, flat and dark, with hollows filled with puddles. Mum never decorated the front with flowers, or bothered to wash or paint the outside. She just didn't have it in her. Her tiny, battered Fiat was parked by the gate. Mum barely drove it now – she barely left the house – but for some reason she seemed reluctant to let it go.

I knocked – there was no point ringing the bell, it hadn't worked for years.

Tugging the door open slowly, Mum's weary eyes focused on me and a hint of a smile settled on her lips. She pulled the door fully open. Today she was dressed in a long flowery dress and oversized cardigan that swamped her tiny body. Her hair, frizzy like mine but blonde to my ginger, was scraped back into a twist at the back of her head.

'Hi, Mum,' I said. 'Aren't you hot dressed like that?'

'You know me, I don't feel the heat.' She peered beyond me. 'I didn't realise how warm it was.'

'It's been like this for weeks.' I frowned. 'When did you last go outside?'

'Oh, a few days ago. Are you coming in, then?' she said, walking back into the house.

I hadn't been here for a month or so. I knew that was bad, but work had been busy, and I had been doing stuff with Richard – and no matter how many excuses I made, coming back here was always going to be difficult. It didn't matter how hard I tried, Mum and I just rubbed each other up the wrong way. It was like we both carried the guilt for still living when Dad wasn't, like we just couldn't be happy together without him.

'Do you want tea?'

'Only if you're making it.'

'I'll take that as a yes, then.'

I followed Mum into the tiny kitchen. As always, it was spotless. As if to make the point, Mum ran a cloth around the surfaces while she waited for the kettle to boil.

While she made the tea, I told her about Will and watched as her face shifted from the politely detached expression she always wore like a shield. She handed me a cup and I saw her hand was shaking.

'He was lucky,' I told her. 'From all accounts, the car was a write-off. He never should have been driving that fast.'

'You don't know that's what happened,' she replied. 'It might not have been his fault.'

'It's the most likely option, Mum. You know he'd been driving like a nutter in it.'

Mum seemed to flinch at that. 'He never even used to be into cars, did he? Never was the type… It's strange how much he changed…'

We walked into her small living room. The TV was turned on low, some cookery programme on. Mum picked up the remote and snapped it off. We both sat on the scuffed leather sofa that she had had since we had moved in here. It had been donated to us after the fire; in fact, a lot of the furniture had been – our beds, the fridge, the coffee table.

'Will he be OK?' Mum asked quietly.

I could see the panic behind her eyes. She loved Will just as much as I did and had probably been just as hurt by our break-up. Unlike me, she had tried to stay in touch with him, convinced that she could still bring the 'old Will' back. Mum thought that was possible, whereas I always knew it wasn't. This was another wedge that had been driven between us, as I felt Mum had taken his side.

'He's awake and he seems fine,' I replied carefully. 'But he has got a bad injury.'

'What sort of injury?'

I hesitated. 'Well, he's lost some of his memory, Mum.' I paused. 'He still thinks we're together.'

'Oh…' She put her cup down on the table. 'Really?'

'It was just so hard, going there and seeing him like that. He looked so vulnerable and sad, and when he started talking to me like... Well, like we were still together, it made everything hurt again.' I stopped myself, shocked at my confession. I never normally opened up to Mum like this, but the emotions were still raw and on the surface. Who else was there to talk to? Vee was busy and I could hardly go to Richard with all of this.

'It must have been hard,' Mum soothed. 'For both of you.'

'And for Nicola. She was there too, but Will didn't even recognise her.'

Mum sniffed. 'Well, that's no bad thing, is it?'

She had only met Nicola once, purely by chance, when she had bumped into the couple in the street, but she hadn't been impressed. She said Nicola had been 'rude' and quick to tug Will away, as if Mum was someone bad to be associated with.

'It can't be easy for her,' I reasoned. 'And it didn't help me being there, muddling Will up even more. I shouldn't have gone.'

'You needed to see him for yourself,' Mum said quietly. 'You had to know.'

'Mum, I still care about him, but that doesn't change anything, you know that.'

'I know. You keep telling me – it just seems such a shame.' She stood up and walked towards the two framed photos on the mantlepiece. She picked up the one on the left, the one I kept begging her to put away. It wasn't fair to Richard to keep seeing it out on display. It was of me and Will the first Christmas we spent together after moving into Nan's flat. We had invited Mum over for dinner – Will's idea, of course. In the photo, he had his arms wrapped around me. We were both wearing party-cracker hats. My face was turned towards his, laughing at some joke he had just made. We had been so blissfully and stupidly happy.

'You were such a good couple,' she said, touching the glass. 'Over ten years together – that's like a marriage, isn't it?'

I sighed. 'Mum, we keep going over this.'

'Childhood sweethearts.' She put the photo down. 'I knew when you were young that you would be together forever. He changed something inside of you, lit up a spark that you needed.'

'Mum!' I could feel myself getting frustrated now. 'I came here to tell you about the accident, to get some support, not to rehash all the old stuff again. Me and Will were over a long time ago. We can't go back after that.'

'I know,' she said, sad now. 'I promised Gayle: I told her I would be there for those boys, always, and I was at the beginning, but I guess I let things slip...'

My anger eased. I nodded. 'You were good to them, Mum.'

Probably better to them than she was to her daughter, but that was a separate issue.

The other photo was of the three of us – me, Will and Jack. I think I was probably about eight, Will nine and Jack twelve. We were sun-kissed and happy, sitting side by side, legs crossed, squinting up as we licked ice creams.

'Sometimes, I just wish I could turn back the time,' she said softly.

I got up to stand behind her and lightly touched her shoulder. 'I know, Mum, but we can't. Things move on.' I paused. 'At least Will is alive; at least Nicola is there to support him. We have to leave them to get on with it now.'

It was the only thing we could do.

I left Mum settled back in front of the TV. She seemed back to her old distant self, but at least today hadn't ended in arguments or escalated emotions. As I walked out of the room, my eyes fell again on the two photos on the mantlepiece. It was hard not to feel nostalgic as I thought of those happier times, but I was happy now. I had the life I needed and wanted, and the security I could never have had with Will. Childhood romances often broke down because they didn't work in real life. We had both grown up, but in different ways.

I stepped outside into the blazing sunshine, sad that Mum wouldn't sit in her small garden. She used to love sunbathing, or at least being out here in the front with Gayle. It wasn't just the fire that made Mum ill, it was losing Gayle too. Her best friend, the person who had given her some of her strength back.

Easing my phone out of my pocket, I checked for messages. There was another from Richard, and I smiled. It was quite sweet.

> Hey Gemma. I hope it all went OK. I've booked a table at Rene's tonight. Thought you could do with a treat. Love you.

There was also a missed call and a message from Vee.

> Hey! I'm sorry I wasn't around earlier. Had a weird morning. Need to talk. Are you around later this week? Weds drink? Vee xx

I replied immediately. I needed a Wednesday catch-up with Vee. If anyone could help me get my head straight, it would be her, but I was also worried and hoped she was OK. I knew the fertility issues were taking their toll on both her and Brandon, and I hated to see how much it was affecting them. They really deserved a break.

There was another missed call, this time from Jack. I was about to play my voicemail when the phone buzzed to life in my hand. He was calling again.

'Jack! You OK? I'm sorry I didn't call – I got distracted.'

'It's all right. I get it. I probably shouldn't have asked you to go.' He paused. 'You OK?'

'Yeah, yeah, getting there.' I started to walk back down the road towards my car.

'I'm back on Osbourne,' I told him. 'Visiting Mum. It always brings back memories.'

'I bet. I haven't been there in years. How's my mum's place?'

I heard the pain in his voice even after all this time. Will always struggled to talk about his mum too. Her death had been like a nuclear explosion in their lives, and the scars had never healed.

'I'm standing outside now. It doesn't really look the same.'

'I hated living there without her. All those years, just me and Will…' Jack took a breath. 'Is your mum keeping well? You need to give her my love.'

'She's OK. Just worried about Will.'

There was a pause. I stood awkwardly outside my car, praying Jack wasn't going to ask me to visit Will again – that would be too hard. I'd have to refuse.

'He called me,' he said finally. 'He's told me he doesn't remember.'

'I know.' My feet scuffed at the kerb. 'He thought we were still together.'

'It's just temporary, right?'

'I–I don't know… I'm guessing so.' I was thinking of the numerous films and dramas I'd seen that featured memory loss as part of the plot. The main character always got their memory back in the end, didn't they?

'I was a bit of a dick to him. He asked me what he'd done, why I wasn't there…' Jack's voice broke a little. 'I know I should come back, I should face him, but this is still Will. It's still the person that caused all this harm.'

'He asked me similar things,' I said quietly. 'I'm guessing he's confused. He wants answers.'

'Did you tell him?'

'No, I couldn't go into all of it again. What's the point?' I paused. 'Did you?'

'Nah, I couldn't face it. Not yet.'

I hesitated, suddenly feeling wobbly. The memories of those few horrible months three years ago were coming crashing down around me. I really didn't want to go back there.

'Gem,' Jack's voice was softer now. 'Are you going to talk to him? Tell him how badly he hurt you?'

'No.' The word flew out before I could stop it.

Because what would be the point? It was done now. There was no going back. Injured or not, Will had still caused too much pain.

And deep down I knew I could never risk letting him back into my life again.

Chapter Nine

Will – 2022

Nicola flung open the car door and made a whooping noise that drilled right into my brain.

'This is it, Will. This is home. Our home! What do you think?'

I staggered out, still clutching my side, which was killing me. The ride up here hadn't exactly been the most comfortable. It seemed my fiancée (God, that sounded so wrong) liked flashy sports cars, and drove them fast and hard. Each bump and quick turn had made my muscles ache and my head thump even more. I had found myself reaching out and gripping the dashboard for support.

'Whoops,' she'd trilled. 'I forgot you might be a bit more sensitive after the crash.'

'I hate speed…'

She'd frowned, which meant this was another part of me I had got wrong. Another part of my personality that I no longer recognised – never mind three years' worth of memory loss, it was like I had woken up a completely different person. But now, after a few blurry days in hospital the doctors had deemed me fit to be discharged.

And now I had been taken here, home. A place where I never, ever thought I'd be seen dead.

It was a new build for a start. I hated bloody new builds, had always preferred older, shabby buildings. Homes with character, charm and a heart. Gem used to say I was a bit pompous about it all.

Gem, shit! I had to stop thinking about her like that.

My house now was in a new estate on the edge of town – identical little boxes with prefabricated plastic fronts and tarmacked front gardens. I was struggling to find any personality, any sense of who was living here. It was just middle-class suburbia with a splash of snobbism.

'We were so lucky to snap up our house off-plan,' Nicola told me.

'Were we?'

She frowned a little. 'Well, in truth, I was. I moved here first, last summer. You followed in December.'

'Ah. I see.'

Nicola had already told me we had started dating in November 2021 (I was still getting used to that date, which felt wrong – still somewhere in the future for me), which meant we had been a couple for eight months. I didn't say anything but, inside, my doubts were tugging at me. Why had I moved in with this woman after only a month of dating? And why the hell had I proposed so soon?

I never normally rushed into things. Well, not the old me anyway...

'It's so quiet here,' Nicola said, as if to remind me once more how lucky I was. 'We don't get any trouble at all.'

'Where's the nearest pub?' I asked hopefully. The estate seemed to be surrounded by a dual carriageway. I hadn't even seen a shop.

'There's no pub near here, Will. The closest one is back into town. They have said they will be building a shop soon, and a school.' She pulled on my arm. 'Come on, you need to look inside. Just seeing the place might help you remember.'

The house was on the corner of sweet-sounding Honeysuckle Crescent. We were in number twenty-one, which was identical to twenty and twenty-two. It was a thin red-brick building with a fake stuck-on porch outside and a tiny white garage attached, which looked far too small for an actual car.

As we stepped inside, I was immediately hit by the smell of polish and cleaner. The hallway was narrow, with a tiled floor that gleamed in the light. A staircase was on my left, covered in thick-looking grey carpet. The decor was all very glam and modern: white wallpaper with delicate silver threads in the design, an ornate mirror on the wall. I almost walked into a huge vase that stood by the door, stuffed full of oversized ferns.

'Isn't it lovely?' Nicola gushed, peeling off her coat and hanging it on a metallic coat stand.

'It... Well, yes, it is.'

She took me on a tour of the place, preening over every room, while I hung back, a stranger in my own life. The living room was just as minimalist and clean as the hall, with spotless leather sofas and colourful scatter cushions. The kitchen was awash with steel and grey, every surface shining, everything looking brand new and expensive. I felt shy as Nicola led me upstairs, showing me first the small spare room that we both used as an office, and then our own bedroom, which was large, with its own en-suite. I stared blankly at the king-sized bed, at the colourful duvet that was pulled tight across and the large, plump pillows that sat upon it. Did I really sleep here? Which side was mine? With Gem, I—

Stop!

I had to stop this!

I walked towards the bedside cabinets. Both had crystal-looking lamps on them, but one side was clearly Nicola's. There was some jewellery scattered on top, body cream and a photo frame. The picture inside was of us.

I lifted it, carefully studying our faces. We were at some event or party; Nicola was in a tight-fitting black dress, her long blonde hair loose and lying like a sheet against her slim tanned shoulders. She was gripping my arm as I stood next to her in some sort of pretentious-looking suit. My hair was slicked back, and my mouth open, as if in mid-shout. I was holding up a glass of champagne.

It was me all right, except it wasn't me. I blinked and put the photo back down.

Why did I look so wrong there?

'That was at your company do,' Nicola said. 'You won best salesman in the south-east. We have your trophy downstairs somewhere. It was a good night. We all got so wasted.'

'Cool,' I said, with little feeling.

I walked to what I assumed was my side of the bed. There wasn't much on the cabinet: a handful of change, one sorry-looking cufflink, lost on its own, and a book, splayed out, clearly half-read. I stared at the title and felt myself die a little more inside.

How to Win in Everything

'Please tell me I wasn't really enjoying this.'

'Oh, you loved it.' Nicola was distracted now. 'Come on, you need to come back downstairs. Let's have something to eat before the others get here.'

'Others?' I looked at her in despair.

Nicola simply giggled softly and took my arm again. 'You needn't look so scared, Will. These are your friends and they've been worried about you. Seeing them again will help you, I'm sure.'

I nodded, even though I really wasn't as convinced.

–

I sat at the breakfast bar, trying to swallow the sandwich that Nicola had made me. It was ham and tomato. Nice. But my guts were twisted up into knots and it was an effort to even chew. This kitchen was so pristine and polished that I was having difficulty finding where I fitted in. I was all muddy shoes, ripped jeans and messy cooking – although, looking down at the clothes Nicola had brought into the hospital for me, that no longer seemed to be my style. I was dressed in designer chinos and a T-shirt that probably cost more than I earned at a shift down The Swan.

'We went shopping just after we got together,' Nicola told me. 'I helped you re-design your look. You were desperate for a change.'

Was I?

I couldn't help thinking about the flat – mine and Gem's flat. How we had made it ours on a shoestring. The furniture had all been found over time, sourced from various charity shops or second-hand places. The decor had been a bit wild – Gem loved bright colours, she said they were healing. I thought of our kitchen, painted yellow, and the rickety old wooden dining table, and suddenly I longed to be back there. Surely this ham sandwich would taste better there too?

'You seem lost in thought,' Nicola said, bringing me over a coffee. I watched as she pulled herself up on the stool opposite me and settled her chin on her hands, as though she was really assessing me.

'It all just feels a bit strange still...' I pushed aside the half-eaten sandwich. 'I'm sorry, Nicola. I don't think I can manage this.'

'Nic,' she said quietly. 'You always call me Nic.'

'Sorry,' I said again, feeling ever more hopeless.

'You're the only person I allow to do that,' she said, a small smile blooming. 'When we first met, I told you I only like to be called Nicola, but you leapt on that. Every bloody minute you'd be saying "Nic this" and "Nic that". I hated it at first, thought you were so annoying...'

'But then...?'

'But then I became intrigued. I liked that you were a bit cheeky, you pushed the boundaries a bit.' She pulled off the crust from my bread and began to nibble it a little. 'I suppose it made you a little different.'

I sat up, feeling strangely proud. It sounded like this version of me had done quite well in winning this pretty woman over.

'And we met through Matty?' I asked again. 'It's odd, because I don't remember ever being friends with him.'

'Oh, you are now! Annoyingly so. And yes, we met through him. You don't remember working for him?'

I shook my head. 'He was just some kid in my year at school...'

I wanted to say more, but she obviously liked him, and I didn't want to upset her. Matty was the annoying kid in school, loud and boastful, always shouting about how much money he had, or what designer clothes he owned, and taking the piss out of those who didn't. I tolerated him because, for the best part, I saw him for what he really was: a skinny, rat-faced kid who was desperate for friends. But

98

Jack hated him, and so did Gem. If he ever walked into The Swan bragging about his latest conquest or his flashy new car, it was difficult to guess who was likely to punch him first.

I really didn't understand how he ended up being my best mate, though. That didn't sit right at all.

'You've been working for Matty's recruitment company for a few years now. I told you, you are one of his best sellers. You even did OK in lockdown, helping people secure new remote jobs. I guess you guys got close then. You all did. All of you lads are forever going out on the lash, or for weekends away. I'm lucky if I get to see you.'

'Did I meet you on one of those nights out?'

Nicola shook her head. 'God no, I wouldn't be seen dead at any of those. No, last year my family had a party. Matty invited you for support, I suppose, or because he didn't have a girlfriend to bring. I caught you sneaking a fag behind our hydrangea bush. I suppose one thing led to another...'

'Instant attraction?' I asked.

'Of course!' Her cheeks were red now, and she dropped the rest of the crust on the plate. 'It's hard, Will, talking about this. It hurts. I hate it that you don't remember these things.'

'I'm sorry,' I said again. 'I wish I could say the right things.'

'It's OK... really. I'm sure things will get better. The doctor seemed convinced, didn't he?'

I shrugged. The doctor hadn't seemed convinced at all. He was non-committal. My feeling was that he didn't bloody know. My brain was either going to wake itself up or it wasn't – it was as simple as that.

'It must be hard for you too,' Nicola said finally.

'Well, yeah. I feel like I've been living another life,' I said quietly. 'It's like, somehow, I crossed the line into another world – one where I'm completely different and doing things in a way I wouldn't normally do. I just feel out of place.'

The memory hit me suddenly, like an icy punch in the chest.

I was talking about parallel worlds with Gem. We had been drinking wine late at night and were lying on the floor of the living room, staring up at the dark splodges on the ceiling, pretending they were stars and planets moving above our heads.

'We are so tiny,' Gem said, pointing. 'Just a speck, really. Nothing at all.'

'We don't really know what we are,' I replied, my eyes heavy with sleep. 'There could be loads of us, living different experiences in loads and loads of universes out there.'

She giggled. 'Are we all lying on the floor, staring at a mouldy ceiling?'

'Maybe, or maybe in one we are staring up at a freshly painted ceiling. A chandelier. Perhaps we are living in luxury.'

'Or perhaps we are out on the streets, staring up at the stars for real.'

I pulled her close, feeling her hot body press against mine. 'As long as in every version we are together.'

Because in that moment I knew that I couldn't bear to be in a world where I wasn't with her, one where we were apart.

And yet, here we were. Apart. Miserable.

Or rather, here I was…

At around four o'clock, just as I had nestled myself in the oversized sofa, ready for some sleep, there was a series of loud knocks on the door. I looked over at Nicola in despair. My head was really hurting and all I wanted to do was rest. Nicola threw down her phone on the cushion beside her and reached over to rub my knee.

'It's just the lads. Remember I said they were coming over?'

'Oh...' My stomach sank. I had kind of hoped they might have forgotten.

'You always meet up with them on Sundays – usually down the pub.' Nicola got up and padded towards the door. 'It's for old times' sake.'

Except it really wasn't.

I stayed on the sofa, feeling a bit like a stranded fish, unable to move. At the door I heard loud, imposing voices – 'where is the old fucker', 'come on Nicola, let us in'.

Matty strode in first. I recognised him instantly, as he hadn't changed from what I could remember. He was still rat-like, with shaggy blond hair, a narrow face and teeth that were slightly too big for his face. When he grinned at me, I was almost blinded by white. OK, that was different! When did he get those done?

Behind him, two other guys bounded in. One was large and looked like a rugby player, with scruffy dark hair and a broken-looking nose. The other was slim and good-looking, with reddish-blond hair and intense eyes that scanned the room.

Matty came straight over to me. He was clutching a six-pack in one hand and a battered card in the other. He shoved the envelope in my direction.

'Shit, Will, you look rough.'

'Matty! That's not nice.' Nicola wandered in behind them and gave Matty a peck on the cheek. I was surprised that someone like her seemed to like someone like him so much.

Matty held up his free hand in mock defence. 'Well, he does, I only speak the truth.'

'I feel like shit, to be honest.' I glanced down at the card. My name was scrawled on the front. There was also a dubious-looking red stain on the envelope, like ketchup had splattered on it.

'It's from all of us at work. We would've got you flowers, but… Well, it didn't seem right.' Matty sat himself in the armchair opposite. The two other men followed suit. Rugby guy perched himself on the arm of the sofa and ginger man pulled up one of the dining chairs.

'Fancy one?' Matty said, holding up a can.

I shook my head and watched as he handed one out to everyone else, Nicola included. I was thirsty but this didn't seem to be the right time to ask for a cup of tea.

'So, you were racing the Merc?' Rugby man asked.

'Pete!' Nicola hissed.

So, the rugby man was Pete, and I guessed that meant ginger guy was Freddie – the names Nicola mentioned yesterday and the very same who'd shown up in my text messages. These were my friends and yet it was like sitting with total strangers.

'Shame about the car, though,' Freddie said. 'Total pussy magnet.'

I felt myself cringe. Did he seriously just say that? I stared at him, but he was grinning back at me like a Cheshire bloody cat.

'Just tell the insurance company that a dog ran out in front of you, or a cat,' Matty said. 'Hopefully, you'll get some bird on the phone and she'll feel sorry for you.'

'I can't remember what happened,' I said coolly.

Pete reached over and tapped my head. I flinched, instantly wanting to punch him.

'Brain-damaged, then, are you?' he said, grinning. 'Gone a bit soft in the head.'

'Pete!' Nicola hissed again. 'Will isn't brain-damaged, he's injured. He's lost some of his memory, that's all. It'll come back in time.'

'Lost your memory?' Pete chuckled. He was still too close, and I could smell the mixture of cheese and beer on his breath. 'Does that mean you can't remember what happened last Saturday night?'

'None of us should remember what happened last Saturday night,' Matty leered.

Pete reached down to his crotch and grabbed it. 'This fella won't forget.'

The lads burst into laughter, and I could feel every part of me shrink and constrict. This was awful. Why did I hang around with such arseholes? Not one of them had even bothered to ask how I was.

'Hopefully, you'll be back in the office soon, eh, Will?' Matty said, winking at me.

I stared back at him, the blood pumping in my head, which was feeling like it might explode. 'I'm not sure, I—'

'He needs rest, Matty. He's been through a huge trauma.'

'Yeah, well, it'll be a trauma for me to be without my top guy for too long.' Matty held up his can towards me. 'You need to get yourself back in the seat as soon as you can, Will. Get yourself back on the horse.' He tapped his head. 'It's just a knock after all, it's not that serious, is it? Just like a big stupid bruise, really.'

I never really liked Matty at school, but now, sitting here, I realised he'd grown into something far worse. He was a successful, controlling, smart-arse of a man – and for some reason he was sitting in my living room, telling me my injury was insignificant.

I don't know if it was the headache, or the lack of sleep, or just the sheer rage at being told such a thing by this shit of a man, but my words shot from me like bullets.

'You know fucking nothing. I wish you'd all just piss off and leave me in peace.'

'W-what did you say?' Matty stuttered, looking shocked.

'I told you to piss off. So do it. Leave me and my stupid bruised brain alone.'

They did go. Reluctantly, moaning under their breath about what a 'grumpy git' I was now, and suggesting I hurry up and take some more drugs to sort myself out.

It was only as the front door shut and Nicola turned around that I saw she was annoyed too.

'I don't know why you like them so much,' I said. 'That Matty is a total idiot.'

She looked at me coldly for a moment before answering. 'That idiot is my older brother, Will.'

And then she walked out of the room, leaving me feeling like the total arsehole.

Before

Gem – 2016

We were still in bed. It was gone ten o'clock in the morning, but neither of us felt any inclination to move. I was so warm and snuggly under the duvet, sipping the tea that Will had slipped out to make, and staring into nothingness. Being lazy for lazy's sake.

'We should get a cat,' Will said.

'A cat? Why?'

'Well, it would be snuggled up next to us now, wouldn't it? Pawing at our laps and demanding attention. Wouldn't that be sweet?'

I considered this for a moment. 'It would more likely scratch at your face, demand to be fed and then wee on the sheets.'

'It wouldn't do that. *Ours* wouldn't do that.'

'Don't you remember Vee's cat? She even named him Pissy McFluff. Bloody thing had such a weak bladder, and a bad temper to boot. It nearly took my eye out once.'

Will put his cup back on the side and settled back against the pillows, his arms behind him. 'Well, like I said, our cat wouldn't be like that. It would be soppy and cute. We'd train it.'

I snorted. 'You can't train a cat!'

'I'm sure you can. The right one, anyway.'

'We could get a dog,' I reasoned.

I liked dogs. They were keen and loyal. Nan had a little Yorkshire terrier for a while, who was already elderly when she got her, but still full of energy and joy. Nan called her Cynthia, after an old friend. I used to love fussing her and taking her for little walks. We were both heartbroken when she died.

'We can't get a dog,' Will said calmly. 'I don't like them.'

I rolled over to face him, my head now resting on his arm. 'You do like them, Will! Just because you hate one breed!'

He frowned. 'Well, you've never been attacked by one before, have you? Bloody things are so unpredictable.'

I began to trace the soft hair on Will's chest. I loved the way they formed a silky line down towards his belly. I felt his body shudder as my fingers traced the route.

'You weren't attacked, though, were you? That dog just jumped up at you.'

I had been nine, Will ten. It had been outside Will's front garden: a big, furry dog had been walking off lead and, for some reason, decided to hurl himself at Will. It had caught Will completely by surprise and he had been knocked to the floor, with this big bear-like creature leering over him. The owner had run over, apologetic, and dragged the dog away – all the while assuring us that he was 'gentle' and over-affectionate, but Will had never quite got over it. He remained convinced the animal had been about to snap his nose off.

'Anyway, we can't have a dog in the flat. It goes against the tenancy agreement.' His voice was quieter now.

My hand was drifting lower, past his stomach and towards his groin. I felt the dip of his lower abdomen and delicately stroked the skin there. Will groaned softly and wrapped an arm around me, pulling me closer.

'We couldn't have a cat either,' I said gently. 'The tenancy agreement says no pets.'

'What about a fish...'

His hand was reaching down towards my breast, circling my nipple. We were both so hot. I kicked off the duvet, feeling an ache between my legs.

'Yeah, we could get a fish...' I whispered, as I pulled myself on top of him, feeling him hard and ready against my thigh. 'We can get anything you want, Will.'

'Right now... all I want is you...' he said, pulling me down lower, forcing himself against me.

Words turned into groans as I melted into him. We stopped talking then.

—

After, I lay on top of Will as he continued to stroke my hair and back. My body was still hot, and shivering from the orgasm. It had been good, but it was always good with Will. I had nothing to compare it with, as Will had been my first partner – but sex with him was always raw, passionate and fast. It left me breathless and shaky afterwards. How could it be any better?

'Are you happy?' Will whispered.

He always asked that.

I nodded and then lifted my head to kiss his dry lips. Will's blue eyes were fixed on mine, and I could see that he had tears in them.

'Are you OK?' I asked, suddenly worried.

His arms linked around my back, pulling me into a tighter hug. I buried my head into his shoulder, breathing in the sweet smell of him.

'It's silly...' he whispered, his mouth pressed up against my neck.

'No, it won't be. Just tell me what's wrong.'

He sighed and the breath carried across my skin, making my senses prickle.

'Will, what is it? You're not normally upset after. Did I do something wrong?'

'No, of course you didn't. It was all perfect. It always is...'

'Then what is it?'

He shifted under me, and I lifted my head again so that I could look him in the eye. He was still visibly upset. I reached over and stroked away a tear. Will didn't usually get emotional like this; if anything, I was always moaning at him for locking his emotions away. My head was swimming with bad thoughts. Was he about to break up with me? Did he have bad news?

'I... I know it sounds crazy, but I just worry, that's all. I have this awful feeling that I can't shake.'

'What feeling?'

'A feeling that this is all too good and that it will be taken away from me.'

'Oh, Will...'

I pulled him back into a hug, and he melted into me. 'You don't need to worry about that. I'm not going anywhere. Nothing is going to get between us.'

'You promise.'

'Of course, I do.'

Because right in that moment, we were perfect. Everything was. How could that possibly change?

Chapter Ten

Gem – 2022

Richard rolled off me with a satisfied sigh. I lay there for a while, watching as he clambered out of bed and made his way to the bathroom to clean himself up, humming softly under his breath.

I knew I had to move. It was Monday morning again. I needed to jump in the shower, clean myself, get ready for work – but my thoughts were unsettled. For the first time, sex with Richard had been stiff and awkward, like going through the motions. It wasn't that I hadn't wanted to – but I certainly hadn't been excited to do it.

It didn't help that I kept thinking about Will. How it had been so different, in bed, with him. How we would giggle and tease each other. Jesus, I could fart in the middle of a session with Will and he wouldn't care. We had been totally relaxed with each other's bodies.

With Richard it was different. The sex was still good, but it was more formal. I almost felt like I was playing a part. I used to think it was because we were still getting used to each other, still a new couple, but we had been together for a while now.

And today, yet again, I hadn't come.

And Richard hadn't even seemed to notice. Or care.

If only I hadn't started remembering again. Thinking about Will and comparing the two – it wasn't helping. I needed to clear my brain out.

'Are you all right?' Richard asked, walking back into the room. He had a towel looped around his hips and a soppy smile on his face. 'I'm about to get in the shower, if you want to join me?'

'No, it's OK. I'll go in after you. I need to wash my hair.'

He shrugged. 'OK, if you're sure.'

'Just be quick, though. I need to leave in an hour…'

I stayed still, listening as the shower turned on and the water drilled against the glass. Richard was probably disappointed that I didn't want to join him, but the truth was I needed some space. The idea of going into school was hard enough – I was fighting the urge to get into the car and keep driving instead. I wanted to escape the thoughts that were constantly circulating in my mind.

My phone buzzed – a message from Vee, reminding me that we were meeting later. I answered keenly. Yes, I needed to see her. A bit of Vee being reassuring and talking sense was just what I needed right now.

I saw there was also a message from Jack.

> Thanks for everything. I shouldn't have asked you to see Will. It wasn't fair of me. Especially now I know his condition. I'll pick things up from now.

I smiled weakly. This was a good thing. At least now I knew Will wouldn't be totally isolated. Jack was a connection to his past, someone else who could help him through this. The only other person would be his old manager, Mel. I knew Will had been very close to her, but I had no idea where she was now. She used to run The Swan but that had long been taken over by a younger couple who'd turned the place into a restaurant and, as far as I knew, Mel had moved out of town.

I thanked Jack and then put my phone back down. A ripple of relief filtered through me. Perhaps now, I could allow myself to move on again. It was probably guilt and worry that were making me think about Will all the time. As I knew he had people looking out for him, I could let him go again.

The shower turned off and Richard called me to take my turn.

–

Under the pulsing water, I closed my eyes. My body was still tense, unsatisfied. I felt like there was a knot in my stomach and a growing pressure building between my legs.

I opened my eyes again and reached for the soap. I rubbed it carefully over my stomach, across my boobs, while my mind wandered, restless and wanting.

I thought of Will. How we used to press ourselves into this shower, giggling under the spray. Will would push me up against the wall and start to stroke my body gently. His fingers would caress my nipples, before he would lightly circle my belly button, taking his time – teasing me with his movements, brushing my thighs and pubic bone – hinting at more. So much more.

With a soft groan, I reached between my legs and, feeling the wetness there, I remembered how Will would touch me – not too soft, not too hard. How he would use his fingers to rub me just how I liked it. How he would find his way inside me, brushing and stroking, seeking that sensitive part that made my back arch and my legs tingle.

I leant back against the tiles and rubbed myself harder, the urgency growing inside of me. The pressure was building, the ache made me feel heavy and desperate. I could picture Will there, with me, his arms wrapped around me, his teeth biting into my shoulder. I groaned. The pressure was building further still, the sensation was overwhelming.

My eyes drifted closed again, finally ready to come. Ready to—

'Gem? Are you OK in there? You've been ages.'

I jolted, pulled my hand away, the image of Will gone in an instant. My clitoris was buzzing, my face burning.

'I'm OK – I'm just coming...' I called back.

Because I had been. For the first time in ages, I'd nearly come – but it was Will's face that had helped me do it.

–

I was grateful it was the last week of term and I didn't have to worry too much about lesson plans. The children were high and excited, and we shared the classes, letting them watch fun films or play outside in the sun. It certainly took the pressure off.

I sat at the back of the room, smiling as the children giggled over the *Minions* movie. I had seen it a million times myself, but it never got boring. Fiona was next to me, as her class was with us. Unlike me, Fiona would not deign to sit on the low cupboards – she was far too stiff and orderly for all of that. Instead, she kept pacing back and forth, unnecessarily checking on her class and frowning at me on occasion, like she was expecting everything to go wrong.

'You look tired, Gemma,' she remarked. 'I suppose you're pleased it's end of term.'

'Yeah, it's been exhausting...' I admitted. 'Do you have anything planned?'

'Oh, I was going to put myself through some training, you know – voluntary stuff to build up my skills. Maybe on mental health, or emotional wellbeing – it's so important, isn't it? Or perhaps help out at the local care home?'

I grinned stiffly. 'Wow, that's amazing.'

'How about you?'

'I dunno – sleep probably.'

Richard and I had talked about going on holiday but hadn't booked anywhere yet. It wasn't as though we didn't have enough money. I was still saving, but for what I wasn't sure. I knew I should be planning to buy my own home, but I had other desires too – to travel the world, to see new places, to finish my writing. When I told Richard these things, he just laughed and said I was being short-sighted. Apparently, the right thing to do now was settle down, not uproot myself. In Richard's eyes, travelling was something you did as a young student, not a thirty-two-year-old woman. He even scoffed when I talked to him about my book.

'Everyone thinks they have a book inside them,' he told me. 'It's better to live in the real world and focus on your career instead of wasting time on pipe dreams.'

I knew he was right, really, but it still stung. Will had always encouraged me, told me to follow my heart. But look what a mess he'd left me in...

'The holidays are always a bit dull,' I said quietly to Fiona. 'Maybe I'll get round to painting the kitchen…'

'Oh, surely you'll do more than that?' Fiona dropped her voice even further. 'From what I've heard, you've been busy with a certain ex-boyfriend?'

I looked up sharply. 'Eh?'

How did Fiona even know about that? And then, of course, it dawned on me. Fiona's flatmate, Erica, worked in the same secondary school as Richard, who often mentioned her name and how the two of them would sit together in the staff room – because they were both maths teachers and understood each other. I knew he messaged her sometimes too. I wasn't remotely jealous, but it irritated me that Richard had obviously been gossiping about me.

'Oh, don't worry, I don't know much,' she said with a snide smile on her face. God, she was really enjoying this.

'There isn't much to know.'

'Really?'

'Really!' I said firmly and then slipped off my seating position to go to speak to little Freddie, who was currently trying to wedge a pencil into his ear. When I returned, Fiona had adopted her 'caring' face. It was enough to turn my stomach.

'It must be hard, though? Having an ex-boyfriend in hospital.'

'It really isn't,' I lied. 'Besides, he's not in hospital now. He's back at home and doing really well by all accounts.'

'Oh? You've spoken to him.'

I could feel my expression harden. Why was Fiona pushing me like this? Was she trying to catch me out? Was there more to Richard and Erica's relationship than I thought?

'Look, Fiona, I'm not sure where you are going with this, but there really is nothing going on. My ex, Will, was in a bad way, but he's recovering. He's being looked after by his girlfriend – his *fiancée*! I've got nothing to do with him now.'

'But it must still be worrying,' Fiona said carefully. 'I know I would be anxious if it was somebody I loved.'

'Somebody I *used to* love,' I shot back.

Fiona nodded slowly, but her eyes were still gleaming. It was all I could do not to punch that stupid expression off her face.

'I see,' she said finally.

Except she didn't, did she?

–

'She really made out that you still love him?'

'Well, yeah, it seemed that way, and all the while bloody Gru was dancing around on the screen in front of us.'

Vee puffed out her cheeks. 'At least you have a few weeks away from her. She does have a point, though.'

'What!'

Vee held out her hands defensively. 'No, no, wait a minute! I mean, maybe she's got a point about doing something this holiday. It's been a tough year, hasn't it? You've been working hard and had such a shock with Will. Maybe a holiday with Richard is what you both need.'

'Maybe, but I can't believe Richard has been moaning about me...' I complained.

Visions of Richard and Erica huddled together in the staff room while he sobbed out his frustrations kept playing out in my mind. It was irritating to say the least.

Vee sighed. 'Gem, it sounds like he was just offloading to a friend. You can't blame him for that, can you?'

'Well, not really.'

'And it's hardly his fault if this friend can't keep her trap shut.'

'Yeah, maybe,' I conceded. 'I could have a look at some holidays tonight, see what deals are out there.'

We were sitting at our usual corner table. I was drinking a vodka, but Vee was sipping a lime soda, claiming she had a headache.

'It's been a long day,' she said, stretching out her legs. 'I can't believe we still have the rest of the week to get through.'

'These past few days have passed in a blur,' I admitted. 'Honestly, I don't know which way is up at the moment.'

'But it's over, right? Jack told you that Will is at home now. He must be on the road to recovery if they discharged him, right?'

'I'm guessing so.' I paused, fiddling with the straw in my drink. 'Jack is picking things up now. He said he'll keep me updated, but I might ask him not to. It's not like I need this, is it? I can't keep myself tied to the guy.'

'You do need a clean break,' Vee said. 'The first time was bad enough. God, that almost destroyed you.'

I didn't want to think back to those dark moments after Will left, but I remembered long days hiding in my bed, not eating or sleeping. Vee had been there, of course, trying to piece me back together – and Jack had been there for a bit too, but he had been broken himself. He couldn't even stand to be in the same country as Will, let alone the same town, so it wasn't long before he took the opportunity to go.

Time didn't heal, but it made things more normal. Gradually, I got used to the fact that I was alone, that the big, ugly space left by Will would be with me forever. Very slowly, I allowed myself to be picked up and dusted down.

That's why I had broken contact completely, refusing to see him or any of his friends. I even avoided Mel, even though I liked her, but I knew she would end up defending her beloved mate. I had kept well away until now.

'It'll be OK,' Vee soothed. 'He'll get his memory back. He'll remember what he did to you, and he will be too ashamed to come near you.'

'Or he'll remember that he fell out of love with me...'

Vee reached over and squeezed my hand. 'He's an idiot. You know that.'

'I've been reading up a bit on memory. It's a really complex thing, the brain. There is still so much we don't understand.' I shook my head. 'There are people with head injuries who never get their full memories back, whereas for others it takes years and years.'

'You shouldn't be reading up on it, though. It's not your problem,' Vee said. 'This is the worry with you, Gem. You can't let these things go.'

'It's hard when it's someone who's been part of your life for so long.' I took a gulp of air. 'It was so strange, Vee. Really surreal. Seeing Will in the hospital, so different. He wasn't like the man he became at the end, he was—'

'What? What was he?'

'He was like the guy I once loved.'

Vee ordered another round of soft drinks, despite my protests, and I ended up sending an apologetic message to Richard, asking him to order some takeaway.

'I'm being such a rubbish girlfriend lately,' I admitted. 'It's not just the Will thing – even before that I wasn't great. Richard keeps trying to pin me down for plans. He wants to talk about holidays, or looking at getting our own place, but I just don't feel ready for any of that.'

'There's no rush, babe. You have to go at your own speed.'

'Except I'm not getting any younger, am I? Look at you and Brandon. You have your own house, your own plans—'

'A baby...'

I froze for a second, trying to gauge if I'd heard that right. Vee was beaming at me; her eyes were bright like sparklers.

'Vee! You're not?'

She instinctively placed a hand on her flat tummy. 'I couldn't tell you before. I really wanted to, but I wanted to do more tests first. We have our twelve-week scan coming up in a few days! I can't believe it's actually worked this time!'

'Oh, Vee!'

I pulled her into a hug, overcome with emotion. I had seen how the long appointments and constant tests had taken their toll on her; both she and Brandon had struggled and questioned if they would ever be parents. And what bloody amazing parents they were going to be! I knew for a fact Vee would be nothing like her alcoholic mum and dad – she would surround a child with love and support. She would be the absolute best.

'I'm so made up for you both,' I said, pulling away from her. We were both crying, so I quickly dug inside my handbag and pulled out some tissues. No good primary school teacher would ever be seen without them.

'And you let me go on and on about Will while you were keeping this good news…' I said, shaking my head. 'You should have told me to shut up.'

'I'd never do that. You needed to offload,' Vee said gently. 'Besides, I hoped this would cheer you up.'

'It really has.'

'Good…' Vee leant forward and grabbed my hand again. 'I'm glad you're so happy for us, because Brandon and I would love you to be our baby's godmother. We don't have much family, so it's important that we have special people in their life.'

'Oh God, Vee, I'd love to!'

I burst into tears again.

–

I drove home, still sniffling and excited to tell Richard my news. My thoughts were already drifting to my upcoming godchild and how I could spoil them. We could go for day trips to the park, or even the zoo. We could take a bus or a train to the beach and eat ice creams while paddling in the sea. I'd never had a little one close to me that I could spoil before and the chance of me being a mum seemed way off in the distance, so the idea of playing such an important part in a child's life meant the world to me.

This was a sign. I could see more clearly now: my future was ahead of me, wide and expansive. I had wonderful friends, a job I was quite good at and a boyfriend I needed to appreciate more. I couldn't afford to let myself be dragged back into the past. That was for old Gemma; I couldn't be that person anymore.

I turned up the car stereo and found myself singing along loudly to an old Britpop anthem. It was still light in the evening and as I drove past dog walkers and joggers, I could feel my muscles relax and my jaw unclench. I had a lovely hot summer in front of me. Tonight, I was going to look into those holidays and see if I could find a villa or apartment somewhere. Richard really wanted to go to Portugal and I knew he would be touched if I sorted something out for us. It would show my commitment.

I would also message Jack and tell him that I didn't want updates on Will's condition. Why would I? I wasn't part of his life now. For both our sakes, I needed to put a stop to all of this.

After parking the car in my usual space, I sat quietly for a moment, pleased that I had made some decisions. It felt like finally I was getting somewhere. And if that snidey cow Fiona had anything else to say about it, I would put her right. I'd tell her that Richard and I had an exciting summer planned and that she should keep her nose out of my bloody business. Hopefully, that would put a stop to her and Erica gossiping.

My phone buzzed then and I picked it up half-heartedly, expecting a follow-up message from Vee, or a text from Richard telling me to hurry up because the curry had arrived.

But instead, it was a number I knew all too well.

I opened the text cautiously, my instincts prickling. The words took a while to sink in, but when they did, they hit me like a wave.

> I can't stop thinking about you, Gem. This feels so wrong. Why are we not together?
> Will

Chapter Eleven

Will – 2022

Oh my God, why the fuck did I send that message?

The thought hit me as soon as I pressed send and saw the words disappear from my screen. My stomach immediately dropped to my feet. What the hell had I been thinking?

The problem was that it had felt so natural. I was sitting on this strange bed, in a strange room, and the only thing I had that made any sense was my phone. There were still things on there that I could connect with. I still had Gem's number for a start. That had to mean something, right? Why hadn't I deleted it? And buried in my saved images were some photos of me and her together. The phone looked expensive and new, so I guessed these pictures must have been saved onto my SIM, or downloaded from social media or something – it didn't really matter, just having them there made the difference. It showed that this 'other me', this 'stranger' still cared for Gem.

For a while I had just stared at the photos, prickling with guilt because Nicola was making us dinner in the kitchen. Was this betrayal? I was looking at pictures of me and my ex. Except, in my head, she wasn't my ex at all.

The photos made me feel sad and confused. I remembered them as clearly as if they had been taken yesterday. In one, we were at a party at Vee's house, snuggled down on her leather sofa, when someone had taken a quick snap of us. We were both looking up, surprised. I had my hand on Gem's knee and she was slightly leaning in towards me. I used to love the top she was wearing – silver sequins and an open strappy back, showing off her beautiful curves. She always felt self-conscious in it, kept pulling her arms across herself, but she had no need. She looked beautiful.

In another photo we were in the park. It was a selfie and I still remember how Gem giggled as she pulled my face closer, her ice-cream breath frosting my ear. We talked a lot that day. Just minutes before that picture was taken, we had made serious plans. Everything was going right and our future was mapped out in front of us.

Except it wasn't, was it? I changed. I'd mucked things up, somehow.

I was working in recruitment now – no longer in touch with Mel, and apparently my best friend was someone who used to irritate the hell out of me.

How did any of this make sense?

Maybe I was still in a coma, and all of this was some kind of dream-induced fuck-up? Or maybe I really had slipped into some kind of parallel world – one where I was, by all accounts, a total arsehole.

All of these thoughts were crazy, but they were no crazier than the situation I was in. How could I be sitting on my so-called fiancée's bed and have no feelings or connection towards her? Instead, every single fibre in me was aching to see Gem again. I just had to. Seeing these photos made me even more convinced of that.

I stared at my blank phone, imagining her opening the message. Another wave of anxiety washed over me.

What had I done.

'Fuck!'

The word flew from my mouth with force, and I hit the bed with frustration. It was only as I turned to get up that I saw Nicola standing in the doorway.

I had no idea how long she'd been there.

'What did you do?'

Her tone was light, but there was a frosty edge there. I pulled myself up. I saw no sense in lying, it wasn't fair. I barely knew this woman, but she obviously cared about me.

'I messaged Gem.'

'You still have her number?' The iciness had gone up a notch.

'Well, yeah. I found it on the phone.'

I saw her shoulders slump. 'You always told me you deleted it.'

'I'm sorry.' I seemed to be saying that a lot lately.

'Why did you message her? What did you say?'

'Does it matter?'

'Will, for fuck's sake, I'm your fiancée.'

God, that word again. I hated how it sounded on her tongue. Too shrill. I picked up my phone and jammed it into my back pocket.

'So first you insult my brother and then you text your ex,' she said coolly.

I rubbed at my head. I couldn't deal with this right now. It was too noisy, too messy.

'I need to get out of here. I need to take a walk,' I said. 'I need to think.'

'No! Will! We need to talk.'

'Not yet, we don't.' I saw the tears in her eyes and felt myself crumble a bit. I really was an arsehole, wasn't I? I was turning into this version of me that I didn't know.

'I'm sorry, Nicola. I'm not trying to hurt you. My head is everywhere so let me just get some space, please?'

'Do you even know where you're going?'

I had managed to get downstairs and was now walking towards the front door. 'Not really, but I'll be OK. I'll work it out.'

'I hope so,' she said quietly. 'And it's Nic, not Nicola.'

'Nic. I'm sorry.' I nodded politely before I slipped out into the cool night air.

Sorry. Sorry.

SORRY!

How many times could I keep saying that? It was beginning to sound so worthless, even in my own head. There was no other word, though, nothing else that I could say to this poor woman, who was looking at me with pain in her eyes, longing for me to remember. Just fucking remember.

And then I was outside, in a part of town that I didn't know – a housing estate that was a maze of bland buildings and freshly tarmacked roads. For all I knew I could be walking around in a great big circle. My rib was killing me, and my eyes were stinging with tears.

I slammed my fist against my head as I walked. My useless bloody brain that was messing everyone around. Why wouldn't it work properly? If it was like a computer that needed rebooting, surely something could help it? Anything was better than hanging around like this, in some kind of cruel limbo.

I whacked my head again, harder, just wishing I could switch it back on and make everything make sense again.

A man walking a dog passed me, stepping out onto the road to give me a wide berth. I saw his eyes search my face, trying to work out if I was a nutter or not. I just hurried on past him. Perhaps I was going crazy. This could be how madness started.

I certainly would go insane, walking around this bloody estate.

I turned out of the close and took a right down an identical street, searching for any signs that I was heading back towards town. I didn't even know where I wanted to go. Somewhere familiar, I supposed. I thought about the park where I used to hang out with Gem, right next to our flat in the tower block. She used to call it the castle. She really did believe Beckett Court was magical. At the time I couldn't understand why a grey, looming building could hold so much sentimental power, but now I did. I ached deep inside of me to go back.

The only other place I wanted to be was in our old street on Osbourne estate. Just thinking about Mum's house made my heart stop for a second. I had to slow my pace and lean against the railings. I still remembered the day Jack and I moved out – I was going to be with Gem and he was renting a smaller flat nearer town. Packing up our stuff had been so hard, especially since we had so many of Mum's things still – her jewellery, her knick-knacks, those stupid Spanish dancer figurines she used to collect, even though she'd never been to Spain. We ended up sitting in the hallway, surrounded by boxes, drinking a cup of tea. We hadn't talked, because we knew it was the end of an era. We were losing our mum all over again. I think closing that front door for the last time had been one of the hardest things we had ever done.

How could I remember that so clearly?! I could still taste the stewed tea that Jack always made, as well as the stink of disinfectant after we'd scrubbed the place from top to bottom – but I couldn't bloody remember the girl I had proposed to, I didn't know the faces of my work colleagues.

'*You'll work it out, Will. You always do. You have the luck of the devil.*'

God – who had said that to me? It was Di, wasn't it? Gem's mum. Years ago, but I could still hear her voice saying it as if she were whispering it in my ear now.

Thinking about that estate had obviously made me think about her too. Gem and Di had a tricky relationship, we all knew that. Gem struggled to understand her at times, was frustrated by Di's flakiness, by the fact that she seemed content to hide herself away and not properly heal. When Gem and I first got together, she had barely been speaking to her mum. She lived at her Nan's and ignored Di's calls, which I hated. I'd already lost my mum and I knew how hard it was not to have that person in your life – the regrets stayed with you forever. I never wanted that to happen to Gem. I'd always loved Di and so did Jack; she was there for us when Mum died, letting us stay over sometimes or cooking us dinners. She understood grief, she knew what a hole it left in your life. She saw the pain in us and tried her best to help.

For a long time, she was the one person, other than Gem, with whom I could talk to about anything.

I blinked, suddenly feeling everything settle and make sense within me. I couldn't be here right now. I couldn't live with Nicola. It wasn't right, it wasn't fair. It was going to make me crazier than I was already.

To have any chance of figuring this out, I needed to be back home. I needed to be somewhere familiar.

With someone who could really help me.

–

'This doesn't make any sense,' Nicola said, watching as I packed up a small amount of clothes. They were mine apparently, although I didn't recognise any of them – all designer labels and jeans that looked far too skinny for my legs.

I knew Nicola had tears in her eyes, so I couldn't look at her. I hated hurting her like this. I didn't want to hurt anyone – I wasn't cut out to play the bastard.

'I told you, it's not for long. Just a day or so…' I tried to keep my voice light. 'I think I need some time alone to get my head around everything.'

'But how does going back to your old estate help? You should be with me.' She was whining now. 'It'll help your memory being here. It'll all start to make sense.'

I zipped up the bag. 'I can't explain. This just feels like the right thing to do. Being here is too weird at the moment. I feel sick, out of sorts, like I can't focus. If my head is spinning like this all the time, how the hell will I get better?'

There was a silence. Maybe she could finally see my point.

'Honestly, Nicola, it won't be for long. I know I need to sort myself out, but being here with you, when I'm like this, just feels cruel. Wrong.'

Because I want to be with someone else, I wanted to say, but of course I kept that firmly to myself.

'How are you even going to get there?' she asked quietly.

'I dunno – walk, I suppose?'

She half-snorted, half-sobbed. 'Will, I can't let you do that. I'll drive you, make sure you're safe.' She paused. 'How do you know this Di will even let you stay?'

I thought of Di's kind face, the way she'd hugged me the last time I saw her. I didn't know how long ago that was, but somehow it didn't matter. In my scrambled brain it felt like yesterday.

'I just know,' I said.

–

I was right. Di welcomed me with literal open arms, pulling me into her house eagerly, as if she was scared the evening air might harm me in some way. I couldn't believe how skinny she was now, how much she had aged. She could only have been in her fifties, but she looked so much older.

Nicola stood awkwardly on the doorstep after dropping my bag down.

'Well, I suppose I'd better go...'

'You can come in?' Di offered. 'Have a cup of tea with us?'

I swear I saw Nicola turn her nose up a little. Was that a tiny little sneer on her face? 'No, it's OK, thanks. I need to get back.'

She glanced at me, and her expression seemed to be asking me to do something – to hug her, or at least kiss her on the cheek. Instead, I awkwardly squeezed her arm.

'I'll message you, yeah?'

'OK...' She frowned. 'This is just a few days, right? Remember you promised.'

'I know. I promise.'

I watched her stride back to the car. Di was behind me, peering over my shoulder. 'She's quite a stunner, isn't she?'

'Yeah, she is.'

I stepped into Di's living room, and I flopped on her sofa. A sigh escaped me, I couldn't help myself. Nothing had changed here. Everything was the same as I remembered: the boxy TV in the corner, the floral wallpaper, the faded cushions. My eyes fell on the photos on her mantlepiece, and I felt my heart constrict. She even still had photos of me and Gem together.

Di walked in, clutching two mugs. She passed one to me.

'You look awful,' she said bluntly.

'Thanks.' I touched my head. 'I think I've had better days.'

'Gem told me about it all,' she said, settling herself in the chair opposite. 'She was quite upset by it, as you can imagine.'

I lowered my head, feeling ashamed. 'I didn't want her to feel like that.'

'It's hard for her, Will. It took her a long time to move on from you, and now you've had this knock and you're acting like you used to. You can understand how confusing that might be.'

'It's not acting, Di.'

'OK, OK…' She sipped at her tea. 'But it might wear off, mightn't it? Your memory could come back, and you'll be him again.'

'Him?' I blinked. 'What do you mean?'

'The wanker that broke Gem's heart.'

'Jesus.' I breathed out.

Di sat back and sighed. 'Look, Will, I'm happy to have you here. I told you long ago that you'd always have a place in my home. It was a promise I made Gayle and I'd never break that. Never. But you have to appreciate that you changed... These last few years, something happened to you. You weren't the Will we all knew and loved.'

'I changed? But how?'

'I dunno, in lots of ways. Gem said you were snappy and tired at first. Then you started picking holes in everything, putting her down, starting arguments. I think she was hoping it was just a phase, but when you—'

She shook her head. 'It's not for me to say.'

'Di, I know I messed up,' I said quietly. 'But I don't know what I did, and it's driving me mad. In my brain, I'm still in love with Gem. I wouldn't hurt her, I'm sure of that.'

'Well, you did,' Di said simply. 'You hurt all of us.'

'I'm so sorry.'

She shrugged. 'It doesn't matter now. It was years ago and I'd rather forget it.'

I had an uncomfortable feeling pressing inside of me, like a weight. It was making me feel sick.

'Di, I feel like I'm in a bloody nightmare.'

Di's face softened a little. 'Seeing you sitting there, you remind me so much of the little boy that used to come and ask for Gem, so sweet and polite.' She sighed. 'I don't know what to say, Will. Maybe this knock has made you see sense. You certainly seemed to be on a path of self-destruction before.'

'I just want Gem,' I whispered, putting my tea down. I couldn't drink it, I was too upset. 'That is why I couldn't stay with Nicola. It felt like I was cheating. It all felt so wrong and I didn't know what else to do.'

Di stood up and placed her hand on my arm. 'You need to sleep, that's what you need to do. You're shattered, I can see it on your face. Sleep, and we'll talk more in the morning.'

'I'm scared, Di...' I said, feeling childlike and pathetic.

'I know you are,' she replied gently, squeezing me. 'I know you are, but don't be. Fate has an answer. We just have to wait to see what it is.'

It was weird being in Di's spare room. A room that used to be Gem's when she was a child. It was still painted the same shade of pale pink, but the posters had been removed, leaving Blu-Tack scars behind. I lay down on the small single bed, feeling exhausted and vulnerable. Was I crazy coming here? I could be curled up in a luxury king-sized bed right now, being looked after by a beautiful woman who obviously loved me. Instead, I was staring up at the cracked ceiling in the room that used to belong to the girl who once said she could never see a future without me. A girl I could still feel in my arms – if I closed my eyes tight, I could still smell the scent of her herbal shampoo, her sweet perfume.

Di was telling me to leave things to fate, but right now fate seemed like a cruel bastard. I wasn't sure I could trust it to do the right thing at all.

I picked up my phone. There were so many apps and things on there that I didn't recognise. I opened up my calendar and scrolled through; apparently, tomorrow I had a lunch meeting with Ben Vixon and then at eight p.m. I was taking Nicola to a show. The next day was stuffed full of sales meetings and client appointments. I wondered who was taking care of them now. When would I be expected back in? Just the thought made my head throb again. How could I go back to a job that I didn't know? I wouldn't have a clue what I was doing.

I closed the calendar and opened my messages again, remembering the text I had sent Gem earlier. That text had led to everything: my overthinking, my eventual meltdown, my walking out on Nicola – but I hadn't even considered what it might have done to Gem. She had a new life now. She had moved on and I was selfishly firing my shit at her.

I wasn't expecting to get a reply, so seeing the unread message made my heart lurch. I couldn't open it for a moment or two. I was too scared of what I might find. Would she tell me where to go? Would she be angry at me for contacting her again?

Finally, after steeling myself for the worst, I opened it.

The message was simple enough, but I had to read it at least four or five times to be sure.

> Let's meet. The park, like old times? 5 p.m. tomorrow.

She wanted to meet. That had to be a sign, right?

Fate was throwing us back together – it had to be – and whatever wrongs I had done in the past, I knew I had to put them right.

Gem was my future. She always had been. Now I just had to persuade her of that.

Before

Gem – 2017

There was a spot in the park that was just ours. It was the tatty old bench beside the duck pond. Most people walked past it because it was so old and tucked up among the trees, but Will and I loved it. It was secluded and calm – our safe haven.

We'd rushed there from the ice-cream van, clutching lollies in our sweaty hands. This place provided the best shade, and we had half a chance of eating our treats before they became melted messes on our laps. Will bit a chunk off his and then screamed in pain as the brain freeze struck him.

'Serves you right.' I giggled. 'You always have to go at everything at 100 miles per hour.'

Will pulled a face, but he knew I was right. I usually was.

Just in front of us the ducks gathered, thinking we had treats for them. Will threw the remainder of his lolly on the ground and watched as a mallard stabbed at it with its beak, rather unenthusiastically.

'I don't think ducks like ice lollies.'

'Really? You don't think…' I frowned. 'You're such a litterbug.'

'Hardly a litterbug, it'll melt in the sun.'

'It's still a waste, though...' I grumbled.

'Not really, I didn't like it much anyway. I only bought it to make you happy...'

'Oh yeah?' I nudged him. 'Buying these wasn't totally your idea, then?'

'Well, it was, yeah, but I dunno – lollies don't taste the same as they did when we were kids, do you know what I mean?'

I studied mine for a moment. It was a strawberry Mivvi and it still tasted pretty much as I expected it to.

'I'm not sure I know what you mean...' I said. 'An ice lolly is an ice lolly.'

'Nah, you don't get it! Lollies just taste so different when you're younger. I swear they are sweeter, more precious, you want to savour every mouthful – like the lollies we used to have on the beach at Bognor.' Will grinned, obviously picturing his perfect seaside scene. 'One day I'll take you. We'll sit on the beach in the blazing sun and you'll see what I mean.'

'But why Bognor?'

'Because my best memories were there, which makes the taste even more special.' He paused. I could tell he was somewhere far away; he did this sometimes, got lost in his past. He never looked unhappy. It was more like he was searching for things that helped him feel grounded again, pieces of his childhood that he knew he couldn't let go of.

'Mum took us there all the time, to a little caravan site near the beach. If we were lucky, we'd have a day trip to Butlins. It was always busy and fun. I can picture her now, laughing at me and Jack, never minding that we had sand in our shoes or got our clothes wet in the sea. Those holidays were magical — and eating lollies on the beach was the most magical part of it.'

'I want to do that with you,' I said. 'It sounds lovely.'

'They will taste better, I promise.'

'What will they taste of, then?' I teased.

Will leant back on the bench, spreading his arms across the back. 'They'll taste of sunshine. Of summer. Of happiness.'

I licked my own lolly again, considering this. 'Well, that does sound nice.'

'And when we have kids of our own, they will be the same. They'll love the lollies we buy them, the happiness it gives them, the memories they'll build. Because taste is just another memory, isn't it? It's another thing we store away and try not to forget — the taste of joy.'

I murmured my agreement, but I was already distracted. Had Will really just mentioned children? He'd never done that before. On the few occasions when I'd broached the subject, Will had dismissed it — telling me the world was far too overpopulated as it was and that he wasn't sure he could be a parent, after going through all the things he had. It was a big responsibility, after all, a huge commitment…

And yet here, he had just uttered the words casually, as if it were a given.

'Our kids?' I repeated softly, taking a bite of my lolly. 'What will they be like?'

'Just perfect,' he replied immediately, wrapping his arms around me. 'Like you.'

Minutes later, Will took out his phone and took a selfie of the both of us, sat there on our favourite spot. My cheeks were still glowing from the hope for the future; Will was still beaming from his happy memories. It had been a good day and, for a long time, that picture was my screensaver. A constant reminder of how lucky I was, of how lucky we both were.

Chapter Twelve

Gem – 2022

I was back here, at the park bench where we used to snuggle, watching the ducks and giggling about the dog walkers that passed. We gave them nicknames, made up ridiculous backstories that made us howl with laughter. I wonder what people used to think of us, the silly couple on the bench. We were always hugging or holding hands – we must have looked so in love, so happy.

I hesitated at the spot, feeling like there was a huge hole in my stomach letting icy air in. I had been avoiding this place for so long. I lived in the flat that we had shared, I still drank in the pub where Will used to work, I still visited the estate where we both grew up. But this place – this place could be avoided.

Why had I even suggested we meet here? Was it just because it was easy, and I'd assumed Will would remember it? Or was there a niggling need to check this out for myself and see how I felt?

And how did I feel?

Hollow.

Sad.

Disappointed.

I was early so I wasn't expecting Will to be there. For a moment or two I hovered by the bench, but it was awkward sitting there by myself, so I stepped towards the shore of the pond and watched the ducks gather in the reeds. They cried out excitedly, thinking that I might have some food for them, and I immediately felt guilty that I had nothing to offer.

'Sorry,' I whispered. 'I haven't even got crumbs in my pocket... which makes a change.'

'Not even an ice lolly?'

I turned, stunned. I hadn't heard Will creep up on me. He was standing just a few inches behind, dressed simply in those too-skinny jeans he now wore and a nice, expensive-looking dark blue T-shirt.

'You remember that, then?' I said, surprised.

'I remember a lot of things from back then.' He stepped a little closer. I could see that his hair was a bit wet, like he'd just stepped out of the shower. He still needed a shave, though; as if conscious of this, he rubbed his hand over his bristles.

'So why here?' he asked.

I shrugged. 'Why not? It's as good a place as any.'

'I guess...'

We stood stiffly for a while and a sadness washed over me. This used to be such a happy spot. I would lean against Will and breathe him in, while watching the ducks swoop and dive in the water. Now the thought of even touching him seemed crazy.

'Shall we sit down?' I said finally.

'Sure, if you think that old thing can still take our weight.'

The bench really was coming to the end of its life now. It was missing one of its inner rungs and the back part was breaking away completely. I lowered myself down on it carefully. It was daft, really, but I would've hated to see

138

this splintered old thing replaced by something new. It was good to have a few things left from the past.

'It's still there,' Will said quietly, sitting himself down beside me.

'What is?' I asked, but already my eyes were following his gaze. Just there, on the wooden rung nearest the back, was the faintest trace of writing. I could picture Will now, taking a black marker pen out of his bag and scrawling our initials into the wood.

'We'd only been together... What? A few months?' he said, smiling. 'I thought it was a bit of a naff thing to do, but I still did it. I wanted something tangible. Every time we came, I would check it was there.'

'I'd forgotten all about it,' I admitted. The letters were so faded now, just light grey streaks that could be easily mistaken as grains in the wood. It was amazing to think how long they had been there, though.

'How's your memory?' I asked carefully. 'Are you remembering any recent things?'

His eyes were still on the graffiti, but he shook his head slowly. 'I can't remember anything. Not recent anyway. My home, my clothes – it's all brand new in my eyes.'

'I guess it will take time. Nicola will help.'

'Well, not at the moment, she won't.' He glanced at me from the side. 'I'm not living there.'

'What?' I replied, stunned. 'Why not?'

'I dunno... It just didn't feel right. It felt like...' His cheeks burnt bright red and he turned away from me. Suddenly, I felt a bit uncomfortable. Why was Will acting so weird with me? Surely, he didn't...

No! I quickly shook that thought away. I couldn't afford to get emotional now.

'So where are you living?'

He coughed, looked down at his feet. 'Well, actually, I'm staying at your mum's for a bit.'

'My mum's!' My voice was louder than I'd intended. 'Why on earth are you there? I mean, you haven't even seen her for years. It makes no sense.'

Will sighed. 'In my head it does. I feel like I was only round there the other week. I can remember sitting with her and talking about my summer – our summer – plans...' He paused. 'I think my memory has stopped there, at that moment. It was early summer, and we were still together. I can recall this mega busy week. Me working in the pub, meeting up with Jack to discuss the band. I remember you were cooking something special...'

I nodded. 'The burnt chicken curry. That was around July time. It was a bit of a disaster.'

'That's right!' He held out his arms in glee. 'You were so apologetic, but it didn't matter, I just...' A frown crossed his face. 'I left, didn't I? I went to the pub that evening to see Mel.'

'Yeah...' I hesitated. 'Will, I'm not sure if I want to go into all of this again.'

Will was staring off into the distance. 'It feels like that week has just happened in my head, like we've only just had that meal, and everything is still OK between us. It's like I'm stuck in the past.' He sighed. 'That's why it made sense to stay at your mum's. Being at Nicola's was too odd, too out of place. I felt like I was messing her around.'

'But you two are engaged,' I insisted softly. 'This is just temporary, Will, I'm sure of it. As you recover, things will start to make sense...'

And you'll fall in love with Nicola again.

I didn't say as much, but we both knew that's what I meant. Will just nodded slowly.

'Maybe,' he said quietly. 'Or maybe I'll just stay as I am.'

It was getting late, and typical for a British summer, the evening air was becoming sharp and cool. I wrapped my arms tightly around myself.

'What's your actual last memory?' I asked.

'It's hard to make out… I remember leaving the flat. I was on a bike, wasn't I? A really old one?'

'Yes, you loved that bloody thing.' Until you moved on to cars, that was. Fast cars with loud engines – the change had been surprising, to say the least.

'I think it was after the meal?' Will screwed up his face to consider this. 'I'm pretty sure I was on my way to The Swan. To work. Everything is a bit muddled after that but I can remember being at work. I can recall Mel's face. I think we were talking. I remember a Madness song playing in the background… but then, nothing…'

I frowned. 'So everything stops the day after the meal? In July 2019?'

'Yeah. Yeah, I think so.'

'It is really odd.' I shuffled on the bench. 'Because that was our last good weekend together. After that it was like you became a different person and everything went wrong.'

'Really? In what way?'

'Well, you just pushed away from me. You made changes to your life, acted differently. You…' I paused, taking a breath. 'You stopped being Will. My Will. And that's why I can't see you again. I can't – this is too hard.'

There wasn't much to say after that. I could see by Will's expression how much my words had affected him. He looked sick, rubbing at his head, as if that could make everything better – like he could suddenly make sense of this mess. But there was no making sense of this.

'I thought...' he mumbled. 'I thought maybe fate had drawn us together again.'

Fate! I almost wanted to scoff. It was clear he had been spending time with my mum. Fate was something she had become obsessed with, when she'd been trying to make sense of the bad things that had happened in our life. That, and spirituality and crystal healing – anything that meant she didn't have to face the brutal reality – that sometimes life was just shit. Sometimes things happened that you didn't want.

Sometimes you just had to be cruel and cold about it all.

I reached forward and took Will's hand in mine. It was surprisingly cold. I wanted to squeeze it, to warm it up, but I also didn't want to send the wrong message. I knew I had to be strong now.

'I'm sorry, Will. This is not what I want. I hate hurting you, but I have a new life now – we both do. You have to accept that.'

'Did you ask me to come here to tell me there's no hope for us?' he asked, the quiet devastation in his voice almost had me wanting to take my words back.

'I needed to see you face to face, somewhere quiet – I don't want to upset you.' I paused, hating the tearing feeling inside my stomach. 'This is the right thing to do, Will. We weren't good for each other.'

'Really?' His eyes were glassy and wide. 'I still can't believe that.'

'You have to believe it. For my sake.'

He nodded, not looking at me. 'OK.'

'I promise, this is for the best.' I got up, feeling stiff and awkward. Every part of me was hurting. I had a sudden urge to sit right down next to him and pull him into my arms, but I couldn't. Not again.

'I'm sorry,' I said instead.

And then I left him and our beauty spot behind, walking quickly so that he couldn't hear the gasp in my breath, or see the tears that were now streaming down my face. I bent my head against the evening breeze and forced myself not to look back. I kept telling myself I was doing the right thing – I knew I was. I was doing the right thing for both of us.

But why did it feel like my heart was breaking all over again?

Before

Gem – 2018

It should have been perfect. The flat was just how I wanted it to be, and Will had even managed to squeeze a real tree into our tiny living room. I draped fairy lights across the bookcase and was playing cheesy Christmas tunes on the highest volume. In the kitchen, the turkey was roasting perfectly. The veg was nearly ready and the best gravy in the world (bought ready-made via the local supermarket) was about to go in the microwave.

My first Christmas hosting and I should have been so happy – except, I wasn't. The big gnawing ball of anxiety and injustice was burning inside me as I checked my watch for the millionth time that day.

'Where is she?'

Will looked apologetic, like it was his fault. He handed me a second glass of wine and told me to entertain Jack and my aunt Lisa, who were both waiting for us in the living room.

'It's nearly two, Will. I told her to be here at eleven,' I snapped. 'Why is she doing this…'

'I should've collected her. That might've been better.'

'She's perfectly capable of walking ten minutes. Besides, that wouldn't have made any difference. She's doing this to hurt me.'

We had agreed, months ago, that we would host our family on Christmas Day at our flat this year. I was sick of the dreary and tiring Christmases at Mum's. It wasn't even like she enjoyed them. She resented cooking the dinner and was usually pissed on the brandy by the time the Queen's speech started. For some reason, Mum saw it as a kind of tradition that she needed to cling on to with her badly bitten nails.

'I've told her why it's better here, so she can relax and not worry about anything,' I said. 'I thought she agreed.'

Will shrugged. 'I guess it must be hard for her, letting go.'

'What am I going to do? The turkey will be all dry and ruined soon...' I peered into the oven, feeling my desperation grow. 'She's not even answering her phone.'

Will was already pulling on his coat. 'I'll go over. I'll find out what's wrong.'

'What if she refuses to come?'

He planted a gentle kiss on my lips. I could taste the Buck's Fizz he had drunk earlier. 'She won't, don't worry. I'll sort it. Just turn the oven on low, and go in the other room and relax...'

'But—'

'No buts.' He held his finger against my lip. 'I'm going to sort it, OK?'

I nodded and felt myself begin to relax. Will had control of this now, so surely everything would be fine.

In the living room, Jack and Lisa were chatting away. They always got on well, used to being the extra guests at Christmas time. Lisa was my dad's older sister and his only living relative. She was a lot older than my mum, as my dad had been – in her late fifties or maybe even early sixties – but she never really talked about her age, being one of those glamorous, stylish women who seemed to defy a number. She had spent most of her life travelling the world as a photographer, and now lived in a small East London flat with her on-off boyfriend Oscar. I loved spending time with her, because she gave me a little insight into my dad's world – a man I barely knew. Judging by the photos I'd seen, she also looked a bit like him, sharing the same sharp jaw, large blue eyes and reddish-blonde hair.

Lisa found Will and Jack charming. I think she liked the fact that they were setting up a band and had big plans. Lisa was a big fan of ambition and creativity.

'Have you heard about this Vic, Gem?' Lisa called out to me as I slipped into the room. 'It sounds like the boys finally have a decent drummer.'

'Does that mean you'll come and see us perform?' Jack asked.

Lisa smiled. 'I might. If you can get me a front-row seat.'

I settled back on the sofa and tried to allow myself to relax, but already I was thinking about Mum again, wondering what excuse she might come up with.

Forty minutes and two drinks later, the letterbox on the front door shook. They were back. I tried to contain my rage as I rushed to let them in; I was sure the dinner was pretty much ruined by now. The turkey would be as dry as dust and the roast potatoes more or less cremated. Even the drink wasn't helping to soothe my mood.

Will swept into the hall with my mum under his arm, like some kind of wounded bird. She was wearing her heavy red winter coat that was far too big for her. Her hair was loose and looked windswept, her face pale without make-up.

'Where have you been?' I hissed.

Will gave me a look. It was a 'hey, not now' look that he often gave me if I was being too moody for his liking. He gently eased the coat off my mum's shoulders and told her to go into the living room.

'Jack'll get you a drink to warm your bones,' he said loud enough so his brother would hear. 'I'll help Gem serve up.'

'There's probably nothing to serve up,' I grumbled as I stormed into the kitchen. 'What was the problem anyway? Was she still sulking because I decided to host this year?'

'Sort of... Maybe...' Will hovered behind me. 'Gem, you have to remember your mum is very unwell. She hasn't been taking her antidepressants and I don't think she's been thinking too clearly...'

I opened the oven, the waft of heat and grease hitting my face full blast – but it was a good distraction from the swirling feelings in my stomach. I could feel the tears beginning to bite. I couldn't let them, not now.

'This is a hard time of year for her,' Will said gently.

I slammed the withered turkey on the side. 'It's hard for me too, Will. That's why I wanted this Christmas to be different. I didn't want to sit around feeling sad all day, wishing Dad was still here. I didn't want to keep talking about the past. I just wanted—'

Will's arms were wrapped around me before the tears could properly hit. I drew myself into him, appreciating the heat, needing his body close to mine.

'What happened?' I finally muttered, lips brushing against Will's garish Christmas jumper. 'What was she like when you found her?'

'She said she took some tablets last night. It wasn't enough to do anything, but it knocked her. When I went over there, she was emotional. She said she had let you down. She's in a pretty dark place.'

'What do I do?' I whispered. 'I'm no good at this, Will. I say all the wrong things. I just get frustrated with her all the time for not getting better. I know it's not her fault, but I can't help it.'

'It's OK, Gem.'

'All I've ever wanted is for things to be normal. For us to be normal and we – we can't...'

Will pulled me in closer and kissed the top of my head.

'What do I do?' I asked again.

'Be there,' he replied. 'Just be there for her. No judgements.'

In the end, the dinner wasn't so bad. OK, the turkey wasn't great, but the expensive gravy helped to moisten it a bit. Jack and Lisa were so pissed that they barely noticed. Mum sat quietly and managed a small plate of food. She didn't talk much, but I was relieved to see her smile a few times. Later, as we settled down to play party games, Mum wrapped a cardigan around herself and sat beside me on the sofa.

'I haven't given you your present yet.'

'Oh,' I replied, surprised. We didn't usually worry about presents now, and I hadn't got anything for her.

'It's OK,' she said softly, passing me a box. 'I didn't really buy you anything. It's just something I think you should have.'

I carefully opened it, my breath catching in my throat. Inside was a gold sovereign ring, threaded onto a delicate gold chain. I pulled it out, holding it carefully between my fingers.

'The ring was your dad's. It was the only jewellery he ever wore. His mum bought it for him.' Mum glanced over at Lisa, who was now dozing on the chair. 'She will tell you when she's not as pissed. Their mum was never one for gifts, so this was extra special.'

I didn't have anything of my dad's. I couldn't quite believe that now I had this, especially as I hadn't even known about it. Mum must have kept it hidden away, like a treasure.

'Thank you,' I whispered.

Her hand touched mine. 'You are so much like him, you really are. I wish he could see. He would be so proud...'

I looked up, saw the tears glistening in her eyes. 'Mum, about earlier, I'm so—'

She squeezed me. 'It's OK, Gem. I get it, I really do.'

'But I should be more understanding.'

'And I should be a better mum.' She nodded towards Will, who was trying to win a game of Guess Who? against Jack. 'I've known that man of yours since he was a boy and I swear every day he gets more precious. You keep hold of him, Gem. The good ones are hard to keep, I should know.'

'He is lovely,' I said, grinning. 'He's good for me.'

'Fate made sure you two came together. You are good for each other – don't ever forget that.'

—

Will and I snuggled up on the sofa once everyone had gone, full of chocolate and Christmas pudding, and warm on wine and Baileys. Will rested his head on mine.

'It's hard, isn't it? Christmas. I mean, it's great and everything, but it's hard too.'

'You must miss your mum,' I said gently.

'I do. I really do.' He paused. 'All of us have people we miss so badly, it's not easy. I can understand why your mum struggles to make it through the day.'

My finger looped through the ring that hung around my neck. 'I've spent so long being angry with her, Will, and I forgot that we are both suffering.'

'It reminds you that people really are precious,' he replied. 'So precious. It's too easy to push those that you love away, but you can't. You need them and they need you.'

He reached down and we kissed for a long time. I sighed as his hands moved over my body, as his mouth came down across my throat and my chest. I groaned as he reached behind me to unzip my dress, helping me to pull it off, his fingers now stroking me urgently.

'Please, Will...' I gasped. 'Never change. Please stay as you are, always.'

He looked up, his cheeky eyes glinting in the light. 'I'm never changing, babe. You're stuck with me, just the fucked-up way that I am.'

'Good.' I giggled, as his hand moved towards the edge of my knickers. 'Good. Because I love this version of you.'

I loved him so bloody much.

Chapter Thirteen

Will – 2022

I didn't like it here. This was always the part of town that I avoided, the flash part that had been built up quickly, totally ignoring the quainter and more historical sections. Here there were only identical, soulless office blocks and coffee houses, with a bland hotel stuck on the corner, facing the traffic.

GM Consulting was one of the shiny, commercial buildings. I could see rows of desks inside, people on phones, someone striding around with his mobile nestled under his chin, waving his arms as if in the middle of something urgent. I couldn't quite compute this place as being somewhere I might've worked. It seemed too sleek and a bit too pretentious. Wasn't recruitment just sales? I couldn't even see myself being any good at that. I could barely sell a pint at The Swan – Mel always told me off for chatting too much, for distracting the punters. For being too lazy.

How the hell did I end up here?

I took a deep gulp of air and them made myself walk in. I wasn't going to gain anything by hovering on the pavement, staring inside like some kind of idiot. I had to confront this.

The interior was as sterile and plush as I'd imagined. I could smell leather and wood, and something deeper, muskier. The office space was large and alive with sound. In every direction I could hear men – and it was mainly men; I only spied one lone woman at the front, sifting through some papers – shouting and talking loudly on their phones. I immediately felt overwhelmed.

The woman looked up as I approached. She had dark hair, cut into a short pixie style, and she smiled brightly in my direction.

'Will! My God! Are you back already?'

'I, er...' I stepped nearer, feeling suddenly self-conscious. 'No. No, I'm not back. I'm here to see Matty.'

Her eyes widened. 'You poor thing. We couldn't believe it when we heard what happened. It's not like you, you're such a safe driver. Well, you always were when I jumped in with you...' She giggled softly. 'I'm just glad you're OK, you know.'

'I'm not really that OK. I knocked my head badly.' I sighed; I didn't know how much she had been told – or even who she was. Was she a friend? Someone I cared about? This whole situation was just making me uncomfortable. 'Is Matty here?'

'Yes, he's in the office. I'll call through, take a seat,' she said, gesturing at the row of soft black chairs that ran alongside her desk. 'Or you might want to go and see the others? Check out what they've been up to?'

I glanced at the main area again; no one had noticed my arrival, and I was reluctant to go and announce myself. Once again, I felt like a stranger in my own life. What could I even say to these people?

'I'll just sit here,' I said, plopping myself down. I felt heavy and tired, and was asking myself for the millionth time why I was here. But Matty kept messaging me. He was my boss and he wanted an update on my condition. It wasn't right to keep him hanging.

And he was also Nicola's brother. I wondered if she had contacted him, told him what a bastard I had been. We had had one brief conversation this morning during which I had agreed to meet Nicola for dinner to 'thrash things out'. I wasn't quite sure what this would involve, but I was guessing it would be tiring and confusing. After seeing Gem last night, I knew that she wanted nothing more to do with me. Maybe she had been right. Maybe as my brain healed, I would find myself falling in love with Nicola again.

Maybe all I needed was time.

'Will?'

Matty was striding towards me, looking every bit the professional with his sharp grey suit and slicked-back hair. Jumping up, I took his outstretched hand. It felt warm and clammy in mine.

'Great to see you back, mate. Recognise the place?'

I shook my head glumly. 'No. Nothing feels familiar, nothing at all.'

He placed his hand on my shoulder and guided me towards the main space. 'Well, you just met Fliss, our receptionist. I'm surprised you don't remember her, but never mind that for now...'

I glanced back at Fliss, who was smiling at me shyly. Something twisted inside me. Had anything happened between us? But when?

'This is the main team,' Matty said, waving his hands across the room. 'The perms team is on the left. The temp team is on the right. That over there,' he pointed at a desk on the far right-hand side, under a huge noticeboard, 'is your desk. You're my main guy in the temp team. My top seller.'

I wasn't sure what to say to that. Was I meant to feel pride? 'Er, that's great.'

I could feel eyes upon me. People were nodding and smiling in my direction, but I could sense their unease. I was the sick man walking back into the office. I guessed I probably looked different, was acting weird too. Nobody liked that, did they? Nobody liked to see people that were behaving so strangely.

Strange. Strangely. Stranger – these words seemed to be haunting me at the moment.

'Come on,' said Matty, possibly guessing I was weirded out. 'Let's go in my office. We have lots to talk about.'

Matty's office was surprisingly small and dingy, with a window that looked out onto the back alley beyond. He didn't seem to mind this, though, as he sat back in his expensive-looking, ergonomic chair and gestured for me to sit opposite him.

'So, mate,' he said, stretching his arms behind his head. 'I'm hoping you've come to tell me when you're coming back. You can't stay on sick pay forever, can you?'

In truth, I hadn't even thought of the money, or even bothered to check my bank balance. All I knew was that I had a wad of cash in my wallet and a shiny-looking card that I couldn't remember owning. Everything was about living day to day now.

'Well, that's why I'm here, Matty,' I said. 'I don't think I will be coming back.'

Matty sat up slowly, his eyes narrowing slightly. 'Will, mate, don't you think you're being a bit hasty here? You've only just come out of hospital. Your head has taken a fair old whack. Surely, you shouldn't be doing anything rash?'

'I don't think this is rash,' I said. 'The truth is, Matty, I don't know how long it will take for me to get better, or if I'll get better at all. I don't even know if I want to get better.'

Matty was staring at me like I had totally lost it. Perhaps I had.

'What I mean is,' I continued hastily, 'I can't remember the person I've become. This man who worked in recruitment, who was a flashy salesman. All I can remember is being a singer in a band. I'm the fella that works shifts in the local pub and barely has a pot to piss in.'

'And you want to go back to that?'

'I don't want to go back. I'm there already,' I replied. 'I don't know if this is for good, or what, but I do know that I can't face coming back here and trying to be someone I'm not.' I glanced back out of the glass door, at the energetic faces of people making calls and securing sales – the thought of being part of that made me feel unsteady.

'Give yourself a bit more time,' Matty soothed. 'I can keep your post open for a bit longer. You're an old friend. Think this over a bit more.'

'No, I've been thinking all night. I've done nothing but think. It's not fair for you to wait around for me to get my shit together.' I shrugged. 'And if anything changes, I can get in contact, can't I?'

Matty nodded. 'Sure – I mean, if I have a vacancy, I'll always consider you. You're one of the best on the job. A total natural.'

'Thanks.'

'What will you do now?'

'I dunno, maybe see if I can get my bar job back. I need to find Mel somehow. I don't suppose you know her number?'

'What, Mel at The Swan? Nah! Last I heard she moved away years ago. It's under new management now.'

'Oh.' I sat back in my seat, feeling a bit hopeless. I was kind of hoping that I could've just waltzed in at the pub and won Mel over with my charm. I really wanted to see her again – some nagging urge inside was telling me it was important.

'I have to say, mate, I feel like you're throwing your life away,' Matty concluded. 'What has Nicola said about all this? I can't imagine she'll be happy about you giving up on the job.'

'I haven't told her yet.' I searched his expression, trying to see if there was any sign that he knew I had walked out last night, but Matty was giving nothing away. He'd make an amazing poker player.

'I stayed away last night,' I said finally, biting the bullet. 'I suppose it's another thing I'm struggling with – the house, Nicola. I just need to give my mind time to process everything.'

'So where are you now?'

'Gem's mum's house.'

'Jesus – Nicola must love that,' Matty replied, and there was the trace of a smile on his face. 'Well, I guess you have to do what you feel is best. It can't be easy. I mean, I've lost a few hours of memory occasionally after a bender, but losing years – that's tough, man.'

I felt myself sag. Matty, surprisingly, was the first person to acknowledge that I really was in a horrible situation. Who would have thought that the annoying runt from school could actually be OK.

'I'm sorry if you think I'm messing Nicola around, though,' I said carefully. 'I can see she's doing a lot for

156

me. She obviously cares and, well… It's making me feel like the biggest shit.'

Matty scoffed. 'Huh. I wouldn't worry too much about that. Our precious Nicola isn't as innocent as you think.'

I stiffened. 'What do you mean?'

Matty got up from his chair and gestured for me to leave with him. 'Look, mate, no offence, but I've got to get on. This office doesn't run itself and now I've got to start looking for your replacement, you know…'

I followed him to the door. 'Matty, what did you mean about Nicola?'

Matty looked back at me, with almost a pained expression. 'Will, I can't go into all of this now, she's my sister. It's not my place. I shouldn't have spoken out of turn, but I just hate seeing you beat yourself up like this.' He paused. 'I just hope – for your sake – that your memory comes back sooner rather than later.'

Chapter Fourteen

Will – 2022

Nicola isn't as innocent as you think.

The statement ran through my head again and again as I sat opposite Nicola in the posh restaurant where she had arranged for us to meet. I was guessing this place was new, as it certainly wasn't somewhere I recognised: a small Italian nestled between the old estate agency and NatWest bank. We were sitting at the back, at a quieter, secluded table – but the place was heaving and I felt conscious of the sheer amount of people around us.

Nicola isn't as innocent as you think.

She was dressed in a tiny black dress. She looked confident and a little bit moody as she sipped her wine and looked me up and down in a not-so-subtle fashion. I was immediately aware that I should've made more effort. A quick bath at Di's, and throwing on the same pair of jeans and a different top clearly didn't meet her expectations.

'I guess you didn't pack much,' she said, taking another sip of her wine. 'But it's hard to see you like this, Will. You always made such an effort with your appearance.'

Did I? I remember the arguments I used to have with Jack, who had always been keen for the band to have a 'look'. He used to complain about the unfairness of me getting the good looks and not making the best of it.

'I'm comfortable like this,' I said and then, after a glance around at all the suited and booted people surrounding us, I quickly added, 'I didn't know we would be meeting somewhere so posh. I expected the pub or something.'

Nicola wrinkled her nose. 'We can hardly talk there, can we?'

I could've argued that it was hard to talk here, with the stupid, over-the-top Italian music playing, but there seemed little point. Instead, I picked up a menu and stared at it blankly.

'I expect you'll be getting the usual risotto?' Nicola asked.

'Will I?'

'Well, yes, you normally do.'

'I don't know what my normal is anymore, Nic.'

Nicola's hand snaked across the table and took hold of mine. 'Oh God, Will, this is so hard. I keep looking at you and expecting you to act and be the same as always. I'm sorry.'

This softening of her attitude made me falter a little, as I hadn't been expecting it. Her smooth skin against mine was so warming, so comforting.

'I hate you being away,' she said quietly. 'It feels so wrong. You should be with me, recovering, not with…'

She left the last part unsaid, but I nodded in understanding. I was staying with my ex-girlfriend's mum. It was weird, whichever way you looked at it.

The waiter came over and asked if we were ready to order. It was clear by the way he greeted us both that we were regulars.

'I haven't seen you in here for ages! I was beginning to worry.'

Nicola giggled nervously. 'Yes, I know, it's been too long. Will has been a bit unwell.'

'I'm sorry to hear that,' the waiter replied soberly. 'I hope you are OK now?'

'Apart from a slightly rattled head...' I mumbled.

I wondered whether it would have been easier if I had broken actual bones or had visible injuries. How could I explain to people that my brain was no longer working properly, that part of my system had completely broken down?

Nicola reached across and squeezed my hand again. 'He's getting better every day. And I thought dinner at Gino's would be just what he needed.'

The waiter grinned and scribbled down Nicola's order enthusiastically. I let her take over, barely acknowledging what she was requesting. To be honest, I was hardly hungry.

I glanced up at Nicola again. She was staring back at me. Her expression was tender, her lips curled into a soft smile. It was hard to think that this woman could be anything but supportive and kind. After all, she was here. She still had time for me, despite me pushing her away. How hard must it be to have your boyfriend, or even your fiancé, wake up from a crash and declare that he no longer knew you?

Nicola isn't as innocent as you think.

I'd loved her once, obviously. I'd loved her enough to propose. There had to be something special about her. And hadn't I just felt a spark of something when she touched my hand? Was that a sign that my memory was beginning to come back? How could I even trust what Matty was telling me? He'd never been a friend, only as a sneaky little runt at school. Maybe he was messing with me. After all, not all brothers and sisters liked each other.

'You look so lost in thought,' Nicola said gently. 'You seem troubled.'

The bread arrived and I picked one bun up half-heartedly, and broke it in two. 'I guess there's a lot to think about.'

'You don't want to tire your brain out too much. It's been through enough already.' Nicola carefully peeled a section of her bread off and popped it into her mouth. 'How was last night? Did you sleep OK?'

'Sort of. I had dreams – a bit weird. They didn't make sense.'

'Really?' Nicola leant forward a little. 'That could be important, Will. You might be getting bits of your memory back. Can you remember anything?'

I shrugged. 'Not really, just flashes. Bright light, loud noise. I could hear shouting, a voice I couldn't make out. I don't know, I think it's just muddled memories.'

Nicola nodded. 'I guess that's to be expected, nothing to be scared of. The doctor said you might have strange flashes of recognition, little things coming back.' She paused. 'But please tell me anything, Will, I might be able to help.'

'I'm not sure anyone can help, really,' I replied.

'I can only try. I want to try.'

I sighed, my body suddenly so heavy, like I was wading through mud. I was so sick of feeling like this.

'You could help with one thing,' I said slowly. 'You could tell me what happened the day of the crash. I have all these pieces of a jigsaw puzzle jumbled up in my head right now, and I need to try to put them back together, try to make sense of what my life was like before...'

I noticed Nicola was fiddling with her hair, twirling it round and round her finger. Her focus looked a little lost, but eventually she nodded.

'We'd been away for the weekend at the Franklin Hotel – you know, the one out in the country, with the big lake and gardens?'

My eyes widened. 'Yeah, it's dead posh, isn't it?'

I'd only ever driven past before. The hotel was a huge Tudor building known for hosting weddings and corporate events. I was pretty sure that guests played croquet on the lawn, or something equally upper class.

'We were there to celebrate our engagement, you know – a romantic weekend. You'd pulled out all the stops: paid for a flashy room, treated us to lovely food. It was great, perfect really. I suppose it was too good to be true...'

'Too good to be true?'

Nicola was staring at the table; she dusted some bread-crumbs onto the floor, not looking at me. 'You were meant to be bringing me back on Monday morning, but we had an argument – it was a stupid one, I can't even remember what it was about. You ended up driving off without me. I had to call Matty to come and pick me up.'

I winced at the selfish behaviour she was describing. 'That sounds like a pretty crappy thing to do.'

She shrugged. 'I was used to it. You can be pretty up and down, Will. You were probably angry when you were driving, not concentrating maybe. I guess that's why you crashed.'

'I sound awful,' I said. To everyone – Gem, Nicola, Jack, Di.

'Not always.' Her smile was sad.

'So why did you put up with it?'

'Because I loved you, stupid,' she said coolly. 'I still love you. The ups are worth it. I just always hoped the downs would eventually stop.'

Dinner arrived and we ate in silence at first. I kept stealing glances at Nicola, but most of the time she seemed absorbed in her food. The tiny frown line on her face suggested she was still worried, or perhaps still frustrated with me. I deserved that. I sounded like I'd been a total jerk towards her. What Matty had said earlier didn't really matter – no woman should have to put up with that.

'I hate hearing how I acted before,' I said, pushing aside my half-eaten dinner. 'It sounds like I was an arsehole to you, to everyone. This is not the person I want to be. It's not the person I believe I am.'

'I don't think you are either,' Nicola replied carefully.

'We got engaged so quickly, didn't we? We had only been together, what…?'

I looked at her hopelessly. I still found the numbers so confusing.

'We've been together long enough, Will, it's hardly a fling. You proposed last month on a weekend away. It was a surprise, but a nice one. We were excited about our wedding.'

Nicola sounded so sad, I flinched. I found myself reaching forward and this time I took her hand. I saw how pretty my mum's ring looked on her finger.

'I wish I could remember giving this to you. It must've been such a special moment.'

'It was.' She smiled. 'You were very old-fashioned and proper. It made me laugh.'

'And did we fall in love quickly?' I asked.

Her fingers curled around mine. 'So quickly. You had been with Gem for a long time, and I knew that, but

163

your relationship was over. Gem had stopped trusting you. She hated your new job and the fact you were working long hours. She was paranoid and accused you of things. You two were arguing all the time and you told me how unhappy you were, that Gem wanted different things. You said you had grown apart.'

'Different things?'

'You know, like travelling. Getting some camper van like a bloody hippie. You didn't want that. You had grown up, you had a steady job, ambition and drive. Gem just wanted to write her book by the seaside and live off silly dreams.'

I looked down at our entwined hands. My head was beginning to thump again. None of this made sense. I had always wanted to travel, since I was a little boy. The camper-van dream had been my dream – I even remember sharing it with Gem. I still wanted that. I could imagine the joy of getting into a beaten-up old vehicle and hitting the road.

And I loved the fact that Gem wrote, and used to encourage her. Why had I changed so much?

'We were good together, Will,' Nicola said quietly. 'And once your memories come back, you'll see. At the moment, you're muddled. You are still living in the world when you were with Gem. But you grew up. You moved on. And soon you will realise that, and everything will make sense.'

'Do you think?' I felt like a child begging his mum for reassurance.

'I know so.' She leant across the table. 'Gem wasn't good for you, Will – you came to realise that – but I am. Together, we were amazing.'

I wasn't expecting her to kiss me, but her lips were warm and welcoming against mine. A longing washed over me, an urge to be held, to be loved, to feel that intimacy again. But there was another sensation there, too, colder and harder – a knowledge that something wasn't right. Something didn't belong.

'You see,' she said, pulling away. 'You see how good we are?'

All I could do was nod, because I didn't even know the right answer anymore.

–

'Are you sure you don't want to come back home?' she asked.

We were standing outside Nicola's car. She pulled me into a hug and gently kissed the side of my neck. 'I'm lonely without you, Will. This doesn't feel right.'

'I just need a few more days, that's all,' I whispered. 'I want to clear my head. I don't want to mess you around.'

She nodded, but I could see the sadness in her eyes. 'I understand. I'm not going to rush you. Hopefully, you will be ready soon.'

I kissed her softly on the lips and watched as she slipped into her car. A mixture of relief and frustration churned inside me. It would've probably been easier just to get in the car beside her, to accept this life I had woken up into, but a bigger part of me was still convinced I was doing the right thing by staying away.

As her car quickly pulled away, I felt my phone buzz inside my pocket. Pulling it out, I saw there were two messages and one missed call. The latter was from Jack, and one of the messages told me I had a voicemail waiting.

I walked away from the restaurant, listening to the familiar sound of Jack's voice fill my ear.

'Will, you OK? I'm feeling bad about our chat the other night. We need to talk properly, so I'm getting a flight home. I've already told Gem. I'll be there for a week or so. We can talk things through, yeah? Maybe sort out what's going on in that head of yours. What was it that Mum used to say…?'

I knew the words before he even said them.

'*You boys need to stick together, whatever. You must always be there for each other.*'

I could hear the wobble in Jack's voice; my own eyes were blurry.

'I'm coming home, Will. I'm coming home.'

A huge wave of relief washed over me. I leant up against a nearby wall and took a few shaky breaths. I needed to hear this. I needed to know that I still had Jack on my side – I felt lost without him.

I opened up the second message hopefully. It was from Gem and my mind immediately kicked into over-drive. Maybe she had done some thinking too? Maybe she regretted what she had said?

> Today was hard, Will. I'm sorry if I hurt you, but please don't contact me again.

My body slammed back against the wall, legs suddenly weak and chest heavy with dread. It was over, it really was.

My brother might be coming back, but Gem was definitely gone. There was no going back.

I had lost her for good.

Later that night, my dreams were disturbing. There were more images this time, confused and disjointed: I was in the driver's seat of a car that was moving too fast. I could feel the panic building as the windscreen mirror loomed in front of me, seeming somehow too big, too horrifying.

The tree. I could see the tree. I knew I was going to hit it.

There was a scream. Too high-pitched for me, surely? But maybe that's how I sounded in the moment.

Shut up!

The tree was coming in fast. Glass, leaves, branches – the overriding sound of screeching tyres and grinding brakes.

And my mind – so still, suddenly. And one thought, just one.

Thank God it's over.

Before

The B&B where we were staying didn't look anything like the website. I stared up at the red-brick building glumly, taking in the nicotine-stained net curtains and overgrown front garden. It looked more like a house of horrors, not a place where I thought we could celebrate our anniversary.

Will's arm circled around me. 'It's all right,' he soothed. 'We're minutes from the sea and the centre. It's not like we need to be here much, is it? Just to sleep…'

'I guess…'

I didn't want to complain too much. This had been Will's idea and I knew he was broke. We both were. It wasn't like we could afford the height of luxury.

We stepped over the loose paving stones and pushed open the surprisingly heavy front door that led into a small, dingy foyer. A woman greeted us with a lacklustre nod. She was one of those people of indeterminate age, with greying hair pulled tight into a ponytail and her face completely free of make-up, apart from a slick of pink lipstick.

'I hope you have a wonderful stay,' she said, as she handed us the key for number ten: the attic room, and apparently one of the special ones. 'Breakfast starts at six a.m. and I'd come down early if you like bacon. We tend to run out.'

Will murmured something next to me and when I caught his eye, I saw he was suppressing a laugh. As if we would stagger down at six a.m.! The idea was to stay out late and lie in without a care in the world. We weren't at work now.

The room itself wasn't too bad: a bit fusty and old-fashioned, but clean at least. The en-suite had a tiny bath with shower over and the king-sized bed was actually two singles pushed together. I inspected the gap that ran down the middle and frowned.

'I hope I don't slip through.'

'You better not.' Will pulled me towards him, burying his face in my neck. 'You can't escape me that easily, Gem.'

We stayed together like that for a while, just in a tight hug, in this new, slightly weird room. Outside, I could hear the seagulls calling. If I really concentrated, I could hear the rush of the sea.

'I want to take you to so many places, Gem,' Will said softly. 'I want to take you all around the world. We can see these things together, experience them...'

'But first we'll start in Brighton?' I giggled.

'Brighton is as good a place to start as any.'

We ended up in a small fish and chip shop along the seafront. I ordered my usual cod and chips, and Will went for the battered sausage. We huddled together on the plastic table outside, trying to shield our food from the rabid seagulls that were threatening to swoop at any moment.

'I wish I could afford to take you out properly,' Will said broodingly.

'I don't need to be taken out properly. This suits me fine.' I liked it there, with the view out to sea. The grey clouds were swirling above the water, merging with the rolling waves. It was cold but calming, and I breathed in the salty air and stretched out my arms.

'This – all of this is enough for me. I don't need fancy restaurants or posh hotels.'

'Really?'

'Really.' I stuffed a chip in my mouth and chewed on it happily. 'Those sorts of places make me nervous; I always feel like I don't belong – like the waiter or hotel owner will know I'm from a council estate and want me to sling my hook. Do you get it?'

Will nodded. 'Oh yeah, I get it.'

'I like to be able to relax, to be myself, and this is just perfect…'

I threw a chip out on the pavement and watched as a flock of seagulls began to shriek and fight over it.

'You shouldn't have done that,' Will said, in a sing-song voice. 'They tell you not to feed the gulls here. It just encourages them.'

'Poor things have to eat…'

He snorted. 'They eat well enough. You're just a soft touch. God knows what you'll be like with our kids.'

I had a chip just ready to go into my mouth. I pulled it back and stared at Will in mock horror.

'Our kids? You're bringing that up again.'

'Yeah, what of it? We'll have two, I reckon. A girl and a boy. The girl will be a gobby little thing, like you, and the boy will be a gifted musician like me.' He grinned. 'Just think, with our genes we could produce the best.'

I couldn't stop the grin that was forming. I had to look away shyly. It wasn't even that I was that bothered about having children. To be honest, working with them every day was pretty much the best form of contraception, but hearing Will say how much he wanted *my* kids was really special.

'The travelling, though? We can't do that with kids.'

I was staring out to sea now. I could just make out a small boat on the horizon and wondered where it was heading. France, probably, but maybe somewhere else. Were the people on board excited about their next adventure?

'We'll still have time to travel, to explore, to do all that,' Will said decisively. 'We have our whole lives ahead of us. Just me and you. What's more exciting than that?'

We had bad sex on the bad beds in the bad hotel that night. To be fair, the sex wasn't that bad, it just started awkwardly as our legs and arms kept disappearing down the crack in the middle. In the end, Will pushed the two single beds apart in frustration and we lay pressed tightly together on one of them. We barely had to move – the sex was lazy and slow as Will moved against me, his face pressed up against my neck. I could feel the beat of his heart against mine. He came first, crying out and then lowering his head against my breast. Moments later, he reached down and tenderly stroked me, his fingers working expertly in the tight space. I came quick and hard, clutching at his body and pulling him towards me in a rush. I never wanted to let him go.

We fell asleep like that, like we once did as teenagers, curled together on Will's tiny bed on the estate. Except now we were both so much bigger, so it was a bit sweatier and tighter for space.

It was early morning when the alarm woke us, high-pitch screeching that pierced through my ears. I immediately sat bolt upright, my body drenched in cold sweat.

That was the fire alarm. We were in the attic room.

There was a fire in this building, and we were trapped.

Images and flashbacks immediately took over: hot flames, thick acrid smoke. Things that I had buried at the back of my mind long ago, things that I thought I had long forgotten.

My body was ice-cold. My heart was thundering in my chest.

'Oh God,' I gasped, clawing at Will's skin. 'There's a fire. We are going to die. We are going to fucking die.'

Will jumped into action, pulling on clothes and then forcing me into a dress, while I sat motionless. He tugged at my frozen body, insisted we move out of the room.

'We need to get out of here.'

'I can't, Will – I can't.'

The fear of seeing flames again, of being exposed to a raging fire, made me remain rigid on the bed. There was no logic to it, of course, but my mind was telling me that there was danger outside the door. All I wanted to do was pull the blankets over my head and hide.

'Gemma.' His voice was loud and firm. He'd never spoken to me like this. 'You're going to take my hand and you are going to follow me, OK? I'm here. I'm with you. You are going to be fine.'

'But I can't see. I can't—'

'Close your eyes, then. I'll lead you.' He took my hand in his. 'You trust me, don't you?'

I swallowed hard, nodded.

'Then follow me.'

So, with my eyes squeezed tightly shut, I followed Will out of the room. My hand remained tightly gripped in his and not once did I believe he would let go. I felt safe. I felt protected.

He guided me out of the fire escape door and onto the stairs, where the morning air hit me. It was so fresh and crisp.

I opened my eyes, tears almost blinding me.

'It's OK, Gem,' he said gently. 'We're out of there now. It's OK.'

After all that, there wasn't even a bloody fire. The alarm had been triggered by the bacon burning in the pan.

Will turned to me afterwards, his eyes glinting with joy.

'No bloody surprise they run out of bacon if they keep burning it all the time.'

But that weekend changed everything for me. It made me realise, perhaps for the first time, how much Will loved me and how he made me feel.

I was safe.

I was loved.

With Will, I was becoming a stronger person.

Chapter Fifteen

Gem – 2022

The shower was perfect. It was just what I needed, at the right temperature and with the right amount of strength. I tipped my head back and allowed the water to strike my body with force, encouraging me to wake the hell up and get on with my day. It was the last day, after all, and then I had the benefit of a long summer holiday – and God, did I need it.

I knew I had been in here far too long. I was waiting for Richard to call through, for him to remind me that we were on a smart meter and time was money, but he was surprisingly quiet. Maybe he realised how much I needed this.

It was good just to stand in this enclosed space and imagine that the water was in some way purifying me and cleansing my thoughts. I couldn't remember ever having had such a confusing couple of weeks. Seeing Will again, up and about in our old favourite spot, had been unnerving. I wasn't even sure why I had arranged to meet him there; it had been a stupid idea. Even harder had been hearing that he wasn't currently with Nicola and was staying with my mum. Wasn't it enough that the ex-boyfriend who had torn my heart to pieces had lost his memory and thought he was still in love with me? I didn't need him shacked up with my mum and making best friends with her too.

I rubbed at my face, feeling the sting in my eyes. I knew I had done the right thing telling him that I didn't want to see him again. He was my past. Everyone said that you should never go back; it was one of those unwritten rules.

But did those rules apply here? When the Will I'd be going back to was the one who made me happiest? The one who still thought we were together. Could I love that Will again?

Even if that was the case, there was still the fact that Will had a head injury. He wasn't well; this wasn't the 'old' Will I was seeing, it was a sick one, a broken one. And if he fully recovered, which I obviously hoped he would, his memory would come back, and he would be back to the man who hurt me.

I turned off the shower, shivering immediately, even though it wasn't even cold. I pulled the thick towel from the shelf and wrapped it around me. The problem with thoughts like these was that they were overwhelming and took over everything else.

I had to remember the now and appreciate what I had.

It was the only thing I could do to stop me going completely insane.

Richard was sitting on the bed. I knew something was wrong, by the sheer fact that he was only dressed in his pants despite the time (Richard was never, ever late, not even on the last day of term). He was stock-still, like he was in shock. I was about to say something, when I noticed he had my phone in his hands.

My phone – what the hell was he doing with that?

'You've been texting him?' he said flatly.

'What?'

I realised how vulnerable I was, standing in a stupid little towel, my hair dripping wet. All I wanted to do was run back into the shower and seek solace in that warm water again.

'Don't even try to deny it, Gem. I read the messages. You arranged to meet him. You even messaged him last night.'

'Who? Will?'

'Of course, fucking Will.' He slammed the phone down on the bed. 'Your ex-boyfriend. The love of your fucking life.'

The words carved through me. I'd never thought Richard was the jealous type – he was always so calm and considerate – but as his eyes caught mine, I could see the hurt blazing there.

'Richard, you shouldn't be going through my phone.'

He shook his head slowly. 'I know. I know I shouldn't, and I hate myself for it, but you've been acting so different, Gem. I just wanted to check. I wanted to reassure myself, but instead…'

I walked towards the bed and carefully picked my phone up. My last message to Will was still on the screen. I read it again, remembering how much it had pained me to send it.

> Today was hard, Will. I'm sorry if I hurt you, but please don't contact me again.

I shoved the screen towards Richard's face.

'Did you even read this properly? Look. Look at what I wrote. I told him not to contact me.'

'That's not the point.' Richard sounded sulky now. 'You still met up with him and didn't tell me. It feels like you're sneaking behind my back.'

'I don't have to report everything I'm doing to you.'

'What? Even if it involves your ex?'

'Yes – my *ex*, and that's the keyword here, Richard. He's my ex and he's that for a reason.' I paused to take a breath. 'Will had something awful happen to him, a major trauma, and he's coming to terms with it, that's all. I met him to try and help. There is nothing to be suspicious about. There is nothing going on.'

He bowed his head. 'I just can't help but worry. You two—'

'You just need to trust me,' I snapped. 'And don't sneak around behind my back. Next time, just ask! I don't give a shit about Will anymore!'

I picked up my clothes and stalked back into the bathroom, where I locked the door and slammed myself down on the toilet seat. The tears came hard and fast. I didn't know if I was angrier at Richard for suspecting me of cheating, or myself for lying to him.

I made it through an emotional day of leavers' assembly and chaotic school performances, and choked out goodbyes to my year group. I was going to miss them. I knew they were only going up a year, but for this year they had been my responsibility, my concern, and now in September I'd have a new batch to worry about, with (according to a rather smug Fiona) a particularly naughty boy called Henry.

Did I even want to do this anymore?

I felt numb as I accepted my gifts of chocolates and candles from the kids and parents. Then, while standing at the school gate waving them off, a mixture of relief and despair crashed through me. What now? How would Richard and I keep ourselves busy for the next six weeks? Did I even want to see him again?

'You look like you need a drink,' Ben whispered to me, offering me a cheeky wink. 'Are you sure we can't tempt you this time?'

I knew the other teachers always went for a last-day-of-term drink at The Swan, and usually I never bothered to join them. For one thing, I couldn't stand the thought of another few hours trapped in the same room as Fiona, and for another I was a total lightweight and bound to make a show of myself. I'd always found it so hard to bond with my colleagues, especially after the messy break-up with Will. It was easier to shut myself away rather than even attempt to reach out to the people around me.

However, today I looked into Ben's friendly eyes and realised all I longed for was company. I couldn't stand the thought of going back to that flat alone and heating myself up a microwave meal. Richard would be out with his lot and wouldn't be back until late. I needed to unwind too.

'Aw, go on, then,' I said, enjoying Ben's surprised reaction. 'But I'm only staying for one.'

–

'It's not bloody fair. It's not.' I was aware that my voice was a bit too loud, a bit too squawky, but I couldn't really control it.

Come to think of it, the room was swirling a bit too. I slammed my hand on the table in an attempt to stabilise myself.

'I didn't ask him to injure his head, did I?' God, my words were slurry. Why was my tongue suddenly too big for my mouth? 'I didn't ask for him to come back into my life! As if I need any of this. Any of!'

'You don't,' Dana soothed, stroking my arm. She had such a lovely Irish accent. I just wanted to close my eyes and drift off to sleep.

'You should tell this Richard of yours to back off a bit,' Ben said, pointing his vape in my direction. 'You can't just turn your feelings off like a light switch. You're bound to still care for this guy, even if he—'

'Was a total shit!' I was too loud again. I noticed Fiona twitch and that made me giggle. She was at the other end of the table with Lucy and Emma, the two quiet Early Years teachers. They were probably the only people polite enough to put up with her.

'He sounded like a shit,' Dana said. 'I only just started at the school when you broke up with Will. I remember what a state you were in.'

'You did look a right mess,' Ben said, nodding. 'One morning you came in still wearing a pyjama top.'

I sniffed dramatically. 'I didn't think anyone noticed.'

'Oh girl! We all noticed.'

'I did love him so much.' I reached for my glass and guzzled some more of the sharp liquid. It burnt my throat and the bottom of my tummy. 'This isn't a single, is it?'

Ben shrugged. 'You needed cheering up.'

'I don't even like drinking that much,' I said, gulping the rest down and then chuckling softly to myself. 'Do you know, it's such a middle-class thing isn't it – to say, "Have a glass of wine, have a gin and drink all your problems away." Yet, when my mum hit the bottle, eyebrows were raised.' I giggled again, but sourly this time. 'But my mum was drinking cheap knock-off gin from the corner shop. Not sitting in bars and pubs with her glamourous friends.'

Dana touched my knee lightly. 'That sounds hard, Gem.'

'Everything is hard,' I muttered. 'I wish things were easier. Years ago, I had it all mapped out. I was with the man I loved, we had plans, I knew what we were going to do, and then almost overnight he became a different person. He didn't want me anymore.'

'But now you have Richard,' Dana soothed.

'You love Richard, right?' Ben added.

'Yeah... yeah I guess I do...'

But it wasn't the same love. Not really. It wasn't fierce wonderful passion. It wasn't laughter and understanding. It wasn't truly knowing that person inside and out – or at least thinking you did.

'Richard is safe,' I said finally.

'Fuck me, he sounds a right catch,' Ben said.

'I need safe, Ben. I need someone to rely on. I need trust...' I squeaked, my voice cracking. I remembered Richard checking my phone and I could feel the tears start up again. 'That's what I thought I needed.'

I picked up a tissue, or what looked like a tissue – it may have been a serviette or something. It felt scrunchy and hard against my face.

'I'm sorry,' I sobbed. 'I didn't mean to ruin your night with my problems. It's just so hard... I'm sorry.' The stupid tissue wasn't doing a good job of mopping up my tears. This is why I didn't usually come out with this lot – I knew I'd end up showing myself up.

I didn't notice Fiona, but suddenly she was looming over me.

'Come on, Gemma. Let's get you home. I think you've had enough.'

'You can't tell me...' I tried to resist, but weirdly one little tug of my arm and Fiona had me up on my feet.

'It's OK,' she said, quite gently for her. 'I'll give you a lift home. It's on my way anyway.'

'But I don't want...'

She pulled me towards her. 'Maybe you don't want to come, but you'll thank me in the morning, I promise. Come on, the car is just outside.'

And just like the domesticated little poodle I was, I found myself following her, a mess of snot, tears and runny mascara.

Perhaps staying in with a microwave meal and my own sad company would've been the better option.

–

The flat was dark and empty when I got in, and misery wrapped around me like a cloak. I wondered what time Richard would come home, or if he would come home at all. He might stay the night with his parents, a grumpy middle-class pair who had never particularly liked me. Or maybe he would stay the night with that female colleague that he seemed close to. What was her name again?

I poured myself a glass of water and chugged it down quickly, hoping it might help to clear my head a little. To be honest, I wasn't sure I even cared where Richard was – but I was here, on my own, with my life crumbling around me again. I hadn't asked for any of this.

I dialled his number without thinking. My fingers were clumsy and my head full as the phone began to ring. I wasn't surprised when he didn't pick up. Will had always liked his sleep, had got into the habit of turning his phone on silent at night – unlike me.

His voicemail kicked in and I left my message. I hated how my words seemed to be curdled with pain. This man was slowly destroying me.

'It's cruel that you are doing this to me, Will,' I croaked. 'It's cruel that you're making me think about you again. Making me think of us. I don't want to do it, but I can't get you out of my head. I can't...'

And then I tumbled onto my sofa, phone still gripped in my hand and a million angry thoughts buzzing around my skull, until the weight of sleep finally allowed me to close my eyes.

Before

Gem – 2019

'I love this place.'

We were on another weekend away and it had been Will's choice once again. This time we were going to his favourite seaside spot: Bognor Regis. The special place he'd come to with his mum.

'It's fun here. Charming, without pretensions,' he said warmly. 'And there's Butlin's on the seafront. What more could you ask for?'

I loved our weekends away. We now tried to do them as often as we could, fitting them around Will's shifts and my ever-growing lesson planning. The idea was to have as many cheap and cheerful breaks as we could, while we still could.

'Come on,' Will said, dragging me towards the crazy golf. 'I bet I can beat you at this easily. You can barely hit straight.'

My competitive spirit was immediately set alight. 'Hand me the bat, sunshine, and just wait and see what I can do.'

'Club,' he told me in a deliberately patronising voice. 'Or a putter. Or a nine iron…'

I nudged him hard in the ribs. 'Unless you want to see this club going somewhere uncomfortable, I'd pack that in.'

183

'Whatever you say, gorgeous...'

The weather was damp and drizzly for early summer, so luckily it was pretty quiet, and we could take our time around the range. Ahead of us, two teenage boys seemed content with hitting the balls with as much force as they could, and behind us, an elderly couple were slower and more ponderous than me. I watched the couple while Will prepared to take his shot. The man had wrapped his arms around the woman's back, guiding her to line up her stroke. Gently, he rocked her from side to side and I watched as his mouth delicately brushed her cheek. They both had white hair, as bright as cotton wool, and their faces were lined and weathered with wisdom and age.

'Look at them,' I whispered to Will.

'Eh?' He was distracted, of course. He hit his ball and then began to crow, amazed by his own accuracy. I tugged at his top.

'I said look at the couple behind us. Discreetly!'

Will whipped his head around, not discreet at all. The couple were now walking arm in arm to the next hole. Her body was slightly bent over, but she still seemed to be floating somehow, like he was carrying her.

'Aren't they gorgeous? I bet they've been together for years.'

'They might have just met last week on Tinder.'

'Will!' I nudged him again. 'I thought you were the romantic.'

'I am.'

He pulled me towards him and planted a small kiss on my nose. His stubble tickled my chin and made me smile.

'I am romantic and that'll be us one day. You can drag me round a golf course when I'm old and incontinent and shouting obscenities at everyone.'

'Sounds bloody perfect.'

He stroked my hair away from my face. 'We can grow old and grumpy together.' He paused. 'But in the meantime, you need to get a bloody move on. It's your shot and I'm beating the crap out of you here.'

He did beat me, of course, which was both disappointing and not totally unexpected. We walked along the seafront, eating our ice creams and disagreeing on the matter.

'Considering I've never even lifted one of those bats before, I think I did all right.'

'Clubs.' Will laughed. 'And I'm hardly a golfing pro.' Will paused a moment to point at a cluster of caravans on the hillside. 'That's where we stayed with Mum,' he said quietly. 'Our last holiday together before…'

I took his hand in mine. 'You must still really miss her.'

'I do, but being here makes me feel close to her. It really does. It was such a happy time.'

'It's good you had those times together.'

I tried not to think of my own mum. I couldn't remember the last time we'd had a decent conversation. We'd certainly never been on holiday together.

'You appreciate it more when they're no longer with you,' Will said. 'That's the sad thing.'

He wrapped his arm around me, and we walked huddled together, the wind trying its best to beat us back.

'Look.' Will pointed. 'There's a fortune-teller hut. Shall we give it a go?'

I hesitated. I'd never been a big fan of these things. Mum was always big into fate and all of that, and it hadn't done her much good.

'Come on,' he said, tugging at me. 'It'll be fun.'

We ran across the road, towards the little tent. Will poked his head inside and then turned excitedly to me.

'She's free. Come on. Maybe she can read our fortune.'

The woman inside was about as stereotypical as you could imagine: white-haired and wizened, and cloaked in an old shawl. We perched on the two stools provided, trying not to catch her sharp gaze. I felt strangely nervous.

She peered into her crystal ball; her nails were painted bright pink and clinked against the glass.

'I see great love,' she said softly. 'It's clear that you are both well suited. The love is strong and true, and your connection is fierce.'

Will nudged me. 'See... fierce connection. I like this woman already.'

But then I saw her frown. She moved away from the ball a little and shook her head.

'What is it?' I demanded. 'What do you see?'

'I'm not sure... It's a bit confusing... I can't really tell.'

'Just tell us,' I insisted.

'The ball is telling me a big change is coming. A bad change.'

I felt myself stiffen.

'And you will fall in love again, both of you.'

'With who?' Will asked.

The woman simply shook her head. 'I'm sorry, that part isn't clear. All I can say for sure is that someone is going to destroy this relationship, and nothing will be the same again afterwards.'

Chapter Sixteen

Will – 2022

I wish I hadn't listened to that bloody voicemail. To hear Gem's voice like that, desperate and needy, clawing into me.

> It's cruel that you are doing this to me, Will. It's cruel that you're making me think about you again. Making me think of us. I don't want to do it, but I can't get you out of my head. I can't…

Maybe it would've been better if I had died in that accident. Anything was better than this. This was an awful kind of limbo, where I was suspended in the past and everyone else around me had moved on. Gem was right, it was cruel. It was cruel for her, and it was bloody cruel for me too.

I was killing both of us.

I didn't even want to go downstairs. I knew facing Di would be hard, and I was right; as soon as she saw my face, she knew something had happened. She settled me down with a strong tea and ordered me to tell her what was going on. Instead of explaining, I simply played Gem's message out loud again. Hearing it again made my breath stop for a moment or two.

'I never meant to hurt her,' I said.

'I believe you,' Di said softly. 'But this must be so hard for her.'

'I think being here is wrong. I should go. I should probably leave this entire bloody town.'

'No, you shouldn't. You're recovering from a major trauma, you need to rest,' Di said firmly. 'Besides, this is your home too.'

'She's with this new fella now, Richard. I guess he makes her happy.'

Di sniffed. 'I'm not so sure about that, Will. Richard was what I would call a lockdown lover. He moved in quickly when the restrictions took hold. I think Gem just went along with it.'

'Lockdown? Restrictions?' I blinked at her; it was like she was from another planet.

Di flapped her hand at me. 'We've no time for that now. I'll explain later. You've got a lot of catching up to do.'

'Don't I just know it.'

'And you're with Nicola, too, remember?' Di added gently. 'How was your date last night?'

I flinched at the word date. In my head, I had only ever dated one woman.

'We just talked. It was OK, a bit odd. I like her – she seems nice. But—'

'But…' Di urged.

'But… I'm not feeling much more than that.' I touched my head. 'Everyone – Gem, Nicola, Matty – seems to think I'll recover my memory and go back to this bloke I'm meant to have been, but I'm not so sure.'

'Why not?'

I frowned; this was the first time I'd articulated these feelings out loud. 'Well, I suppose because I don't recognise this bloke they're describing. It doesn't sound like me at all. Apparently, I'm some hotshot sales guy that shags around and treats women badly. I'm someone who abandoned my music for money. Someone who shat all over my brother and the girl I loved most in the world—' I stopped, as I could feel myself choking up. 'It doesn't make sense, Di. You know me. You saw me grow up. Does it sound like me?'

'No,' said Di decisively, and I was thrown. I stared back at her, blinking away my tears. Did someone finally believe me?

'I didn't believe it at the time,' Di said slowly. 'When Gem started mentioning the changes in your behaviour, the staying out late, the being argumentative, I started to think something else was happening – I don't know, maybe you were ill or something, or stressed. But you hurting Jack and Gem like that...' She brought her hands together. 'That wasn't you, Will. You even fell out with Mel. You always put those three above and beyond everything else. I think something happened, something bad.'

A cold chill passed through me. 'OK, you say that. But what? What happened?'

She shook her head. 'It must be in your memories somewhere.'

I half-laughed. 'Fucking hell, if we're relying on them, we really are screwed.'

Di sat back in her chair, studying me, eyes searching mine. I had never seen her look so serious. This was the thin, bird-like woman that I had often found shaking in her living room. The woman who turned to anything to take away her pain – alcohol, painkillers, sleeping pills – but could never confront her true demons. Yet here she was, her gaze picking me apart while looking determined to be the one who would help put me together again.

'Will,' she said softly. 'What can you remember? What is your last proper memory?'

'It's so confusing Di. I see things in my dreams. I think it's the crash. I can hear sounds, can see things coming towards glass…'

Di held out her hand. 'No, before that. What was your last clear memory when you woke up? You thought you were in 2019, didn't you? What was the last thing you could remember from then?'

I closed my eyes for a moment. 'I'm not sure. I've talked this through with Gem too, and it's a bit murky… but I'm pretty sure it was at The Swan. I can hear music playing and I can smell beer.' I paused. 'I can hear Mel, she's talking to me. She's saying something to me over and over and over. I think she's angry.'

'Can you remember why?'

I shook my head. 'It's all distorted, Di. I can't make it out.'

I wanted to bang my head to make the thoughts make sense, but I knew that wouldn't help.

'Well, distorted or not, that's where the answer lies,' Di said calmly. 'Mel is the last person you remember from your old self, the self before you changed. Maybe you need to see her to help bring everything back.'

I sat there, stunned. Mel. Of course. I had so wanted to speak to her after the accident and had been upset to find her number no longer on my phone. How the hell was I going to find her now? Mel had been like my burly big sister. The one who had taken me under her wing and forced me to have some direction in my life. The woman who understood me probably just as much as Gem did.

Once, I had had both these strong women in my life and now I had neither. Just that fact made me feel unbalanced and lost.

'She doesn't work at The Swan anymore, Di,' I said. 'Apparently, she's moved away. I've got no clue where she is.'

Di was already digging through the nearby sideboard. 'She's not gone far, though, only over to Farnleigh. She popped over to see me when she left, gave me a flyer. Told me to come and see her when I could.' Di chuckled softly. 'Never mind that I barely leave this house, let alone the town.'

'You've got her details?' I was confused. As far as I was aware, the two weren't even friends.

Di still had her head half-buried in the sideboard. 'Yeah, Mel was one of the few people who would check in on me now and again, make sure I was OK. I suppose she understood addicts, working in a bloody pub – she saw the loneliness we all share...'

'Oh, Di—'

She flapped her hand in my direction. 'No, I don't want to hear any of your sympathy. This is not the time. We're working on getting your head sorted first.'

I looked at her sadly. How many times had I sat in this room and felt pity claw inside me towards this tiny, frail woman who barely seemed able to look after herself? I knew Gem had struggled with it over the years. In fact, it was one of the few things we had argued about, but I never saw the neglectful, bad mother that she described. I just saw a woman wrecked by pain. A woman whose life was destroyed in one night, and all because—

'Here it is. Aren't you glad I keep everything!' She chuckled, holding aloft a creased leaflet. 'Gem always tells me off for not clearing stuff out, but you never know when you might need it.'

Taking the leaflet from her hand, I carefully uncrumpled it. It was an advert for a country pub out in the sticks that apparently offered hog roasts, curry nights and Elvis evenings. What a mix. The number provided was for the pub itself – The Jolly Sailor, Mel's apparent new ship. Even just thinking of her there made my heart lift with hope.

'Will she still be there?'

Di shrugged. 'Who knows? But if you don't try, you won't know, will you?'

A minute later, I was in Di's small hall, making the call. After a few rings, a gruff voice answered.

'Is Mel there?' I asked.

'Who's asking?'

'Will. Will Manning.' I paused. I had no idea who this was. A new bar manager? A lodger? Unless Mel's sexuality had changed, it certainly wasn't her lover. 'I'm an old friend.'

'Oh, right, I see.' The man's voice softened a little. 'Well, she's not here at the moment. She's gone to stay at a friend's. I'm overseeing things here for a bit. Can I help at all?'

'No, it's Mel I need to talk to.'

'Can I give her your number? She can call you back as soon as she returns.'

'Yes, yes of course.' I stammered out my number. 'And can you tell her one other thing for me?'

'What's that?'

'Tell her it's the old Will,' I said quietly. 'The one she worked with. The one she liked.'

'Right. OK, I'll tell her.'

I just hoped he'd remember this last detail, because the Will I'd become didn't seem to be very popular at all.

–

I didn't go out all day. I couldn't face it. Being in Gem's old bedroom was comforting, if not a little creepy. While I lay on the bed, trying desperately to clear my mind, it was almost like the ghost of child Gem was looking down at me scornfully, telling me to get my shit together. Surely, if I relaxed, *something* would begin to make sense?

Instead, all I did was sleep. Blurry, mixed-up dreams haunted me. Yet again, I was in a car. I could feel the seat beat tight across my chest, hear the rush of the engine, but there was something else too – another sound. Another sensation.

Was it tugging? A pulling? What the hell was it?

I woke up sharply, feeling disorientated at first, and a little bit hungry. I realised that I could hear voices downstairs and my heart lurched when I realised who it was.

Gem.

I wondered if I should stay here, in this safe, quiet space. I didn't want to face her again, not after that voicemail. I didn't want to subject myself to that pain, to that hurt. I also didn't like her seeing me in her mum's house, like some kind of saddo who had nowhere better to go. She had never understood the bond I'd had with Di; it had always made her a little bitter that I could get something from Di that she never could.

I was better off up here, away from her.

However, I didn't have much choice when Di's shrill voice called up the stairs, ordering me down there. I had to man up and face the music.

Gem was standing in the hall, dressed in a pretty floral dress. Her hair was pulled away from her face in a loose ponytail and her cheeks looked flushed, like she had just been running. She looked up at me and then away again.

'Hey,' I said quietly.

'Hey,' she replied.

Di stood between us, like a faded fairy godmother. She smiled weakly. 'I was just saying to Gem that I think you both need to talk, properly talk, and not here.'

'So where?' I asked.

Gem finally looked up and caught my eye. 'Let's go to The Swan,' she said.

To the place that used to mean everything to me.

Before

Will – 2019

'Look at this, bruv. It's amazing.'

Jack shoved his phone towards me. The email was already loaded up. It took me a while to read the words, to take it all in, especially as the pub was heaving and noisy as usual.

'He's an influential man out there, Will,' Aby said softly. 'He'll fix up loads of dates in the States.'

'This could be our big break,' Jack said, the excitement distorting his voice. 'This is what we've been waiting for.'

The words in the message were exciting – 'sell-out gigs', 'large crowds', 'guaranteed rewards', 'loving your sound'. I passed the phone back and nodded keenly. This was really picking up steam now.

'It's great, it really is. How soon do they want us out there?'

'Late summer, I think.' Jack reached across to Aby and stroked her leg. 'We have this diamond to thank, of course. She's been sharing our demos everywhere.'

Aby rolled her eyes. 'It was no effort. You guys have the raw sound Americans are killing for at the moment.'

I smiled but couldn't quite find the words to thank her. I loved Aby, but there was something about her smug look that suddenly irritated me. I watched as her carefully manicured hand rested on top of Jack's – like I'd seen it rest on many men at the bar, especially after a few drinks. Working here meant I witnessed a lot of revealing behaviours. Aby wore the pretty, innocent mask well, but I could see her for what she really was.

'I'll have to talk to Gem, of course,' I said. 'But I'm sure she will be happy too. We've been dreaming about doing something different this summer.'

'This summer is going to change our lives. I can feel it,' Jack said, his happiness radiating from him. 'You wait – it's all coming soon.'

I rushed back to the bar before Mel could moan at me. She turned a blind eye at my breaks but not if I took the piss. I told her the news and she gave me a hug, told me how proud she was of me. However, I soon noticed that Mel's gaze was fixed on a figure sitting hunched on their own by the door.

'She's back.' Mel sighed. 'It's every night now.'

Di. As usual, it was a gin she was nursing, probably a double.

'I'll talk to her,' I said softly. 'I'll try and persuade her to go home.'

Mel touched my hand. 'It's good you look out for her. Does Gem know how bad she's getting?'

I shrugged. 'I've talked to her, yeah, but she gets angry. In her eyes, her mum is just getting worse and worse. Her patience is wearing thin.'

Mel sighed. 'Everyone makes mistakes. Gem needs to realise that.'

'I know.'

'There's so much trauma going on there: two women who need each other, yet keep pushing each other away. It's sad. I wish I still had my mum,' Mel said.

I turned to Mel. She hadn't been her bubbly self today; it wasn't like her to be so philosophical.

'What's up?' I asked. 'I can see something is bothering you, and it's not just Di.'

Mel frowned. 'Oh, it's something and nothing.'

'It's clearly not – what's happened?'

Mel bent down and retrieved a letter from under the bar. She shoved it in my direction. 'I received this today. I still can't get my head around it.'

Carefully, I unfolded it. The first word that hit me was 'disqualified'.

'What is this?' I asked stupidly.

'I've been banned from driving. Too many speeding offences,' Mel said glumly. 'I know I've been an idiot, but I didn't expect this to happen. You know how much I love my car.'

I did. Mel had an old battered MR2 that she took out every chance she got, especially when she was feeling stressed. Although, that was probably how she ended up with the ban.

'Oh, Mel.' I pulled her towards me. 'I'm sorry, mate.'

'And now I'm hearing I will be losing my best barman too.' Mel sniffed. 'Also, who is going to look after Di when you're gone, eh? Because she can't carry on like this. She really can't.'

–

I softened Gem with news of the band first. As I expected, she was delighted and pulled me into a fierce hug.

'Oh Will, this is so good! This is what you've both dreamt of. I can save some money, come with you for a bit. It'll be great for my writing.'

'I'd love that.'

'This could be the start of our adventures,' she said, tugging at my top. 'We could travel after, maybe? I could leave my job—'

I laughed, pulled away. 'Let's just see how it goes, but yes, it could open up loads of opportunities.'

Gem spun round on the spot. 'I have to tell Vee and Bran. They won't believe it. Well, they will, but you know what I mean—'

'Gem. There's something else.' My tone was firm enough that it made her stop and look at me. Her eyes were wide with worry.

'Don't you want me to come?' she asked.

'Of course, I do, but...' I bit my lip. 'It's Di, Gem. I'm worried about her. She's drinking again.'

'Oh.' Gem's face fell, her eyes now cold. 'What a surprise. She goes from hiding in the house to dosing herself up with pills and then sitting in the pub and drowning her sorrows.'

'Gem, she can't help it. She is suffering. She can't deal with what happened, and your relationship—'

'What about our relationship?' Gem snapped. 'You can't understand that, Will. No one can.'

'If we went to America and left her, there would be no one around to look after her.'

Gem said nothing but I could see tears glinting in her eyes.

'Mel has offered to help,' I said. 'But I hate how bad your relationship with your mum is. I think it's making things worse. You need to forgive her.'

'You don't know what you're saying, Will.'

Gem stormed out and strode into the bathroom. I heard the taps running and the sound of her stifled tears. With a sigh, I went over and rapped gently on the door.

'Gem, please don't do this. Don't shut me out.'

'You don't understand.'

'Then tell me!'

Silence.

'Gem, please, this is me here. After all we've been through, you can tell me anything.'

Silence.

'Gem—'

'She killed him.' Her voice was so quiet that I had to push my ear up to the wood to hear it. 'She fell asleep with a cigarette in her hand and started the fire. She could have killed us all, but instead she just killed him. My dad. For that, I can never forgive her.'

Chapter Seventeen

Will – 2022

I didn't really want to go – after all, what was the point? We were going round and round in so many circles that it was making me feel sick. Gem didn't want anything more to do with me and who could blame her? But until I spoke to Mel, I wasn't even sure how I could make things any better. First, I needed to get my head round what had happened to me. What had made me change so dramatically?

A question was sitting uncomfortably in my mind. What if Gem had done something to me, something that had upset and wound me up so badly that I couldn't deal with it? Was that why I ended up at The Swan with Mel? Did I confess something to her?

Did I make a decision to change? To put an end to the great thing I had with Gem?

Or maybe…

'Will?'

Gem was looking at me with a nervous expression, her eyes wide and her face drawn. I guessed she hadn't slept too well either if the dark circles under her eyes were anything to go by.

'Will, I'm sorry. I don't really know why I'm here,' she said softly. 'I just couldn't leave things as they were. I thought maybe I could help you, as a friend…'

A friend. Wow! That hurt more than I was expecting.

'You know...' she continued. 'I might be able to help you remember something. It must be so hard for you.'

I nodded. 'It is.'

She touched my hand. I tried to ignore the tingle that fed right down to my bone. I told myself I was imagining it, that it was nothing.

'We'll go to The Swan,' she said. 'That pub meant so much to you. To us. It might help you.'

'OK,' I said, not feeling so sure. 'Let's try.'

On the way out, Di pulled my arm, holding me back. Gem was already outside, clearly glad to be out of there.

'Give her time, Will,' she said quietly. 'She struggles to deal with bad news. You need to give her time to adjust to all of this.'

'Like you do,' I said back, sharper than I'd intended. I saw the brief stab of pain in Di's eyes before she looked away.

'I know,' she said. 'And it's my biggest regret that I never won Gem's trust back. I'm still hoping that maybe one day...' She looked up and held my gaze. 'But I don't think it's too late for you, Will. What you two had was so special, but you need to fight for her. You need to show her that you're not that man anymore.'

I nodded weakly and left the house, but how could I show Gemma anything, when I didn't even know who I was anymore?

The walk to The Swan was as familiar to me as an old nursery rhyme. I remembered all the years we had turned out of this estate, cut across the park, past the small row of neighbourhood shops towards the hulking structure that was the pub.

It had never been a good-looking building: a flat-roofed box surrounded by a sea of tarmac. It used to have hanging baskets outside to make it look more welcoming – but these had all been removed now. The swinging sign outside had also changed. I looked up at it grimly.

'The Swan Inn? Not just The Swan?'

Gem shrugged. 'The new owners have changed it a bit. It won't be quite like you remember, I guess.'

We hadn't exchanged a single word on the way there and proceeded to walk through the door of the pub in silence. I had never known us be so awkward and this made me sad more than anything else. It was like a huge invisible wedge was sitting between us, forcing us apart, and I had no clue how to push it away.

My phone rang just as we entered and I looked at Gem, embarrassed for a moment – I didn't recognise the number and thought I should take it. It would probably be the police following up, or maybe the hospital with another appointment to look at my battered brain. Gem waved at me to take the call and stepped aside, giving me a little bit of privacy.

I certainly didn't recognise the voice on the other end of the phone, and I listened numbly as they spoke at me, not really able to process what was being said. When I finally hung up, I must have looked a little pale or sick, because Gem came back up beside me.

'Everything OK?'

I shoved my phone in my pocket, not even wanting to look at the thing. 'Yeah, everything's fine,' I lied.

Gem led me into the main bar area, and my stomach dropped. This wasn't the pub I knew at all. I stared bleakly at the bar, the one I'd worked behind, where I had laughed and joked with Mel – and it looked completely different.

The old, splintered wood had been replaced by glass and plush cushioned panels. The pub itself no longer had a worn green carpet (stained by puke, beer and crisps). It was now shiny floorboards and gleaming white walls. Every table was stainless steel, surrounded by soft, posh-looking chairs in bright fabrics.

'Shit,' I whispered. 'Is this even the same place?'

'The rumour is they're struggling,' Gem said, a tiny, wry smile appearing. 'The locals don't want fancy meals and club nights. They miss the dartboard and the bands.'

'The bands?'

I walked across to where the stage had once stood, but it was gone. An aching sensation took over and I almost wanted to drop to my knees. How could this all have happened without me knowing? Except I did know, didn't I? Another me knew this place like this.

'The nights we played here,' I said. 'We used to pack the place out.'

'I know,' Gem's voice was soft. 'I know you did.'

'And now look...' I spun round. OK, it was afternoon, but apart from an old man reading a paper in the corner, the place was completely empty.

'It's different now,' Gem replied. 'So many things are, Will. But you need to see it. It might help you remember.'

'I don't remember this. I don't want to remember,' I said. 'I just want everything to be like it was before.'

–

We sat with our drinks. At least that hadn't changed – Gem still loved a gin and tonic. There was music playing, but nothing that I recognised, and this made me feel even more frustrated. If a band hadn't been playing, I used to hijack the jukebox to make sure only decent tracks were chosen – there was no sign of that anywhere now.

'Who was the phone call from?' Gem asked finally. 'If you don't mind me asking.'

I hesitated for a second. 'It was just the bank. They have a few concerns they need to clear up.'

Gem raised an eyebrow. 'Everything OK?'

I took another slug of my drink. 'I hope so.'

In all honesty, I still hadn't really taken in what they had told me – the brief conversation hadn't quite sunk into my brain. All I could remember were words like 'concerning' and 'extended overdraft', and a now a hollow pit had opened in my chest.

'Did you hear back from the police? Are they still looking into the accident?'

I shrugged. 'There are no witnesses. The only person hurt was me and I had no drugs or drink in my system. I think it might be written off as an accident. It's not like I can help them…'

She nodded, seeming to pick up on my signal that I didn't want to say anything more on the matter.

'This place has no vibe,' I said. 'When did it change?'

Gem seemed to consider this for a moment. 'Shortly after Mel left – the new owners wanted to make it fresh and modern.' She took a sip of her drink, her eyes still on me. 'I hated coming here afterwards. It never felt the same, but you loved it. You said it was even better. I never understood that.'

'I did?' I looked around, confused. 'When did Mel leave?'

Gem screwed her face up, clearly trying to remember. 'Well, it must have been three years or so ago. You guys had that row—'

'Row?' I interrupted her. 'What row? What was that about?'

'I don't know, Will. You wouldn't tell me. You started acting weird after that, you left your job here and were really rude about Mel. You said she was lazy and bossy.'

I shook my head, denial flooding my veins. 'No. No, I'd never say anything like that about Mel.'

I loved her like a sister. I knew that. Yeah, she had been irritating sometimes, but she had also been fun. The person I could rely on to make me belly laugh; the one who held me when I had too many beers that night and got upset over Mum. I could still picture her here now, sly smile on her face, her dimpled cheeks, the blonde fringe that fell against her eyes in a blunt edge. This was where she was meant to be – here in the pub, with me.

'I really need to talk to Mel,' I said, more to myself than anything. 'I need to find out what happened.'

Gem shrugged. 'If you say so. Like I said, you were different after that argument, that's when you started being mean to me. Picking faults in everything I did.'

'Being mean…' The ice in my belly was back. 'What the hell, Gem?'

She shook her head. 'I don't want to go over it all again. You not remembering is such a headfuck, Will. I can't make any sense of it. I can't believe you don't know what sort of person you ended up being.'

I leant forward and reached for her hand, and to my surprise she didn't pull away. 'But don't you see? This is all beginning to add up now. My last memory is being here in the pub with Mel, three years ago. I think it was that night. The night of the row.'

'I don't know what you mean, Will.'

'I mean that I think something happened that night, something significant. It made me change, and it made Mel sell up and move on. Don't you see? There has to be a link!'

Gem took another sip of her drink and then seemed to shudder as if the words were ice flowing down her spine. 'I don't know, Will, but maybe you're right. I never understood why you started to act differently, like...' She chewed her lip, as though trying to find the right words. 'It was like the person I'd known since childhood had suddenly been replaced with someone else. You were different. Even your eyes...'

'My eyes?'

She flinched. 'I dunno. It sounds daft now, but they seemed colder – just not you.'

'And now?' I asked quietly, leaning in towards her. She looked across at me and I could see her own tears building. 'How do my eyes look now?'

'Will...' she whispered, her eyes flicking away from mine again. 'This is not easy for me. I have to think of Richard. I'm with him now, and all this stuff is so confusing. It's so—'

'I get that,' I said gently. 'But I need to know; I need to know what you see.'

She took a sharp breath, but then her gaze drifted back to me again. It was so familiar, so kind, like staring into a reflection that I had known forever. I could have sat here for the rest of my life, just like this, and been happy.

'I see...' She paused. 'I see you...'

'Old me?'

'Old you. Will.' A tiny smile. 'My Will.'

It would've only taken a tiny move – I could have gently tilted my head towards hers, rested my lips on hers.

I saw her mouth open slightly, like she was ready for it too. I could see the softness in her eyes.

'Gem...'

'Will! There you are!'

We both snapped back in our seats like the elastic between us had been cut. Gem looked immediately guilty, rubbing at her face like I'd actually touched it, and I felt a wave of sadness that someone I loved could react in such a way. I turned my head, no longer able to look at her, and saw my older brother striding towards me.

Gem jumped up. 'Jack! I didn't know you'd be back so soon.'

Jack swamped her with a bear hug. 'I got here as soon as I could. A flight back to London, quick night in some godawful hotel and then I got the first train down here.'

He stood back and we found ourselves looking at each other for the first time in years, even though for me it only felt like days ago. The Jack that I remembered had been laughing and joking with me. As far as I recalled, we had serious plans to take the band on tour. However, I knew now that this memory was wrong and I had messed things up. I had hurt Jack in the worst possible way, and he hadn't been able to forgive me.

It was clear to see that now. Jack looked so different. His hair, which had always been neat and short, was long and scruffy around his neck. He was much thinner – I couldn't make out his beer gut at all – and he was hanging back from me as if he was wary, like I was a spider that might attack at any second.

Gem seemed to pick up on the tension. 'I'm going to go,' she said. 'Leave you boys to catch up.'

'You don't have to, Gem,' Jack told her.

Gem grabbed her bag. 'No, it's OK. You have a lot to talk about.' She glanced at me again and I saw something pass in her expression. What was that? Confusion? Regret?

God, please don't let it be regret.

'We'll catch up soon, Will,' she said briskly and then that was it – she was out the door. I watched her leave and felt the emptiness inside me open up again. It was like a gale-force wind was blowing right through me.

Jack gestured towards my drink. 'Want another one?'

I glanced at the pint and nodded. 'Yeah. Go on, then.'

I wasn't quite sure how this was going to go but I hoped that beer might help.

–

'You look better than I expected,' he said stiffly. 'I mean, I don't know what I was expecting.'

I touched my head instinctively. 'It took a bit of a knock. My ribs, too, but I think it's my brain that got the worst of it.'

'Maybe it knocked some sense into you.'

I smiled wanly but there was no warmth in Jack's words.

'Do you know what happened yet?' he asked. 'Why you crashed?'

I took a sip of my beer. I didn't even like the taste much. 'No, I can't remember. There were no witnesses at all. I guess I took the corner too fast.'

'Idiot.' This time there was a glimmer of a smile.

'Yeah, I know. That's me.'

The silence hung between us, heavy and awkward. I shifted in my seat, uncomfortable and tired. There was so much I wanted to say, so much I wanted to ask, but I didn't even know where to start.

Finally, I coughed, tried to make a start.

'Jack, I've been talking to Gem about all of this. I think something happened to me, before the accident. I've lost three years' worth of memory, but the last thing I remember is being here at The Swan, with Mel. Everything before that was good, I was happy. I was with Gem; I was sound with you. Gem thinks something happened that night – because afterwards I was different. I started to act like I wasn't me anymore.'

'And you can't remember any part of that?' Jack asked.

'No, it's completely wiped.' I frowned. 'The only thing I think I remember is related to the accident, but it's really vague. I can feel a car moving fast, can feel someone tugging at me – I can't quite make it out.'

'It was probably the people that rescued you,' Jack reasoned. 'Maybe you came to after you banged your head and that's why you can remember it a bit.'

I blew out a breath. 'Yeah, that makes sense.'

'And there's nothing to say you won't get those years you lost back,' Jack said gravely. 'Overnight you could turn into a complete arsehole again.'

With a wince, I sighed. 'There is a risk of that, I suppose, but I don't think so.' I rubbed at my head again, like it could help. 'I can't explain it properly, but now I feel like how I'm supposed to be. I'm back to myself. I can't believe for one second that I was mentally well before. Maybe I had had some kind of breakdown?'

Jack snorted. 'Overnight? I dunno. I think it's more likely that there was a part of you we never realised was there. Maybe you buried it after Mum died. Maybe you did have a row with Mel or something and it made that

209

side of you come out. I think you must have been good at pretending you were something you weren't.'

His words carved into me. This was awful.

'I'm not pretending now, Jack,' I said quietly but firmly. 'This is me.'

'OK.' He shrugged, not looking convinced. 'So what will you do next?'

'I have to speak to Mel. I have to find out what happened between us.' I paused. 'And I have to win you and Gem back.'

Jack sighed. 'Well, you know I've always told you to follow your gut, Will. You have to do what you think is best but please promise me one thing...'

'What's that?'

'You won't hurt that poor girl again.'

After that, we carried on talking – it was hard, stilted at first. Jack told me about the band, about their tour of America. It had been a bit hit-and-miss, but with some successes.

'I've met a girl out there,' he said with a half-smile, like he was shy and proud all at once. 'Jamie.'

'Wow, mate, that's great.' I gripped my glass and took another gulp of beer. In my head, of course, he was still with Aby – his beloved Aby. 'But Aby – what happened there? Do you still hear from her?'

'Aby?' His eyes darkened for a moment and then he shook the expression away. 'No, Will. I don't.'

'Oh my God, I'm so sorry.'

Jack stared at me hard. 'Christ, being back here is more difficult than I'd imagined. Having to see you like this again – it brings it all back...'

'Jack,' I croaked, barely able to get the words out. 'What did I do? I need to know.'

Jack shook his head slowly. 'You destroyed everything, Will. In one shitty night – you ruined it all.'

Before

Jack – August 2019

'Are you sure I can't convince you to take a sick day?'

It was so tempting. Aby was standing in the kitchen, dressed to kill as usual in a short dress and high heels. Her hair was loose and messy, and her lips sweet and glossy. She was looking at me in that cute, big-eyed girl way that always seemed to hit me right in the groin.

'I can't, babe.' I pulled her towards me, drinking in the smell of her perfume, her hair, of her. 'We need the money for America.'

Aby groaned softly. 'You're just too good,' she said as she pulled herself away.

All I wanted to do was tug her back into the bedroom and have another hot, sticky session between the sheets. But there was no way I could justify it. Our tour was only weeks away and it made sense to earn what we could in this time.

'You'll probably just be bored with us anyway,' Aby said as she walked towards the door. 'Me and the girls, driving you mad with our gossip.'

'Yeah, probably.' I laughed. 'Have fun, though. Don't do anything I wouldn't do.'

I left the flat quickly before she could tempt me any more.

The truth was I could never get bored with Aby. That was the thing I loved most about her. She kept me on my toes.

She made everything fun.

Not everyone got me and Aby. I knew that and was thinking about it as I walked to work. It was difficult to ignore the comments that had been made. Most of them were just little digs from lads: Deano going on about Aby's flirting and 'wandering hands'. I laughed it off. That was just the way she was. She didn't mean any harm by it. The doubt still niggled, though. Only a few days ago, Mel had taken me to one side and told me she had heard rumours.

'There's talk Aby has been getting close to a few men,' she said. 'You know I don't like to gossip, but...'

I had shrugged her off. 'Well, you are gossiping. Listening to the pub rumour mills. Aby isn't like that.'

Mel had pulled a 'suit yourself' face and wandered off, leaving me feeling frustrated and a little bit concerned.

Was I being a mug? Had I failed to see the signs? Aby was so kind and loving. We got on well, laughed loads and the sex was good too. Why would I have reason to doubt our relationship?

I reached for my phone, still feeling insecurity gnaw at me. The screensaver was a picture of us together, sun-kissed in Greece and grinning in a selfie pose. I traced the image with my finger for a moment, wondering if I should call her. Check what she was up to.

Check. The word hung heavily in my mind. Wasn't that what Dad used to do to Mum all the time, kept calling and checking where she was, while he was shagging around behind her back? When he left, I was only young, but I still remembered Mum crying in the kitchen, telling me that she had loved our dad but could never trust him.

213

'Without trust you have nothing,' she told me tearfully. 'Love will never be enough.'

I stared blankly at the screen for a minute or so longer, and then I quickly scrolled down and found the number.

I knew who to call.

'Jack?'

'Yeah, Will – you there?'

There was loads of background noise and it was hard to hear him very well. I moved away from the road to try to help.

'Yeah, yeah. You OK?'

'I guess. I'm just on my way to work.'

'Ah, right... cool.'

A flicker of irritation. Will knew we needed money for the tour, yet it seemed I was the only one working my arse off for it. In the last couple of weeks, Will hadn't even bothered to contact me. In fact, according to Gem, he had been out most nights getting drunk.

'You out again, then?' I asked.

'Yeah, with Matty and some of his lot.'

'Matty?' I screwed my face up. Will had never had time for him before. 'I didn't know you were friends.'

'Yeah, the last couple of weeks we've been hanging out.' Will sniffed. 'He's cool, bruv. I reckon he might even be able to get me a solid a job at his recruitment agency.'

'A job? But we've got the tour coming up.'

'Ah yeah, of course...'

Will broke away and I could hear him laughing with someone else. There were whoops and cheers in the background, and loud music drilling through.

'Will? Will, are you still there?'

'Yeah, bruv, sorry – but look I'm on a night out, yeah? It's hard to talk. We can catch up later.'

We could, I thought, except we hadn't seemed to have done this recently.

'You might see Aby when you're out,' I said quietly.

'Oh cool, I'll look out for her.'

'Maybe you could keep an eye on her,' I said, hating myself. 'Make sure she's OK.'

Will's laugh was brutal. 'Oh, it's like that, is it?'

'No, it's not, I just—'

'Don't worry, bruv. I'll keep an eye on her. I'll make sure she behaves herself.'

The line went dead.

–

Maybe it was the difficult call with Will, or perhaps the worry about Aby – whatever it was had had a huge effect on my guts. For the first three hours at my current job in the factory, I managed to ignore the sharp pains in my stomach as I loaded products into vans for transport. However, by midnight I was a sweaty, pale mess. My supervisor took one look at me and ordered me to go home.

There was a missed call from Gem on my phone, but I swiped past it. It was too late to ring her back and I felt too rough. I assumed that she was still worried about Will. So was I. If he was thinking of taking this new job, that meant he no longer wanted to tour, which didn't make sense. He loved the band as much as I did. It was part of us.

I couldn't understand how he could've changed so suddenly.

I let myself into the flat quietly, not knowing if Aby was back or not. If she was, I didn't want to disturb her.

Climbing up the stairs, exhausted and aching, my stomach still hard and sore, I saw that the light in the bedroom was on; Aby was possibly passed-out drunk. Or maybe she was scrolling on her phone, perhaps even texting me.

I went to push the door open, and I heard the giggle. And then the groan.

A man's groan.

It took far too long for me to comprehend what I was seeing as I stepped into the room. My brain couldn't make sense of it all. Suddenly, the pain in my stomach was gone. It was like someone had taken an ice-cold knife and sliced all my organs away.

For there, on the bed, was my brother. Fucking my girlfriend.

Chapter Eighteen

Gem – 2022

'Are you OK to come over about seven? Brandon wants to eat early – he's convinced that if I eat late the baby will suffer or something...'

'Seven?' I was flailing, desperately trying to remember what on earth I had organised. I heard Vee take a sharp breath on the other end of the phone.

'Dinner tonight, Gem. You remember? I messaged you about it days ago. To celebrate our news?'

I couldn't fail to notice the emphasis she placed on the word *news*. Vee knew that my mind had been totally elsewhere these past few weeks. It was like I had no room to think about anything else.

'Vee, I'm sorry, of course tonight. You know we'll be there.'

I stole a glance at the bedroom, where Richard was getting ready for his run. We'd barely spoken, moving around the flat like two ghosts trying to avoid one another. Last night, he had even stayed out late and ended up sleeping on the sofa, which was so unlike him.

But who could blame him? Richard could see the change in me. He knew something had shifted. None of this was fair, to any of us.

I thought of the pub yesterday, and how I had sat so close to Will. How I had looked deep into his eyes for the first time in so long and all the emotions I thought I'd buried forever had crashed to the surface. Everything I had fought so hard to suppress – that heartache I had battled to overcome, the scars that I had learnt to ignore – all of it was back on show. I had never felt so vulnerable, so scared.

And yes, so excited. Dare I admit that I felt alive again, like a giddy teen once more? This wasn't how I was with Richard, no matter how hard I tried, but I did care about him so much. He had been such a stable presence in my life and reassuring. I owed it to him to try and sort this mess out.

'Gem? Are you still there?'

'Yes... Yes, sorry...'

'God, I swear talking to you is getting harder and harder,' Vee said, and there was a small, forced laugh, and I felt an immediate twinge of guilt.

'Vee, I'm so sorry! I will be there, don't worry. I'm looking forward to it. I'll nip to Sainsbury's on the way and grab us a dessert, yeah?'

'Not chocolate, though... that grosses me out at the moment.'

'Not chocolate. No problem.'

'And Richard is coming?' Vee asked softly.

I hesitated, my gaze drifting towards the closed door again. The truth was, I hadn't even told him about it, but I knew how much he loved Vee and Brandon – he wouldn't upset them. Richard was good at putting on an act if he needed to.

'You need to come,' Vee said firmly. 'I have a present especially for you, godmother.'

Godmother! That word still made me grin from ear to ear.

'Oh my God, what?'

Vee giggled. 'You'll just have to wait and see – make sure you are on time, OK? And, Gem?'

'What?'

'Try to forget about Will for one night, please.'

Forget! That word was being used so much. Memory was a dangerous thing – how could anyone really let go of the thoughts and feelings that have been a part of them for so long? It was like trying to remove the roots from a plant and expect it still to flourish. Will would always be part of me, no matter what, and in his mind, I was still in his present. He still loved me.

How could I forget that? It was bloody impossible.

As if on cue, as soon as I'd finished my call with Vee, my phone buzzed. I knew it was Will before I even looked down at the screen. This was an intuition we used to have: knowing when he was close, finishing each other's sentences, feeling his pain.

It was a voice note. I pressed the phone to my ear, unable to hide my smile when I heard his voice again.

It was great to see you yesterday. Sorry you had to rush off. Me and Jack have been catching up. It's not easy, I guess you can imagine. I'm only beginning to realise how awful I was to you. He told me about Aby. I can't believe I did that. It still hasn't sunk in. I'm so sorry.

I know it's not enough, but Gem, I really am sorry. Something still doesn't feel right. I'm hoping to get some more answers.

I typed back my reply.

> I'm glad you and Jack are talking. Don't apologise. You can't apologise for something you don't remember. I hope you find the answers you are looking for.

His answer came almost straight away.

> I'll keep you posted. What are you up to today? XXX

The three little kisses, so harmless – but that was how Will used to sign off all his messages to me, except towards the end, when he changed and became cold.

> I'm going to dinner at Vee's. Maybe we can catch up again soon.

I kept my replies short and to the point. In truth, I ached to see him again, but I knew this wasn't good for me. It didn't matter what Will was saying right now, or how he was acting – he was still recovering from an accident. He was shaken up and not thinking straight. There was no guarantee he wouldn't go back to how he was before, or that he wouldn't hurt me again.

> I'll look forward to that xxx

'I bet you would,' I muttered under my breath, still unable to suppress my grin. Brain injury or no brain injury, Will was still a cheeky sod.

'Who's that you're texting?'

I looked up and saw Richard in the doorway. He was dressed in his running gear – shorts and tight T-shirt – and clutching his shoes in his hand.

I threw my phone back onto the sofa and tried to look casual. The last thing I needed was another row about Will. Richard wouldn't understand.

'It's just Vee – she wanted to make sure we were OK for tonight still?'

'Tonight?' Richard frowned. 'Had we planned something?'

I had to rely on Richard's hopeless memory now, feeling a bit guilty as I forced a grin. 'Yeah, I told you ages ago. Vee's arranged a dinner tonight to celebrate their pregnancy.'

I saw Richard's shoulders relax a little. 'Aw, yeah, that would be nice. It feels like so long since I saw those guys.' He walked into the room and sat down carefully beside me. 'Sorry I didn't come into the bedroom last night, but I got back so late...'

'Yeah.' I shrugged. 'I figured. It doesn't matter.'

Richard put his hand on my knee and gently squeezed it. 'Gem, I know I've been a bit of an arse these last few days. It's just this stuff with Will, it's hard, you know. It's been messing with my head a bit.'

He was looking at me in that completely loving and open way that he had, and I could feel myself begin to crack. It wasn't fair that he was thinking he was some paranoid idiot – after all, I couldn't deny this was messing with me too.

'Richard, I—'

'No. You don't need to apologise,' he said, shutting me down. 'Last night I did a lot of thinking. I know that this must be hard for you. Will was a big deal in your life, wasn't he? Of course, you're going to worry about him, still care about him.'

I nodded, tears pricking my eyes.

'But Gem, don't forget this was the man who hurt you. Do you remember how I had to fix you?'

I flinched, not sure I liked being compared to a damaged doll. Yeah, I had been in a bad place after Will. My trust had been completely destroyed and I wasn't even sure I wanted to be in a relationship again. It was only through gentle persuasion and support that Richard convinced me to open my heart.

'I know he hurt me,' I said carefully. 'I'm aware of what happened in my own life, Richard. But you're right – this whole experience has been weird and stressful. I feel like I'm living two lives.'

He hesitated, but then leant forward. 'I get it – I understand. This is a totally unexpected situation, but at the same time I don't want you to forget that I'm here. I'm with you, Gem, and I care about you so much. You know that.'

I smiled. Damn, Richard was so sweet. 'I care about you, too, Richard.'

He moved towards me. The kiss was nice and light, bringing with it a reminder that I was safe, I was loved in this relationship. This was good, I had to remind myself – what I had with Richard was solid and kind and real. It wasn't built on flimsy dreams and broken promises.

And yet...

I pulled gently away, shaking away the doubts. 'Thank you, Richard.'

'For what?'

'I dunno. For just understanding – or at least for trying to understand.'

His expression was serious. 'I really am trying to, Gem. But I also need your help in return. You can't give Will too much of yourself. You'll end up forgetting all the bad things he did to you; you'll be blinded by sentiment and the fact that you feel sorry for him.'

'I don't feel sorry for him,' I said firmly.

'Are you sure you don't?' Richard asked searchingly. 'Look, just think about it, Gem. Will has had a major trauma. He's vulnerable, scared and probably taking lots of strong medication. I know what a big heart you have, how hard it would be to walk away from someone like that.'

'I'm only trying to help him.'

'And you also have to be careful. Is this really Will that you are dealing with? He can't remember anything except you, so he's clinging on because you're the only thing that makes sense at the moment. How do you know he's not using you?'

I shook my head. I didn't have an answer for that.

'You're exhausted, Gem. This is meant to be your holiday; you don't need this stress in your life. Isn't there someone else who can help Will? Someone who is less likely to get hurt by all of this?'

With some reluctance, I nodded. 'Yes, there are other people. Will's brother is home now, and those guys were always so close before... Well, before any of the stuff happened – and Will is staying with my mum.'

'Your mum?' Richard looked visibly shocked. 'How on earth did that happen? I thought he had a girlfriend.'

'Well, like you said, it's complicated. Will is pushing away the people he doesn't remember.' I caught Richard's frown and continued. 'It's no good looking at me like that, Richard. I wasn't happy about Will staying with Mum either. But those two have always been close. I swear she'd prefer him to be her own child.'

'I'm sure that's not true… Your mum is probably just trying to help.' Richard squeezed my knee again. 'Look, what you need is a break from Will. After tonight, shall we look at booking that holiday?'

'Yeah, sure.'

Richard began to pull on his running shoes, still chatting brightly as he did so. 'I'm looking forward to tonight – seeing Vee again. She must be so thrilled about the baby. It's lovely seeing those guys get exactly what they want. Properly settling down.'

'It is,' I smiled.

Richard jumped up and then planted a small kiss on my head. 'That'll be us one day, Gem. You'll see. We'll have it all sorted too.'

I watched as he left the room, wishing I had the same enthusiasm, and wondered why the smile on my face felt painted on.

As he called, 'Love you,' from the door, I realised I couldn't bring myself to return the words.

It was like they were stuck inside of me.

–

'Yay, so good to see you both!'

Vee planted a kiss on both our cheeks and then guided us into her house. I always loved it here. Their home was a tiny terraced house on a busy street, but Vee had managed to make it look like one of those places featured in interior magazines. The downstairs was very white and open plan, with an extended kitchen and bifold doors leading out into the neat, well-maintained garden. It was nothing like the rundown council house where Vee had grown up; everything here looked opulent and modern.

Brandon was busy in the kitchen as we walked in. I could immediately smell his curry; he was famously good at whipping them up. He beamed as we came over to him.

'Guys! So good to see you.' He clapped Richard on the back. 'How have you been?'

I liked Brandon. He was a six-foot gentle giant who looked like he should be out on the rugby pitch, but actually hated most sport. I knew his job involved something to do with finance or money, but I switched off any time he tried to explain it to me. All I knew was that he made Vee happy. In the early days, Will and I used to double-date with them a lot – Will and Brandon immediately connected over a love of retro music. Brandon was always a bit in awe of Will's musical talent and he was genuinely upset when we broke up. I think that's why it took him longer to get on with Richard and perhaps why, subconsciously, I kept Richard away a bit. I didn't want him to be existing in anyone's shadow.

'I was saying to Gem that we should do more stuff together,' Richard said earnestly. I noticed Brandon nod along, but something in his eyes told me he wasn't as keen. Had I ever noticed before how stiff he was around Richard? How his smile seemed flatter?

Vee tugged my arm. 'Let's go outside. Leave the boys to chat.'

I followed her out to the patio. She already had some Pimm's mixed up in a jug and she poured me a glass.

'I miss this stuff already,' she said, passing it to me. 'Orange juice doesn't quite have the same kick.'

I sat myself down on the nearest chair, my thoughts still caught up in the scene unfolding in the kitchen.

'Vee, does Brandon like Richard?'

'Eh?' Vee looked at me surprised. 'Where did that come from?'

'I was just wondering...'

'Of course, he does. He thinks he's a nice guy.'

Nice. I sipped my drink. Nice wasn't really the word I was looking for, but I guessed that would have to do for now.

'That's good.' I paused. 'It's just he doesn't seem to like him as much as he did Will. You remember how those two were? Always laughing and joking around. Brandon now just seems a bit more... I don't know, stiff?'

Vee seemed to consider this. 'Yeah, I guess you're right, but Brandon just really gelled with Will – after all, we've all known each other for so long. He was gutted when you guys split up. Also, he cares so much about you. He's probably always going to be a bit defensive because no one matches up to Brandon's high standards.'

I laughed. 'I'm too good for anyone else.'

'Something like that,' Vee said. 'Anyway, it doesn't matter what Brandon thinks. His judgement isn't that great – look at his shit choice of clothes and shoes.' She pulled a face. 'If he hadn't pulled me, I'd be seriously questioning his taste. You need to chill out, Gem. As long as you get on with Richard, that's the only thing that matters.'

In the kitchen I could hear Richard telling Brandon about the latest football results; he never seemed to get it that Brandon hated the sport. Nevertheless, Brandon seemed to be joining in fine. Vee was right: I really needed to chill out.

Vee lowered her voice. 'Have you thought any more about the Will situation?'

I sighed. 'It's just so complicated, Vee. When I see him, he's so different. I can't turn my back on him when he's like this.' I sucked in a breath. 'I just wonder whether, I dunno, maybe we can be friends now.'

Vee actually snorted. 'You and Will – friends? Are you serious? It was always all or nothing with you guys. I'm not sure how you could be anything else.'

'Well, I'm not sure I can walk away from him, though,' I said. 'I guess I'll just have to see what happens. His brain is likely to recover. He might go back to how he was before and none of this will matter. But—'

'But, what?'

I was about to tell Vee about Will's theory that something had happened to him three years ago – something that had made him change – but looking across at her concerned expression, I stopped myself. I didn't want to worry her any more.

'Today isn't meant to be about me, Vee,' I said gently. 'This is about you – about you and the baby. I promise you, I'm going to be fine.'

'I hope so,' Vee replied. 'Because I need my godmother on top form.'

Vee reached over to the table and picked up a silver envelope that I hadn't noticed there before; it had my name on it.

'What's this?' I asked, as she passed it to me.

'A present. Just a tiny thing,' Vee said shyly. 'I hope you like it.'

I heard a noise and looked up to see Richard behind me, clutching a beer. He kissed my head lightly. 'What's this? Exchanging birthday cards early?'

'I don't know what it is.' I giggled.

I ran my finger under the flap and eased it open. Almost immediately, I recognised what it was and a tiny gasp escaped me.

'Oh Vee, this is so precious.'

'Your little god-daughter or godson,' Vee said, her eyes tearing up. 'I wanted you to have a copy. You are as much a part of this as we are.'

I stared at the ultrasound image, at the tiny white blurry lines that clearly formed a child. I ran my finger across it, hardly able to believe it. After so long, he or she was finally here. They were real.

'It's beautiful,' I whispered. I slipped the image back into the envelope and then into my bag for safekeeping. Richard squeezed my shoulder.

'That really is a wonderful thing,' he said.

I nodded. 'It's the best thing ever.' I was the proudest godmother alive.

Before

Will – July 2019

Vee had gone to town – her house was spotless, the dining table laid out as if she was expecting royalty, and the kitchen was full of enticing food smells.

I strolled over to her and kissed her cheek. Her skin had a slight sweaty sheen.

'You've done too much,' I said. 'We were only expecting drinks and a few snacks.'

Vee batted me away. 'You know I like spoiling you guys!'

'And who is going to try and stop her?' Bran asked, strolling in from the living room. We immediately gave each other a hug, his big bearlike hands rapping me on the back.

Gem had already rolled up her sleeves and was helping Vee with the last bits of the meal. I grinned in her direction. We'd had a bet that Vee would put on at least three courses. Looking at the food already bubbling away, it was possible we were on for a four-courser.

I followed Bran out into the garden. The evening was thick with heat. I sat opposite him on one of their fancy reclining chairs, nothing like the tatty plastic ones that Gem and I had out on our balcony.

'She's still struggling, you know,' Bran said quietly.

I cast an eye back towards the kitchen. You wouldn't have guessed – Vee was dancing in front of the oven, giggling with Gem, and she looked the picture of happiness.

'I keep trying to say the right thing, but what can you say, really?' Bran shrugged. 'Her moods are so dark. She's so snappy. Sometimes I feel like I'm in the way.'

'That's not true, mate, she's potty about you. She always has been.'

Bran sat back in his chair, stared up at the sky. 'I just wish she didn't clam up so much, you know?'

'Yeah, I get that.'

I didn't really, though. I looked back at Gem in the kitchen and all I could see was a laughing, easy-going girl. Yeah, we had our ups and downs, but Gem didn't keep anything from me. She was as open as a book.

'You'll be all right, Bran,' I said. 'You two always are.'

'Yeah, I know.' He shot me a weak smile. 'The four of us always will be, won't we? The four musketeers. I can't see it ever changing.'

The meal was perfect, as expected. The company even better. I felt full and satisfied, with Gem's arm curled around my back, and I saw Bran flash me a knowing smile, indicating that shared sense of contentment. We both understood what we had and appreciated it. Vee was quieter during the meal, and I noticed she was fiddling with her hair more than usual. When she made moves to clear up, I offered to help, and ordered Gem and Bran outside to enjoy the last of the sunshine.

'You want me on my own?' Vee said. 'Should I be concerned?'

I busied myself scraping the plates and loading the dishwasher, not wanting to be too full on.

'You didn't eat much tonight.'

'I'm just not hungry.' She wiped the countertops with a cloth. 'It's no big deal.'

'And… I dunno…' I shrugged. 'You don't really seem here tonight?'

Vee turned. Her eyes glinted with mirth. 'Oh, I'm sorry, Will, wasn't I the perfect hostess?'

'Of course, you were.'

'I cooked all of this food, I made the house nice, I painted on my biggest smile—'

The mask slipped, and tears trembled on her lashes. Her mouth opened and closed as she gripped the nearby chair.

'Vee, you don't have to pretend around us. You know that.'

She stared at me, wide-eyed. 'But I like to pretend, Will. That way I can forget.'

I walked over to her and delicately pulled her into a hug. Her head sank onto my shoulder as if she were weightless.

'Talk to me, Vee,' I said gently. 'I want to know what's going on with you.'

'Do you?' she whispered.

'Yes, I do.' I stroked the top of her head. 'You're one of my oldest friends, Vee. We all care about you so much. I hate to see you like this.'

'Like what?'

'Like a shadow of your former self.' I paused. 'It reminds me of how my mum was, when she was ill. She kept pretending everything was OK, forcing that smile on her face, but I could see she was breaking apart underneath it all. She couldn't fool me, even though she wanted to.'

'I'm not trying to fool anyone, Will. It's just so hard...'
Vee's voice broke and I pulled her closer towards me.

'I know you're not, Vee. I just hate seeing you in pain like this.'

She sighed, her breath fluttering against my shirt. Her fingers clenched and unclenched around my arm.

'I lost another baby,' she said finally, her words bleeding into my chest. 'The fifth one now, Will. I hadn't even told Bran. What's the point? My body can never keep hold of them. I'm useless. A failure.'

I pulled away, stared down at her. 'You are not useless, Vee. Don't ever think that.'

She swiped at her nose. 'What else is there to think? All I want to be is a mum. Everything else – all of this is irrelevant. I'm irrelevant.'

'Vee, that's bollocks. You are one of the most relevant people I know. We all love you. And Bran – my God, he's beside himself trying to work out what's wrong with you.'

'Really?' She sniffed.

'Really! You need to talk to him. He'd want to know this, he'd want to support you.' I stroked her arm gently. 'I promise you, Vee. He will help you. You just have to let him in.'

She nodded meekly. 'I will. I'm going to, but I just can't find the words.'

'Tell him what you told me. You're not alone with this, Vee, please remember that.'

She sucked in a shaky breath. 'Thanks, Will, thanks for this – it was good.'

'It's what I'm here for.' I smiled weakly. 'I can be a grown-up sometimes.'

She grinned back at me, blinking away her tears. 'Yeah, maybe you can. Gem is a lucky girl.'

'And I'm a lucky guy,' I replied. 'And one day, Vee, I swear you are going to be one hell of an amazing mum.'

Later, in bed, Gem pulled me towards her.

'I know what you said to Vee today. She told me before we left.'

'She was so upset; I didn't really know what to do.'

Gem kissed me on the lips. Gentle, but so perfect. 'You did the exact right thing. You listened to her; you held her – it was what she needed at that moment.'

'She should've talked to you or Bran.'

Gem stroked my arm. 'She told me about the baby but not that she had lost it.' Her voice softened. 'I had no idea. It only happened yesterday. She knew how excited I was about the pregnancy, and I guess she didn't want to upset me.'

'That's awful.'

'I feel so bad. We talked earlier and I'm going to meet up with her tomorrow, to try and help her through this.'

'Poor Vee,' I said.

'I know.' Gem pulled herself up on her arms and peered down at me. 'But you did a really good thing today and I wanted to thank you.'

'Oh yeah… how?'

Her fingers delicately tickled my stomach. I could feel myself getting aroused and groaned quietly.

'Well… yes, that…' she whispered. 'But also, I'm going to make you a special meal next weekend.'

'Next weekend?' My mind was blurry as her hand kept moving. 'But hang on, isn't that the 18th of July…?'

'The anniversary, yes.' She paused, and so did her hand. 'But I want to change what that date means. I need to start to do special things instead, mark it in a different way.'

'I'm happy to oblige, but only if you're sure?'

She carefully clambered on top of my body, lowering her hips slowly against my already erect penis.

'Oh, believe me. I'm sure.'

Chapter Nineteen

Will – 2022

I'd slept badly. Really badly. Maybe it was because of my emotional meeting with Jack yesterday, but more likely it was due to the dreams that seemed to be taking over my nights. Last night had been more intense than ever – it was still the same thing: I'm in a car, hurtling at speed towards bushes, a fence, something else that looks like a tree. I know I'm going to hit it. I try to take control, but I can't. I can't stop what is happening.

Everything is rushing towards me so fast – and then there is the sound. The awful sound of metal hitting wood at full throttle. A splintering of glass.

Me, shouting.

I can't make out what I'm saying but I'm definitely shouting.

And there – somewhere in the distance – is something else.

Someone else is screaming.

Someone is screaming my name.

The shower did nothing to help clear my head. I could still hear the voice, somewhere in my subconscious, shouting at me, but I couldn't work out who it was.

Had someone else been with me that morning?

As I stepped out and began to dry myself, I tried desperately to think back to the dream, to try and wrestle the part of my brain that had completely closed down. I was remembering the crash now, a bit at least, so surely more would come back?

But why had I felt so powerless? And who did that other voice belong to?

My instinct told me I should ring Gem and tell her what I remembered. She was always the sensible one, always knew what to do, but I hesitated. I had to give her space; I didn't want to overwhelm her. There was also a part of me that felt I needed more proof to show Gem that I was really the old me again and there wasn't any risk of me turning into the man I'd become in the last three years.

I went back into Gem's old bedroom and threw myself on her bed. My phone was flashing, so I read through my updates. As usual, there was a message from Nicola.

> Hey babe – how did you sleep? Maybe we can go for lunch tomorrow. I know just the place. This flat is so empty without you Xx

I texted her back:

> Sounds good xx

Nicola tended to text every morning and night. I still hated how numb I felt towards the woman I was meant to be with now. Perhaps I really was an arsehole? Did I deserve to be with anyone?

Jack had left a voice note and, listening to his gruff, yet friendly, tone immediately made me relax a little.

> Hey bro! Last night was good, better than I thought it would be, actually. It made me realise how much I'd missed you. These past few years have been – well, tough… It's typical that it's taken a bang to your head to bring us back together. I always said you had that coming to you… Anyway, I'm catching up with some of the fellas, but I'm around, OK? Just call me if you need me.

I smiled. Just knowing that Jack was close made me feel good. I didn't know how I'd coped without him for so long.

The last update was a missed call from a number I didn't recognise. I hoped it wasn't the bank again, on at me about the poor state of my finances. I quickly dialled to listen to the voicemail, and a rush of emotions hit me when I heard her voice. It was only once the message ended that I realised I had been holding my breath the entire time.

I played it again and tried to listen to Mel properly this time.

> Will, fuck! I wasn't expecting to hear from you again. I thought we had said all we needed to say to each other. I can't say I relish the thought of another argu-ment… but look, if it's important, come and see me, yeah? I'm at the pub today. I'm sure you can find it OK. I can't say I'll be glad to see you, but I'm not going to push you away either…

There was a pause – a slight cough and then:

> You hurt me, Will. All that stuff you said. I always
> thought we looked after each other, especially
> considering all I did for you after your Mum died… I
> just hope you're not coming to look for more trouble.

I threw the phone on the bed and then lay down beside it. As I stared up at the Artex ceiling, I kept replaying Mel's words in my head. It was clear that we'd had an argument. But what the hell was it over? Mel and I had always scraped along perfectly fine. I couldn't remember us falling out over anything before.

Downstairs I could hear the loud laughter of morning TV. I knew Di would be sat there, transfixed. Suddenly, this house felt too small, too claustrophobic. Everywhere I looked there were memories of Gem – a reminder of how much my world had become messed up.

Despite my suddenly pounding head and the reluctance in Mel's voice, I knew I had to go and see her – and sooner rather than later.

–

Di looked at me blankly when I said I was going to Mel's pub.

'Will, it's in the middle of nowhere. How will you get there?'

'Well, I was kind of hoping you would take me.'

I saw Di shrink back in her seat a little and suck in her cheeks. 'I barely use my car now and when I do, it's only for little trips to the supermarket.'

'Please, Di,' I said. 'I know this is hard for you. A big ask, but I need to do this, and I could use the support too. I'm not sure Mel even wants to see me.'

'Will, I—'

'It'll do you good, Di. You'll get away from this crap for a little while.' I gestured at the TV. 'And I'll navigate. It'll only take twenty minutes in the car. You can play all your crappy 1980s music and I won't complain.'

Di laughed. 'What? Even the cheesy stuff?'

'Even that.'

She sighed and then began to ease herself up. 'OK, let me get changed, but we're not stopping for long, right? I want to be back for my quiz show this afternoon.'

'OK, Di.'

She nodded quickly and then reached up to pat my cheeks. 'I dunno, Will. You have a way of persuading people to do things, did you know that?'

'It's my cheeky charm, Di.'

'No...' she said, still smiling. 'It's just you.'

–

Sitting in the car with Di, I was beginning to wonder why I had begged her to give me a lift. I had only experienced her driving a few times previously – on odd trips to the shops with Gem years ago – but I didn't remember her being so crazy behind the wheel.

'Di, are you sure it was me that crashed the car and not you?' I said, gripping the side of my seat as we tore around another corner sharply.

'We can always drive back home if you're not happy,' Di said, grinning. I think, secretly, she was quite enjoying herself. This was the first time she had been out for a while, and it was clearly good for her.

On my lap, my phone buzzed. Di peered across. 'Is that my Gem?'

'Yeah.' I scanned the text. I couldn't help messaging her earlier. I just had to know what she was up to, still unused to her not being beside me. 'She's going to Vee's for some dinner party,' I said. 'God, Vee never changes, does she? She used to love throwing those things.'

'Have you not been in touch with Vee?' Di asked.

I shook my head. 'No. I thought about it, but Vee's number isn't saved on my phone anymore so I'm guessing I pissed her off too.' My finger traced the screen thoughtfully. Vee had been a good friend once, part of my life too. We had grown up together. I loved her for being slightly wacky and much stronger than any of us. I also loved her because she loved Gem so much.

'The Vee I remember would probably want to chew my balls off for hurting Gem.'

'You're right there,' Di said, crunching the gears once again. 'Gem went wild after you changed, but Vee took her under her wing, of course, and sorted her out. I'm not sure how she would feel about all of this.'

'No, nor am I.'

We were flying down country roads now, which was giving me a weird mixture of relief and panic. The relief was due to the fact that Di was on a relatively straight patch and, surely, a bit safer. The panic was coming from deeper inside me. I figured it was some instinct kicking in within me, making me want to fling open the door and chuck myself out.

Di seemed to notice. 'Are you OK?'

'It's this road... I don't know.'

I sat back and closed my eyes, trying not to overthink, but this road was too familiar. I had blanked out the details of the accident: everything Nicola and the police had told me had blurred into a mush – but I knew without even looking that this was where I crashed.

'Oh, Will,' Di said quickly. 'I didn't think. This is the road, isn't it? I should've taken the longer route. I should've cut across town. I didn't think...'

I couldn't answer. I couldn't say a word.

As my eyes opened again, everything came back to me in a rush. It was so fast; it took my breath away.

The day of the crash was slowly taking shape in my mind: images were forming and sounds were becoming a little clearer.

'Will, are you OK?'

'Yes, yes, I'm fine.'

I stared out of the window, feeling strangely calmer now. The flashbacks still weren't in the right order, just a mess of broken-up scenes — shattered glass, blood, screaming, branches through the windscreen. A howling noise. And something else, something that I hadn't seen before.

I wasn't scared anymore; I was just stunned. As we whipped past trees and fields, I noticed I was taking long, deep breaths. I stared down at my hands and realised they were shaking.

'Will? I can pull over if you want.' Di was clearly worried.

'No, please don't. Just get to Mel's,' I said as calmly as I could.

I still couldn't quite process exactly what had happened, but an uneasy feeling had settled deep inside me. It was like the pieces of the jigsaw were slowly coming together.

And I wasn't sure if I was ready to face the truth yet.

–

We found Mel's pub, The Jolly Sailor, relatively easily and I was happy to clamber out of the car and step into the fresh air. We really were out in the sticks. The Jolly Sailor was anchored in the corner of the small village, facing a neatly trimmed green and backing on to woodland and more fields. The pub garden, despite it only being late morning, was already quite busy with families and a couple of dogs running around.

Di came up beside me, smiling.

'That was actually better than I expected, Will.'

I wished I felt the same way. I was still processing stuff, thinking about that drive and what had come back to me. It was weird how so much made sense now. It gave me a strange feeling of comfort, despite also making me feel quite unnerved.

'Nice place,' Di said, looking across at the pub. 'Very different from The Swan, eh?'

I nodded. It was a really nice place. I wasn't an expert, so I couldn't age the building, but it was clearly old – the timber frame and thatched roof gave that away. Whereas The Swan was all hard lines and dark windows, this place looked soft and welcoming – the perfect village pub. I frowned; I just couldn't picture Mel somewhere so quaint. She always liked noise and chaos, and this place was the complete opposite of that! It was all fresh air, sweet families and old charm.

Di touched my arm. 'Are you sure you're OK, Will? You were so quiet in the car, and I do worry about you. You are recovering after all.'

'I'm fine, Di. Honestly.' I took a breath. 'This place just isn't what I was expecting, that's all.'

'I guess people move on.'

'I know.' I just hadn't realised how fast. And how much…

I led Di through the main door of the pub, pleased to see that inside was a little quieter than outside. The exposed beams and open fireplaces gave it that olde-worlde feel. It would have been a perfect pub to go to at Christmas. I imagined snuggling up with Gem in one of the cosy corners and then quickly pushed the image away.

Each table had a thick menu planted on top, next to a vase that held a single flower. I picked up one of the menus and leafed through it.

'Look, Di – duck bloody pâté and risotto to follow. I remember suggesting we do burger and chips at The Swan and Mel nearly laughing her head off. Told me cooking was—'

'Too much stress! Yeah, and I was probably right about that.'

I turned around. Standing behind me was Mel, intimidating even at her five-foot height. I was relieved that she really didn't look that different. Her hair was still bleached blonde, though styled into a sharper and shorter cut than I remembered. Her eyes were still heavily made-up with dark liner and her lips were painted bright red. The only clear difference was the scowl on her face and the fact that her arms were folded tightly across her chest.

'It looks good, Mel,' I said, throwing the menu back down. 'All of this. The menu, the pub, the decor. It's all—'

'Different?' She nodded. 'I needed a change, and this was it.'

'It's wonderful, Mel,' Di said.

Mel turned towards Di stiffly. 'What are you doing here?'

Di seemed to flinch at Mel's rather brittle tone. 'I came with Will, Mel. Someone had to bring him. You always told me to come and visit...'

'Yeah, so we could talk about everything.' Mel's eyes flickered towards me and then back to Di again. 'Did you drive here? Seriously?'

Di nodded. 'Yes. Yes, I did.'

I noticed her voice was thinner now, less certain. She sat herself down on one of the nearby chairs, as if suddenly tired.

Mel snorted. 'You couldn't face driving your flash car over here, Will?'

The scorn in her voice was alarming.

'No, I didn't fancy it,' I said quietly. 'I smashed it into a tree and my head alongside it.'

Mel's face paled. 'I'm sorry. I didn't know.'

'That's why we're here, Mel,' Di said softly. 'Will has been in a bad way. He's hit his head and lost his memory. Three years of it, in fact. The last thing he remembers from that time is talking to you.'

'I think something happened,' I said. 'Something that changed me.'

'Oh Jesus.' Mel rubbed her face. 'And that's why you came here?'

I shrugged. 'All I can remember is you shouting at me. Or at someone. I thought you might be able to help me work it all out.'

'Oh, I can,' Mel said. 'I can help you perfectly well. But there's someone here who can help you even better. Somebody who was there that night too.'

I blinked as Mel glared directly at Di. Di was staring back at Mel, a puzzled expression taking over her face.

'Are you telling me you can't remember what happened either, Di?' Mel said sadly. 'Well, maybe it's time for me to remind you.'

Before

Mel – July 2019

I'd been watching her for most of the evening. I'd had an uneasy feeling from the moment she walked in, quietly ordered a double gin and tonic and then slipped into one of the corner booths.

'What's the date today?' I whispered to Leon, who was on shift with me that night.

'The 18th, why?'

'No reason...' My gaze drifted towards Di again. I wiped down the bar as I watched her gulp down her drink. All the time, she was staring blankly into space. Sighing, I decided to approach her. It wasn't what I usually did. Running a busy pub, you soon got used to leaving people alone in their own thoughts. It's never a good idea to interrupt someone's misery – after all, we all need our time to wallow. But there was something about Di that was making me uneasy. She wasn't a chatty regular, but I knew her history – Will had told me enough. I also knew that she only drank like this when she was in a really bad place.

'Are you OK, love?' I asked, walking over.

Di looked up, blinking. Her eyes were red-rimmed, her nose a bit snotty. 'I'm fine,' she said, swiping a sleeve across her nostrils. She then lifted her glass. 'I could use another one of these, though.'

I shrugged and called over to Leon to serve her another, and one for me too. Then I slid into the seat opposite.

Once closer, I could really smell the booze on her. She had clearly been drinking before coming in here and her hand shook as she downed the rest of her gin and tonic. I immediately regretted my decision to order her another.

'It's the anniversary, isn't it?' I said gently. 'Today. It's the anniversary of the fire.'

'Yeah…' She pushed the glass across the table. 'You think it will get easier. But it doesn't.'

'I can only imagine.'

'Every year I drag myself through it, but this time…' She shook her head. 'This time I can't see the point.'

Leon brought the drinks over and flashed me a 'is this is OK?' look. I pulled a face and stood up. What other option was there? At least this way she was safe, she was with us. I didn't want her wandering off and coming to harm.

'Call Will,' I whispered to Leon. 'He'll know what to do.'

'Isn't he having a romantic evening with Gem tonight?' Leon asked.

He was. That was why Leon was working this shift and not Will – but I looked at Di's sad face and empty eyes, and I felt a stab of anxiety. She really wasn't right.

'We can't leave her. She needs family, and Will is the closest to her. He knows how to calm her. I'll stay with her until he comes.'

Di seemed to bristle at the last sentence.

'You don't have to watch over me,' she said softly, her words slurring. 'I'm not some sad, old dog.'

'I just want to be here for you, that's all,' I replied.

'I don't need anybody.'

'Well, I think you do.'

'I don't want to talk.'

'That's fine. I'll just sit and watch you, then.'

She sighed heavily, frowning at me, and then slugged more of her drink. 'Annoying bugger, aren't you?'

I sat and waited while Leon made the call. I knew Will would come; I had no doubt. Will always did the right thing. While I waited, Di did talk. She talked a lot – about her life before, about Gem, about her sad thoughts, but there was only one thing that stood out in my mind.

She sat forward, took my hand in hers and then, quietly, told me the truth of what had happened.

'I killed him. It was me. One cigarette that I took up to bed.' Her hand was quivering in my grip; I tried to steady it, but I couldn't. 'I told Gem once and she could never forgive me. It changed everything between us.'

'Oh Di…' I breathed out – it was a lot to take in. My next words were clumsy, but I didn't really think. 'Were you drunk?'

Di looked at me for a moment. I saw pain there, real pain. Then she pushed back the table and stood up.

'I need to get out of here,' she said.

'No, you don't need to do that. Stay here. Talk to me some more.'

Di was already moving towards the door, and I let her go, assuming she would make her way home and I could send Will after her, but then I noticed she was reaching inside her bag. I saw the glint of metal and my heart started to pound. Why had she taken out her car keys? She only lived around the corner. Surely, she didn't drive here? She couldn't get back in the car in that state.

I stumbled after her, now in a panic. A customer stepped between us, asking if I was all right, and I had to politely tell him everything was fine, but by then Di was already out of the door.

Outside, it was a surprisingly cold night for July. I looked around blindly for her. She was staggering towards her battered Fiat, keys clasped in her hand. I ran towards her and grabbed the keys from her grasp. She wasn't expecting it and wobbled on the spot.

'What are you doing? I can drive...'

'No. No you can't, Di – I can smell you from here.'

'Well, I'm not walking,' she said, and I could see tears in her eyes. 'I need to get home now. I'm not leaving the car here. I don't trust pub car parks.'

It was a stupid, reckless decision, but all I wanted to do was get her home safe. I guided her into the car, slipped the key into the ignition and tried to ignore the nagging doubt in my head.

I was banned. I shouldn't be behind the wheel, but I only had to drive down a few streets. Where was the harm in that? Nobody would know.

As I pulled away, Di started moaning again. She complained that her seat belt was too tight and tugged on it; she said she was feeling sick. My eyes were only drawn away for a few seconds as I turned to try to placate her. I just wanted her to sit still, to stop wriggling.

I didn't see the bike coming round the corner. I certainly hit the brake far too late, my feet getting caught in the pedals. I remember looking up blindly, my hands clutching the steering wheel. I felt the car strike something. A dark body bounced against the bonnet and then fell heavily onto the tarmac. I saw the head slamming against the ground in a sickening fashion. It felt like it all happened in slow motion, but it could only have been a matter of seconds.

A matter of seconds that changed everything.

My stomach was rolling, acid burning in my throat. I staggered out of my seat, leaving Di behind. She was oblivious, still clawing at her belt and calling me names. She had no clue what had just happened.

But I knew. I knew what I had done and the panic inside me was escalating. I rushed to the body and pulled on his coat. He groaned before slowly pushing himself up into a seated position.

Will stared up at me, looking dazed. A tiny spot of blood glistened on his hairline like a rich jewel. He wasn't wearing his helmet. Like me, he had acted without thinking in his rush to help Di.

'I'm sorry. I'm so sorry. I just wanted to get her home. Are you OK? Oh my God, are you hurt?' My words were loud, almost angry. I stared back at Di, who seemed to have blacked out in her seat. This was all her fault. I'd only been trying to help. 'Shall I call an ambulance?'

Will staggered up, clutching his head.

'I'm fine,' he muttered. 'At least, I will be…'

I wanted to take him back to the pub, but he kept insisting he was OK. The doors were wide open and I could hear the strains of a Madness tune coming through. The juxtaposition of that happy song against this awful scene seemed all wrong.

'We need to take her home.' He pointed at Di. 'We're not leaving her like that.'

'But are you OK?' I tried to look at his head, but he pushed me away.

'I'm fine, stop fussing. It was a knock, that's all.'

He insisted we take Di home and sat himself in the driver's seat. He would drive, he told me. He was more than capable of doing that.

We drove the short distance in silence. I sat in the back seat, my mind awash with confusing thoughts and my hands still shaking. There was so much I wanted to say, but there was something about Will's stern expression and his stiff posture that made me hold back. He was angry, I could see that. He was angry that I had driven without a licence.

But surely he would forgive me soon? I was only thankful that he wasn't badly hurt.

Will took Di into her house. I waited in the car, counting down the minutes and running through the accident over and over again. If only I had waited for him. If only I had left Di alone in the first place. I blinked back tears and took a deep breath. Will was my friend; I knew he would understand eventually.

I jumped when Will opened the door forcefully. He sat heavily in the front seat and sighed.

'Is Di OK?' I asked.

Silence.

'Will, I'm so sorry. I know I shouldn't have driven the car. I'm so sorry I hurt you. Please—'

He turned to look at me. His eyes were hard and his tone, when he spoke, was hostile.

'You ran me over, Mel. I'm not going to forget that easily,' he said carefully. 'In fact, it's going to take a lot to forgive you for this.'

And after that, everything changed.

Chapter Twenty

Will – 2022

'You ran me over? I can't believe this,' I said slowly. 'I hit my head. Didn't I get it checked out in the end?'

'No...' Mel looked shifty. 'You didn't seem that injured, and I wasn't going to push it. I had a driving ban, Will. Do you know what would have happened to me if anyone had found out? You seemed fine. There was practically no blood. I wasn't driving fast—'

'But I could've been badly injured.' I said. 'It could have been what changed me.'

'I know, and you were so angry with me. We had a row at the time, you had a go at me for taking the risk.'

I touched my head instinctively. Was that what I had begun to remember?

Mel sighed. 'I told you to go to the hospital a few days afterwards, when you started getting headaches and your mood seemed to get worse. You weren't the same at all – you were so snappy and cold. I knew then that something might be wrong, but you refused to go. You wouldn't listen to me.'

'What did I do that night? After we dropped Di off.'

'We went back to the pub,' Mel said. 'You insisted, said it would help the headache that you had. You said I owed you a drink and you ended up having quite a few. You slept over in the end.'

'I don't remember any of this,' Di said quietly. 'But all of this is my fault.'

'It wasn't your fault, Di,' I said flatly. 'It's a bloody mess, though.'

'It wasn't mine either,' Mel insisted. 'Not really. I was just trying to do the right thing. I kept hoping you would get back to your old self over time, Will, but you just seemed to get worse and worse.'

Di shook her head sadly. 'I can't believe I didn't know any of this, although I do think in some way I did. I had a feeling I'd done something wrong, but I wasn't sure what.'

'Shit!' I breathed out hard. 'This explains why I felt the need to come to see you, Mel. I must have known the answers were with you.'

Mel lowered her head – at least she had the decency to look guilty about it. I wasn't even sure what to say next. I got up and started pacing the floor.

'I'm sorry,' Di whispered finally. 'I know I was drinking a lot back then. It was all getting too much for me.'

'But you stopped, didn't you?' Mel said. 'That seemed to be the line in the sand for you. Every time I visited you afterwards you were sober.'

Di nodded. 'Not being able to remember was terrifying. I never want to be in that position again.'

I stared back at Di wordlessly. At least that was something I could understand.

'Why did you keep visiting Di?' I asked Mel sharply. 'Was it because you cared, or did you have an ulterior motive?'

All this time I'd thought Mel must have had a good reason to be angry with me, but it was clearly her own guilt that had made her snappy.

Mel sighed. 'I was angry with Di and, yes, I admit that. But I also wanted to help her come off the drink. I couldn't let this horrible thing be for nothing.'

'Will, you must have been so angry with me,' Di whispered.

I shook my head in instant denial, but maybe the arse-hole in me did want to punish Di?

Mel touched my arm. 'You weren't angry with Di, Will. You wanted to protect her. You didn't want her to get into trouble or for Gem to find out and have another reason to fall out with her. You were putting other people ahead of yourself.'

'For all the good it did me,' I muttered.

Mel sighed. 'I knew you were struggling. The injury had given you headaches, but you wouldn't get it checked out. You weren't sleeping properly and were bad-tempered. Then the next thing I hear, you got drunk one night with Aby and ended up sleeping with her. That was the end of everything. I tried to talk to you about it and we had an awful row. You said some bad things, really bad things.'

'Like what?'

Mel blinked at me. 'That was when you told me I should leave. You threatened to tell people what I had done to you. You said you'd go to the police, make Di back up your statement. I couldn't risk that. That's why I decided to sell up.'

'God.' I felt sick. 'I couldn't have been thinking prop-erly to say things like that to you... To sleep with Aby.'

'Poor Gem didn't know what was going on. You weren't often at home and then when you were, you were horrible towards her. You weren't acting like yourself at all, but that could have been concussion, I suppose.' Mel ran her fingers through her hair. 'I didn't really make the connection at the time. I thought you were stressed, maybe drinking too much.'

'You should have known me better than that, Mel,' I said quietly. 'You of all people.' I slumped back in the chair, my body suddenly so heavy, my head so confused. 'That person just isn't me,' I whispered. 'I swear.'

'It wasn't you,' Mel said. 'Everyone noticed. Within a few months, it was like the old you had been replaced by this different version. Once you and Gem split up, you decided to reinvent yourself. You resigned from the bar, started hanging around with that Matty all the time and then you were working for him. All you seemed to care about was money and going out.'

'Maybe it helped me cope with what I had lost,' I said quietly. 'It seems like in the space of a few months I destroyed everything I cared about.'

'But you're forgetting something,' Di said, reaching forward and touching my hand.

'What?' I said, frowning. 'Of course, I'm forgetting something, Di. It's what I seem to be doing best at the moment.'

Di flinched but carried on. 'Will, you banged your head, and it was the bang on the head that changed things. You were in pain and grumpy. You never got yourself checked over.'

'So? We know this already.' I shrugged glumly. 'I keep banging my head. What of it?'

'What if your most recent accident did more than wipe your memory?' Di said softly. 'What if it actually reset you in some way?'

–

In the car on the way back, Di's driving was noticeably tamer. I could tell she was mulling things over. She had that thoughtful look on her face, the same one she had when she was watching her favourite quiz show on TV.

'What?' I asked eventually.

She chewed on her bottom lip. 'I dunno, Will. This… All of this, it's going to be a lot for Gem to take in.'

'She's not a child, Di,' I replied, a little bit too bitterly. 'Besides, you were the one who told me to go and see Mel. To find out what happened…'

'Yes, I know… I know I did,' Di said. 'I guess I must've known that Mel knew the truth, even though it's hurt both of us.'

After a small pause, she asked, 'Will you forgive her?'

'Yeah… I guess. I just need some time.' Leaving had been awkward. I knew Mel wanted more reassurance, a hug maybe, but I wasn't ready to give her that yet. 'She made a bloody stupid mistake, but I know she was trying to do the right thing. The trouble is, her mistake cost me dearly.'

Silence stretched between us, and I felt a horrible twinge in my stomach, the same one that kept coming back. It was that painful feeling of loss, of losing control. I turned away from Di and blinked my tears away as I stared numbly out of the window. Why did it seem like everyone I loved was slipping away from me? Even Di now seemed out of my reach.

Di sighed. 'Will, love, don't get upset. I probably shouldn't be thinking out loud like this.'

'You just don't want Gem to know that you played a part in all of this,' I said sulkily.

'I don't care anymore,' Di said softly. 'Gemma has drifted so far away from me that I'm not sure what I can do to repair our relationship and, to be fair, I deserve anything that is coming my way. I can't have more lies, I just can't.'

The silence continued to yawn between us.

'I'm just trying to see it from Gem's point of view, that's all, Will. It's going to be scary. A lot for her to consider. She took so long getting over you. She decided that whatever she thought you were – whatever dream man she had deemed you to be – she must have got it wrong, and that the true you came out eventually, and that side of you hurt, humiliated and betrayed her. She moved on with her life. She healed. Why should she risk that all for you?'

'I get that, Di. I do,' I whispered. 'But that wasn't me before, was it? I hurt my head. I was injured then too. I think you're right. I think the car accident has reset me. It's put me back to how I used to be.'

'I know, Will.' Di's voice was soothing. 'And I think you might be right. But don't rush into this, OK? Don't be reckless with your words. Remember that Gem is a new person too now. She might not be quite how you remember either.'

–

Back at Di's, I paced Gem's old bedroom, trying to think of what to do for the best. My head was whirring. I couldn't get any of my thoughts straight. I spent some time online, looking up brain injuries, seeing if it was possible for a personality to change afterwards. I was soon swept up, reading about people whose lives had changed. Some, like me, had become short-tempered or appeared 'different' to their loved ones. Others had suddenly developed new skills – speaking in different languages or accents, or having a talent they didn't possess before.

I put down my phone, my mind buzzing with inform-ation. I'd had two knocks to the head, not one. The first had altered my personality and the second had brought me back to me – could Di be right? Could the second injury have reset me in some way?

Eventually, I slipped out, leaving Di cosy in her chair, wrapped up in the safety of afternoon TV.

I just needed to walk. To think, away from everyone.

I went where my feet took me, across the estate. I passed our old childhood house and had to stop, my heart beating hard in my chest. It had changed quite a bit, but not enough for it not to stir up emotions inside me. I could still see my mum, standing by the front door, waiting for me and Jack to get home from school. I remembered the smell of the deep fat fryer, or Mum's stupid potpourri that she insisted on putting in the hall. I still remembered the smell of her…

I tore myself away, barely able to stand being there again. She was someone else I had lost. My anchor. She had loved Gem as much as I did. I had no idea what she would make of all this mess. Knowing Mum, she would ruffle my hair and tell me it would all be better in the morning. Except, it wasn't going to be, was it?

I dimly thought of calling Jack, but soon changed my mind. Jack was busy with his own stuff. He was only starting to warm towards me. If I asked too much of him too soon, I might end up pushing him away again.

But Gem, she would listen. She would hear the whole story before she made a judgement.

I kept walking, past the old park, past our school and up towards The Swan. God, that place. If only I'd known how important this pub had been in the whole story. I stared at the stupid ugly building and felt numb.

It meant nothing to me now.

I kept walking, thoughts tumbling and free-falling; my body was stiff and my eyes dry, almost unblinking.

I kept walking until I ended up there.

At Vee's.

It was Bran who answered the door. I saw his look of confusion first and then the sudden break of his smile. He always was a big bear of a man, full of affection, bad jokes and vice-like hugs. I felt a rush of warmth as he gripped me in his arms, almost squashing me with those stupidly large biceps of his.

'Will! Vee told me you were out of hospital.' He pushed me back and looked me up and down. 'How are you? It sounded pretty serious.'

My hand instinctively touched the front of my head. It was like I expected a big bump to be there, like those giant goose-eggs they show in cartoons. The reality was that the bruising was all under my hair and much deeper. It's often the wounds you can't see that are the worst ones of all.

'I guess it was serious. I took quite a knock, but I'm still here, so...' I shrugged.

'I should've come and visited you.' Bran looked sad. 'But it was awkward, you know. How things were before the crash...'

'Well... I don't really know,' I said. 'But I'm beginning to find out. I'm guessing I was a wanker to you too.'

Bran rubbed his beard. 'Not so much me, but when Vee had a go at you for hurting Gem... you weren't so nice. I had to step in then.' His eyes were busy assessing me, like he was really trying to work out if this was for real. 'Have you really forgotten it all?'

'Yeah, three years of it. I'm beginning to think that's a good thing, though.' I smiled sheepishly.

Bran reached across and squeezed my shoulder. 'It's good to see you, mate, it really is and I'm sorry you've been through it all.' He paused and looked back over his shoulder. 'Look, I don't know what you're doing here, but it's a little bit awkward. We're—'

'It's OK.' I held my hands up. 'I'm not stopping long. I just need to say one thing to Gem.'

Bran frowned. 'I'm not sure, mate. Richard is here and—'

'It'll only take a few minutes. Please, Bran, I'm not here to cause trouble.' I lowered my voice. 'Come on, this is me, you know me! The old me! I just need to do this one thing.'

Bran seemed to hesitate again and then a tiny smile slipped back on his face.

'OK, then, come on in, but don't blame me if they're a bit, well, hostile.'

I stepped into the hall, closing the door behind me. I could hear the bright chatter coming from Vee's extended kitchen.

'Bran! Who is it?' she called. 'You've been ages.'

'Just coming,' Bran called back. He turned back to me, his eyes glinting. 'At least you'll give me a break from

260

Richard's boring stories. I was beginning to lose the will to live.'

I had timed it well. They had already finished dinner. Gem and her bloke, Richard, were sitting facing me as I walked into the kitchen. They didn't notice me at first as I followed Bran through the doorway. This fella, Richard, was sitting back on his chair, holding his glass of wine in a lazy way, while telling Vee all about some kind of crypto-currency that he was looking into. Gem's gaze was caught elsewhere, as if in a daydream. She was fiddling with her necklace, the one that held her dad's gold sovereign ring. I knew that look on her face: she was bored. That man with the crisply ironed shirt and freshly shaven face was boring the shit out of her.

I also couldn't quite believe how different he was to me. He was clearly taller than me, and lanky, and had that kind of well-oiled look that salesmen have. He would probably be better suited to a desk next to Matty than I was.

Brandon coughed nervously. 'Look who I found.'

All eyes suddenly turned in my direction. Vee swivelled in her chair, mouth dropping into a perfect circle of shock. Gem was simply staring at me; her eyes were bright but there was no smile there. Richard – well, his expression was the most surprising of all. He was grinning at me like a Cheshire bloody cat.

'Will!' Vee breathed. 'What on earth?'

'I'm sorry to interrupt,' I replied carefully. 'This looks like a lovely dinner party you're having here.'

I felt a little sad. I thought of the times Gem and I used to come to these nights. How we would secretly giggle at Vee's slightly over-the-top efforts to look like the perfect middle-class housewife, while also feeling a deep affection for the girl who had made her life so good.

'Will.' Vee's voice had a warning to it. 'You shouldn't be here, not now.'

'No, it's OK, Vee!' Richard said brightly. He stood up and held his hand out for me to shake. 'We had to meet sometime, didn't we, Will? So why not now?'

I took his hand. It was limp and made me feel a bit queasy. I caught Gem's eye and raised an eyebrow.

Seriously?! This guy?

'So, why are you here, Will?' Richard asked in an overly sweet tone. 'You can see the dinner has been eaten. There isn't much here for you, I'm afraid. Why, there isn't even an extra chair!'

I pulled my hand away, like I was worried he might contaminate me.

'We can bring another chair to the table,' Bran said lightly. 'And there's plenty of booze if you fancy some-thing?'

'No, that's OK, mate,' I replied. 'Like I said, I'm not stopping.'

Gem shifted in her seat. 'Why are you here?' she asked. Her tone was gentle, but her eyes were pleading with me.

I took a sharp breath. I had to get this done – I *had* to do this.

'I have to talk to you, Gem,' I said. 'There's something you need to know.'

'And it couldn't wait?'

I ignored the impatient tut from Vee and tried not to feel a bit smug when I saw Richard's grin slip away.

'No,' I said firmly. 'It can't.'

Chapter Twenty-one

I honestly didn't have a clue what was going on.

When Will walked in, I felt a prickle of anxiety inside my stomach, but there was also an overwhelming sense of relief. I couldn't deny that it was good to see him. He was even dressed a bit like his old self. OK, his jeans were still those fancy designer ones, but I saw he'd thrown on a scruffy T-shirt that looked like it had been slept in. His stubble was growing back, too.

I could feel Richard stiffen beside me. I was expecting him to say something, maybe even challenge Will – but when he shook his hand and greeted him in that smug, over-the-top way, something curdled within me.

It was like I had only just noticed that the milk was starting to go off.

And then Will told me he had to talk to me. That he couldn't wait.

'I'm not sure, Will…' I said, looking around me. 'This isn't really the time, is it?'

'I couldn't wait, Gem. I'm sorry.'

Richard placed a hand on my knee. It was only a light touch, but it still made me squirm.

'You've interrupted our evening, Will,' he said evenly.

'Yes, I know that.' Will was staring at me now. I'd always loved his dark-blue eyes – I thought they showed that he was sincere and honest. Today they seemed even more open, like Will was totally exposed to me. Suddenly, I could see how awkward this was for him, standing in the kitchen of former friends – no longer feeling liked and accepted by them – and being challenged by a man he didn't even know.

I stood up.

'It's fine, Richard,' I said. 'Vee, is it OK if we go into your living room?'

Vee nodded, but her expression was grim. 'If you need me—'

I laughed lightly. 'I'll be fine, honestly. Like Will said, this won't take long.'

Will followed me into the next room. I closed the door gently behind us. We stood awkwardly for a while, then Will took a few steps forward, looking around the room with a wide-eyed stare.

'Wow, they've done this up nice.'

It had only been recently decorated, to be fair. After all the disappointments of failing to conceive, Vee had thrown herself into her passion for interior design. The carpet was cream and luxurious; the brand-new leather sofa was white, crisp and clean. Bookcases filled one wall, while another was covered in beautiful artwork.

'It's certainly not suitable for—' I caught myself. I couldn't tell Will about the baby; Vee had only just told me. I felt sad for a moment, realising that, in the past, Will would have been included in the announcement and would've been just as excited as me. Would Vee have made him a godparent too?

'Not suitable for what?' Will asked.

I smiled. 'Not suitable for scum like us, so we better not stay in here too long, eh? Wouldn't like to break something.'

Will grinned back at me. He walked around the room, taking it all in. 'I remember this house, of course I do, but Vee and Bran had only been here a year or so then. Wasn't this room painted green?'

'Yeah, she used to call it the ugly room.'

'I never minded it. I always thought it was quite hippyish,' Will said nostalgically. 'This house always had a good vibe. I'm pleased Vee and Bran are still so happy, that some things are as they should be.'

'Will—'

'No, please.' He held out a hand as if to silence me. 'You need to hear what I discovered today, when I spoke to Mel.'

'Did she tell you what happened that night?' I said, now intrigued. 'Did something really happen at the pub?'

Will sighed. 'Gem, I lied. This may take longer than a few minutes – so, scum or not, you better sit down and I'll explain as best I can.'

–

'I-I can't quite work this out,' I said quietly. I couldn't even get the words out properly; my mind was swirling too much. 'You're telling me that Mel actually ran you over? And my mum was the cause of it all and you never told me?'

'I don't know, Gem, but I'm guessing I didn't want to tell you, not at the time. You would have been heart-broken.' He paused, his brow creased with concern. 'It was the anniversary, wasn't it? You already blamed your mum for that. What good would it have done if I'd told you that she had been involved with this too?'

'But you were injured, and it was probably that injury that made you change.'

Will was sitting next to me, a few inches of space between us. 'I didn't think I was injured at the time, though. I thought I was fine.'

'But you weren't. You knocked your head.' I blew out a breath, completely overwhelmed by everything. 'I remember you were having headaches. And you were sleeping badly, but you told me that was stress. I knew you were keeping something from me, though...'

'That's why we started arguing, I guess?'

'Well, yeah – that and the fact you were so distant. Always in the pub. And then you had the night with Aby...'

Will flinched. 'I know. I'm so sorry. I can't excuse that.'

I shook my head. 'No, you can't.'

'Mel said I was in a lot of pain and quite nasty after. I'm guessing the knock itself and the discomfort shifted my personality.'

'I'm trying to remember.' I closed my eyes briefly. 'That night, you did stay away – which was odd, because you never normally did that. You didn't tell me where you went and that was the start of our arguments.'

'How did I seem to you?'

'God, Will, this was three years ago.' I sighed. 'But there was a sudden change in your behaviour – yes, all of a sudden you were staying out all the time. You snapped when I spoke to you. God, I just wish you'd spoken to me about it all.'

Will looked so sad. 'I don't know why I didn't, Gem. I must have thought I was doing the right thing at first. I was trying to protect you and your mum.'

'Oh, my mum...' I half-laughed. 'Can that woman surprise me anymore?'

Appearing torn, Will said, 'She wasn't thinking straight, Gem. She'd been drinking. But from what I've heard she hasn't had a drink since.'

I nodded. That was true at least. The one small thing I could grab on to.

'So, you are saying you've had two potential head injuries in the space of three years,' I concluded finally, trying to wrap my mind around it all.

'It's crazy, isn't it? But, yeah, that's what I'm saying.' He paused. 'And I reckon the second injury has done something more than make me lose my memory. I think it caused some kind of reset in my brain.'

'Will...' I almost wanted to laugh. 'You're not some kind of computer.'

'I've looked it up, Gem. It's not as crazy as it sounds. People have changed after head injuries – some have been able to speak different languages suddenly. Why is it so unbelievable that my personality would alter the first time and then be restored by a second, bigger injury?'

'I-I don't know...' I frowned at him. 'Have you even spoken to a doctor about this?'

'No, but I will. Although, my last scan showed my brain is healing as expected, so I'm not sure whether they can help with this. Any previous injury will probably not show now.' Will had inched closer to me. He laid his hand carefully on my leg. 'Gem, they might not understand it either. I know the consultant told me before that brains are extremely complex and even the leading experts don't know everything about them. But this makes sense to me. I feel like who I am is me right now. Whatever the past three years were, I don't know – it's like a stranger had taken my place.'

'It's convenient that you've lost your memory for those years, though, isn't it?' I said, feeling myself stiffen. 'What if this is you trying to excuse that bad behaviour as being no fault of your own? What if, even if only subconsciously, you have realised what a complete shit you were and are now trying to find a way to convince me that you've changed? Again.'

'Gem...' Will sighed. 'I'm not trying to trick you. I'm as confused as you are. All I know is I've had two bad knocks. I don't know why I can't remember those years – maybe you're right, maybe it is a subconscious thing. Maybe I don't want to remember the man I became.'

'This is so much to take in.' My voice shook with all the emotions that were waging a war inside of me. 'I'm not even sure what you want from me. You come bursting in here, uninvited, and you want to tell me all of this when it could have waited. I just don't know—'

'I came here because I needed you to know.' Will took my hand in his and squeezed it. 'I needed you to know that I'm back. That I'm the man you love, the man you've always loved. I'm sorry for any pain I've put you through, but you can't say you don't still have feelings for me. You can't!'

'Will...' I was floundering. I knew I should pull away, but something kept me rooted on that sofa, with my hand closely held in his.

'You don't love that man,' Will continued, his gaze boring into mine. 'Don't even pretend that you do! I saw the way you looked at him. I know you, Gem. I can still see something in your eyes when you look at me. I know I'm not imagining it.'

I immediately looked away. 'This isn't fair.'

'No, it's not,' Will said quietly. 'None of this is fair. On you, on me. On Nicola or Richard. But I can't help the way I feel, Gem, and I nearly died on that road, when I crashed into that tree. I can't believe I survived but won't end up with the woman I love. That doesn't make sense.'

'The trouble is,' I whispered, 'I'm not sure I could ever love you again, Will. It's been too long. It was all so painful.'

'But it never used to be, did it? Before my first injury, it was perfect. Admit that.'

'I – well, yes. It was…'

I wasn't expecting him to move towards me, and yet I didn't pull away when he did. His lips were suddenly on mine and my stomach lifted, like it used to when I was younger. The kiss was gentle at first, but then within seconds his hands were on my face, buried in my hair. I heard him sigh as I responded, feeling his mouth press against mine, more urgent and faster.

It was so familiar. So wonderful. My skin was tingling all over, my body alight.

His fingers traced down the line of my neck, his body moving closer towards me so that I could smell him. I couldn't stop myself from relaxing with the familiarity of it all, the memories, the connection.

Oh God.

No. No. This wasn't right.

This was too soon.

I pulled away.

Will looked at me, his eyes so kind. His hand lingered on my neck, gently stroking the skin there.

'I've never forgotten that,' he whispered. 'How perfect you are. How perfect we are, Gem. Can't you see? It's fate. We're meant to be together.'

I gently but firmly pushed him off me. 'Will, I can't do this now. I can't. I have to get my head around it all. I can't rush into it – it's just too confusing...' My words came out like bullets. I felt so flustered. I could see Will was hurt, but he nodded his acceptance.

'It's OK, I get it. I shouldn't have rushed you. Even your mum said I needed to be careful.'

'My mum?' My tone was sharp. 'Bloody hell, Will. Have you been discussing this all with her? After everything she's done?'

His eyes widened, realising his mistake. 'Well, she came with me today, Gem. She was a great help.'

I pulled a face. I couldn't help it. The closeness between my mum and Will would always drive me mad, and now I'd found out she might be the reason why we broke up. It was almost too much to bear.

'I'm sorry,' Will whispered. He placed his hand back on my leg and gently squeezed it. 'But I mean what I said, Gem. You're perfect, you always have been. I love you and I always have.'

I didn't know what to say. I simply shook my head.

'I'm going to go now, Gem. I came tonight to say my bit but now I'm going to leave you in peace. The next part is up to you. If you want to come back to me, I'm waiting for you. But if you want to make it work with Richard, then I understand.'

It was only as Will got up to leave that I looked up towards the glass doors to the kitchen.

Richard was standing there, staring into the room, and I had no idea how long he'd been watching.

Before

Gem – July 2019

I had to face it: I would never be up to Vee's standard. My chicken curry was bubbling away nicely but it had caught a bit and burnt. I had also cheated and resorted to microwave rice. I knew Will wouldn't mind. Tonight wasn't about the food anyway. Not really.

Moving around the kitchen in my tight slinky black dress wasn't easy. In all honesty, it was a touch small for me, but I didn't care. I liked the way it made my boobs look. I liked how it made me feel powerful and sexy.

'Are you sure you don't want me to help?'

Will was sitting at our small dining table; the candles were flickering delicately in front of him. He shifted in the seat, awkward, like he was about to get up – but I batted him back.

'Leave it! I'm fine. I want to treat you.'

'You should be relaxing today, not me.'

I smiled thinly and then turned back to the food, busying myself by dishing up. Despite the wine, my hands were still shaking a little. It was so silly really. Today was just another day. I had to forget the date. The fire had happened so many years ago now, why couldn't I let it go?

'Have you spoken to your mum?' Will asked.

'I tried calling but she didn't pick up.'

I didn't mention how relieved I'd been. I couldn't face a long conversation with her today – the tears and the drawn-out memories were so wearing. It felt like our lives had been completely defined by that one night.

'Oh...' I could almost hear Will's brain ticking over. 'I hope she's OK.'

I slopped out the curry onto the plate, wondering how it was that I couldn't serve anything perfectly. It always looked such a mess. The rice beeped in the microwave. I pulled it out, opening the packet too fast and letting the steam catch my face.

'Gem? Do you think she's OK?'

More slop on the plate. I stared at the creation in front of me and sighed. This wasn't going exactly as I'd planned.

'This is our night. Ours,' I said, my voice brittle. 'Can we please talk about something else?'

And so, we did. I drank more wine while Will barely touched his. He was too focused on his food, which he called 'the best yet' as he picked out the burnt bits. I knew he was lying but loved him even more for it. My gaze kept creeping over to the one small photograph on the bookcase that I avoided looking at most days. Mum and Dad together, with me as a baby. Once, there had been three of us. Once upon a time, things had been normal. My hand instinctively went to Dad's necklace, a reminder he was still there with me.

Will touched my knee. 'You don't have to do this, you know?'

'Do what?'

'Pretend everything is OK.' He smiled tenderly. 'I never expect this day to be easy for you. I just want to support you.'

I lowered my fork. I wasn't very hungry, and the curry was pretty rank.

'Maybe next year we could go away?' I offered. 'I think always being here, in the same town, doesn't help.'

Will nodded. 'We can go away. Every year, if that helps?'

I could feel myself warming to the idea. 'You always talk about that camper van – maybe one year we should just do it.'

'That sounds like a plan.'

Will's phone buzzed suddenly on the table beside him, and we both looked at it, surprised. He glanced at the screen and frowned.

'It's Leon, from the pub.'

'Why is he calling? You're not due in tonight.'

'I dunno, but I should answer. Maybe something's happened.'

I watched as he took the call, as he muttered responses, his voice growing more serious with every second. Finally, he ended with the words: 'I'm coming.'

My heart dropped. 'What is it?'

'Mel needs me.' He shook his head, not catching my eye. 'I have to go and help her. It won't take long.'

'No.' I knew I sounded awful. Spoilt, stubborn even. 'You're not working today. This is our night. She's...'

I stared at my wine. How many glasses had I had now? I already felt tipsy.

He leant over and gently kissed my cheek.

'I won't be long,' he repeated. 'Let me just make sure she's OK. You understand, don't you?'

'I guess...'

'Keep the food warm for me, Gem. I'll be back before you know it.'

Those were the last words he said before he slipped out into the cool summer night, leaving me behind with a headful of memories and a sour taste in my mouth.

Later still, I would wake in a cold bed and stare blankly at the space beside me, wondering where my man had gone. What was keeping him away?

And why did I have a horrible feeling that this date had, yet again, created more heartache?

Chapter Twenty-two

Will — 2022

I chose to take the long route back, thinking it might help to clear my thoughts a bit. Sadly, it did little of the sort. My thoughts were like a jar stuffed full of marbles: there was nowhere for them to move easily. I felt like I was being overpowered by the sheer weight and pressure of them all.

What had I done?

What if Gem pushed me further away? Had I messed it up completely?

Could I even give her what she wanted?

I thought of the kiss, and a combination of excitement and fear overcame me. It'd felt so good. So real. So right.

But what the hell had I done?

Walking down the roads and paths of the estate that I had known all my life just made me feel sadder somehow — like I was a ghost trapped in a place that had once been familiar. A part of me knew I no longer belonged here; I had chosen to move on. Even if I didn't understand or agree with the reasons for it, I had moved away from here for three years — I'd lived a different life. All I wanted was to turn the clock back, but as I passed by another newly painted house that I didn't recognise, another corner shop that had been turned into a charity shop, my heart sank.

I sat for a moment on the bench that was placed outside the community centre. This had always been the place where drunks gathered in the daytime, watching the world go by. I never really understood it before, how someone could just sit and stare at the scenery around them, but right now it made sense. It was weirdly calming, just watching as people ambled past. A couple strolled right past me, their arms looped around each other, their faces lit up in laughter and hope. The girl stumbled over one of the stupid loose paving slabs and cried out briefly, before the guy's hand snatched at her arm, tugging her back into position. They giggled – the silliness of nearly falling, the gratefulness of being caught.

I had to look away again. Something was choking me up.

The small parade of shops across the way from me hadn't changed much, and that gave me a brief sense of relief. The tatty old hairdresser was still there – the one where Gem had got a dodgy haircut when she was eighteen. God, she cried over that for days! The kebab shop was still on the corner, with its spinning greasy leg of meat that I doubt had been changed for over twenty years. The only thing I didn't remember was the betting shop, instead of the laundrette.

I'd loved that laundrette. I suppose people didn't use them so much these days, but Jack and I were thankful for the place after our ancient washing machine packed in. For months we'd save up our change and then lug our dirty clothes in black sacks over there. At first, I hated it. I was scared one of my mates would spot us. What a show-up to have to wash your pants in a public place. But later, as time went on, I enjoyed our trips. Jack was always so busy at work in those days, so it was one of the few times we could sit and be together – staring at those spinning machines, the scent of fabric conditioner washing over us.

'One day,' Jack had said, pointing at the turning drum, 'I'll have a top-of-the-range one of these. And a tumble dryer.'

'What about a dishwasher?' I stared down at my hands. They were red and peeling from the cheap washing-up liquid we used.

'Yeah, that and all.' Jack laughed. 'One day we'll have it all.'

It was only a few months after that that Di found out about our trips and put a stop to it. Soon it was me lugging our washing over to Di and sitting with her over a biscuit and cup of tea, while I waited for it to be done.

I liked spending time with Di – of course I did. It was warm and comfortable, and she refused payment, but part of me still missed those strange old times with Jack, sitting side by side on a hard bench, staring at a whizzing machine.

Now I found myself staring at the bright white building where it used to be. It looked gaudy and too dazzling, and I felt sad that the laundrette had gone.

No – more than that, I felt angry.

Little bits of my past were slowly being erased and there was nothing I could do about it.

–

I was surprised to find Di still awake; it had taken me a good hour to walk back with all the stopping and detours, but she was curled up on the sofa, staring at the TV. I popped my head around the door.

'I think I'll go straight up.'

'No – no, don't, Will.' She reached over to the remote control and turned the TV off. 'Please come in for a bit. I don't want you to avoid me.'

'I'm not avoiding you,' I said, but I didn't step over the threshold.

Di sat up and pushed her hair away from her face. Shadows were stretched across her features, and her eyes looked heavy and dull.

'Where did you go?' she asked.

'To Vee's.' I saw her eyes widen a little and continued, 'I had to see Gem, Di. I told you. I needed to talk to her.'

'You told her?'

I nodded slowly. 'She didn't really say much.'

'No, that doesn't surprise me.' Di sounded sad, tired. 'I don't think she expects much of me, but I'm glad she knows. I'm glad I know. I hate it that we were all in the dark for so long.'

'It happened, Di,' I said softly. 'It was a long time ago. There's no point us going over it.'

'It's true. I did stop drinking after.' Di was rubbing her hands now, no longer looking at me. 'I didn't know what happened that night at the pub, but I knew it was something bad. To lose your memory like that is scary and I knew I couldn't let that happen again to me.'

'That's why you understood what I've been going through,' I said. 'You've been the main person to stand by me.'

She nodded. 'As soon as Gem told me, I felt sick. Unless you've been through it, you can't possibly understand what it's like to root around in the darkness for things that aren't there. I only had it for a day – I can't even imagine what losing years is like.'

I stepped into the living room and perched on the arm of the sofa. 'It's just awful,' I said finally. 'I'm getting flashes now. Tiny ones, but they still don't seem to fit in with the life I thought I had. I can briefly picture myself at a desk or drinking with men I don't know. Or in my car...'

I flinched again, remembering my last dream. The sensation of crashing, of shouting and something tugging at me. It was quite overwhelming. Sickening even.

'I guess I must have been happy in my own way, but it's like my life branched off in a direction I didn't want it to. This accident has made me realise that.'

'I know you want Gem back,' Di said. 'But does she want you back?'

'I don't know. I've laid it all out for her. I've told her how things stand and how I feel.' I paused, giving myself a chance to get everything straight in my head. 'But this is about more than Gem. I realised that while I was walking back tonight. This is about reconnecting with the stuff from my past. I need to be the person I believe I truly am.'

Di smiled sadly. 'I understand that, Will, and this is coming from someone who has lived most of their life in fear. I don't think I've ever been able to face who I really am.'

'You need to try, Di,' I said, more urgently now. 'Look around you. Look at this safe little world you've produced for yourself. It's suffocating you. Hiding away doesn't make the past disappear, it doesn't make people forget.'

'I want to forget,' she whispered, her voice breaking.

I got up and reached for her hand. It was so delicate in mine; I was scared I might break her if I squeezed too tight.

'Forgetting isn't the answer,' I said gently. 'Forgetting doesn't make things go away, you know that as much as me. It just leaves a big hole in your life, an absence that feels wrong and unsettling. The only way you can move forward is by forgiving yourself.'

I saw her eyes were bright with tears. She blinked them away. 'Is that what you're going to do, Will?' she asked.

'I'm going to try,' I said.

'And what if Gem says no? What will you do then?'

'Then I will start again without her,' I said quietly. 'But far away from here. I don't think my heart could take being here without her. I think I would need to move on, once and for all.'

–

Before I even tried to attempt to get some sleep, I sent Jack a message, telling him I needed to see him in the morning. The image of us sitting side by side at the laundrette hadn't left me. We had been through so much together. *Too* much together.

I needed him.

My second message was to Nicola. I spent longer on this one, deleting my first draft and taking time over my second. I knew I needed to see her. I needed to be straight with her and I didn't want to give away too much with the words I chose, in case I hurt her. I felt like I barely knew the woman, but we had clearly been close. She deserved answers.

I put down the phone and crawled into bed, quietly pleased I had at least made an attempt to put things right. I didn't expect to drift off so quickly. Most nights, it took me hours, staring up at Gem's old ceiling, thinking the same sad old thoughts. But tonight, as soon as my eyes closed, my muscles relaxed slowly into the bed, the darkness came and dreams soon took over.

Fuck. No.

No.

I am in the car. I can feel the sensation of speed, the power of the engine around me. I'm clutching the wheel.

My head is pounding. Such a bad headache. The sun is making it worse, so much worse. It flashes too bright and briefly stuns me so I reach up to shield my face and rub at my eye. Take the pain away.

Just shut up — shut up! What is that noise?

I try to turn but my neck is stiff. My eyes are blinking in the bright light. My mouth tastes of shit.

The car is hurtling in a different direction. I try to grab the wheel again, but it's too late — I can see the bushes looming, their branches suddenly ripping against the sides like open arms.

I see the tree — tall and unforgiving. Waiting for me. A final gift.

My grip tightens. I scream, I think? I hear screams, anyway. But my mind is surprisingly clear.

All I can think as I slam into the trunk is: thank God it's over.

It's over.

I woke up in a cold sweat. The dream that had caught me in its horrible, twisty claws had finally let me free, but there was no sweet release — just a nauseating, gut-clenching sensation. I rushed to Di's bathroom, thinking for a moment that I was about to be sick, but nothing came up. Instead, I dry-heaved into the bowl, coughing hopelessly while tears stung my eyes.

I remembered everything about the crash and the events leading up to it.

Everything.

Getting in the car. The journey. The speed. Even the cheesy bloody music that was playing too loudly in the background.

I remembered it all and now I had no clue what I was going to do next.

Chapter Twenty-three

It was pretty rubbish after Will left. The entire atmosphere in the house had changed, as if we were all carefully sidestepping each other, too frightened to say the wrong thing. Brandon was stupidly apologetic for letting him in; Vee was raging and being far too protective over me – and Richard was quiet. Too bloody quiet. He was once again sitting at the dining table, sipping his wine and staring at me.

How much had he seen? Had he seen the kiss or just us talking after?

How the hell had I got into this bloody mess?

I couldn't even be bothered to address him. Instead, I grabbed myself another drink and slugged it back by the sink. Too much had happened in too short a space of time. My ex-boyfriend had just told me he'd been run over years ago! It was like something from a bloody awful soap opera and, on top of that, he had kissed me.

Worse still – I hadn't pulled away.

I took another slug of my drink, feeling a sick sensation rise inside me. This was all so bad, such a bloody mess. When did my life get into such a chaotic, laughable state?

'Gem! Come here!'

Vee more or less dragged me back out into the back garden where we had sat only hours earlier, happily chatting about her new baby. Now the energy was different. Vee was pacing up and down the patio, looking like she might kill someone.

I pulled the door closed and sat myself down on the nearby seat.

'It's times like these I wish I smoked,' I said.

Vee glared at me. 'You're not the only one.' She sat opposite me and leant forward. I could smell the cranberry juice on her breath. 'What's going on, Gem? Why are you still letting Will in your life like this?'

'It's complicated...' I felt helpless. 'I can't turn my feelings off.'

'Don't you remember what he did to you?' she hissed. 'Let me remind you: he shagged his brother's girlfriend, he humiliated you, he stayed away from home for days on end and he spoke to you like shit.'

'I know, I know all this...' I sat back. 'You don't need to remind me, Vee. This isn't exactly stuff I'm ever going to get over.'

'You were broken,' she continued, on an obvious rant now. 'Totally broken. In pieces. It was me and Bran who had to peel you off the floor and try to put you back together again. All those years you were with Will, all those years you loved him, and he threw it all in your face.'

'But Vee...' I sighed, body and mind suddenly weighed down by the events of this evening. 'There's more to it.'

I gave her the abridged version and watched her eyebrows rise as I talked about my drunken mother, Mel's mistake and Will's injury. I saw the scorn flash across her face when I mentioned how Will had struggled to cope and pushed us all away.

'Well, I did wonder if he was brain-damaged when he started hanging around with that rat, Matty.'

'It does make sense, all of it,' I replied. 'For so long I couldn't work out why Will had changed, and what had caused it to happen so quickly. We talked about it, didn't we? We said he must have had some kind of breakdown, some kind of life crisis.'

'To be honest, isn't that more likely?' Vee said coolly. 'Will had a lot of stress in his life. He lost his mum young and he was always broke, waiting for that bloody band to take off. I think it's more likely he thought that another life was more exciting than the one he was living.'

'Jeez, thanks.'

I rubbed my face, letting those words hit me like darts. I knew Will and I didn't have the most rock-and-roll lifestyle. It was simple – but it was ours. I never had any indication that it wasn't what Will wanted. If anything, he was the stay-at-home type of guy. When Jack started getting excited about the potential American tour, it was Will who had had cold feet. He'd been worried about the travelling, about the unknown. Funny, really, he never needed to worry – because by the time the tour actually happened, he and Jack were no longer talking, and Jack had done everything he could to get away from him.

'Look, I didn't mean that,' Vee said gently. 'I'm sorry, Gem. You guys had a great life together, we all know that. All I meant was—'

'I know what you meant, but I'm not sure it's true,' I interrupted. 'We were strong. We always were. There was a bond between us that I was sure would never break, and when it did...' I shook my head. 'What Will is saying is making sense to me. This first head injury was unreported, so he never got it checked. God knows what it did to him. Is it so unreasonable to think that he might have changed because of it?'

Vee shrugged. 'No, I guess not.'

'And you loved him as much as I did. You know what a great guy Will was – how important he was to all of us.'

Vee bowed her head. 'I know. I would love that guy to come back.'

'Well, now there's every chance that he is back. The man I loved is back.'

Vee was staring at me. I could see tears glinting in her eyes. 'You know how much I loved Will, Gem. I want this to be true too, but I don't want you to be hurt – that's all.'

I reached across and took her hand in mine. 'It's OK. I'm looking after myself, I promise.'

She smiled weakly. 'What are you going to do next?'

'About Will? I'm not sure.' I paused. 'But I do know I need to sort something else out.'

–

He wasn't happy, of course he wasn't. What else was I expecting? I explained the whole story to Richard, everything Will had said. I didn't mention the kiss. I still wasn't sure what he'd seen, but I felt it was unnecessary to bring more complications to an already heated conversation.

'This is crazy, Gem. Crazy!' He spluttered. 'I can't even believe you're thinking straight right now.'

We were back at the flat. *My* flat. The emphasis on it being mine had never felt so strong. I needed to be here by myself. I needed Richard gone. I wanted to be alone so I could think straight.

It had dawned on me at Vee's that I had gone too quickly from one relationship to another. I'd barely given myself a chance to heal from Will when I met Richard and allowed myself to go on a few dates with him. I suppose at the time I thought it was a good thing. Even Vee had encouraged it – 'You get over someone by getting under someone else,' she had said, and for a time it did work. Richard was so different from Will in every way. I could at least make out that I was moving on, especially when I found out that Will had done just that with Nicola. I knew it was pathetic and, looking back, it hadn't been fair to Richard at all – but I really thought I had been doing the right thing.

'I need to get my head straight,' I said firmly. 'This – all of this – is so confusing. I don't know what I want anymore.'

'Are you saying that you want to be with him?' Richard spat.

'No. I'm not saying that at all,' I replied firmly. 'But seeing Will like this, being close to him, has brought back a lot of feelings I thought I'd forgotten. It's made me question stuff.' I looked at him weakly. What did he want me to say? Did he really want me to hurt him?

'Are you saying you don't want to be with me?'

My eyes drifted down at the floor, to the swirly patterned carpet that Will and I had always laughed at but I had never been able to get rid of because it reminded me too much of Nan. Every part of this flat, every fibre of it, had a connection back to me, Will and my family.

'Richard, it's not fair,' I said finally. 'I can't keep being with you, pretending—'

'Pretending.' His voice was ice-cold. 'Have you been pretending this entire time?'

I slumped in my chair. 'No, not pretending. I haven't been. I've enjoyed it all – I've enjoyed us. But now, I'm just not sure it's enough.'

'Just because your ex has come along with a half-baked sob story.' Richard tutted under his breath.

'Honestly, Gem, you really will fall for anything, you know that?'

'I'm not falling for anything!'

'Oh yeah?' He was glaring at me with a snidey expression that I didn't even recognise. 'Did you know that I spoke to Will's girlfriend, Nicola? I knew she worked at the estate agency in town, so she was easy enough to trace.'

I was stunned into momentary silence. 'Why did you do that?'

'I wanted to get her take on things,' he replied coolly. 'I guessed she was feeling pretty shitty about it all, like I was, and I was right. We had both been pushed aside, while you two decided to relive your little fairy story. We decided to meet for a drink and share our experiences. The thing is, Nicola had a different view on the situation. Quite a different view, actually.'

I was still reeling from the fact he'd tracked down Nicola and spoken to her about this, about us. 'What did she say?'

'She told me she kicked Will out. She said that she couldn't cope with his mood swings since his accident and didn't much fancy being his nursemaid. According to Nicola, Will is having all sorts of delusions and false memories. She doesn't trust a word he says. In fact, she's quite worried about you…'

I felt numb. 'Richard, why are you telling me this?'

'I'm telling you this because I think you're making a big mistake. I think Will is conning you. He's created this little backstory so that you'll feel sorry for him and believe he's changed. He wants another victim now that his girlfriend has dumped him. He can't bear the idea of being alone.'

'I don't think that's true, Richard. I really think—'

Richard held out his hand to stop me. 'I don't need to hear any more, Gem. You've got to make your own mind up about all of this, but I just wish you'd take my advice and stop living in the past. You have someone now who loves you. Who will treat you right.' He bent down and kissed my forehead lightly. 'I'm going to move out for a bit, like you asked, give you some space, but I will be waiting. I love you, Gem, and I would never hurt you like that man did.'

And then quietly, without any fuss, he left the room.

—

I drank from a can of beer in the kitchen, while he packed his stuff up. I must have looked like a right heartless bitch, sitting there in my nice dress, with a lager stuffed in my hand – but I never was a classy one. The drink soothed me, mixing headily with the wine I had drunk at Vee's. I stared around the small room and wondered hopelessly how I had got into this mess.

I'd never asked for any of it. Not one bit.

I took another slug.

All I could think about was that kiss, and how good it had felt. I thought I'd forgotten what it was like to be that close to Will, to feel him against me, but now that it had happened again, every muscle in my body was aching for him even more.

Could Richard be right? Could Will be tricking me? Had Nicola really left him because of his unpredictable behaviour? That certainly matched the Will of before. I thought that he had been different recently, but I'd only seen him in short bursts of time.

Maybe he hadn't changed at all.

I put my beer down, feeling suddenly queasy. My vision was cloudy, and my head was already beginning to throb. I just wanted Richard gone so that I could curl up and sleep.

And then tomorrow... Tomorrow I would get to the bottom of this.

Before

Gem – July 2019

I woke up in the morning to an empty, cold bed. My stomach was raw and hollow, my head throbbing badly. I checked my phone, thinking that Will might have called – but there was nothing. My body was tense with fear as I walked through the flat. The remains of our 'special dinner' were still left on the side, and I felt queasy just looking at it.

Was Will OK? Had he been hurt? Where the hell was he?

I tried calling him again, but it just rang out. My throat was dry as I dialled Mel's number, and I licked my chapped lips.

'Gem?' She seemed surprised, or maybe flustered. 'Are you OK?'

'I'm sorry it's so early…' I stammered. 'I just wondered if you'd seen Will – the last I'd heard, he'd—'

'Oh!' She laughed awkwardly. 'Yeah, it's all right. He's here. He crashed out on the sofa. He probably didn't hear his phone.'

I thanked Mel stiffly, the throb in my head increasing. So, he'd stayed at the pub, probably getting drunk with Leon and Mel. I wouldn't have minded normally but he knew yesterday was an important night for me. I stared down at the creased, tight black dress that I'd slept in, suddenly feeling foolish and exposed.

Did Will even care about me at all?

He came back home later that morning. He couldn't even look at me, just sloped off to the kitchen to fetch some water, without a word.

'Where have you been?' I demanded. I couldn't help the anger that was building inside me, gaining energy when I saw the sulky, uncaring expression on his face.

'There was trouble at the pub. Mel was a bit upset so I offered to stay. I'm sorry.'

I watched him slug back his drink, hating the jealous feelings that were bothering me. I knew Mel and Will were close, and I knew Mel would have no interest in him, and yet...

'Why didn't you call me?' I asked. 'I was really worried.'

'I fell asleep. It's no big deal.'

He walked back into the living room slowly. He still looked exhausted. 'Have we got painkillers anywhere? I've taken some paracetamol already, but maybe I could have some ibuprofen...'

'I-I don't know...' I was still shocked by his sheer flippancy. 'Were you drinking?'

'Well, yeah. We had a few...'

He wasn't catching my eye. Something was off, I could feel it instinctively. My mouth still felt so dry, my stomach unsettled.

'I wanted you last night, Will. You know how important it was to me.'

'I know...' He rubbed his face. 'I was only helping Mel out, but I got caught up in other stuff.'

'How was she?' My voice was flat.

'Fine. It was no big deal, just some drunks that were acting up. Leon was exaggerating. I'll probably pop in and see her later on. Make sure she's OK.'

'Why?'

'Because that's the right thing to do.'

'Will, I—'

He slammed down his glass. His eyes seemed darker somehow, less warm. It was hard to look at them for long.

'Gem, I can't hear this right now. I need to get some sleep.'

'But you said you'd slept at the pub.'

Will ignored me and charged into the bedroom. I shook when he shut the door loudly.

He slept all day. That evening he barely spoke. Instead, he grunted words at me, swallowed a fistful of pills, and by seven he was back at The Swan for his shift.

I was left confused, angry and unsettled. I considered messaging Mel, but what would be the point? I would only end up looking silly and paranoid.

Later on, when I was taking the bins out, I saw Will's bike left carelessly by the bin store. The front looked bent and was badly marked.

Had he come off it drunk? Was that why he was angry?

The next day, I tried talking to Will again, but he wasn't interested.

'I can't stand your nagging,' he moaned. 'It hurts my head.'

He'd never accused me of that before.

'Something has happened, Will. Something has changed about you.'

Will just laughed. 'You're paranoid.' He sneered.

But I knew I wasn't. I knew I would be proved right – I just didn't expect it to be in such a life-changing way.

Chapter Twenty-four

Will – 2022

'Trust you to want to meet here – you always were a sentimental bastard.'

Jack pulled himself up next me, on the low-rising brick wall opposite our old house. To the left was the scrappy bit of green where we used to knock a ball about or make up crazy games with rules that were too long and too complicated for us to ever stick to.

'We were happy here, weren't we?' I said, nodding towards the tatty old house. I couldn't even stand to think of anyone else being there; that realisation was too hard to take in.

'It was a good place. Lots of happy memories,' Jack replied gently. 'I remember the fight I had with the council to keep us there. Thank God, Mum had the foresight to sign the tenancy over to me before she died. I like thinking that we kept the good feelings going in that house, even afterwards.'

'We did.' I nodded. 'You shouldn't have moved out. You'd still be there now.'

Jack shrugged. 'It wouldn't have been right without you, mate. It was our home. Our childhood home. I could never imagine it being anything else.'

'I keep thinking back to those days, though, and how easy everything was, at least before Mum died. We were so laid-back, so full of promise. We had all our dreams of making it big.' I paused, realising I was rambling a bit. 'We never would have expected this, would we? Us falling out and not talking? Me turning into someone I barely recognise, ending up making friends with people I'd not normally spend five minutes with...'

'What's all this about, Will?' Jack asked. 'You said you need to tell me something urgently. What is it?'

I told him.

I told him about Di and Mel. About my head injury. About the drinking. About the mess my life had suddenly become. It sounded like a daft plot for a film, but instead it was my life. My stupid, painful life.

Jack breathed out slowly and then swore under his breath.

'Will – seriously, mate? I can't believe so much happened.'

'And now my memory is coming back,' I added. 'Or at least some of it is. I remember the accident and some of the events leading up to it.'

Jack nudged me. 'Well, that's good, isn't it? Aren't you relieved?'

'I guess, but it's not quite what I was expecting.' I shifted on the brick wall, suddenly feeling uncomfortable on this hard surface. 'It's making me pretty certain about some things, but it's also very unnerving. I've got a little glimpse into how I was acting – it feels unfamiliar and...' I shook my head, unable to find the right word.

'Scary?' Jack offered.

'Yeah – scary. Really bloody scary.' I rubbed my legs, trying to make sense of what I was about to say. 'Jack, I hate myself for what I did to you. To Gem. To everyone who cared for me. I'm pretty sure I couldn't help it, but that doesn't mean I shouldn't feel bad for the pain I caused. When I think of Aby...'

Jack frowned. 'Well, according to her, you were both very drunk. Not that it changes anything.'

'No, of course it doesn't.' I heaved out a breath. 'We always had a code, didn't we, Jack? Even as kids, we would look out for each other.'

'Yeah. That's true enough. Mum would've slammed our heads together if we didn't.'

'And I broke that code, destroying the great thing we had.' I felt myself choke up. 'Jack, I know it's going to be hard, but I need you to forgive me. I really do. There's so much going on right now, so much that I can't get my head around, and I feel so lost. All I want is you and Gem and—'

Jack's hand reached across and gripped mine. He squeezed it tight.

'Will, it's OK. I can see the pain you're in and you don't need to put yourself through this anymore.' He coughed awkwardly. 'I broke the code too. I was too pig-headed, too angry to see that something was wrong. I should have noticed you weren't yourself. I should've worked it out – but instead, I ran away.'

'I don't blame you.'

'But I blame me,' Jack said firmly. 'I'm your older brother. I'm your mate. I'm the shitty little voice in your conscience keeping you on the straight and narrow, and I should have been there.'

I bowed my head, feeling a bit overcome with emotion.

Jack leant forward and whispered in my ear, 'I should have been here.'

We sat in silence for a bit, side by side, on the same wall where Jack had once pushed me off as a kid and I'd grazed my knee (but never told Mum because I would've hated to get him in trouble). The same wall where we had sat together eating ice creams freshly bought from the ice-cream truck.

The same wall where I'd told Jack, all those years ago, that I had fallen in love with Gem. That she was the girl for me, and I was certain I would marry her. I think Jack had laughed at the time. After all, I'd just been a kid – no more than ten years old.

But I wasn't laughing, because I knew it was true.

I still knew.

'Jack, I've told Gem we need to be together.'

'You did what?'

'I gatecrashed Vee's posh little dinner party. I took Gem aside and I told her,' I said. 'I don't know if I messed up, but I couldn't stand not saying anything. I couldn't stay quiet. And now the ball is in her court. It's up to her what she does next.'

'And what are you going to do if Gem decides she doesn't want you?' Jack asked plainly. 'Because after all, you couldn't blame her, Will. She has every reason to stick her finger up at you and move on.'

'The guy she's with is an idiot,' I told him.

Jack snorted. 'That is as may be, but he's Gem's idiot. She's with him for a reason. You can't muscle into that.'

'I know – and I'm not,' I said. 'I told you. It's up to her. If she's not interested, I'll understand. I have a back-up plan.'

'Which is?'

I smiled. 'I want to go back to our other happy place, Jack. I think that's the answer. I think, perhaps, if I have no future here, I need to start again.'

'Aw... our other happy place.' Jack's eyes lit up at the reminder. 'Bognor Regis is a good place, that's for sure, but you don't need to run, Will. You have enough people who love you here – Di, me, Nicola!'

I laughed. 'Di needs Gem, not me – and me being here is getting in the way of that. You need to go back to America, Jack. There's nothing here for you now, but the band is doing well. You need to capitalise on that while you can.'

'You could come with me,' Jack suggested quietly. 'The band was always meant to be us two. We can do that again.'

'No.' I was firm now. 'The band was always more your dream than mine. You know that as much as I do. I just loved being part of it at the time. I have other things I want to do – that I need to do – and I don't want to hold you back.'

Jack nodded slowly. 'That's fair enough. But I need you to know the offer is there.'

'I know. And I appreciate it.'

'I like being around you again,' Jack said softly. 'It's nice, you know.'

'I like it too,' I said. 'Really like it. We were always stronger together, weren't we?'

Jack nodded. He was fiddling with the cord on his sweatshirt and staring out towards the old house. 'You know, I don't have to go back just yet. The band is on a rest break anyway. We're not due to tour again for a few weeks.'

'Haven't you got other things to get back for?' I asked. 'What about your new girlfriend?'

Jack shrugged. 'Not really, nothing that can't wait. And Jamie will understand. I think being here with my kid brother is more important, don't you?'

I smiled. I didn't need to answer that.

'So, what about Nicola?' Jack asked carefully. 'I mean, she is still your girlfriend, isn't she? Doesn't she deserve to know what's going on?'

'Yeah,' I said coolly. 'And that's what I'll be sorting out next.'

–

Nicola seemed surprised that I wanted to come over. She offered to pick me up, but I refused and instead asked for the address so that I could get a cab. It seemed so crazy that I still didn't know the address of the place where I had been living for so long.

I wondered idly whether eventually all my memories would come back, and I might recall a time when I actually felt something for Nicola. Right now, that seemed unlikely. Although, in fairness, I was telling myself a lie. I did feel something towards Nicola.

I hated her.

I felt sick even as I rang the doorbell. There was nothing about this place that made me long to be back. If anything, I would've quite happily run back to the safety of Di's cramped and cosy home. But I knew I had to face this. The time was right.

Nicola let me in, greeting me warmly. She was dressed casually in jeans and a tight white jumper, which I guessed were much more expensive than they looked. When she smiled, it seemed stiff and awkward. As she leant in to kiss my cheek, I flinched. It wasn't just the touch, it was her scent – light, sweet, slightly sickly. I'd noticed it before, but this time it was more of a punch in the guts.

Nicola's face turned towards mine, shouting, screaming, her arm reaching forward. That smell. That perfume…

'What is it?' Nicola said, looking hurt. 'What have I done?'

'I told you I needed to talk,' I replied. 'I can explain it all then.'

Nicola stared at me for a moment or two and then simply nodded. I numbly followed her into the minimalistic and pretty characterless lounge. I reckoned Vee would like it here. It looked like it belonged in some glossy magazine.

I sat down gingerly on the armchair and Nicola perched on the sofa, looking smaller and thinner than I remembered. I wondered whether she was eating properly, or had she always been like this? It was still so awful to stare back at a face and just not know them at all.

But maybe I never knew Nicola. Not really. She was full of surprises.

'I remember the accident,' I said finally.

Nicola didn't reply at first. I saw one eyebrow rise slightly. She lifted her hand and brushed a long nail against her lips, as if she was about to chew it.

'Oh…' she said finally. 'What do you remember, then?'

'I remember a lot,' I said calmly. 'I remember that me and you had been in a hotel overnight. It didn't go so well, did it? We'd been arguing…'

Nicola continued to stare at me.

'What were we arguing about?' I asked.

She wrinkled her nose. 'It was something and nothing, Will. God, I can barely remember.'

'But I do, Nicola – I remember.' I leant forward. 'And it wasn't something and nothing.'

A tiny smile drifted on her face. 'OK, Will, so tell me. What was it?'

I matched her smile with a bigger one, though it was entirely devoid of humour. In my mind, it was as though the clouds were slowly clearing. There wasn't sunshine coming through, but something else: an icy awareness, both startling and freeing at the same time.

'I remember you shouting, Nicola. You were unhappy with me. You were demanding more attention, more fuss.' I paused. 'More money. You liked me to spend money on you, didn't you?'

She shrugged. 'What woman doesn't? It's hardly a crime.'

'But it was too much, wasn't it? You were running me dry. All those little trips, the expensive clothes and meals out. I've already had a call from the bank, telling me I need a meeting to discuss the state of my finances. At first, I didn't understand why I was in such a bad way – but now I remember.'

Nicola pulled a face. 'You loved spending the money as much as me, Will. Don't lay that all on me.'

'But you wanted more.' I pointed towards her hand. 'You wanted that, didn't you? You wanted my ring. And I wasn't prepared to give it to you.'

Nicola stared down at her finger. 'That's not true, Will. You proposed. You've forgotten.'

'No, I don't think I have. Because I can remember this argument very well now. It all came back in tiny fragments and then eventually as a whole.' I caught her eye, held her gaze. 'I never proposed to you, Nicola. You made that all up.'

I could have left it there. It was enough, after all. A massive lie that Nicola had invented while she stood at my bedside in hospital. I wondered how she got that ring on her finger. Did she sneak into my things to get it? Did she pluck my mum's precious ring out of the box and place it on her own hand? Did she examine it with that sickly grin on her face, making up a story in her head of how I proposed? Maybe she even started to believe it – truly believe that that ring belonged with her.

A ring that was always meant for someone else.

I could picture our argument clearly now. We were in a hotel room and it was early morning. I was tired and stressed, and my head was pounding. Nicola was sitting on the end of the bed, looking sulky.

'I didn't even want to talk about this,' I said. 'But you keep going on and on at me, asking me if I'm happy. I'm telling you now – I'm not.'

'I thought you'd liked coming here,' she whined. 'It was meant to be a romantic trip.'

'We can't keep booking these weekends away, Nic,' I'd replied in a voice that I barely recognised. It was gruff and abrupt, like I was talking to someone who didn't really matter. 'You're killing my credit card. I can't afford this.'

'You're killing the fun.' She shook back her hair and pouted slightly. 'I thought you were a new man now, Will. Someone who lived life on the edge, who took the bull by the horns. I thought you had shed your boring, stuffy image.'

I was pacing the room. I remembered the headache was getting worse, throbbing against my temples in a constant sickening beat. I wanted to take something for it, to make that pain go away, but I also wanted more. I wanted quiet and peace.

'I can't do this anymore, Nic. This isn't fun. This is just crazy, it's relentless.' I shook my head. 'I don't even know who I am anymore.'

Nicola stood up, arms crossed tightly across her body. 'You can't keep doing this, Will. Breaking up, making up. This isn't some kind of game.'

I spun round to face her. 'Isn't it? I feel like my life is a game to you. That you enjoy picking me up and placing me wherever you want me to be. I'm just another accessory to you, aren't I, Nic? Nothing more.'

'The next thing you're going to say is that you wish you were still with her,' Nicola spat. 'Don't you dare say that.'

'Well, maybe I do,' I shot back. 'What I had with Gem was real. This...'

I gestured around the room, at the expensive furnishings, at the empty bottle of champagne that we had managed to drink last night, despite my reservations, at the crumpled silky sheets.

'This is just a sham,' I said finally.

I saw the spark in her eyes. I wasn't sure if it was anger or pain. She glowered at me.

'I'm not going to marry you, Nic,' I continued. 'I don't care what you said last night, all those plans, all those big ideas. I just can't do it. I can't. This is too much for me.'

I rubbed my head.

'I make you happy, Will,' she said.

'No, you don't. That's the thing.' I was feeling so sick, the room was swirling. 'I don't think I've felt happy in a long time. This isn't fair on either of us, Nic. I'm sorry. It's over.'

I looked at Nicola now, defiance clear in the line of her shoulders even as she seemed to be getting smaller and smaller in my eyes.

'I broke up with you that morning,' I said coolly. 'I broke up with you, because I knew my life was escalating into something I didn't want. I was trying to put the brakes on it. I'd had enough.'

'You didn't know what you were saying,' Nicola muttered, but she didn't look sad. She looked anxious, as she bothered her teeth with the side of her nail again.

'I told you – I remember it all,' I continued. 'It was bad enough that you lied about us being together still, that you made out that we were engaged. I guess I could forgive that. I could convince myself that you cared about me and did it for some misguided sense of love. But you didn't ever really love me, did you, Nic? You just liked me because I splashed the cash on you. I lived the crazy life you wanted to be part of.'

Nicola shook her head. 'This is insane, Will. I think we need to take you back to the hospital. Maybe the accident has made you misremember things. You are confused and it's making you think—'

'No!' I slammed my hand on the arm of the chair. I'd had enough of this now. I couldn't stand to hear her lies a second longer. 'You have to stop this! You have to admit the truth. I know what you did, Nicola. I know what you did to me.'

Nicola stared back at me, her eyes brimming with tears. 'Will, I—'

'I know what you did that morning. Now, are you going to start telling the truth? Or am I?'

Chapter Twenty-five

Nicola – 2022

I didn't really like Will when I first met him. He was just some scruffy friend my brother had brought along to my parents' party. I mean, he was good-looking enough in a cute, rock-star kind of way, but that had never been my vibe. His attitude was shit, though, all sulky dark looks and slurred words. He barely paid me any attention when I first approached him. He was sneaking a quick fag behind a bush, totally uninterested in the huge bash that was being thrown. I wasn't even sure why he was there; it was pathetic, really.

'You leave Will alone,' Matty warned when he caught me eyeing him up. 'He's been through enough. He wouldn't be interested in you anyway…'

'Oh. You want to bet?'

To be honest, that was the only incentive I needed. If I was going to piss Matty off by pulling his sad little mate, then it was worth doing. It was just a shame the guy was totally caught up in his own misery and heartbreak. He hardly paid me any attention at all.

I'm not going to lie, I didn't like that much. But I've never been one to give up easily.

My first night with Will was pretty uneventful: he ended up unconscious on my bed after one too many shots and a sobbing fit, during which he bored me senseless, telling me the history of him and Gem. Seriously, you'd think those two were Romeo and bloody Juliet the way he went on – and, meantime, I just looked at him sympathetically and thought about the look on Matty's face when I told him that I'd ended up with Will in my bed. The truth was, he had barely even touched me. When he woke up, he was moaning again, feeling sorry for himself, and clutching his head and telling me he was in pain. He kept going on about these stupid headaches he'd been having.

I texted Matty, telling him what I'd done, but I embellished it a bit (what girl doesn't?). Matty wasn't impressed: one night meant nothing in his eyes – it only mattered if I got a few dates with him. He told me Will wouldn't take someone 'like me' seriously, and that only made me more determined. I was sick of Matty dismissing me, thinking I could never settle down. He always teased me for it and so did my parents – telling me I was too 'reckless' and constantly joking about my hopeless dating record. I suppose the anger kicked in a bit. Why couldn't someone like Will fall for me? After all, he was lucky to have me.

I decided it was time for me to stop screwing around, and Will could be the one to help me do it. I liked the fact that he wasn't clingy like the men I usually dated. Will was slightly aloof and a bit moody – it made me want him more. Most men had fallen over backwards to get me to commit, so I knew that after a little time Will would be the same.

The problem was, Will had somebody else on his mind.

'Do you think I should contact Gem?' he asked, showing me her picture, which was still saved as his screensaver. 'I messed up so badly – I'm not even sure how it got so bad. If I had just been honest with her from the start...'

I knew this was the weak point here – Gem. I wasn't going to stand a chance with Will if he was still obsessed with his ex. I had to make sure he kept away from her.

'She wouldn't want to know,' I told him gently. 'She'd never understand, someone like Gem. Do you really think she'd forgive you for hurting her like you did? Do you even deserve her?'

I saw the crack in his expression. This was killing him, but I pressed on. This man had to let go of his pathetic dreams. How many people stayed with their first love anyway? It was all a bit too Mills & Boon for me.

'She might understand...' he said. 'If I explained and told her I could change. That night with Aby was a mistake. I was so drunk...'

He swallowed down a fistful of painkillers. I could see his head was bothering him, but I assumed it was a hangover.

'She wouldn't and you couldn't risk it anyway. If you truly love someone, you let them go.'

He went quiet then. I knew I'd hit a nerve.

I didn't have to be so cruel. I could have helped him; he was clearly a man struggling with heartbreak, a man who seemed to be very low and often in pain. I could have told him to see a doctor, to get some advice, but I did none of those things. Instead, I continued to sow the seeds of doubt while being the sweet, loyal girl he could talk to. I knew that, eventually, he would see I was the better option.

'She doesn't want you back,' I told him. 'I heard her slagging you off in the pub, she was drunk and telling anyone that would listen that your relationship had been

307

on the rocks for years. She said she was relieved that you weren't with her now.'

I knew I was hurting him, but I also knew I had to break the ties between them. People are so easy to manipulate when you know how. It doesn't matter if you have to tell a few lies along the way. I was only saying what others suspected. Why else would their relationship have broken down so easily? It couldn't have been that perfect.

Will was full of bitterness and tears, but fear of rejection stopped him reaching out to Gem. Slowly but surely, he started to listen to me; after all, I was one of the few people who would put up with him now. His own brother had deserted him after his clumsy drunken fling with his girlfriend.

'I'll look after you,' I told Will, sensing the child in him crying out for something more. 'I can help you move on.'

He liked that. When he pulled me towards him, I felt something shift inside me, an emotion that I'd never felt before. That night we had the best sex I'd ever had. Raw and unforgiving, as he pressed me up against the wall of the kitchen. We were so hungry for each other that we'd barely had a chance to take our clothes off. Suddenly, it wasn't just about proving a point. I realised I was falling for Will.

I was also glad that Will was working with my brother. It was another connection that we had and the money he was earning meant that could fit in with my lifestyle. I began to reform Will, turning him into the man I had always imagined myself to be with. I bought his clothes and styled him, and he looked so much better under my care. He was so docile and compliant by then, it was easy. I kept him steady.

Matty offered Will the job at the agency and I persuaded Will to take it – he would need money if he was going to keep up with me.

Once Will started working with Matty, things changed again. Will realised he was good at it – I guess the anger and frustration that always seemed to bubble just below the surface had to go somewhere and they were channelled into his desire to make sales. He started earning good money and got a thrill from that, buying me nice things and taking me out to fancy restaurants. Most days he made me feel good, but sometimes he didn't.

His moods were like storms – sudden and brutal. I never knew when to expect them, but they left me feeling lost and isolated. He would look at me as if I were a stranger. I hated it, but at the same time I couldn't let go of him. It was like an addiction I needed to feed. I needed him to love me.

'I don't know why you're with me,' he said once. 'I can't feel that way about you. You know that. I'm not capable of loving anyone else.'

It stung. It really did. I wanted to be just as important to him as Gem had been. I wanted to matter. Pretty pathetic, when you think about it.

But deep inside, I was convinced that eventually things would work out and that we were meant to be. It sounds super corny now, but Will was the first man who made me want to settle down – that had to count for something, didn't it? I hated how jealous I felt towards Gem, and how Will seemed to be drawn to her like a magnet. I did everything I could to try to break that bond and make him see that he had a new life now, a better one – with me. If that meant putting up with his drinking with the lads or him being a bit mean to me at times, then so be it. As the months passed, Will seemed to be more settled and I felt like we were getting somewhere.

Just before the accident, Will cut out drinking. He'd had a scare after a party at work, and had come home looking pale and shaken.

'The lads said I had a fit,' he said. 'I was passed out on the office floor. I must've looked a right sight.'

'Did you go to hospital?' I asked.

'No, Matty said it was best not to. They don't need to know about our little after-hours parties, do they?' He smiled sadly. 'It's OK, I'm fine now.'

Except, he wasn't fine. He couldn't eat properly for days, he was shaking and he started complaining about his head again. It kept him up at night.

'I don't feel the same,' he grumbled, rubbing at his temples. 'Everything feels wrong.'

I was worried. I told him to go to the doctor, but he wouldn't listen; I could feel Will slipping away from me. He was on his phone a lot, looking at old photos. I once saw him type out a message to Gem and then quickly delete it when he noticed me nearby.

I was going to lose him. I could feel it. The thought of being alone again made me feel exposed, angry. I couldn't let that happen.

I booked the hotel in desperation. I thought a romantic night away was all we needed. I was going to tell him how much he meant to me and outline all my plans: we could get engaged, move away, start a new life together.

It was meant to be the solution to everything.

But it ended up being the start of the nightmare.

—

Will was sitting and looking at me now, his expression serious and distant. I knew he'd never loved me, but there had been a time when I thought he might grow to. I guess it's the hope that keeps you hanging on. Or drives you crazy. One of them, anyway.

I honestly did think he might adapt to the life I had pushed him into and finally become the man I needed him to be.

I was wrong.

'Just tell me,' he said tiredly. 'Tell me why you did it.'

There was no point in lying anymore. He was beginning to remember it all. Soon, it would all come back, I was sure of it, either in a rush all at once or as a slow drip – bit by bit. The truth always revealed itself eventually, I should have known that.

Either way, I was screwed. There was no going back.

So, I told him. I told him everything.

But I still had an ace card left to play.

Chapter Twenty-six

Gem – 2022

I woke up with a dry mouth, a headache and a sore neck from the stupidly awkward position I'd ended up sleeping in. I pulled myself out of bed, groaning and blinking for a moment at the empty space beside me, before I remembered. Richard was gone.

Sadness was a dull ache pulling at my stomach. I missed the warmth of his body, the comfort of knowing he was just there. God, I even missed the too-strong tea that he brought in every morning.

What was I doing? Was I cracking up completely? Pushing away a decent man for some kind of fantasy? None of this was healthy.

I glanced at my phone. There was a sweet message from Vee, reminding me that she was there if I needed her. There was also a text from Richard, telling me he was staying at his mate's house and 'hoped I'd slept OK'. Most surprising of all, there was a text from my mum.

She hated her phone and never texted. I read the message a few times, feeling a little anxious as the words washed over me.

I'm worried about you, Gem. You and Will. You are both going through so much. I'm here if you need me. I need you to know that just because Will is here, it doesn't mean I'm not there for you too.

I sniffed as I read it again. She was there for me? Really? When had my mum ever been there for me? She had always been too trapped in her world, too swamped in her own grief.

That was why it was easier for her to have Will there. Good old strong Will. He'd never given her a moment's grief. He'd never asked too much from her. He'd just been her constant support – something I could never be.

I was pretty sure Mum would take Will's side over anything. She hadn't even been there for me when Will and I broke up, too busy having another one of her own crises. I'd rung her, only days after Will had left me. My heart had been torn in two, my world broken – but Mum's first response had been telling.

'*Oh God, how is Will? He can't be thinking right to have done something like this.*'

Mum could never see Will as the bad guy; she would never be able to be objective.

I was on my own with this, as I couldn't keep bothering Vee and Brandon. This was my problem, my decision, and I had to choose what I was going to do next.

No one was going to interfere with it or offer their helpful advice. Only I could work out my next best move.

The shower helped a bit – at least, it helped to hammer against my sore muscles and relax me a little. I stayed in there far longer than usual, drenching my skin in the expensive gel that Richard had got me for Christmas and I had been scared to waste. It smelt so good, I wished I'd used it before now.

After drying myself and dressing in comfortable, ugly clothes, I considered having something to eat, but my stomach was still full of knots. I knew that nothing would settle it properly, so I made myself drink some orange juice instead, hoping the vitamins might reinvigorate me. I kept scanning my phone, half-expecting Will to message me, but there was nothing. It seemed he was sticking to his word and leaving me in peace. I was pleased in a way, but also a little disappointed. It was frustrating how dependent I was becoming on him again, how much I needed to hear from him.

The flat was too empty, too quiet, and no amount of dire daytime TV was going to distract me. I briefly scanned holidays online, gazing wistfully at the villas and beaches. It had only been a few days ago when Richard and I had been discussing our summer plans. Now, looking at these pretty and exotic places just made me feel sad.

I closed the laptop and stared bleakly around my flat, suddenly aware of how small and routine everything had become. Even this – my flat – had been part of me for so long that I felt I was part of the fixtures and fittings.

I was stale and I was stuck, not moving forward. I loved Will – I knew that. I knew I probably always would, but did that mean he was the right person to be with forever? Wasn't life about change? About taking new opportunities and running with them?

I couldn't keep going back to my safety net, to the things that were familiar. I wasn't even sure that was healthy.

It was like I was choking in here. The flat was too small, too stuffy, and I was consumed by memories, by expectation, by broken promises.

I had to get out. I wasn't sure where to go – but I had to leave.

Pulling on my trainers, I picked up my bag and slammed the door. For the first time in my life, I was glad to see the back of the place.

I ended up at the cafe on the High Street, huddled in the corner with a warm cup of coffee and staring out at the world beyond. My phone stayed buried in my pocket – I could do without the distractions.

'Gem? Fancy seeing you here.'

I looked up and my heart immediately dropped. Fiona! She was the last person I needed to see right now, but my smile immediately slipped into place, even as I fought the urge to get up and leave.

'Oh hi, Fiona. How are you?'

She was holding a large mug of tea in one hand and a plate with a slice of cake on it in the other. She slipped into the seat opposite me without bothering to ask if anyone else was sitting there; her knees brushed against mine, and I pushed back my chair a little, bristling at the intrusion.

'Holidays are great, aren't they,' she said, stabbing at her cake. It was a gooey chocolate one. Usually I'd be craving a slice, but today my tummy flipped in response. 'A chance to have some "me time".'

I stared back at her, wondering if she understood the irony in her statement. 'Yeah... I guess... I thought you were doing lots of voluntary work?'

Fiona had the decency to blush a little. 'Oh yes... that. Well, I am. Soon, but I'm at a loose end for a couple of weeks at least.'

I nodded. 'Of course.'

'I'm guessing you have lots of plans, don't you? You and Richard?' she said, smiling. 'I suppose that's a nice benefit of you both being teachers.'

I hesitated before answering, remembering that Richard was friends with her housemate. How much did she know already? Had she only sat next to me to get more gossip? I stirred my coffee slowly.

'Have you? Any plans?' she probed.

'I'm just taking every day as it comes,' I said. 'How about you?'

'Oh – nothing too exciting, not yet anyway.' She stabbed at the cake again. 'Do you want some of this? It's really nice.'

I touched my stomach. It still felt so tight and sore. 'No, no, it's OK. Thank you.'

Fiona paused, her fork still hovering mid-air. 'Gemma, I have to say, you don't look yourself. In fact, I've been saying for weeks that you haven't looked right at all. Is everything OK?'

I sighed; I was so confused. But the last thing I wanted to do was spill my guts out to Fiona, especially knowing that her flatmate knew Richard.

'I have to make some decisions, that's all,' I said finally. 'And it's hard to know which way to go. I guess you could say I'm a bit overwhelmed.'

'Ah, I see.' Fiona nodded, a crumb of cake resting on her lip. 'Maybe you should do what my nan always advised me to do in these sorts of situations.'

I resisted the urge to roll my eyes. 'Oh yeah, what's that?'

'Wait to see what fate throws at you. You're bound to get a sign. Something that will show you the right way to go.'

For the first time in a long while I found myself smiling genuinely at Fiona. The word fate again: my mum had always believed in it, and Will too. Maybe it was my turn.

'Do you know what?' I said. 'That kind of makes sense. I might try that.'

She waved her fork in response. 'Sometimes it's the only way. Follow the signs, Gemma. It's the only way to know what's best for your heart.'

–

A sign, Fiona had said. A sign. There I was, thinking something might show up and make things easier for me, but I certainly wasn't expecting to see one soon.

And the last person I expected to see was Nicola, but there she was, walking up the path outside my flat, looking a little lost and upset. I stiffened immediately, not even sure I wanted her to notice me, but it was too late – Nicola was soon waving at me and calling my name loudly. I could hardly run away.

'Gem! Oh God, I caught you. What a relief! I thought you were out. I just tried your door.'

'I was out,' I said needlessly. 'But I'm back now. Are you OK, Nicola?'

Her eyes were wide and watery, but she attempted a weak grin. 'Not really, Gem. Is it OK if we go inside? I really need to speak to you.'

What else could I do?

I invited her in.

Chapter Twenty-seven

Gem – 2022

Nicola was not acting her normal self. In fact, she was a bit of a sloppy, mucky mess. Her make-up was already bleeding around her eyes, and her hair looked ruffled and not as silky as usual. I wondered if she had slept properly. I think for the first time in forever, I looked better than her.

'I don't have much to offer you,' I said, glancing around my poky kitchen. 'I have tea, coffee... Beer?'

Her tiny nose wrinkled a little. 'Coffee... I guess.'

I picked up the jar and saw her body stiffen a little. Of course, she never drank instant.

'Sorry – I don't drink this much. Richard used to, before he got into his power smoothies, but he's taken his blender with him.' I was waffling, I knew. I made our drinks as I talked, trying to ignore the fact that my voice was a little more high-pitched than normal. A bit wobbly.

'He's taken so much. I forgot how much he had. It's funny how stuff accumulates over time, isn't it? A person moves in with you, first of all with just a suitcase, but suddenly they have box after box of stuff. It's crazy—'

'I didn't know Richard had gone.' Nicola's voice was haughty. She took my proffered coffee and stared at it blankly for a moment or two, before placing it carefully on the counter. She leant up against the side, her crop top riding up to reveal her slim, tight stomach. I felt a twinge of envy, thinking of Will's arms circling her waist. Of him kissing her neck, her chest...

'What happened?' she asked, snapping me back into reality.

'I... Well, we just needed some space.'

She nodded. 'Same as us, then, I guess. You know Will is living with your mum?'

I sipped my own coffee. It tasted rank. I remembered that this was why I stuck to the coffee-shop stuff. 'Yeah, I know. I can't say I'm too happy about it, but my mum and Will have always been close.'

'Yeah, well I'm not happy about it either, but what can you do...'

Nicola stared down at the floor. Her foot was carefully circling the tiles. She had tiny feet. I bet she was one of those girls that did ballet as a kid. She would be there with her delicate posing and pointing, while I was crashing through fields trying to learn football.

'Nicola – no offence, but why are you here?'

She looked up again and smiled weakly. 'You never liked me, did you, Gemma?'

I frowned. 'Well, not exactly. It's not personal, Nicola, but I don't even know you – and you are dating my ex.'

'That's true, but I think we have more in common than you think. We're both strong women – both have our own place, our own careers. We wouldn't let a man get to us, would we?'

I stared at Nicola, not sure where this was going. I hoped she didn't have a clue how long it took me to get over Will. Even though Vee and Brandon knew the truth, had seen the broken me, I had done well to cover it up –

to make out that I was strong and in control. It was the pretending that had kept me going.

'Are you going to take him back?' she asked finally. 'Please tell me honestly.'

'Nicola, I—'

She held out her hand. 'It's OK. I'm not too bothered if you are. I'm not here to start a fight or anything like that, I promise. I know he still loves you. I think he always has.' Her head dipped a little and she gave it a tiny shake. 'But I need to know if you are thinking of going back to him.'

I shrugged; my entire body was weary and overloaded. 'Maybe... I don't know. It's not that easy.'

'But you're thinking about it?'

What was the point in lying? My answer came out like a breath.

'Yes, yes I am.'

She nodded crisply. 'In that case there's something you need to know, Gemma. But I don't think you are going to like this very much.'

Nicola led me into the living room and gestured for me to sit down.

'What I'm going to show you, I need you to keep to yourself. If you tell Will, or anyone...' Her voice broke briefly. 'I need to trust you.'

'You can trust me,' I whispered. My heart was beating so fast. I wasn't sure what was happening, but I got the feeling it wouldn't be good. I waited, while Nicola stared at me for a moment or so longer and then peeled up her top.

And then I gasped.

Along her right side was a set of bruises. They were faded with time but still large and ugly. A graze also cut across her hip and more bruising looked to be evident across her ribs.

'What the hell happened to you?' I asked.

She pulled the top down, looking suddenly self-conscious. 'I didn't want to show you, Gem. But I think it's important you see, especially if you are thinking of going back to him.'

My hand fluttered towards my mouth. 'Are you saying... Are you saying that Will did this to you?'

I couldn't get my head round this at all. Will had never been violent to me, never. Angry – yes. Dismissive, cold and distant – but never violent. This wasn't even making sense.

Tears were streaming down Nicola's face. She sat herself carefully down on the seat opposite me.

'I didn't want to tell you; I knew you'd get upset,' she repeated.

'Of course, I'm upset. I don't understand how, or why...' I shook my head. 'Will has never done anything like that to me.'

'Me neither.' She rubbed at her eyes. 'But he changed, over time... You know how he was getting. You know how bad his moods were, and eventually he just snapped.'

'What happened?'

She sighed. 'It was the night before the accident. We had a big row. It was my fault, probably. I was pushing him – I felt like he was drifting away from me a bit, wasn't interested in anything, really, and he was starting to talk about you again.'

'He was?' I couldn't help my response. I saw Nicola's eyes glint briefly.

'Yeah, he was. It was driving me mad. I felt like I couldn't live up to your standards, no matter how hard I tried.'

I had to fight back a laugh. Seriously! Nicola was so glamourous and put-together, yet here she was declaring that she was trying to live up to my standards.

'I was pushing Will,' Nicola continued. 'I kept on at him, asking him when we were going to move things forward. Get engaged, that sort of thing...'

'But I thought you were...' My gaze drifted towards her hand, and I saw that Will's mum's ring was no longer there.

'Oh,' I said quietly. 'I'm sorry.'

But was I? Why had she been wearing it in hospital? Had she taken it to try and trick Will? That would've been pretty sick if she had...

'I tried it on,' she said, as if reading my mind. 'While Will was in hospital, I tried it on and imagined what life might have been like. I just forgot to take it off. Then when I was told he had lost his memory...' Her shoulders slumped, and she sniffed loudly. 'I should have said something then, I know, but it felt so right to have the ring in place. I'd dreamt about being engaged to Will; I knew it would only be a matter of time.'

My mouth dropped open in utter shock at her audacity. I couldn't even begin to find the words to respond to what she was telling me.

'You don't understand, Gem. It's been hard for me too.'

'You faked your engagement!'

'I know. I know...' Her voice was barely a whisper. 'I just got carried away in the lie. When Will saw the ring and accepted we were engaged, I didn't see the harm. I

322

thought maybe it might be something good that could come out of the accident – something positive...'

I blew out a breath. 'But now you're telling me he hurt you the night before the accident?'

She nodded slowly, not looking at me. 'Yeah. The row got bad. I said some stuff I shouldn't have; he said some more things. I went into the bathroom, and he followed me in. He ended up shoving me and I fell against the bath.' She flinched, as if she was reliving the experience. 'It was reckless and scary, and I think Will felt bad about it after, but...'

'But what?'

'It shows you what he is capable of.'

I hesitated. This was so hard to hear. It didn't sound right, not one part of it – and yet a nagging doubt was gnawing deep inside my brain. Will had changed, we all knew that. He claimed it was the first accident that had caused it, but had it made him lash out in rage too?

'He says he's different now?' I whispered. It sounded like a question, almost as if I hoped Nicola would have the answer.

'Yeah, he says that,' she replied softly. 'He says a lot of things, Gem. He's scared of being alone. He wants things to be back to normal, but you have to be realistic here. This man has a brain injury. He's not been acting reasonably for some time. You only see him for short bursts, so you don't know what he's really capable of.'

'Have you noticed anything different? More recently?' I asked.

Nicola straightened up on her seat. 'Yesterday I saw him, Gem, and he was horrible again. Angry and nasty and—'

'And what?'

She closed her eyes briefly and when she opened them again, I saw the panic in her expression.

'Scary, Gem. He was really scary,' she said finally. 'It's made me realise that he will never change. Nothing positive can come from this...'

I think that was the moment when my broken heart, which I had spent so long piecing back together, finally splintered into an unholy mess.

–

She left and I was alone again. I moved mechanically, flushing that godawful coffee down the sink and then getting myself a cold beer instead. It was still early, but who cared! I was on holiday. I'd just been told horrific news. I needed something to take the edge off.

While I drank, I weighed up the options. Could Nicola be telling me the truth? I couldn't deny the bruises that were presented to me – and why would a woman lie about such things? I'd seen what Vee had gone through when her parents had fought. I knew what destruction and pain this could cause. I also knew it wasn't something I could even risk putting myself through.

'Oh Will,' I whispered out loud. 'What happened to you?'

I couldn't call him. I didn't want to confront him. There was a risk that he could get angry with Nicola again, and what would he say anyway? I knew he would deny it, so how would that be helpful? I knew how much he had changed, and I was already worried that his moods could get worse. Nicola was right: I'd only been seeing Will in snatched moments; I wasn't living with him day in, day out, when he was exposed to real-life pressures.

I couldn't risk all the protection I had built up for myself, for the sake of chasing a stupid fairy-tale ending. I had to listen to what life was presenting me with. Fiona, as annoying as she was, was probably right: I had to follow the signs. And the signs weren't looking very good.

It was all too much.

I slugged my beer some more and then pulled out my phone. The tears were blurring my eyes a little, but I knew what I had to do. I needed to take back control. My message to Will was short and not at all sweet:

> Will – I'm sorry. I can't see you anymore.
> I have my reasons, but I can't go into them right now. Just please believe me that they are good ones.
> This is really hard. I hope you let me go in peace.
> Gem x

And then I put my head on the table and cried.

Before

Gem – August 2019

'I'm so sorry, Gem. I didn't want to be the one to tell you.'

I put my phone down calmly. No tears would come. I felt completely motionless, almost robotic.

I walked into the bedroom where Will was sleeping off another drinking session. In the space of a few weeks, this man I had known for so long had turned into a stranger. Now he spent his spare time drinking with that knob Matty and his friends. He had given up his job at The Swan. There was talk he had fallen out with Mel.

And now this.

'That was Jack on the phone.' My voice was loud. Will stirred, groaning a little. His hand reached up to rub his eyes and he pulled himself up a little.

'What?'

'I said, that was Jack on the phone.'

'So?' Will stared at me coldly. I was getting used to that look. It didn't make me shiver anymore; it just made me sad.

'So, he told me you two had words last night. He told me he's now going on tour without you.'

Will pulled a face, his 'not bothered' expression. 'He was being an idiot last night. You should be pleased, anyway. You didn't what me to go.'

'That isn't true.'

Will knew I'd planned to go with them, I had been excited. This tour could've taken his career, our life, into a new direction. Yet now, it felt like everything was crumbling into this one, awful point.

'I want you to leave, Will.'

He sat up. 'You what?'

'You heard. I want you to leave – for good. It's over.'

'Have you lost your mind?'

'No, no I haven't…' I spoke slowly, trying desperately to keep my voice level. 'But I actually think you might have.'

'Me and Jack'll be all right. I'll speak to him, I'll sort it out,' Will said, pulling himself off the bed. 'It's all something over nothing.'

'So, sleeping with Jack's girlfriend was nothing?' My words were ice now. 'I want you to get out, Will, and never come back. We're through. I can't do this anymore.'

–

I sat frozen on the sofa while he packed up his things. My mind was racing. Jack thought Will and Aby had been a drunken one-off fling, but I wasn't so sure. Something had been going on for weeks; something had changed.

It didn't matter either way. Jack was as broken as me. He had been in tears on the phone, told me about the row he and Will had had, and the nasty things Will had said to him.

We were both done. We had to move on, before this man destroyed us even more.

Will came out of the bedroom, clutching a holdall. The rest of his things he could collect later.

'I'm sorry, Gem,' he managed; he looked pale, ill. 'I don't even know what I'm thinking at the moment.'

'I'm sorry too,' I whispered.

'I didn't mean to hurt you. I just feel so...' He shook his head. 'It seems silly saying it.'

'What?'

'I feel jumbled up. Confused. I'm not sure what I want at the moment.'

That stung. I flinched but refused to cry. Not in front of him.

'Is it really over?' he asked quietly.

I stared at his face. That face I had known since we were children. The one I had loved for so long. I reached out and touched his cheek briefly, but there was no tenderness there.

'You are a stranger now,' I said softly. 'I don't know who you are. You are a stranger with Will's face.'

He left without fuss and once the door closed, I allowed myself to collapse.

In just a few weeks my entire world had been destroyed.

Chapter Twenty-eight

'I shouldn't have asked you to help me.'

'It's OK, really. What else was I going to do with my day anyway? At least we have Di, in the car. I wouldn't fancy lugging this lot back on the bus.'

I grinned. Jack was currently carrying two battered-looking and very overfilled boxes. They were stuffed full of items that I didn't even recognise – flashy trainers, a weird-looking juicer, a chest expander. I saw Jack peer over the edge of the top one as we walked.

'You really were a bit of a health freak, weren't you. There are about six boxes of protein powder in here. Who even needs that much!'

'I told Nicola not to pack that stuff,' I replied. 'She might as well have thrown it away.'

To be fair, I'd told Nicola not to pack any of it. I was happy to come here and collect whatever I needed – a few clothes, some shoes, my toiletries – but it looked like she had gone mad, throwing my stuff into various bags and boxes. I was clutching two bin bags rammed full of designer clothes that I probably wouldn't wear again. It wasn't that they weren't good quality, but rather that they were just too fancy for me. I didn't even know what had happened to my sports tops and trackie bottoms. I was betting my favourite Liverpool top had made its way into the bin.

'I guess you should be thankful she didn't tear the lot up,' Jack said. 'I mean, that look on her face...'

I grimaced a little. It hadn't been pleasant. Nicola seemed to be fluctuating from upset and sulky to angry and dismissive. I had tried again to talk to her, to take her to one side in the house and tell her that it was OK, that I wasn't bothered about what had happened. I was sick of focusing on the past – a past that was lurking too deep in the shadows for me. All I wanted to do was move forward.

'I won't forgive you for this,' Nicola had hissed, as I walked down the hall clutching the last of my things. 'I won't ever forgive you for deserting me like this.'

'You know I didn't want it to be like this, but it's best for both of us,' I said. 'Surely you can't believe we could have carried on after what you did.'

'You're toxic, do you know that, Will?' she shouted as I reached the front door. 'Toxic. Everyone you go near, you hurt.'

'I heard what she said,' Jack said a little while later. 'It wasn't nice.'

I paused, placing the heavy bags down on the path and giving myself a moment to flex my aching arms. 'It's OK. It's what I expected. She's hardly going to be happy about all of this, is she?'

But I had to admit that last comment had hurt. Was she right? Was I toxic?

'But if what you say about her is true... If what you remember...' Jack shook his head in obvious frustration. I could tell he had that look on his face, the one that meant he was getting worked up and wanted to defend me.

'I don't want to do anything more, Jack. The police have dropped the case against me. They have ruled it was an accidental crash, so it's best to leave it at that.'

'If they knew the truth it would be different, though,' Jack said. 'She could have killed you, Will.'

'But she didn't, did she?'

I thought of Nicola, standing alone in the house, staring at me with a false sense of entitlement. I knew she felt awful. She might act like a confident woman, with the nice house and flash car, but I could see the fragile person behind it all. It's funny how being in a delicate state yourself makes you recognise it more in others. I could see that Nicola really cared for me, possibly even loved me, and whatever she had done, it had been out of misguided beliefs rather than dangerous intentions.

I hadn't been a good boyfriend to Nicola and that was because she wasn't really with me. She had dated the damaged, broken version of me. I couldn't even begin to imagine how hard that must have been for her. I thought of the accident and still felt a trickle of fear run through my body, mixed with a hint of anger. She shouldn't have done what she did. However, the accident gave me my life back – and for that reason, I had something to thank her for. I was back now. I wanted to focus on my future, not my past.

'I've hurt her enough already,' I said quietly. 'I don't need to do anything more.'

Di was playing heavy-rock music in the car and sitting back in her seat with quite a peaceful look on her face.

Jack opened the boot and heaved in my boxes. I threw in my bags.

'It's not much to show for a man of my age, is it?' I said, staring grimly into the space.

'You should see me: I travel even lighter.' Jack slammed the boot down hard. 'It's not about the things, is it? It's about the people around you and the life you choose to live. Don't you remember your plans to travel the country in a camper van?'

I laughed. 'God, yeah. I haven't given up on that one yet.'

Jack squeezed my arm. 'Good, because maybe that's what you need, eh? A fresh start. A fresh perspective?'

'Yeah, maybe you're right.'

My hand instinctively brushed the phone in my pocket. I still hadn't heard from Gem. I didn't know what she was thinking or how she felt after the kiss. So much relied on her decision. I felt like she held the coin that would decide what I would do next – heads. Or tails.

Which one would it be?

Di turned down the volume and smiled as we piled back in the car.

'That was quick. I take it her ladyship didn't have much to say.'

Jack pushed himself into the back seat. 'Oh, she had a few things to say to Will, all right.'

'Well, I suppose that's to be expected,' Di reasoned.

'She even had a pop at you,' Jack added. I glared at him through the windscreen mirror; Di didn't need to hear all of that.

'Oh yeah? What did she say?'

'Oh, nothing much.' Jack was clearly trying to play it down. 'Something about Will going back to Gem's mum because he didn't have one of his own. I don't think Nicola understands the relationship we all have.'

I nodded, just glad that Jack had left out 'Gem's mental mum' from his explanation.

Di started the car. 'I guess it's hard for her, isn't it? She's having to face up to a lot of what she's done.'

Jack flashed me a look and I pulled a face. I hadn't told her the full extent of what had happened yet and what I remembered. I wasn't quite sure how she would take it. There had been so many revelations recently.

Di clearly caught our exchange. 'What's going on with the face pulling? Is there something you wanted to tell me?'

I slumped back into my seat. 'Yeah, maybe later, Di. When we get home, eh? I'm gagging for a tea.'

Di nodded stiffly but her expression was grim. 'OK, but don't leave it too long. We've had enough secrets between us.'

She was right, of course she was, and the comment hung heavily between us. There had been secrets, deceptions and hidden memories – which had all led to this almighty mess I was in right now.

'I just want an easy life, Di,' I muttered.

'Amen to that!' Jack replied.

We drove away in silence, Di's radio turned down and our own conversation muted. I knew I had lots of talking to do, so it was nice to appreciate the quiet while I could. In my pocket, my phone remained still – no buzz of a text or chime for a call. In my mind's eye I could see the coin still spinning in mid-flight. Spinning and spinning, and I had no clue which way it was about to land.

Back at Di's house, I put my stuff in Gem's tiny room, apologising out loud for filling it full of rubbish. I only knew this room as a tidy, ordered place. Somewhere Gem would occasionally stay if her nan was poorly or if her mum had persuaded her to remain the night. It had never really looked like a teenager's room and had always seemed a bit sad to me – faded posters of popstars that Gem had long grown out of, teddies that she no longer needed to cuddle, a pink duvet that she'd hated for being too babyish.

This room should have had Gem in it. She should have grown up in here. Instead, she'd packed up her things at thirteen and slipped away. Now it would be vacated again while it stored all of my worldly goods, things that I didn't even think I wanted.

Was this room destined to be a halfway house? A place for people to pass through and never stay? There was a sense of that here. A sense of time passing, and nothing being resolved. I thought I liked this bedroom when I first stayed here, but I was wrong. I hated it.

It represented everything that was miserable in my life right now.

–

'I'm not going to stay much longer, Di,' I said, sitting down next to her on the sofa. 'I've been here long enough as it is already. I need to move on.'

'Oh.' Di reached for her tea. She had made us both one, as she always did. I watched as she blew on the surface and then took a long sip. She always seemed to be able to drink the stuff red-hot, while I had to leave mine until it was practically cold.

'Where will you go?' she asked. 'What about your stuff?'

'It depends...' My hand touched my pocket instinctively. 'There's somewhere I'd like to go. I've talked to Jack about it too, but...'

Di followed my gaze. 'But you'd like to take Gem too?'

My shoulders sagged a little. 'Yeah, I would like that, but Gem has to want it too. I'm waiting for a text from her. Or a call – something. She needs to tell me what she wants.'

'Maybe she doesn't know.'

'Then I'll give her time.' I shrugged. 'I seem to have plenty of that all of a sudden.'

Di wrapped her hands around her cup and sat back a little. 'You've been through so much, Will. Mel knocking you over, getting yourself in another car accident – not being able to remember. I can't believe how calm you are about everything.'

'It's just how I am.' I frowned. 'Isn't it?'

Di nodded. 'That's why I should've known there was something wrong with you before. If only my own brain had been working properly. I should've known that you would never have changed like that! Not unless something bad had happened to you. You've always been so stoic. You've been mine and Gem's rock. Even when your mum died...'

Her voice broke. I reached over and squeezed her shoulder. She flapped her hand, showing me she could continue.

'Even when your mum died, you carried on. You finished school, you stuck by Gem, you refused to be drawn into negative thinking.'

'I couldn't, Di. Mum always told me to live my best life and that's what I've tried to do.' I paused. 'Even though it feels like it's been two lives at the moment.'

'You've almost been given a gift,' Di said softly. 'You've seen what your life could have been like if you took a different direction. Now you have a chance to live how you really want to.'

335

With Gem, I thought. That's the only way I want to. With Gem. If she said no to me, I wasn't sure I could be so positive.

'Do you remember everything now?' Di asked.

I shook my head. 'No, but more stuff is coming back. I don't know if it'll all come, who knows.'

'What really happened on the morning of the accident?' Di asked softly. 'Nicola was there, wasn't she?'

I nodded.

'Did she cause the accident?'

I nodded again, feeling the tears in my eyes. I hated reliving it, but I had no choice. It haunted my dreams now.

'What happened, Will?' Di repeated, firmer this time.

I rubbed my eyes. I was so tired. Tired of this, tired of explaining, tired of even thinking about it all – but I knew I had to confirm Di's gut instinct. The fact that she'd guessed that the accident wasn't my fault just confirmed everything I already knew about her – she had always believed in me. She had never given up.

'We had had a row,' I said. 'I don't remember all of it, only flashes, but it happened the night before. Nicola was pushing to move the relationship to something more serious. I think I only saw it as something...' I sighed. I didn't even know what I saw it as. Fun? A stopgap? Something to take my mind off Gem and the injury I was concealing from everyone?

'Anyway, whatever it was, it wasn't enough for Nicola,' I said quietly. 'I feel bad about that. She probably felt let down, I suppose. She wanted to be engaged. She wanted—'

'To be more important than Gemma?' Di said.

I nodded. 'Yeah, I guess so. Gem was the block between us. I'm guessing I wasn't really ready to be with anyone. Not then, anyway. I think I told her so that night, that I wanted to end it. I think I realised that we weren't going anywhere.'

'And she didn't take it too well?'

My thoughts drifted, my dreams coming back to the forefront. It was so much clearer now – the car journey home that morning. I could even remember my splitting headache, the sickness that was washing over me, the film of sweat that was clinging to my skin.

And I remembered Nicola sitting beside me.

'I wasn't feeling well,' I said. 'I didn't want to drive, but Nicola was too busy sulking about our argument. She told me her eyes were sore, so I had no choice but to take the wheel. I remember my head was pounding – I wasn't right.'

Di's hand flew up to her mouth. 'Oh, Will – it's worse than I thought, did that first accident cause lasting damage? Was that the reason you crashed the car?'

'No, no, it wasn't that,' I said. 'But my sore head led to another argument. Nicola was telling me I was putting it on, trying to get sympathy. She reckoned I was going to go crying back to Gem and tell her how poorly I was.' I shook my head. 'It just shows you how she didn't know me at all! I never wanted to tell Gem, I didn't want to worry her.'

Di's head dropped. 'I know you didn't. I can see that. It makes everything much worse.'

'Di, even I didn't know how injured I was. I just thought my headaches were caused by stress and hangovers from too many nights out. I tried to ignore Nicola, but she was going on and on at me that morning. Her voice

337

was getting louder, more of a screech – I can remember how that shot through my brain. It really hurt! She was saying all sorts, calling me a waster and a loser, and telling me she was better off alone than with me. I could deal with all of that – it was water off a duck's back. But then she said something I couldn't forgive.'

Di's eyes darkened. 'What did she say?'

'She said I might as well go back to that common slag, Gem. She was all I deserved.' I took a sharp breath, those words reverberating around my head. 'I snapped. As we were turning that sharp bend, I shouted at Nicola. I told her what I thought of her – that I never loved her. That I hadn't been thinking straight.'

I could picture it now. It's funny how something that had been lost had come back much sharper. I could smell Nicola's sweet perfume as she shifted closer in her seat. I could see the road ahead, winding and twisting. The trees on the edge leaning over, an old farm building as we swept by, brambles spilling into our path. I remembered the sun glinting low in the sky, catching my eyes and making me squint briefly. I remembered reaching up to protect my eyes from the glare, to stop the brightness hurting my head even more.

And that's when she did it.

'She screamed and then she grabbed the wheel. I only had one hand on it at the time, so my control wasn't good. She was so quick – lightning-quick – and in moments we were tearing off the road towards that tree.'

'Oh my God!' Di was shaking. She reached towards me, pressed her hand into mine. 'She tried to kill both of you.'

'I don't know. I don't think she was thinking straight. All I know is that the car hit that tree and knocked me unconscious, and Nicola – well, she was surprisingly OK. A few bruises to her side, a sore rib, but that was it. She walked away.'

'And left you,' Di whispered. 'She left you there, in the car. And all this time allowed you to think it was your fault.'

'She got out and called Matty, apparently, and he picked her up, further on from the accident. She had already called the emergency services – apparently that redeems her in her eyes.' I scoffed. 'And I ended up in hospital with concussion, bust ribs and a bleed on my brain that maybe had already been there for months, slowly eating away at my memory, at me. Perhaps the crash made it worse, or maybe it just revealed it. In a strange way, Nicola saved my life that day.'

Di squeezed my hand. 'That's all we can be thankful for, Will. From this bloody mess, we've got you back. We've got Will back.'

I touched my pocket again, willing it to buzz. 'Yeah, I'm back,' I whispered.

I just wished Gem was too.

–

It was a relief, telling Di. Talking it all through again made everything so much more solid in my mind. Di told me I had to tell Gem too, but right now I knew I had thrown too much at her already. She needed time and I had to give her that. This accident had been about me and Nicola, and I'd put that to rest now. I wasn't going to report Nicola; I knew I had caused her enough hurt.

I just needed never to see her again.

All I wanted to do was go to bed and sleep. To have a night uninterrupted by nightmares. To be free from my past.

I was about to slip upstairs to the bedroom when the doorbell rang. I was surprised. Although it wasn't late, Di didn't usually have visitors past seven. In fact, she barely had any visitors at all. She was in the bath, so I had no option but to answer it.

As I pulled the door open, I couldn't believe who I saw standing there.

Richard.

'Hello, Will,' he said. 'Just the person.'

I stared at his face just a few seconds too long, not quite able to work out why he was there, on the doorstep. Then, as if on cue, my phone buzzed in my pocket. Instinctively, I reached for it, pulling it out.

Gem.

> Will – I'm sorry. I can't see you anymore.
> I have my reasons, but I can't go into them
> right now. Just please believe me that they
> are good ones.
> This is really hard. I hope you let me go in
> peace.
> Gem x

I stared back at Richard, tears fresh in my eyes. Was this why he was here? Had he come to jeer? To make this a million times worse?

'Was that Gem?' he asked. His face was serious, his eyes kind. All I could do was nod. My mouth was numb.

'I think I can guess what she's said from your face,' he said, sighing. 'Will, that's why I'm here. I need to explain.'

'Explain what?' I muttered.

'I need to explain why you can never see Gem again.'

Chapter Twenty-nine

Gem — 2022

I hadn't been looking forward to being back in this place, but I needn't have worried. Despite the glaring bright lights and clinical smell, this department had an altogether different vibe. Vee was sitting next to me, subconsciously rubbing her non-existent bump. This was a simple check-up due to Vee's history of miscarriages — routine bloods, that sort of thing. Vee had said that she was fine going alone, but I insisted on keeping her company. I knew how grim it could be waiting around, especially on your own. The little waiting area was packed full of women in various stages of pregnancy, some looking more accustomed to it than others. One woman was huddled in the corner — her skin had a waxy, sickly sheen to it, and her hair looked greasy and was dragged tightly away from her face. She had been staring at her phone for ages but had barely moved. She looked completely zoned out.

I nudged Vee. 'That'll be me if I ever end up pregnant. I wouldn't so much bloom as slowly rot.'

Vee rolled her eyes. 'You don't know that. For all you know, you could be a natural.'

'What, like my mum?'

I folded my arms across my chest, drawing them tight as if I could keep the anger inside. That was the trouble, wasn't it? Some people shouldn't be allowed to be parents. Just look at the destruction they caused.

'Your mum went through a lot, Gem. You know that. It's a hard thing to live with.'

'She just kept mucking up,' I muttered. 'She fell asleep with a fag in her hand, who does that? She killed her own husband and then, years later, she helped to injure my own boyfriend and was so drunk she couldn't even remember.'

Vee tutted softly under her breath. 'Your life is like something from a soap opera.'

'It's not funny.'

'No, I know it's not. I'm sorry.'

I sat back on the hard plastic chair. Opposite me, the clock ticked far too slowly – we still had a ten-minute wait. I stared numbly at the posters, the ones that warned about HPV and abusive relationships. I wondered if life was just so much simpler if you stayed single.

'For what it's worth, me and Brandon always said you'd make a great mum,' Vee said suddenly. 'I wish he was here, you know? I get it that he has a deadline, and this is just a routine thing, but after all we've been through…'

I reached across and grabbed her hand. 'You're still scared. I get that.'

'All those miscarriages. All those missed chances for love. Every time it happened, a little bit of hope died within me.' Vee circled her hand across her tummy, pausing for a moment. 'It could have pushed us apart, you know? We rowed so often, we cried so many times, but I do truly believe that Brandon and I are stronger together.'

'You are,' I said. 'I believe that too.'

'And I believe it of you and Will too,' she said firmly. 'I think you're meant to be.'

I hesitated, not sure what to say. In the car, on the way up here, I'd told Vee about Nicola's little visit, about her disclosure to me. Vee hadn't said much in reply – she seemed to be taking it all in, or maybe she was too angry to respond. I knew she would hate to think of anyone being hurt.

'But I told you what Nicola said. She showed me the bruises.'

Vee shrugged. 'They could be from something else, Gem. Why are you so quick to believe her? This is Will we are talking about – Will! We both know he's not violent!'

'But what about his injury...'

'Even when he changed, he didn't hurt you, did he? You never felt at risk, did you?'

I shook my head. No, I didn't. Yes, he had made me feel sad and frustrated, but I'd never felt scared.

'I was so quick to accept it as truth,' I whispered. 'She seemed so convincing.'

'I'm sure she did. This is Nicola after all, but I think you need to be careful what you believe.'

'I'm not sure what is real anymore, Vee, that's the problem.'

Vee was about to answer when her name was called by the nurse. I jumped up with her, but Vee planted a small kiss on my cheek.

'I'll be fine. You wait here, have a think. I've got this.'

As I watched her walk away, I heard my phone buzz. Reaching for it, I half-expected it to be Will, asking me why I had sent him such a cold message.

But it wasn't Will. It was the last person I expected to hear from.

'Matty?'

'Gem, I'm glad I caught you. Is this a good time?'

I stared around the small waiting room and cupped my hand around the phone, hoping Vee wouldn't come back in. 'Hang on, let me just pop outside.'

The corridor stank of bleach. I stood near a window that was slightly ajar, dragging in a few gulps of air. I dug at the loose paint on the sill, my mind already jumping ahead a few thousand steps.

'Matty, how did you even get my number?'

Matty sighed. 'Well, it's a bit against the book, but you signed up with our agency a few years ago for temp work, do you remember?'

I screwed my eyes shut. Oh yes, I did. It was when Will and I had been talking about giving everything up for the tour. I was all set to work weekends to raise some extra funds. We even considered buying that camper van afterwards. I must have only been registered with Matty a month or so, before everything changed with Will, before all our dreams went up in smoke.

'I hope you don't mind,' Matty continued softly. 'I mean, I could say I'm ringing you to check if you still want to be on our database?'

'But you're not calling about that,' I said. My heart fluttered suddenly. 'Oh my God, is it Nicola? Is she all right?'

Matty coughed. 'Well, yes, it is about Nicola, but I'm not sure she's all right—'

'She came to see me. She told me what happened with Will.' My gaze drifted back to the waiting room. I needed to get back to Vee. 'Look, Matty, I don't want to be drawn into all of this. I told Nicola I would stay away from Will. He's obviously not in the right place at the moment. I suggest she does the same.'

'Will didn't hit her,' Matty said flatly.

I gripped the phone a little too tightly. 'What? What did you say?'

'I said, Will didn't hit her.' Matty sighed. 'Oh, this is such a bloody mess! I'm so sick of cleaning up her mess. First, she nearly kills the bloke and then she blames him. It's not right!'

'Hang on.' I could feel the words catching in my throat. 'What do you mean, she nearly killed him?'

'Nicola caused the car crash. They were having some argument and she grabbed the wheel – veered them straight into the tree.'

'But she wasn't in the car. Will was found alone.'

'I rescued her, didn't I? Like I always do. Nicola messes up and her big brother comes to clean it all up. She's always been like this, Gem, ever since she was a little girl. She needs attention constantly, has to be the centre of drama. I've convinced myself that she will grow up one of these days, but I'm not sure when that'll happen. It's just—'

'So, the bruises...' I interrupted. 'The bruises were from the crash?'

Not Will's fist.

'Yeah,' Matty said quietly. 'She wouldn't get checked over, but I think her ribs took quite a knock.'

'Did she tell you why she blamed Will?'

'I went to see her, to check on her last night. She was in a bit of a state, had been drinking for hours. She wasn't making a lot of sense at first, told me she "had done everything she could" to keep Will. And she was sobbing about why he didn't love her. In the end she got a bit angry, started ranting about you.'

'Me! What have I done?'

'Nothing – except be the woman Will loves.' Matty paused. 'Eventually, she told me what she said about him.

She was trying to scare you off. She probably wouldn't have confessed to me if she hadn't been so wasted. I was so angry with her. I'm sick of her dramas.'

I leant up against the wall, thankful for the cold plaster against my skin. How could I have even believed Nicola? What did that say about me? I knew Will, didn't I? I knew he would never be violent.

I knew that much about him at least. So, why did I even doubt him?

'Oh Matty,' I breathed. 'I've messed up.'

'Nicola is a great actress. She's convinced me of worse things,' Matty said. 'When she told me what she'd done, I couldn't let it slide. Will's a good guy, you know? I can see that. Even through his bad patch, I could see he was a decent fella, really. He was just lost.'

Bad patch.

Lost.

I ran my tongue silently over the words.

'It was like he was lost,' I whispered. 'And now he's found again.'

—

I drove Vee back to her place, my head totally lost in thought. Luckily, she was busy enough, caught up in her own excitement. The checks had gone well; everything was going as it should be, and Vee was now excitedly planning baby names and what buggy she should buy.

'You'll have to sort out my baby shower,' she said. 'And the christening after that. You'll have lots of responsibility.'

I smiled. 'It'll be a pleasure.'

Vee stroked her bump. 'I feel like she is coming at just the right time, you know? It's like everything is aligning as it should. It's going to be a good phase.'

'She?' I raised an eyebrow.

Vee blushed a little. 'It's just a feeling. I could be wrong – but I'm feeling very femme.' We both giggled and Vee gently laid her hand on my knee. 'I know you're worried, Gem, and I know I've warned you off before, but maybe you do need to follow your heart on this one.'

I looked at her. 'You've always been telling me never to go back, though?'

She nodded. 'Yeah, going back is never a good idea, but I don't think you are in this case. It's more like you've gone in a circle. You're starting over again.'

'But what if he hurts me again?'

'Then you'll know to walk away,' she said softly. 'But if you let him go now, you'll spend the rest of your life wondering if it was a huge mistake.'

–

I stood outside the house for a while, almost too nervous to ring the doorbell or to step inside. How crazy was that? This was my mum's house – *my* house for so long – and yet right now I felt like a stranger about to impose.

I stared up at the thin, bleak building. How much had I hated this place growing up? It seemed to cocoon me and Mum together, trapping us in our grief. I don't think we ever moved on here, and instead, I ended up running away from the claustrophobic walls and dark shadows, and my mum dug herself deeper inside.

I guess we had different ways of coping. Will had always tried to tell me that. He insisted that the reason he spent so much time with my mum was because he felt like she was badly misunderstood.

'Your mum hates herself so much,' he used to say. 'She can't ever face what happened to your dad and what she caused – so she's slowly destroying herself.'

I understood that. I really did, and there was so much of me that wanted to reach out and help her. After all, we only had each other. We had to look after one another. Sadly, the angry side of me had remained dominant – constantly clawing at me, demanding more.

Blinking at the front door, I felt a little unsteady. The thoughts of the past were quite overpowering – the anger, the bitterness and remorse. And now I was here, hoping to see Will, to talk to the man I had pushed away. The one I had struggled to forgive – even though he had easily forgiven my mother for nearly destroying his life in one stupid drunken moment.

Will had opened up his heart. He had turned to the past and welcomed it back with open arms. He had grabbed on to the good memories like a kid clinging on to a kite on a windy day. He wasn't focusing on the pain, on the upset, on the challenges that lay ahead.

He just wanted the now. He'd always been like that, living in the moment; it was the thing I had once loved so much about him.

I swallowed hard.

Still loved. I still loved him.

The front door opened without me even needing to press the doorbell. In my dreams, of course, it would have been Will standing there, with his arms wide open, ready to take me back.

Instead, it was Mum. Her face was grave, her eyes watery. I saw the quiver in her lips.

'I'm too late, aren't I?' I whispered.

She nodded slowly.

'I'm sorry, love. He's gone.'

It was warm inside, cosy. I think I'd ignored this before – always found it too stuffy and cluttered, but right now the heat and comfort were what I longed for. I sank down on the worn sofa and tucked my legs under me. Mum said nothing. I could hear her in the kitchen making tea – the thing she always did when she felt nervous or under pressure.

I pushed my head back against the cushions and closed my eyes. Was it crazy that I could smell him in the air? His aftershave. That shower gel he always used. Maybe he had sat here, in this exact spot, before he left.

Maybe he closed his eyes and thought of me?

Mum nudged my arm. I opened my eyes and took the tea she was offering, even though I wasn't thirsty at all. If anything, I felt sick.

'When did he go?' I asked.

'Not long ago, an hour or so. He was going to Jack's hotel and then on from there.'

'Where are they going?'

'I don't know. He didn't say.' Mum sat herself down in the chair and started to fiddle with the hem of her skirt. 'I did ask, of course, but he said it was better that I didn't know. He wanted to be with Jack. He said that he needed to be away from you.'

She whispered the last part, but it still managed to sear through my heart. I put my cup on the table, realising my hands were shaking too much to hold it.

'Did he hear about Nicola visiting? Did he know what she said?'

Mum frowned at me. 'No, love, I don't think he did. Will and Nicola saw each other yesterday. Will packed up his stuff and left. He said she was quite nasty. Said all kinds of things, but she was hurt, he understood that—'

'She said things to me.' I shook my head, hearing my voice wobble. 'Oh Mum, I listened to her. I listened to all of her venom, and I pushed Will away.'

'Oh love, I'm sure you didn't.'

She got up, a little awkwardly at first, and then carefully pulled me towards her. I couldn't remember the last time my mum had held me like that. I leant up against her breast, my tears flowing, exhaustion overwhelming me.

'Mum, what have I done?'

'It'll be OK, lovely. It'll be OK.'

'Did he say anything? Anything at all?'

Mum pushed back the hair from my face. 'No, not really. He just made the decision to go and that was it. I told him he should call you, I hoped he would. But he said he couldn't do that. He said you both needed time apart.'

'It must have been my text,' I said. 'It couldn't have been anything else.'

Mum had stopped rubbing my head. She was staring off into space, a small frown appearing.

'Actually, now I come to think of it, there might have been something happening to make Will go. He had a visitor.'

'Who?' I demanded. And then, in sheer impatience, shouted even louder than I meant to, 'Who, Mum, who was it?'

'It was Richard. He came to see Will last night.'

Chapter Thirty

Gem – 2022

Time seemed to be the one thing that had haunted me these last few weeks – the sense that me and Will kept missing our moments together and had different perceptions of reality. And now, I'd finally realised that none of that mattered – the past, or the future, or where either of us thought we were in the world was irrelevant. All that mattered was the here and now and the feelings we had for each other in that one, single moment. But it was too late, and I seemed to be running out of time itself.

Instead, I was tracking down Richard – the last thing I had planned today, but he had been keen enough to meet up.

'Let's meet at The Swan,' he said. 'We can talk there.'

Part of me hated the fact that he was picking a place that he knew had meant so much to me and Will, but I was beyond arguing. I needed to know why he had gone round to see Will and what he had said that had made him take flight so quickly.

'Honestly, with him and Nicola confusing things, it's no wonder we keep messing up,' I muttered to Mum as I rushed to the front door. 'I'm beginning to think those two are suited to each other.'

'Or maybe they are just two people who got caught in the middle of something that they could never understand,' Mum replied. 'It can't ever have been easy for either of them – playing second best.'

She planted a small kiss on my cheek as I went to leave. I think we were both surprised and my hand floated up to touch the spot, almost as if I'd been slapped.

'I always care about you, Gem. You might not think so, but I do.'

'I only hope you're right,' I said, trying to ignore the nagging doubts in my head.

'Sometimes I am,' she said gently. 'Although I've been wrong a lot, I know.'

'I'm sorry, Mum,' I said finally. 'I know I should have been there for you more. I always found it so hard.'

'I was hard to deal with, I know that.'

'But now I can see,' I said, 'I can understand what Will kept telling me over the years.'

'What's that?' Her voice was barely more than a whisper.

'I can see how much I need my mum,' I said. 'And I can see how precious you really are.'

Mum drew me into a hug, so tight it nearly took my breath away, but it was what I needed. I think it was what we both needed.

'I understand why you couldn't forgive me, after the fire,' Mum whispered. 'You never wanted to talk about it and that really got to me, but I need you to know it was an accident. I was working such long hours, I was caring for you, I was exhausted. I just fell asleep—'

'And Dad? Wasn't he working?' I asked, realising I'd never explored these things before.

'Your dad didn't do as much as he could,' Mum said carefully. 'He liked to be looked after, shall we say. He didn't believe in sharing childcare. It wasn't the easiest life.'

'Mum, I never knew. I always thought—'

'It didn't matter. I didn't want you to think badly of your dad. It was easier for you to blame me, and I felt bad enough about it, so you couldn't really make me feel worse.'

'All these years...' I shook my head sadly. 'You never put yourself first.'

'I just wanted you to be happy. That's all I've ever wanted.'

'I love you,' I whispered, realising I had never said those words to her before.

'I love you too, Gemma, more than you'll ever know.' She pulled me away from her and nodded towards the door. 'Now hurry up and meet Richard. Find out what's going on. It's not too late to sort this out.'

–

Richard had already ordered me a gin and was sitting close to where the old stage used to be. Now it was a polished platform, used mainly for DJs who came in for the weekly disco. I stood by the door for a moment and remembered lingering by the old wooden deck. I was always right at the front, ready to see Jack and Will perform. In those days the pub had been full and crowded, stinking of sweat, leather and spilt beer. Will always used to joke that it was a 'real pub, spit and sawdust'.

Now it was all clean edges, chrome and a stink of polish. There was no spit. No sawdust. No band. No Will.

'Hey! Gem!'

Richard was waving me over. I noticed he was wearing the blue polo shirt I bought him. It went well with his eyes. His hair was shorter too and he was clean-shaven. He looked good. Wholesome. Intelligent. Kind.

I walked to the table and forced a smile. 'Thanks for agreeing to meet me,' I said. I took the drink he offered and guzzled it, hungry like a baby. Richard watched me, amused.

'You needed that, then?'

'You could say that.'

The chair I was sitting on was a bit rickety and wobbled as I moved, but I tried to ignore it. I put the drink back down and I scanned the room. It was always so quiet in here these days.

'This place isn't the same,' I muttered.

'Oh...' Richard seemed disappointed. 'I quite like it. I only came to The Swan a few times in the old days, but it was always so rowdy. It's quite classy in here now.'

'Classy?' I raised an eyebrow. 'Richard, it's fake. It's a pub sat right on the Osbourne estate. It's never going to be classy here. They're not serving their public.'

'Or maybe their public need to be more aspirational.' Richard sniffed. 'We shouldn't be dumbing down.'

I felt myself stiffen. 'It's not about dumbing down, Richard. It's about fitting in. I don't fit in here. This isn't me.' I poked at the fake potted plant that was dangling on the windowsill next to us. 'All of this is so – well, so unnecessary.'

'I'm sorry.' Richard reached for my hand. 'Maybe I shouldn't have suggested here. I just thought you liked it.'

I pulled my hand away and buried it in my lap. I was too hot in here, too uncomfortable, and the stupid chair was driving me nuts.

'Gem,' Richard said softly. 'I'm glad you called. I was hoping you'd see sense. We need to talk about everything, about us. I don't think I've been supportive enough. I should have—'

'Why did you see Will?' I said, interrupting him.

'What?'

'You heard.' My tone was flat, emotionless. In all honesty, I was exhausted. 'I know you went, Richard, so don't try to deny it. My mum saw you leave. You must've said something serious, something to really upset him, because he's gone.'

I saw something there, something in Richard's eyes – a little sparkle. He quickly looked away, keen for me not to notice, and swiped at his mouth.

'I just talked to him, that's all. Man to man.'

'Richard, please don't lie to me.' I could feel my frustration bubbling over, threatening to spill into pure rage. 'I know you did more than talk. I'm going to call Will myself and ask him, but I'd rather hear it from you first.'

I could see Richard hesitate; I knew he was deliberating. Should he be honest? Would I really speak to Will?

He looked back at me, and his eyes were glinting.

'What did you do?' I repeated, my voice rising. 'Tell me.'

'I showed him Vee's scan,' he said finally, quietly. 'I showed him Vee's scan and I told him it was ours. I begged him not to destroy our family.'

I couldn't react at first. The words were there, but they were hot and angry in my mouth. I slugged down the rest of my drink and pushed my glass aside, almost knocking it over in my frustration.

'I did it for us,' Richard said, his eyes wide and pleading. 'I knew you weren't thinking rationally so I needed to do something drastic. I needed something to get Will to leave. I know it was extreme—'

'Extreme!' I hissed at him. 'You lied, Richard. How did you even get the scan anyway?'

'I took it from your bag,' he said. 'I took it days ago. You've been so preoccupied that you didn't even notice.'

His reply sliced through me. I thought of Vee, of how proud she had been of that scan, and I'd just shoved it away and not looked at it again. He was right, I was an awful person not to notice it had gone.

Everything was such a bloody mess.

'I'm being honest now, Gem,' Richard said, almost begging. 'I shouldn't have done what I did, but I panicked. I was scared you were going to go back to him.'

'That doesn't excuse your behaviour.'

'I know it doesn't.' I'd never seen Richard look so desperate. 'But try and see things from my perspective, Gem – I was going out of my mind. All you seemed to care about was Will, it was like he was worming his way back into your life again. I felt like I couldn't compete.'

I shook my head. I couldn't speak.

'I love you, Gem. I love you so much. I'm good for you. I'll look after you, you know that.' He paused. 'Remember it was me who helped you before. I was the one that fixed you.'

'I. Fixed. Myself,' I said coldly. 'I didn't need anyone doing it for me.'

'But I was there for you,' he insisted. 'I've always been there for you.'

'Everyone has lied,' I said, my mouth dry, despite the drink. I licked at my lips. 'Everyone has lied to me: you, Nicola, Mel. The only person who hasn't in all of this is Will. In fact, he has done all he can to uncover the truth.'

'He will hurt you again.'

I sighed. 'Yeah – yeah, he might. But you know what? He might not. I've spent the last few weeks convincing myself that he is still this bad person, that he is still capable of hurting me, but what if I've been wrong and he's been right all this time? We were together for years, Richard, and for all of that time, he was nothing but amazing to me. He was kind, loyal, considerate, funny...'

Richard bowed his head. 'I'm not sure I want to hear this.'

'It was only for a few weeks that he was different. A few weeks when everything went to shit.' I shook my head. 'And now I know why, and it wasn't his fault. None of this was.'

Richard's voice was quiet. 'You were never going to take me back, were you?'

I held his gaze. I could see now what my mum had meant before: other people had been caught up in our mess and hurt. It wasn't fair, not really.

'I loved being with you, Richard. I really did. You were there for me when I needed you and you did help me rebuild. But—'

'I'm not Will,' he concluded flatly.

'You're not Will,' I said.

Richard sat back in his chair. He rubbed his face, seeming to consider all of this for a moment – then he slowly nodded.

'I tried, Gem,' he said softly. 'I tried to make you love me.'

'You can't make something happen if it's not meant to be. You'll just end up breaking it.' I paused, as I could see the pain in Richard's eyes and I felt myself soften. 'I'm sorry.'

'What are you going to do now?' he asked.

'I'm going to try and unravel all this mess. I'm going to say I'm sorry to Will. I'm going to try and put things right.'

Richard nodded again. He slowly reached into his pocket, drew out a folded piece of paper and passed it to me. It was the scan. I took it back gratefully, clutching it close to my heart.

'Do what you need to do, Gem,' he said kindly. 'I'm sorry too for doing what I did. I thought I was doing the right thing, but you're right, I could never compete with that man and, to be honest, it was exhausting trying to.' Then he got up and slowly left the pub.

I sat for a while, carefully unfolding the scan photo and pressing out the creases. My finger traced the fine lines of the image, wondering what my godson or god-daughter would be like. I wanted them to meet a happy me, a sorted me.

It was time for me to listen to my heart for once.

Reaching for my phone, I scrolled down to Will's number. The hesitation was there for a moment or two. I felt shy, unsure. I didn't know where he was or if he even wanted to hear from me but, finally, I decided to bite the bullet and press call.

He answered within two rings.

'Gem?'

'Will. Where are you?'

A beat. 'I'm going away for a bit, Gem. I need to get my head together.'

'Your poor head.' I couldn't help smiling. 'It really has taken some knocks recently.'

'You're telling me.'

I knew he was smiling back. I could tell he was. In the background I could hear a rustling sound. Talking.

'Are you on a train?' I asked.

He sighed. 'Gem, it's better you don't know. I think we need some time apart.'

'But that's the thing, Will, I don't think we do.' I knew the words were rushing from me. 'I'm not pregnant! Richard made that up. He showed you Vee's scan. She's the one who's pregnant.'

'Vee?' Will breathed out. 'Really?'

'Yes, really! Her and Brandon have been trying for years, you must remember. It started before your first accident.'

'I remember.' He paused. 'Congratulations to them. That's amazing news.'

'I didn't mean to send you the message I did, Will. I was confused – upset. Nicola had been to see me and she said things.'

'What did she say?'

'She said – well, she showed me her bruises. She said you had pushed her.'

Silence.

'Will, I'm sorry, I shouldn't have believed her. I was in shock, I think, and then I spoke to Matty and he told me the truth.'

'But you believed her at first?' Will's voice was cooler. 'You still thought I could have hurt her.'

'I-I don't know, Will. It was all so confusing. Your injury – Nicola was so convincing, I just—'

'Thought the worst?'

Silence again. I clutched the phone, feeling my tears build.

'Will, I'm so sorry. I got this wrong. I can see now. I understand that you weren't you before. That first accident changed you – you did things that you wouldn't normally do, and I do think you're different now. I can see it.'

Silence still. God, what was he thinking?

'Will,' I whispered. 'I love you. I miss you so much.'

'I love you too, Gem.' He paused. 'But we shouldn't be together.'

What?

I pulled the phone away for a moment, drew a shaky breath and then, finally, I managed to squeak, 'Will, I don't understand. You wanted this. You want us. You know we are better together.'

I heard him sniff and then heard the quiver in his words. 'I did think that. I still do, but this isn't fair on you, Gem. I can't guarantee that I'm better. I could still mess up – I could still make a mistake.'

'But Will—'

'No.' His voice was firm now. 'You need to let me go, Gem. I'm blocking your number now. I'm ending this. You need to move on. You don't need this broken version of me.'

And then he hung up, leaving me in pieces.

Will had gone and I had no clue where he was or if I would ever see him again.

Chapter Thirty-one

Will – 2022

I thumped down the phone and sat back with a groan. Opposite me, Jack glanced over, his expression grim.

'That sounded tough, bruv.'

'It was.' I screwed my face up, as if doing that could push away the images of Gem. Images that I wanted gone from my brain.

'Are you sure that was the right thing to do?' Jack paused. 'I mean, it sounded quite drastic.'

'I told you, I have to do this,' I replied stiffly. 'I can't keep messing the girl around. I feel like I'm a liability to everyone right now.'

Luckily, the train carriage was empty. I pressed my head up against the window, liking the sensation of the vibrations jolting through me. The scenery flashed past. We had passed through London now and were deep in the countryside, fields opening up on either side of the carriage. I could almost see my freedom stretching out in front of me.

A new start. A new future.

This was the right thing to do.

Jack was fiddling with his phone, and I could see his frown was back. He'd been like this all morning, quiet and unsure. I knew there was something bugging him.

'Who keeps contacting you?' I asked him finally. 'You've been on that thing all day.'

Jack put the phone down and attempted to straighten his expression into something that half-resembled relaxed.

'It's just the band. It's nothing important.'

'What do they want? I thought you said you had a few weeks off.'

'A few weeks, yeah,' Jack said. 'But we have new dates coming up. They'll need me back for rehearsals soon. That's if I go back—'

'Of course you're going back,' I snapped. 'You don't have to stay with me long. You didn't even need to come with me now.'

Jack leant forward. 'I wanted to come, you know that. I'm looking forward to this as much as you are.'

I smiled weakly. I was glad – this mattered to me. Despite all of the chaos, I was clinging on to this trip and what it offered us. It was the last bit of hope I had.

'I said before, you can come with me,' Jack said.

'Where? To America?'

'Yeah, where else, Mars?'

'How would that even work? I haven't got a job.'

'You can come back to the band,' Jack replied. 'You're the best lead guitarist I know. Deano is OK, but not a patch on you.'

It was difficult not to feel smug. I'd never liked that Deano – he was always an annoying bastard.

'So, what happens to Deano?' I asked. 'It's not like he's going to be happy with me kicking him out.'

'We don't have to kick him out. He's a decent rhythm guitarist too. To be fair, he just likes being in the band, I don't think he cares too much what his role is.'

I shrugged. 'Well, I guess I could think about it.'

'But that's only if you're really done with Gem. If you're sure?'

I had to admit, the thought of being back in the band with Jack was exciting; I could feel warmth in my fingers again – a longing to pick up the guitar and get back on the stage. How had I managed to ignore that for so long?

'It's how it should be, us two together,' Jack said quietly. 'It never felt right, even though we were doing OK out there – it never felt right without you. I felt a bit lost.'

'Well, you would be. I was the talent.'

Jack stuck his finger up. We both laughed and I sat back in my seat.

'I'm surprised you can forgive me, though – for what I did. You loved Aby so much.'

Jack stared down at his lap. 'I didn't think I'd ever forgive you. That's why I went away, I had to. I wanted to kill you at the time. It felt like you didn't even care.'

'It wasn't really me, Jack. I'd never do anything to hurt you.'

'Aby would, though.' He sighed. 'I knew that, really. There were rumours that she had slept with other men while we were together, but I just ignored them. I believed her when she said she only really loved me. But sleeping with you – it was the final straw.'

I shook my head. 'I hate thinking I did that, Jack. I'm glad I can't remember that bit.'

'I wish I didn't,' he muttered softly.

I pressed my head up against the window again, watching as the world sped past me. I had lost three years of my life. So little made sense at the moment, and it still felt like my world was tipping and twisting out of my control.

Jack leant forward and nudged my arm.

'I'm glad you're back, Will. Like, properly back.'

I could see a spark of warmth in Jack's eyes. And there was something else there: hope.

What was that old saying? It's the hope that keeps you going.

'So am I, mate,' I said. 'So am I.'

A little later, Jack nudged me again.

'Gem is calling me. I should answer.'

I took the phone from him and ended the call. 'No, you shouldn't. I told you, I don't want her to know where we are.'

Jack looked uneasy. 'Bruv, this feels cruel. What do I say to her if she messages?'

'Just ignore her for now. Or turn your phone off.' I glared at him. 'Please, Jack, I'm doing this for Gem. It's killing me, but I'm doing the right thing.'

Jack sighed. 'Well, only if you're sure...'

It was the last thing I was – but I had to keep convincing myself.

–

Hours later, tired and slightly beaten, we arrived at our final destination: Bognor. We walked briskly to the nearest taxi rank, loaded our bags in the cab and delivered our instructions. As I settled in the back of the warm car, it was all I could do not to fall asleep.

'I still can't believe we managed to book this place,' Jack said. 'It's the summer holidays, we were lucky it was available.'

'Fate was on our side,' I replied. 'We are clearly destined to come back here.'

I did question whether that was true when the taxi pulled into the small caravan site. As I stepped outside,

I couldn't help feeling a sense of disappointment. This wasn't as I remembered it.

The caravans were set out in long lines, and they looked tired and worn with age. By the car park there was a small clubhouse, with dark windows and cheesy-sounding music coming out of it. I could smell fried onions and cheese. My stomach growled instinctively, which surprised me, as I didn't feel particularly hungry.

'Aw, the clubhouse. You remember?' Jack said, heaving his bag on his back. 'I remember you sitting outside on the steps over there, moaning about missing Gem and feeling homesick...'

I picked up my own bag and frowned. 'We're here to forget about all of that, Jack. This is about us. Our childhood.'

'That's all well and good,' Jack said. 'Except Gem was part of our childhood too, wasn't she?'

I stood blinking at the clubhouse lights, remembering how it had felt being here as a young boy. I'd barely known Gem then, of course, but she had suddenly become such a big part of my life – and being on holiday without her had worried me; I'd kept thinking of her back home, arguing with her mum.

I had missed her.

'It just seems to me that this is the worst possible place to come if you want to forget about the girl,' Jack said. 'She's with you everywhere here.'

The caravan wasn't as I remembered either. It was smaller and greyer than I recalled, and far more cramped inside. They'd obviously changed the decor over the years too: the floral, slightly naff sofas that I had pictured had been replaced by cheap leather, and the small, portable TV in the corner was now a flat widescreen. The only thing that was the same were the few chintzy ornaments and the dolly sitting on the toilet roll.

'Do you remember how much Mum hated that thing?' Jack said, pointing at it. 'It really freaked her out.'

'It's not exactly normal to have a doll with a bog roll up her bottom,' I replied, remembering that it had creeped me out too. 'Jack, I can see why this place wasn't rented out. It's not exactly well-loved, is it?'

'To be fair, it wasn't when we came here before. Don't you remember how crap the mattresses were?' Jack went to inspect the beds. He pummelled both of them and pulled a face. 'I think these are the same ones.'

'It's weird, I always saw this as the best holiday ever. When I pictured the caravan in my head, it was bright – perfect. We loved it here.'

Jack perched on the end of the bed. 'We loved it here because it was sunny, do you remember? A really hot summer. And we loved it here because it was our last holiday with Mum. She did everything she could to make sure we had a great time. We played games all the time, we went out, we laughed.' Jack paused. 'I think we remember this place as a great holiday because we are remembering her at her happiest.'

I couldn't reply to that. I was staring around the small space, fascinated by the fact that memories could be so easily shaped by those who were with you in them.

'We were so loved, weren't we, Jack?' I said finally. 'We were so lucky.'

Jack stared back at me, his eyes glistening.

'We were the luckiest boys alive that summer.'

–

Later, Jack went to the clubhouse for a drink and something to eat. He insisted that I go with him, but I was too exhausted, and the thought of eating made me squirm.

'I'll bring you back a burger,' he said. 'You need to eat. You're still recovering.'

I nodded numbly – anything to stop him nagging. As much as I'd wanted him here, I was glad of the peace, and relief swamped me when he closed the door.

I lay on the cracked sofa and tried to find something to watch on the dodgy TV. The signal was awful, and the channels were limited. I ended up with some antique programme, which I stared at blankly, soon realising that none of the information was going in.

My phone was beside me. It would've been so easy to reach out for it – to type out a message to Gem and tell her I couldn't stop thinking about her. Tell her I didn't mean to push her away.

Outside, the wind swirled leaves through the air. For the first time in ages my head throbbed. No matter what I did, no matter what distraction I tried to use, I couldn't stop the same thoughts from overtaking my mind.

What if I had got this wrong?

What if Gem and I could make it work?

What if…

What if…

They were the worst two words in the world.

Chapter Thirty-two

Gem – 2022

Oh God, I was really doing this.

But I couldn't leave things as they were, especially after the phone call last night.

After I left the pub, I'd curled up on my sofa, flicking through the old photo album that Will and I had put together years ago. Seeing all those images again had been hard. Me and Will as kids on the estate. Me and Will in the flat, with my nan, fussing over her. Me and Will moving in here. Me and Will on holiday, weekends away, nights out.

So many memories. For so long, I felt like I'd known Will better than I knew myself – and it turned out that one stupid night, one mistake, had changed all that.

If only I'd known before, maybe I could've helped Will.

But another thought hit me as I lingered on a final picture of me and Will together, our last happy shot – if we hadn't broken up, Will would never have been in that car accident with Nicola, and his mind would never have reset.

No matter how hard it was to accept, I had to acknowledge that fate might have played a part in all of this. Perhaps this was how it was always meant to be.

And Will's second accident meant that he was able to return to being the man I loved. The one I remembered.

Now, fate was urging me to take him back – to let him into my heart once more. As I stared at the picture of us together, laughing and cuddled up, I could feel warmth spread across my body.

It was always meant to be this way.

My phone rang a few hours later. I was surprised and hopeful. The disappointment came a split second after that, when I realised that it wasn't Will. However, it was the next best thing.

'Jack?' He had finally phoned me back.

The background was so noisy that I was tempted to pull the phone away from my ear. Was that a band playing? They sounded awful.

'Gem… Gem, sorry, I can't hear you very well. Hang on, I'll step outside.'

I waited, listening to the noises of footsteps, chatter, a door slamming. My heart was pounding. Jack was with Will, wasn't he? Was everything all right?

'Gem, I'm sorry.' Jack was clearer now. He coughed. 'I had to call; I'm sorry I missed you earlier. Will asked me to ignore you, but I can't listen to him. I had to speak to you.'

'Is it Will? Is he OK?'

'Yeah – oh God, yeah. He's fine. He's just chilling back in the caravan.'

'The caravan?' I frowned, confused. 'Wait? Are you on holiday or something?'

A boys' holiday. I tried not to let the weight of this sink in. Will clearly wasn't that upset over me, then.

'Well, yes… but…' Jack sounded confused. 'It's not what you think, Gem. We're in Bognor.'

'Bognor.' I paused. 'Oh, you mean where you went before.'

I picked up the photo album again, began flicking through – right back to the beginning. There was a picture there that I loved of Jack and Will together. They had been so young and tanned. I remember how much I'd missed Will then. He'd only been away for two weeks but it felt like two months. We were just friends then, of course, nothing more – but something fierce burnt between us. An electric force that was difficult to ignore. We were never good apart; we were never happy.

My finger traced the photo.

'You went there just before your mum died. I remember.'

'That's right. It was such a special holiday. For both of us. We came a few times before that too, it was a great place to be. A family place.' Jack took a shaky breath. 'Will wanted us to come back, just for a few days. He needs to clear his head.'

'I know.' I heard the quiver in my voice. 'He told me he's better off without me.'

'That's what he keeps telling me: that he might hurt you again. That he can't be sure he's the man he used to be. He seemed so convinced, and that's the only reason I suggested it...'

'Suggested what?'

He drew a breath. 'Suggested that he should come with me to America. Rejoin the band, the tour. I didn't think he'd accept – I was kind of testing him, I suppose – but he did.'

'Oh...'

It was as if all of the air had been sucked out of me. I closed my eyes briefly, wondering what life would be like with Will so far away. I'd already lost three years – could I bear to lose any more?

'Gem?' Jack said softly. 'Are you still there?'

'Yeah. Yeah, I am.'

'It doesn't have to be this way. You can still change his mind, I think.'

'How? How the hell do I do that? I've already called him. I told him how I felt, but it wasn't enough…'

'I don't know, but…' I could hear Jack walking up and down, the beat of the music behind him. 'I just know my brother and I can see how unhappy he is. He's just not the same without you.'

It felt like my heart was being broken and pieced back together all at the same time. 'What do I do, Jack?'

'Do what you think is right, Gem. That's all you can do.'

So here I was now, driving to the South Coast – I had to see Will again and tell him how I was feeling. I wasn't sure if he'd be willing to listen. I wasn't even sure if he was going to change his mind; the only thing I was sure about was how I felt.

And I wasn't about to ignore that ever again.

–

I arrived at five o'clock in the afternoon, having only taken one break in a tiny service station en route. I hadn't been able to eat, my stomach was too churned up for all of that. As I pulled into the car park, my head kept going over the same questions and the same worries. Was I even right to be coming here? Will should be going to America with his brother. He needed to be in that band, he was so talented.

Was fate steering us on a different path again?

I stepped out of the car and reached for my phone to ring Jack and ask him where their caravan was. Instead, my gaze fell on the clubhouse: a strange, tatty-looking building with a worn-out sign painted on the front – and on the steps sat Will.

I was frozen for a moment. He looked so lost, sitting there. His hair had grown longer these past few weeks and he was wearing it like he used to. He was dressed casually, almost scruffily. His face was lined with stubble.

My Will.

I walked towards him.

He looked up, held up his hand to shade his eyes from the sun.

'Gem?'

'That's me.'

I stood before him, suddenly feeling daft and awkward. How could he even want me? I was dumpy and plain, nothing special.

'You're here.' He rubbed at his face. 'I was thinking of you, and you came.'

'You were thinking of me?'

'When we came here before, I used to sit on these steps whenever I missed you. I'd stare out at the drive and wish that I could magic up your appearance.'

'And now here I am.'

'And now, here you are,' he repeated.

I sat down next to him. There were just inches between us. I could feel the buzz of electricity and shivered.

'Jack called me,' I said. 'He told me you were here.'

'Oh.' Will's voice was casual. 'What else did he say?'

'He said you were going to America with him.'

Will nodded slowly. 'I did say I would, yeah.' He paused. 'What do you think about that?'

'I think that I would miss you.'

He didn't speak, kicking at the dirt and grit with his trainers.

'But you should go,' I said finally. 'I've come here to say goodbye. I didn't want to do it over the phone. I wanted to do it here and now.'

He lifted his head, and his eyes finally met mine. Those eyes always made me go soft inside, and there was no change today.

'I'm going to miss you too, Gem.'

I gently placed my hand on his knee. I felt him tremble. 'This doesn't have to be the end, Will. I know you think you need to push me away, but you don't. We both need time – that's true. We both need to deal with what's happened.'

Will sighed. 'Gem, all I want is to be with you, you know that. But I'm so scared. I might change again as my memory comes back. I might not be the man you loved.'

'Will, you were always the man I loved. I realise that now. The love has never gone.' I leant into him, feeling his solidness. 'We don't know what tomorrow might bring, but instead of fearing it, why don't we just run with it, give in to fate?'

'So, what happens now, Gem? What do we do?'

'You go to America and try it out there. See how the tour goes. Rebuild your relationship with Jack. Have some bloody fun!'

'And what about you?' he asked quietly.

'I've realised that I need a change too. I'm in a job that I don't really love, living in a flat that is full of old memories, and I feel like I've just been through two really brutal break-ups.'

'I'm sorry,' Will said, his voice breaking. 'I wish I could take back that hurt, that pain—'

I squeezed his leg. 'It's OK. It's in the past now, but that's the thing – I need to stop living in the past and clinging on to dreams that I never fulfil. I need to start focusing on the future.'

'You need to get that camper van,' Will mused. 'Travel the world like you always said.'

I nodded excitedly. 'Yes! That's what I want to do. I still have some money from when Nan died. I was saving it towards a deposit on a flat, but I've realised I don't want to be sensible like Richard. I want to explore. My mum is much stronger now, she's in touch with Mel and already making plans to visit her more. I've spoken to Vee and she's excited for me to go. I can still support her, wherever I am. I can still be a good godmother.' I heard my voice break a little. 'But I need to see if there is a life for me outside of Crowbridge.'

'There is more to life than little old Crowbridge,' Will agreed. 'Although I do love the place. Will you write, Gem? Please tell me you'll use the time to get your book finished.'

I grinned. Will, unlike others, had always believed in my writing. 'I will. I have this amazing plot now – about a boy and a girl who were in love, but one accident changed everything.'

'Two accidents,' Will reminded me. We both chuckled. 'You are so brave,' he said. 'Giving up everything and starting again.'

'You're brave too,' I said. 'It hasn't been easy for either of us. But we have a second chance at living our lives properly, so let's grab it.'

Will turned towards me. He gently placed his hands on my face and guided my lips towards his. This kiss was much more tender than the one before. I could feel my body heat up. A surge of lust and desire pounded through me, but I had to push it back down. It wasn't right to explore this now. I gently pulled away.

'I'll miss you,' Will whispered. 'Every day, I'll miss you.'

'I'll miss you too,' I replied, my voice catching. 'But who's to say where we will be in a year's time.'

'Maybe we can be here?' he suggested suddenly, sitting up straight and pointing at the spot. 'We could be right here. In a year's time?'

'On the 18th of July,' I added. 'We could meet here then.'

'On the 18th of July.' He nodded. 'It's a date.'

'I was wrong about that date,' I said. 'I always thought it was the worst thing ever, but I've realised it could be a good omen too.'

'Because it's when I smashed my head?'

'No, because it's when I found somebody I used to love.'

Will pulled me closer towards him.

'Somebody you will always love,' he replied. 'And somebody who will always love you.'

Acknowledgements

This is hard. There are so many people that I want to thank, and I have a terrible fear that I might forget someone – but it's lovely to have the opportunity to try and document those that have helped me along the way. Writing can be such an isolating process and it's so important to have people around who believe in you, keep you motivated and laughing, and feed you biscuits where necessary. I know I wouldn't have got this book written without these important people in my life.

First, I would love to thank the wonderful team at Canelo, especially Emily Bedford, who believed in this book as much as I do and brings such wonderful passion and excitement to the mix. I'm so excited to be working with you all and hope that this is the start of an amazing journey together.

I'd also like to thank my fab agent, Elizabeth Counsell, who loved *Somebody I Used to Love* right from the start, and has offered me continued advice and guidance. It is truly appreciated.

As always, I wouldn't be where I am today without my amazing family. I wrote *Somebody I Used to Love* after a particularly difficult time in my life and it was their love and support which has kept me going. Thank you to my other half Tom, for being my editor, my counsellor, my best friend and chief tea-maker. Thank you to Ella and

Ethan for putting up with an ever-distracted mum and continuing to shine in your own respects. Thank you also to my brothers and sisters and my lovely mum – I know how lucky I am to have you.

I am also very fortunate to have amazing authors that I can call friends. As always, I thank the gorgeous Placers for their wisdom, wit and wonders (I honestly think you keep me sane) and the Savvys for being a great support throughout and also to my Debut 2022 group for being an awesome bunch of people. A special shout out to early beta readers Victoria Scott and Lisa Glass, and a big thank you to Emma Pass, Sarah Harris, Rachel Ward, Becca Day and Natali Simmonds for the chats when I needed them.

I'm so lucky to have wonderful and encouraging friends and also appreciate the support they give me. Thank you in particular to Amanda, Jodie and Gemma for the coffees and giggles. I've also been lucky to become part of a wonderful local improvisation group – so thank you to all the Dingbats for crazy times and the genuine friendships that I've made (particular big hugs go to my fab group Strangest Things). Also, a shout out to the amazing guys at Pitchy Breath Theatre and thank you to our wonderful bookclub, run by Karen, who is one of the most supportive and enthusiastic people I know.

A shout out, too, to the wonderful librarians, teachers, bloggers and reviewers who have championed me over the years and to every amazing reader who has picked up one of my books. I know I wouldn't be here without you.

If I've forgotten anyone, it's only because of my tired, peri-menopausal brain and not because I don't love and appreciate you.

I will always be forever grateful x